# *From* SILT *and* ASHES

# *From* SILT *and* ASHES

## HAVAH'S JOURNEY

ROCHELLE WISOFF-FIELDS

OPEN ROAD INTEGRATED MEDIA
NEW YORK

ISBN: 978-1-5040-7771-2

This edition published in 2022 by Open Road Integrated Media, Inc.
180 Maiden Lane
New York, NY 10038
www.openroadmedia.com

*To Shannon, Travis and Christian*

# *From* Silt *and* Ashes

# PART I

## *Life After Death*

# CHAPTER ONE

*Kansas City, Missouri, January 1904*

Police! Open the door!"

Her body shook, more from horror than cold. She drew up her knees, cowered in a corner of the room and stared at the bloodstains on the floral wallpaper. The back of her head ached where he had yanked her hair and dragged her to the floor. A bitter wind blew through the broken window. She shivered. Her knuckles smarted from a large gash across them. She wrapped her nightgown hem around her hand.

Tears burned her eyes and she shut them tight, leaning her head against the wall. "Will it ever end?"

The pounding at the door grew louder. "Last warning. Open up or we'll break the door down."

The clock on the mantel chimed three. She looked around the room. How could she explain the overturned chairs and shattered glass? Ridiculous. Preposterous. No one would ever believe her.

Grabbing the arm of the sofa, Havah struggled to her feet, hobbled to the door and pulled it open. A sharp gust stung her cheeks. Behind her, her husband Arel's breath warmed her neck. A dour middle aged woman she recognized as her next door neighbor stood between two uniformed policemen. She pointed a bony finger over Havah's shoulder at Arel.

"That's him, Officer. He's the one."

The sight of uniforms terrified Havah. In the old country uniforms at the door meant one thing. Would these men finish the destruction she herself had caused? Would they haul her beloved off to jail? Or worse, would they kill her outright?

These thoughts surged through her until the shorter of the two policemen pulled his coat collar up around his ears and said, "I don't mean to intrude on this little melodrama but it's colder than an undertaker's heart out here. Could we please come inside?"

Havah coaxed her stone lips to smile and stepped back. "How rude of me."

Her neighbor and the policemen filed into the living room. She shut the door behind them. The taller officer, an imposing presence with dark skin, fascinated her. Although she had read about them in Professor Dietrich's books about Africa and American history, she had never met a Negro face to face.

At once, his kind expression and gentle manners allayed her deepest fears. He bowed at the waist. "Please excuse our rudeness, ma'am. I'm Officer Lafayette Tillman and this is my partner, Pat Mulligan."

"I am Havah Gitterman and this is my husband Arel."

With a raised eyebrow Officer Mulligan gave a curt nod and walked to the middle of the demolished room. He knelt, picked up a butcher knife and inspected it.

"Blood on the handle. Someone's luckier than a four leaf clover to be alive. What do you think, Tillman?"

The neighbor's mouth puckered between her weathered cheeks. She glared at Arel and thrust a spear like finger in his direction. "I'm telling you, Officer, I hear this commotion almost every night. That beast is beating up on this poor helpless little gal. It's a crying shame, her being in a family way and crippled besides! Why he oughta be horsewhipped! Just look at them scars, any dang fool can tell he's a brawler."

Arel's gray eyes turned black. He tugged his nightcap trying to hide the scars that trailed from his forehead to his chin. His thin lips tightened over his clamped teeth.

Havah's chest buzzed like an angry hornet. How dare this wicked woman make such accusations! Clenching her good hand into a fist, Havah tripped toward her, but Arel's fingers tightened around her shoulder.

"Now, now, Mrs. Hutton, let's not jump to hasty conclusions." The brown skinned officer took the knife from his partner and ran his bronze fingers over the edge of the blade. Then his gaze fell to Havah's hand. "It could've been a terrible tragedy. At least there's no blood on the blade. Mr. Gitterman, did you try to kill your wife?"

"I think I tried to kill *him*." Havah hung her head and blinked at the red stains on the floor. Her lips quivered.

"You *think*?" Officer Mulligan twirled the end of his moustache.

"Please understand. She does not remember doing these things." Arel held up his hands.

"Yeah. Right. I say we take them both down to the station and book 'em. It's as plain as cow plop on your shoe: fighting and disturbing the peace."

Under the threat of arrest, a heated flush rose from Havah's neck. Her temples thudded.

She stamped her foot. "We did *not* fight."

"Well, if you wasn't feuding, dearie, what in tarnation was you doing? It sure don't look like you two was spooning!" Mrs. Hutton bent down, picked up a cushion and tossed it onto the sofa.

Havah brushed pieces of glass from the sofa. "Sit. Please sit."

Muttering under her breath, Mrs. Hutton plunked down in a rocking chair in front of the fireplace. "Dang foreigners wake me with their squabbling; now she wants me to listen to her jaw all night."

"We come . . . came to America from Kishinev, Moldavia . . . last September. That is only . . ." Havah counted on her fingers. "October, November, December, January . . . four months and a little more. We . . . my husband, his family and me."

Officer Mulligan gritted his teeth. He stood and took a step toward the door. "With all due respect, ma'am, we ain't about hearing your whole life's story. Just tell us what happened here—*tonight,* Mrs. Gitterman."

Arel pulled her onto his lap in an overstuffed chair. "Please to sit, sir. Arguing with my wife, it does no good."

"That how ya got them scars, mister?" With a wheezing chuckle, Officer Mulligan, took a tin from his pocket, pinched a wad of snuff between his thumb and forefinger and crammed it into his mouth. He maneuvered it to his inner cheek with his tongue.

"My Havaleh, she is a gentle woman—when she is awake."

"The worst wounds are here because even Dr. Nikolai cannot sew them up and make them heal. At night I dream I am in Kishinev." She tapped her forehead.

After he studied the shattered window for a moment, Officer Mulligan tucked his tobacco tin back into his pocket. "So you're saying you did all *this* in your sleep? Sounds kind of farfetched, if you ask me."

Officer Tillman did not seem to share his partner's impatience. He propped his head on his hand, resting his elbow on the arm of the sofa, his onyx eyes focused on Havah.

"Kishinev? That's in Eastern Europe. I read about the—the pogrom, they called it, in the *New York Times*. President Roosevelt tried to make the Czar denounce it. Were you there?"

Her courage bolstered by his kindly concern, Havah continued. "Christians say we killed their Christ so they kill us. Czar Nicholas, he should die three times. With his head buried in the dirt like an onion, he did nothing to stop it."

She turned to Mrs. Hutton. "You think my Arel is, as you say, a brawler? Not so. Three men at once, with sticks and knives, they cut him and beat him until he drowns in his own blood. We, all of us, are left to die. And the police? They turn their heads like they don't see monsters slaughter babies."

"Forever more!" Mrs. Hutton's face paled to silver gray in the dim light and her mouth dropped open.

"Sweet Canaan land!" Officer Tillman's baritone voice hushed to a thundering whisper. "Who could call themselves Christian and do such things?"

"Thank you, Mrs. Hutton." Standing in the entryway, Havah waved.

After touching the mezuzah on the jamb, she kissed her fingertips. With a knot forming in his throat, Arel watched her trace the Hebrew letter *"sheen"* that stood for "*Shaddai*," Almighty, with her index finger. The weathered tube, one of her most prized possessions, contained a parchment scroll inscribed with Hebrew verses from the Torah. Her brother David had carved it long ago. It was one of the few things she salvaged from the ruins of her village.

Arel settled back against the sofa cushions. He stretched out his feet to warm them in front of the blaze in the fireplace. "Wasn't it kind of the officers to kindle a fire for us? Police in the old country would've thrown us *into* the fire."

Her attention still on Mrs. Hutton, Havah slammed the door. "Busybody."

"She meant no harm, Havah, and to be fair, she did dress your wound."

"Iodine and bandages, I could've done it myself. I don't need her pity."

"She swept up the glass and even washed the stains off the wall-paper and how many times did she apologize?"

"I can take care of my own house." Havah stuffed her hand into her pocket. Hobbling to the divan she plopped down beside him. "I'm no cripple."

Early morning light and blustery wind swept through the broken picture window. "I need to put something over that before we freeze." He stretched his arms over his head. "Then it's off to work for me."

"Don't go." She snuggled her head against his chest. "Stay home with me, please."

"I have to earn a living," he sat back and riffled his hand through her ink black tendrils, "for my bride." Pressing his other hand against her belly, he did not have to wait long for his unborn child to kick. "For my son."

Her teeth chattered and vibrated against his ribs. He took the crocheted afghan, a housewarming gift from Mrs. Hutton, from the back of the sofa and tucked it around her. "Go back to bed, Havah."

"What if I fall asleep and burn the house down?"

A log in the fireplace rolled off another amid a fountain of spark and flame. Smoke billows choked him. He groped for an answer.

"I'm going to ask Auntie Fruma and Papa to move in with us."

"But they're such a comfort to your sister. The kids adore them, and I don't need a nursemaid."

"Is that so?" He pulled a pair of woolen socks from his pocket and patted his lap.

"Did you see the way the policeman and that old crone ogled?" With a painful grimace she laid her legs across his knees and eased back against the armrest.

"They've just never seen such a pretty lady." He raised her leg in both of his hands and kissed it.

"Pretty freak is more like it. It's ugly."

"No, it's not. It's a medal of honor." He massaged her disfigured right foot. "Does this hurt?"

"It feels nice."

His mind reeled back to their wedding night, less than a year ago, when he had asked to see it. She had pulled the covers over her head and said, "Don't look. You'll never want to share my bed again."

With unrelenting stubbornness he had wheedled, joshed and hounded. Finally she allowed him to slide off her stocking while she held her breath, her eyes black with terror.

Gangrene had robbed her of a third of her foot. Scars, like seams on trousers, lined her withered arch and her three gnarled toes looked like claws. Although he had laughed and proclaimed his undying love, nothing could have prepared him for the sight. It took everything in his power to hide his shock.

"My bride, you are altogether lovely."

After a year of marriage he had become accustomed to it. It was simply a part of her. He slipped the thick stockings over her foot and kneaded it with his thumbs. "I've loved you since the first time I laid eyes on you."

"That explains why you married Gittel and not me."

"Please, Havaleh, not now."

"I know what you're going to say. You were betrothed since you were children. You had no choice." She curled up under the afghan and pulled her foot from his grasp. "Arranged marriages, *feh!*"

"That's it." His jaws tightened and he sprang off the couch.

"Where are you going?"

Exhausted and longing to slip between their feather mattress and down comforter, he moved to the steps leading up their bedroom. "I'm going to get dressed, fix the window and then go to work where I can have some peace."

She tossed the afghan aside, stood and hobbled after him. "I'm ugly. I'm fat. You don't love me anymore, do you?"

"What do you think?" He swept her up in his arms, dried her tears with his lips and carried her up the stairs. "I did love Gittel."

"So did I. She was my sister."

"Admit it, Havah. If she hadn't died when she did, you would have married Ulrich."

# CHAPTER TWO

Sweet linseed oil aroma filled Havah as she poured it onto a soft rag and polished the oak mantel over the fireplace. Her sore knuckles throbbed. She set the bottle of oil on an end table.

Voracious readers, she and Arel had packed the bookshelves on either side of the fireplace with their favorites, Shakespeare, Dickens, Tolstoy, Sholom Aleikhem and Mark Twain to name a few.

"The dishes are washed, dried and put away." Shayndel Abromovich, Arel's sister, sauntered into the room. Her round cheeks flushed and her wavy blonde hair gleamed in the afternoon sunlight pouring through the new window glass.

"I didn't invite you over to do my work."

"Let your hand heal, then you can come next door to my house and wash my dishes to your heart's content."

"Where are the twins?"

"Itzak took them on a cabinet delivery. He thought they'd enjoy the sunshine."

With her hand resting on her expanded midsection Shayndel dropped down on the sofa and sighed. "Two months to go. I hope it's a girl this time. Havah, did you ever in your dreams think one day we would be together in America?"

"Not in *my* dreams."

"You know what I mean, little sister. I don't know what I'd have done if Itzak and I had stayed in the old country. I would've died of a broken heart."

"Me, too."

"Have you heard from your professor?"

"I got a letter this morning." Havah took an envelope from her pocket.

"How is he?"

"He's so lonesome. Oh, he doesn't say so, but I can tell by the way he talks about his wife and how much he misses her. She's been gone thirteen years. It's a pity he never remarried."

Shayndel fixed her cerulean eyes on Havah and lowered her voice. "You know he's still in love with you."

Hot blood rushed to Havah's face. Despite her fierce devotion to Arel, the thought of Ulrich's unrequited love afforded her unconfessed pleasure. To avoid any further conversation, she took a book from the shelf and opened it.

Instead of taking her mind off him, *Alice's Adventures in Wonderland* only sent her mind back three years to his mansion's library in Kishinev, to the summer of 1902. It was a day about which she had no intention of telling even her best friend. The memory still left her breathless.

One afternoon he had handed her the same book. "Here's a new textbook for your English lessons; something a little more advanced for my prized pupil."

Heart sore at losing Arel to Gittel and then Gittel to childbirth, she thumbed through the book. Learning English no longer mattered. What good would learning the language do her in Moldavia? She scoffed at a drawing of a rabbit blowing a horn and sporting a ruffled collar.

"This isn't a textbook. It's a silly book for children."

An elegantly attired man of wealth and six-foot stature, he surprised her when he wreathed his lips into a silly smile and he crossed his eyes. "There's none as old as he who forgets how to be a child."

"Is that a quote from one of those authors?" She pointed to the loaded bookshelves and tilted her head.

"*Nein.* It's straight from the mouth of Ulrich Dietrich, your humble teacher." He clicked his heels and bowed.

Two glass marbles, one green, one yellow, escaped from his waistcoat pocket and bounced across the hardwood floor. Dropping to his knees, he crawled after the renegade orbs.

At the very moment he slapped his hand over them, he hit his head into the side of his desk. He collapsed and rolled over onto his back, clutching his prey, eyes shut.

"Ulrich?" Holding her breath, she knelt beside him and tapped his forehead. "Speak to me."

With a mischievous grin he opened his eyes and lifted his head and shoulders off the floor. Startled, she lost her balance and pitched forward. In a moment of abandon that still sent pleasant shivers up her spine, he kissed her.

# CHAPTER THREE

It was only a dream."

Ulrich's hands trembled as he threw back the bedcovers and rolled out of bed. The cold floor chilled his bare feet. Donning a dressing gown and a pair of slippers, he padded down the hall to his study, pushing his hair, damp with sweat, off his forehead. He struck a match on the sole of his slipper and lit an oil lamp. The soft light cast shadows on the walls and gave them a gentle radiance.

It had been three months since he had moved into the modest Victorian home in Streatham on the outskirts of London, yet half of his belongings remained in wooden crates and steamer trunks.

"Don't you think it's time to finish unpacking?"

He turned his head to see his housemate, Nikolai, huddled in a high backed chair in a corner of the room, wrapped in a quilt. His pale blond hair hung in his half-closed eyes. An opened book lay face down on his lap and his eyeglasses were cocked on top of his head.

"If you'd invest in incandescent lights, you'd run less risk of a house fire." Nikolai pointed to the lump of wax on the table beside him that had, earlier in the evening, been a candle.

"Who needs incandescent lights? Ha! Those hideous bulbs and wires would destroy the charm of this lovely old house."

"It *is* the twentieth century, my friend."

"Dr. Nikolai Derevenko, always the voice of reason. Is something wrong?"

"No. I'm just catching up on a little reading, that's all."

Picking up a glass from the table, Ulrich took a whiff of the powdery residue at the bottom. "Bicarbonate of soda?"

"I have a touch of dyspepsia."

"Did you lose a patient?"

"Why do you ask?" Nikolai shut his book.

"I've seen the look before."

"It was a textbook case, a simple bump on the head, nothing more." Nikolai's square jaw tightened and a seditious tear trickled from his eye. He grasped the padded arms of the chair as if he could bend them with his bare hands. "No reason for the child to die."

"Ah, that explains it."

"Children aren't meant to die, Ulrich." Nikolai released the chair arms, wiped his eyes on his sleeve, put on his spectacles and cleared his throat with an obvious cough. "If you want, I can give you something to help you sleep."

"'Physician, heal thyself.' It's freezing in here." Ulrich moved to the marble framed fireplace and squatted. He took some logs from the wrought iron holder and he piled them in. "Havah would like this room."

"I can see her curled up on one of these fine red chairs of yours, reading by the fire."

"She adored them. She said she imagined King David's throne was very much like them."

Ulrich crumpled a piece of paper and tucked it between the logs. He struck a match on the hearth and tossed it on top of the pile. Crouching, he fanned reluctant flames and surveyed the semi-darkened library.

Rows of half vacant bookshelves lined an entire wall on either side of the fireplace. In one corner sat one of the few pieces of furniture he had shipped from Eastern Europe—an oak desk with intricate carvings on the legs. A baby grand piano imposed its polished presence in the opposite corner.

Two oval-backed, red brocade chairs, like royalty, occupied the expanse of floor graced by a fringed Persian rug directly in front of the fireplace. An oak table that matched the desk stood between them with four brass candlesticks and a framed photograph of Havah and Arel on their wedding day. Nikolai sarcastically referred to the layout as "Havah's shrine."

"There's no room for dancing like the old place, but plenty big enough for two devil-may-care bachelors," said Ulrich with a stiff smile.

"More like two stodgy old spinsters in neckties and trousers, I'd say." Nikolai yawned and rose from his chair. He tucked his book under his arm, his stolid composure reclaimed. "It's a comfortable room."

Wisps of memory, like fog rising from a stream in the early morning, took Ulrich to Kishinev where he gave piano lessons, concerts and entertained guests in his prodigious ballroom. In his mind's eye he saw the Abromovich children, Ruth and Rukhel, bright-eyed twins always chattering and giggling, Zelig, the bespectacled youth with a pronounced overbite who wanted to be a rabbi when he grew up and everybody's favorite son, little Tuli, the artist.

"I miss them." He stood and wiped soot from his hands.

Ulrich could hear Evron, their father, the gentle tailor, play his clarinet, and his brother Itzak, the cabinetmaker, his violin.

"Damnable waste," whispered Nikolai.

Picking up a letter from his desk, Ulrich held it to his nose and breathed in the aroma of rose water. He pictured Havah sitting at the kitchen table, pen in hand, munching raisins, black waves cascading over her shoulders.

Nikolai walked to the desk, picked up the envelope and squinted. "'Kansas City, Missouri. U.S.A.'"

"The postman delivered it yesterday afternoon."

"What does she have to say?"

"Here, I'll read it to you.

*Friday, 29 January, 1904*

*Dearest Ulrich, my angel and friend,*

*I am hoping happiness for you. You, above all people, deserve it.*

*I miss hearing you play. Perhaps one day you will come here for a concert.*

*Can you understand it, my writing?"*

For a moment he stopped to study her even letters. The memory of her battle with her knife-slashed hand still pained him. No longer able to perform simple tasks such as writing or even holding a spoon, she forced her left hand, with unyielding diligence, into submission. After all of that, she still had impeccable penmanship.

*"Please tell Dr. Nikolai for me to say hello. I owe him my life.*

*"I am happy to say I am no longer ill and my son kicks me day and night."*

His lips curving into something between a tenuous smile and a grimace, Nikolai peered over his spectacles. He set the envelope back on the desk. "She owes me nothing. When's the blessed event again?"

"Sometime in March."

"When you write, tell her how happy I am for them." His voice sounded flimsy and artificial.

"Write and tell her yourself."

"I hate to write. Go on."

"She continues to play the piano."

"Good exercise for that hand. How's Arel?"

"Splendid." Ulrich tossed the letter back on the desk. "He's simply splendid."

"Is something wrong?"

"No."

"Don't lie to me. I've seen the look before."

At a loss for rebuttal, Ulrich bristled. He sighed, sat down at the piano and played the opening chords of a Chopin nocturne. The diaphanous melody both cheered and flooded him with sorrow, until he hit a sour note.

"She gives me too much credit. What good did I really do, Nikolai?"

"You paid their way to America. You gave eight people—*including Havah*—a better life."

"It was only last Easter. Those butchers used that sacred day as an excuse." Ulrich pressed the palms of his hands against his eyes and rubbed. "If only I'd been there instead of traipsing off like a—a selfish vagabond on holiday."

"Then what? That pack of rabid dogs wouldn't have thought twice about killing you. You're only one man, not God!"

"You're one to cast stones, Doctor. Here you are, sitting up half the night, swilling bicarbonate and weeping for a stranger's child you couldn't save."

"Touché," whispered Nikolai. For a few moments he stared into the fire in silence. Then he turned back to Ulrich. "Professor, let her go."

# CHAPTER FOUR

With a leather portfolio under his arm and his medical bag in his hand, Nikolai wandered London's streets. Since his chief errand was accomplished he had no particular destination, so he seized the opportunity for an afternoon of sightseeing.

Passengers crowded themselves into square compartments atop coaches whose side and back banners advertised such necessities as Lipton's Teas and Nestlé's Milk. Above all else, London's churches fascinated him with their clock towers. A man never needed to ask the time in Britain.

Now and then, he paused to read shop signs. One particular shop caught his interest with its display of paints and drawing papers. He read the sign aloud, "L. Cornelisson and Son. Artist Colourman."

Something banged into his knees, causing him to drop his bag and portfolio. Kneeling to retrieve them, he looked into the brown eyes of a tiny girl; her dark spiral curls beribboned with a huge bow. She wagged a pudgy finger and cocked her head like a matronly school teacher reprimanding a recalcitrant pupil.

"Hey there, Mister, watch where I'm going."

A young woman whisked the child into her arms. "Apologize to the nice gentleman this instant!"

"No harm, madam." After he retrieved his bags he stood, touched his hat brim with his fingertips and bowed.

The woman appeared to be at least seven months along. She blushed, turned and hurried off into the fog.

Although he had not admitted it to Ulrich, a niggling fear tore at him. He worried about Havah's compromised health. Had it not been less than a year since the horrendous massacre in Kishinev's Jewish quarter? Given her size and the extent of her injuries, the pragmatic physician wished she had allowed more time to recuperate before conception.

Suddenly a flagrant dervish of henna hair and purple feathers in chartreuse skirts swirled past him. Floundering in a wake of strong perfume, he sneezed and opened the door for her.

"Allow me."

Curious to know what a woman of her ilk would want in an artist shop, he followed her. He removed his hat, pushed back his straight hair, stepped over the threshold and shut the door behind him. The pungent aromas of pigment, art paper and varnish filled the air.

"How might I help you, sir?" asked a rail thin man whose spectacles rested halfway down his narrow nose. He curved his meager lips into the slightest of smiles. His forklike fingers wielded a pestle. Blue and orange powders combined to make brown in the stone mortar.

"I am just—how you say it—browsing."

"I can help you with anything what ails you, guv." The woman, who had pushed past him, wrapped her fingers around his arm. Her periwinkle eyes sparkled and her crimson mouth stretched into a predatory grin. She pointed to his medical bag with a cackle.

"How's your bedside manner, Doctor Handsome?" Winking, she bumped her hip against his. "If you knows what I mean."

English nuances, particularly the slang-riddled cockney dialect, frustrated Nikolai. Outside of medical terminology, he struggled with everyday conversation. He pulled his arm from her grasp and cleared his throat.

"If you are in need of medical assistance, I could, perhaps, see you in my clinic at St. Thomas this Monday coming."

The feathers on her hat waggled like flocking birds ready to take wing. Her raucous laughter bounced off the walls and his discomfort mounted. Any moment the buttons of her overtaxed blouse, a scant covering for her jiggling bosom, would spring off.

"Where're you from, Doctor?"

"I am from Russia."

"I thought so. I have a friend what talks like you. Hey, ain't we met before?"

"I doubt it, Mrs.—"

"Miss. Miss Mary Alice Tanner. You sure we ain't never met? You does look familiar." She shrugged. "No matter. I'd best be about me business. Can't forget me little Dodger's birthday, can I?"

"Please to explain. What is a 'Dodger'?"

Her expression changed from vulturous to maternal. "It's what I calls me nephew. He ain't really no kin to me, but I loves him like he's me own. Going to be a great artist when he grows up, he is. Thirteen this next Wednesday."

"My son will be thirteen next Wednesday."

"Going to have a big party for him, I'll wager."

"My Solnyshko, my little sun, he is gone these past seven years."

Her smile dissolved and her charcoal smudged eyes brimmed. "How awful for you and your missus."

"She is also gone."

He walked beside the likeable woman past shelves loaded with ink jars and pencils in silence. She stopped and picked up a wooden handled brush with sable bristles. Grabbing his wrist, she led him to the sales counter.

"Let me show you something."

Unsure of what she meant to show him, he pulled back his hand. He heaved a sigh of relief when, like a cunning magician, she flourished her hand over a newly framed painting of her. It was a remarkable likeness, which captured her apparent inner beauty and indicated great skill for an adult, let alone a thirteen-year-old boy.

"Blessed little rotter done it for me birthday. Ain't no one ever give me the time of day before, let alone a present."

With a sudden affinity for a child he had never met, Nikolai set his portfolio on the counter. "Now I show you."

He unbuckled the straps and pulled out two framed pictures, both drawn by six-year-old boys. One was a sketch of a man on a merry-go-round and the other depicted a boy with yellow hair on his father's shoulders.

"Tuli was a sweet boy. We ride carousel together in Kishinev, so he drew this picture." He pointed to the first drawing and then caressed the second with his fingertips. "My son, he drew this."

His thoughts full of the boy he longed for, he moved to one of the shelves and flipped open a wooden box filled with a colorful array of paints. He closed it, carried it to the clerk and fished his wallet from his pocket.

After paying for her frame and the set of paints, he placed it in Miss Tanner's hands. "Tell your Dodger for me, 'Happy Birthday.'"

# CHAPTER FIVE

Sarah Tulschinsky, Arel's older sister, fascinated Havah. Her crooked-toothed smile eclipsed her hollow cheeks. Skinny, with a thatch of kinky black hair and round eyes, she lacked Shayndel's physical attributes.

Arel said he could not recall ever hearing Sarah raise her voice, until seven years ago. Always the dutiful daughter, she did whatever she was told until her father arranged for her to marry a man twice her age. With shrieks of rage that shocked everyone, she stuffed her few belongings into a carpetbag and left home. The few kopeks she had scrimped together from mending clothes paid her passage to America.

Amid stench and disease in the ship's steerage, she met her beloved Wolf. Married soon after their arrival in New York, they followed their dreams to Kansas City where they lived in a flea-infested shack among the impoverished unwashed in a settlement known as McClure Flats. Side-by-side, she and Wolf established his tailor shop. Within two years, they saved enough money to move from the slums into a two-story home.

At her insistence, the Tuesday afternoon synagogue ladies' sewing circle gathered in her living room to make and mend clothing for Jewish emigrants. She claimed it was the least she could do in return for the freedoms she enjoyed.

In spite of five-year-old twins, her house was immaculate. Not one of the tatted doilies that graced her tables and sofa was out of place. Havah would dare anyone to find so much as a dust speck on Sarah's polished furniture.

Sunlight poured through the long windows and glinted off the needle between Sarah's slender fingers. Hunched over a child-size dress, her straight stitches rivaled Arel's sewing machine. She reached over and touched Havah's elbow.

"How's your hand, little sister?"

"It's much better, thank you. Ouch!"

Poking her needle through the fabric, Havah jabbed it into her finger. Pain shot through her already injured hand. The button she was trying to sew onto a shirt fell off her lap and rolled under her chair.

Sarah set the dress aside, knelt and snapped up the renegade button. "You'll get better with practice. Shayndel tells me you weren't always left handed."

"It doesn't matter which hand I use. I'm hopeless."

"My mother used to say, 'Never give up, even if it takes a hundred years.'"

"I'm afraid it'll take me *two* hundred years." Havah sighed and resumed her quarrel with the obstinate button.

"*Nu?* When are these two little ones going to show their precious faces?"

Nettie Weinberg, a plump woman with sorrel hair piled atop her head and cinnamon brown eyes sat between Havah and Shayndel on the sofa and patted their mountainous bellies.

Vivacious and warm, Nettie had been the first outside of family to welcome the Gitterman clan to America. On countless occasions, she and her husband George kept the Shayndel's sons so they would not be underfoot during the unpacking. From their first meeting, Havah and Nettie were fast friends.

"Auntie Fruma says another month. She was the midwife in Svechka, you know." Shayndel finished repairing a blouse's lace collar and folded it into a square. "She delivered all the babies there, including me.

"She never gave up on me." Sarah's eyes misted and she hugged her sewing to her breast. "I wish she'd been here when I had the twins."

"Perhaps one day I'll be in need of her assistance." Nettie heaved a wistful sigh and resumed her sewing.

"Must you all speak Yiddish?" Zelda Mayer's strident voice grated in Havah's ears. "This is America, you know."

Since their first meeting a year ago at a synagogue, Havah had little tolerance for the otherwise attractive socialite. That night, ignorant that anyone among the new arrivals understood English, Zelda vociferously criticized Sarah for turning her fine home in to a boarding house for "*shtetl* peasants." Under her rouge, her cheeks had turned white when Havah told her off in English.

All morning Zelda stitched little and boasted much. She and her husband Sol, a successful business owner, were going to build in Hyde Park, a prestigious new Kansas City neighborhood. Every so often she cast a sidelong disdainful glance in Havah's direction.

Unable to contain her irritation any longer, Havah eased herself off the sofa, picked up her teacup from the end table and walked across the room. After taking one last sip, she poured the remainder into Zelda's lap and said, "*Tzu fil koved iz a halbeh shand.* Too much glory is half disgrace."

# CHAPTER SIX

The baby lodged his foot under Havah's rib. She pressed her hand against her side in an attempt to move him. Perhaps someday he would be a rabbi like both of his grandfathers, or he could be a doctor like Dr. Nikolai. He could be anything he wanted since he would be a freeborn American.

The aroma of chocolate filled her kitchen. She swirled a wooden spoon through the cocoa and took a deep breath. Her mouth watered in anticipation.

"I fear you've made a terrible enemy, little sister." Shayndel leaned back in her chair with her hands behind her and rubbed her lower back.

"Twice I've looked the Angel of Death in the face and spit in his eye. What is Zelda Mayer to me? She's a mosquito. Take that, Mrs. High Society!" Havah banged the spoon on the edge of the pot. "Splat!"

She spun on her heel, tossed the spoon into the sink and glanced out the window. Shayndel's four-year-old sons, Mendel and David, named for Havah's deceased brothers, played in the snow with five-year-old Gwendolyn Mayer.

Their round cheeks deep pink from the cold, the Abromovich twins were anything but identical. Like Shayndel, David's eyes were sky blue and his hair golden. Mendel was a smaller version of Itzak with tight black curls and eyes as dark as coffee beans.

"Let's drink hot chocolate before those kids swoop in on us like baby vultures." Havah extinguished the fire and then poured the cocoa into two cups, then set them on the table.

"If you dislike Zelda so much, why do you nursemaid her daughter? This is the third time this week."

"Wendy's lonely. Sol asked if she could come over to play with the boys while Zelda went to one of her meetings. For him, I said yes. Why did such a nice man marry such a disagreeable woman?"

"Maybe it was an arranged marriage? They are from Poland, you know."

At the mention of the old country, Havah paused to listen to the ghosts. Tears ran down her cheeks and fell into her cocoa. "I still can't believe they're gone. Angels."

"Try not to think about them."

"How can you say that? None of us should ever forget."

"It's not as if we could." Shayndel's eyes brimmed. "At night when he thinks no one's awake, my Itzak weeps for them. In his sleep, he calls out his brother's name."

"Evron was a great man, a good father and husband. I'll always be grateful for the way he and Katya took me in when they had so little room for themselves." Wiping her eyes, Havah sipped her drink and savored it on her tongue. "Life is like cocoa and sugar. We take the bitter and sweet."

"I'm sorry you've been through such horrid things."

"I am a stronger person because of them."

"Yes, you're strong enough to break windows in the middle of the night."

"David, I'm telling!" Wendy's shrill voice broke into the conversation. "You big fat liar!"

"I'd better break this up." Shayndel sprang from her chair.

"No. Wendy's my responsibility." Havah rose and hobbled to the window. The glare on the snow nearly blinded her as she squinted to see David and Wendy rolling on the ground. Havah grabbed her shawl, swung open the back door and stepped out into the snow.

"Take it back or I'll make you!" David brandished his fist above his head.

Havah rushed to grab him. Thrown off balance by her added weight, she slipped and landed on her backside. Cold snow penetrated her flimsy shawl and slush filled her shoes. Her unborn baby thrashed and somersaulted. She rose on both elbows.

"David, you know better than to hit young ladies."

"She's no lady."

"Why is David a liar, Wendy?" Havah bit her lip.

"He says President Roosevelt gave him a silver dollar!"

"What would you say, if I tell you he's not a liar?"

* * *

Wrapped in a blanket, Havah sat on the sofa in front of the fireplace absorbing the radiant heat from the flames. The children's wet clothes were draped over the mantel. She hoped Wendy's dress would be dry before Sol came for her.

On one side, Wendy huddled against Havah. David snuggled up to her on the other. Mendel slept, curled like a kitten in the overstuffed chair. The baby had finally settled and Havah fought to keep her eyes open.

"Tell me about the silver dollar." Wendy's sharp voice went up an octave and pierced Havah's ears like needles.

"You must be very quiet." Taking a deep breath to mask her annoyance, Havah forced a smile and pressed her finger to her lips. "Shhhh."

"Okay." Even when she whispered, the girl screeched. "Tell me . . . pleeeeeeze."

"That's better. The registry hall on Ellis Island is the biggest building I've ever seen. It's filled with people from all over world, hundreds of them, and like the Tower of Babel, many speaking, no one understanding.

"David is three at the time and doesn't speak English yet. The only thing he knows how to say was 'Statue of Liberty.'"

"Now I talk English real good," said David.

"I've spoken English ever since I be'd a baby." With her dark curls and the way she cocked her head when she spoke, Wendy looked like a miniature version of Zelda.

"You were born in America where *everyone* speaks English," said Havah, "but Mendel and David were born in Moldavia, far away on the other side of the world."

"Betcha can't speak Yiddish, Wendy." David stuck out his tongue.

"My mommy says Yiddish is for *shebble pheasants*."

Ignoring her, Havah continued, "I have to stand in line to buy tickets for the train to Kansas City. All of a sudden David's mama comes to me and says he's run off. So I give up my place and search for him."

"Were you mad?"

"Mad? Furious! I swear if I find him, first I'll give him a spanking he'll remember until he's an old gray man."

"Goody. Did you find him first?"

"Nope. Mr. Roosevelt does. Slam! Bam! David runs right into him."

"Was *he* mad?"

"No. He picks him up and says, 'I have a son just like this fine young man.'"

"Was it scary to meet the President?"

"I didn't know he was the President."

"That's silly. Everyone knows the President!"

"You forget, little Miss Mayer, in the old country, I never saw a picture of him. Important government people in Europe don't walk among common folk like us."

Havah remembered the tears in Mr. Roosevelt's kindly blue eyes when she told him how she had survived certain death. He welcomed her to America and said he hoped she would find a safe haven.

"Are you going to finish telling the story or aren't you?" Wendy poked her shoulder.

"Yes, yes, of course. Where was I? He sits down and talks to me like an old friend. Then he takes me to the ticket counter and tells the man to give me eight tickets to Kansas City.

"Also he gives me this to dry my tears." Havah took a handkerchief from her apron pocket. Unfolding it, she showed Wendy the letters that had been embroidered with gold thread on the corner. "See? 'T' for Theodore and 'R' for Roosevelt."

"Wow! Wait 'til I tell Mommy!"

# CHAPTER SEVEN

The aromas of roasted chicken and sponge cake mingled in the air even though supper had long since been eaten. Laughter came from the kitchen where Arel helped his stepmother Fruma Ya'el with the dishes. Disregarding Havah's protests he insisted she rest her swollen feet and read to his father.

Resigned, she settled back on the sofa and thumbed through her Psalm book to find just the right one. The Hebrew letters, like familiar friends in this yet foreign land, danced in celebration across the yellowed pages. The ancient writings, particularly the ones penned by King David, comforted her.

*"Gahm kee elekh bagay tsalmahvet, Even though I walk through the valley of the shadow of death—lo eerah rah kee atah eemahdee, I will not fear evil for You are with me."*

"I hear sadness, my little scholar."

Despite his blindness, Yussel Gitterman's eyes remained as gray and clear as his son's. His white beard gleamed in the lamplight. He cocked his head to one side.

"Soon my baby will be born." With her fingertips she traced the outline of a tiny foot through her blouse. "He'll never know his grandfather."

"Nu? What am I? His maiden aunt?"

"You know what I mean."

"Don't worry. Your son will know his grandfather through the stories we'll tell him, you and I. Your papa Shimon Cohen, now there was a *somebody*. Everyone was entitled to his opinion. And such opinions, I can tell you! Once he made up his mind, there was no arguing. Even the Baal Shem Tov wouldn't have a chance with him. One time, in Talmud Torah class . . ."

Havah's heavy eyelids fluttered and the living room faded into a colorful haze. As Yussel's voice intoned like a steady rain, she drifted back to her childhood . . . with Papa . . .  dear, sweet Papa.

The Heder teacher's face turned crimson. He narrowed his eyes and glared at five-year-old Havah as if she were a piglet about to be dumped on his doorstep. Then he clenched his tobacco-stained teeth and spat a brown glob on the doorstep.

Up until this moment she had been excited to learn to read the Torah, the words that came from Adoshem's own mouth. Huddled against Papa's shoulder she hid her eyes in his coat folds.

"You can't be serious, Rabbi Shimon. She's a girl."

"So she is." Papa's arm tightened around her. "My daughter's mind is every whit as keen as her brother Mendel's."

"To be certain she's a bright one, and one day she'll be a most excellent wife and mother. Perhaps she'll even marry a rabbi herself *but*, Rebbe, to come to Heder with boys? It's not right."

"Where does the Torah say it's wrong for a girl to learn?"

"Rabbi Ben Hyrcanus clearly stated in the Talmud that to teach a daughter Torah is *tiflut*, obscenity. And did he not also say that the words of the Torah should be burned rather than be entrusted to a woman? Rabbi, you of all people should know this."

"As far as I'm concerned it's opinion and rubbish! Didn't the prophet Yo'el write 'your sons *and* daughters shall prophecy'? Miriam and Deborah—were they not judges in Israel?"

"You win, Rebbe."

"I always do."

The soft couch embraced Fruma Ya'el's tired back. Snuggling against her husband, she watched Arel carry Havah up the stairs to their bedroom.

"I'm afraid I put her to sleep with my chatter," said Yussel.

"Nonsense. She's exhausted. I only hope she sleeps tonight without a nightmare."

Yussel skimmed Fruma Ya'el's lips with his index finger and then leaned forward for a kiss. He tugged a lock of her shoulder length hair. "It feels soft. You know I've never seen it, but even with those flowery scarves you wore then you were a beauty. To tell the truth I had a bit of a crush on you even then."

"For shame! We were both married to other people, may they rest in peace."

He shrugged. "You want I should lie?"

"Stop! Aidel was my best friend."

"And Hershel was mine. I think they would approve."

Years before, when Arel and Gittel, Fruma Ya'el's daughter, were children, an epidemic swept through Svechka. The fever took not only Yussel's wife Aidel, but his eyesight as well. The closest thing to a doctor in the village, Fruma Ya'el nursed him and many others back to health.

When her husband Hershel suffered a heart attack two years ago, Yussel waited less than six months to ask for her hand. By then she had also lost Gittel. The prospect of life alone terrified her, so she accepted his proposal.

A wayward lock of hair tickled her forehead. She tucked it behind her ear. "I'll never get used to them, these modern American ways."

"What's really vexing you?"

"What if both of our grandbabies should come at the same time?"

"Sarah will help. If memory serves, she's learned all about being a midwife from her Auntie Fruma. Nothing to worry about."

"I'm worried." Fruma Ya'el twined her fingers between Yussel's. "From the first day Havah appeared at my door in Arel's arms, half dead from her narrow escape, she became my daughter, as dear to me as my own Gittel, may she rest in peace."

"I remember that *Shabbes* morning. What a Sabbath! We found her collapsed on the synagogue steps. And who else could tend to her wounds better than our Fruma?"

"Did I tell you that Gittel tried to back out of her marriage to Arel the night before the wedding?"

"And I tried to convince him to run away with Havah the same night."

"Yussel Gitterman, you didn't!"

"Why not? He loved her. She loved him."

"You know good and well why not." Settling back against a cushion, Fruma Ya'el sighed. "If she hadn't run off she'd never have met Professor Dietrich. What a kind, gentle man was he to give her so much. I don't know what I'll do if . . ."

"If she dies in childbirth? She won't. She's young."

"Yes, she is, but not strong. Remember how the children all came down with German measles when we first arrived in Kansas City? In three days they're over it, but not Havah. If being in a family way wasn't enough. She was so ill she couldn't get out of bed for two weeks." Fruma Ya'el grasped Yussel's wrist and lowered her voice to a whisper. "When her time comes, even the youngest and strongest woman wrestles with the Angel of Death. Sometimes he wins."

# CHAPTER EIGHT

Seated at the piano, Ulrich held Havah's rosewater-scented letter to his nose. For a moment he savored it like fine wine then laid it on the end table next to his deceased wife's picture. Picking up the framed photograph, he kissed her image.

"Valerica, queen of the angels, you left too soon."

Heaving a resigned sigh, he placed his fingers on the keyboard to practice a piece for an upcoming concert. Just as he played the opening notes, Nikolai straggled into the library. Dark hollows framed his blue gray eyes. Ulrich turned from the piano.

"What happened, Kolyah?"

"Do me a favor and just kill me." Dropping his medical bag on the floor, Nikolai sat on the sofa with a groan.

"Here's what you need." Ulrich opened the end table drawer, pulled out Nikolai's flute case and held it out to him. "Music hath charms to soothe the savage breast."

"Let me be for a moment. For the past hour, I've had to listen to the complaints of a fat aristocrat who thinks she is at death's door when all she really needs is castor oil and a good swift kick in that ample area she sits upon."

"You work too hard. Methinks the doctor should prescribe a social life for himself. Find a good woman."

Nikolai threw a sofa cushion which narrowly missed Ulrich's head, bounced, hit the piano keys and generated a mélange of sour notes. With a grimace, Nikolai stretched his arms over his head. He rose and walked to the bookcase where he took a crystal decanter from a shelf and poured a glass of sherry.

"Methinks Professor Recluse would do well to mind his own affairs and take his own advice." He swallowed the sherry with a single gulp.

"I've been in love twice. Never again. Besides, most of the women I've met in London are mindless flibbertigibbets who wouldn't know Charles Dickens, the author, from Henry Dickens, the chimney sweep."

"Touché."

Nikolai poured a second glass and pointed to the envelope on the table. "What's in the letter? Good news I hope?"

"No news yet, I'm afraid. She and Shayndel are running a race to see who gives birth first."

The doorbell rang. Ulrich started and looked at the clock. "Who on earth would that be at this hour?"

"I'll see to it. The way my luck's been running today, it's 'Lady Aristocrat' wanting me to treat her immediately for some incurable disease she just read about and is certain she's dying of." Nikolai set down his glass and left the room.

A few moments later an angry female voice resounded from the foyer. "Are you Professor Dietrich?"

"You'll find him in his study, Madame. It's the first door on your right. Whom shall I say is calling?"

The words had barely left Nikolai's mouth when a lavender perfumed whirlwind, heels pounding a staccato beat on the hardwood floor, stormed into Ulrich's study.

"Professor Dietrich, I presume?"

"At your service, Fraulein." He stood, clicked his heels and bowed.

Under a straw hat her emerald eyes flashed and a profusion of strawberry blonde waves and ringlets bobbed around the young woman's heart shaped face. Her blouse's lace collar accentuated a graceful neck. He found himself completely captivated.

"How dare you give a failing mark to one of the most brilliant musicians of our time!"

"And just who might this 'brilliant musician' be?"

"Quinnon Flannery."

"I'm sorry, Frau Flannery, I had no idea he was married to such a charming lady."

"Epstein."

"I beg your pardon?"

"My last name is Epstein. *Mrs.* Catherine Flannery *Epstein*!"

"Then you're not Quinnon's wife? You're too young to be his mother."

"I'm his blasted sister and guardian, you dolt. My brother has *never* received a failing grade."

"Yes, it's an unfortunate situation. The truth is I didn't *give* your brother his failing mark, he *earned* it. Quinnon is talented, but even the most gifted musicians need to put forth a certain amount of effort. The world will never hand out accolades to the undeserving, and neither, Frau Epstein, shall I."

"Are you insinuating my brother is lazy?"

"No, madam," said Ulrich. "I'm not *insinuating*, I'm saying it straightaway. If your precious baby brother doesn't start working more and playing less, he'll not only fail my class, he'll be expelled as well."

Her lips paled and her anger abated like a snuffed candle. She nearly collapsed on one of the red chairs, hiding her face in her hands. Unsettled, Ulrich knelt beside her and pulled a handkerchief from his pocket.

"Is there anything I can do to help, Frau Epstein?"

"I promised Mum I'd look after him and I can scarce look after myself." She raised her head and dabbed her eyes. "I owe you an apology, Professor. You see, my brother is what you might call 'willful.' And since our parents both passed away it's fallen to me to raise him."

"What about your husband?"

"I'm a widow. Quinnon and I are quite alone in this world."

"May I offer you my condolences, Frau Epstein." Ulrich's throat tightened and sweat trickled down his neck.

"Please call me Catherine. I hate the name Epstein." She held out her gloved hand.

He took it and held it to his lips. "Only if you'll call me Ulrich."

Her round cheeks flushed. She smiled, revealing captivating dimples and a charming overbite. Something about her made him feel as though he had returned home after an arduous journey.

Reluctantly, he released her hand, then walked with backward steps to the piano and flipped Valerica's picture.

"Tell me, Catherine, do you have plans for this evening?"

"I've made a date with David Copperfield. Why?"

"I beg your pardon?"

"Surely you've heard of the book by Charles Dickens. My only plan is to nestle into my favorite chair and read." His heart fluttered against his ribcage like someone risen from the dead. "Are you hungry?"

"I'm positively famished."

"I know of a café that's open late and serves marvelous food. May I buy you supper?"

On the way out, he passed Nikolai who shook his head and whispered under his breath, "Never again."

# CHAPTER NINE

Itzak Abromovich's laughter sated Havah like a cool drink of water on a sweltering August day. Short and stout as a bear cub, his eyes twinkled like midnight stars. He could always find amusement, even in the worst situations. Sometimes she wished Arel could be a little more like him.

"That was the best *Shabbes* dinner I've ever had." Itzak pushed back his chair and patted his stomach.

"You say that every Friday night," said Shayndel.

"That's because it gets better every week."

Since moving into their own homes three months prior, Shayndel and Havah took turns with Sarah hosting Sabbath dinner. Havah loved their new tradition.

"Next week it's my turn to host—ouch!" A sudden kick to her ribs quelled Havah's appetite. She set down her fork.

"You shouldn't plan too far ahead. If I stuck a pin in you, you'd pop like a balloon. *Bam!*" Sarah's husband Wolf snapped his fingers.

"Wolf, that's rude!" exclaimed Sarah.

"Those babies won't wait much longer. A week at the most I'd say," said Fruma Ya'el.

"Come out, come out, Baby Cousin." Sarah and Wolf's five-year-old daughter Evalyne lay her head on Havah's belly. "I can hear him swimming inside you, Auntie."

Her twin brother, Jeffrey, snickered and rolled his eyes. "Girls are so dopey."

With childlike excitement, Itzak jumped up from his chair. "Speaking of babies, I have something to show everyone."

In a flurry of giggles and overlapping conversations, most of the family, save Havah and Shayndel, followed him to the living room.

Havah reached for her cane beside the chair and struggled to stand. Swollen ankles made it more difficult than ever to walk and the baby's added weight put more stress on her back.

On the other side of the table, Shayndel stood and then grabbed the back of a chair with one hand, her other on her stomach. She bit her lip and answered Havah's unvoiced question. "Just a hard kick, that's all."

"You wouldn't lie to me, would you?"

"Go on. I'll be along in a minute. I promise."

Reluctant to leave her, Havah followed everyone to the living room where they gathered around something in front of the fireplace.

Itzak and Shayndel's house had been built by the same builders and were mirror images of each other—the only difference between them was décor.

Both dining rooms had ornate tables and chairs to match, for Itzak made his living as a cabinetmaker. When Arel had tried to pay Itzak for the set, he folded the money and stuffed it back into Arel's pocket.

"A man should never make a profit from his own family."

In the old country such finery was affordable only by the wealthy, and even then there was no such thing as electricity or indoor plumbing where her people were concerned. It never ceased to fill Havah with wonder.

"Little Brother, you've outdone yourself." Wolf knelt beside two cradles, one made of oak and the other of walnut. "It's no wonder your business is already successful."

"I wouldn't be doing nearly as well if it hadn't been for Sol Mayer's influence and backing." Itzak sat down on the floor between the cradles.

"And well he should. The wardrobe you built for Zelda is an amazing piece of furniture."

"Not too shabby for a '*shtetl* peasant', eh? Havah, you should choose since it's your first child."

"What if you should have two babies again?" She pointed to Mendel and David, sound asleep on the sofa.

"One can sleep in a washtub until I can make another cradle. Now choose."

"I like the lighter one with birds. It matches my cane."

"Did you make this, too, Uncle Izzy?" Evalyne traced the vine with intricate leaves and flowers that wound around the cane until they came to the handle, a carved eagle's head.

"Do chickens have beaks?" asked Itzak.

"Last year, he made this for me." As if it were a child, Havah caressed the cane. "He's a special man, your uncle. When he's sad he makes others happy."

A pinch in her lower back made Havah flinch. Nothing to worry about she told herself. Over the past nine months she had experienced a host of new twinges and pains. She could never be sure if they resulted from injuries suffered in Kishinev or from her son finding new places to explore. She eased down onto the sofa next to Arel.

Evalyne wedged in between them and laid her head on Havah's stomach.

"Evie, let Auntie have some peace. You've been all over her tonight." Sarah frowned.

"Please let her stay. She's comfortable," said Havah.

"Auntie Havah shared a bed with Ruth and Rukhel in Kishinev, and usually by sunrise their little brother, Tuli, would join them, so she's used to being crowded by little ones," said Itzak as he headed for the stairs with the walnut cradle under his arm.

"Do you miss those boys and girls in Kishinev, Auntie?" Evalyne's round eyes, brimming with curiosity, seemed to pop out of her slender face.

"Would you miss your nose if it fell off?" asked Havah.

Sarah held her finger to her lips. "Evie, you'll wear Auntie out with your questions."

"How else will she learn? She can never ask me too many questions."

"She's a bright one, my granddaughter." Yussel tapped his cane on the floor. "She'll be starting school soon, yes?"

After one last draw on his pipe, Wolf emptied it into an ashtray on the end table. He leaned back on the sofa and stretched his lanky arms over his head and his long legs out in front of him.

"Auntie Havah reads the Torah in Hebrew, doesn't she?" Evalyne stuck out her lower lip.

"Public school is a wonderful thing," he said. "The twins will learn to read and write like American children. There's talk at the synagogue of starting a Talmud Torah class as well. It will be like *heder* in the old country, so Jeffrey will learn Hebrew, too."

"What about me?" Evalyne sat up straight.

"Talmud Torah classes are for boys, sweetheart."

"Auntie Havah reads the Torah in Hebrew, doesn't she?" Evalyne stuck out her lower lip.

"Yes, I do. Is this not America? Why shouldn't Evie know what her brother does?" Havah rose and arched her back in an attempt to find some relief.

"Are you saying we should be without tradition like the gentiles?" asked Wolf with a growl in his voice as he stood.

"I'm saying, our traditions should include women and girls."

"Then your tradition contradicts Talmud!"

"My papa used to say the Talmud is just a bunch of rabbinic opinions."

"They're damn good ones at that, and I'll thank you to keep your ideas to yourself where my daughter's concerned."

Havah's stomach tightened. She pressed her lips together, sat on the sofa and held her breath until the pain eased.

"Papa! Papa, don't yell at Auntie." Sobs convulsed Evalyne's thin shoulders as she sprang from the couch and threw her spindly arms around his knees. "Say you're sorry, Papa."

Sweeping his daughter up into his arms, Wolf muttered, "Sorry," but his dark eyes still blazed without apology.

Arel clapped his hand over Havah's mouth before she could answer and said, "Please. It's Shabbes. Peace. You know how it is with women, Wolf. After all, she *is* in a family way."

Havah stared at her exhausted reflection in the mirror above the dressing table. With a vengeful tug at a snarl she parted her knee-length hair down the middle and plaited it into two braids.

"What's the matter? You haven't said a word since we came home." In his nightshirt and cap, Arel knelt beside her and said, "Talk to me."

"All right." She threw her hairbrush to the floor. "'You know how women are, Wolf. After all she *is* in a family way.' Does that sound familiar?"

"Is *that* all that's vexing you?" He stood and moved toward her, arms outstretched.

"Is that *all*? Let me tell you—*ow*!" A cramp, worse than all the others combined, took her breath.

When at last the pain subsided, she took a deep breath. A pounding at the front door interrupted her reply. The pounding grew louder. He grabbed his bathrobe and raced down the stairs. She hobbled close behind. Fully dressed, Fruma Ya'el beat them both to the door and flung it open. On the front porch, looking like a boy separated from his mother in the woods, stood Itzak with a groggy son on each arm.

"Mama's getting a baby," said David.

"She says any minute," said Mendel.

"Put the boys in the extra bedroom upstairs." Fruma Ya'el took Mendel from Itzak and handed him to Arel. "Itzak, how far apart are her pains?"

David yawned and held up three fingers. "This many."

Glad to have something to offset her anger at Arel, Havah followed Fruma Ya'el and Sarah. When they entered the bedroom, arms loaded with bed linens, towels and blankets, Shayndel forced a smile, which quickly faded. She moaned and grasped the bed frame behind her.

After a moment her fingers eased open and she smiled again. "That was a hard one."

Clad in robe and slippers, Sarah sat on the bed beside her and wiped her brow with a damp towel. "How long have you been in labor?"

"Not long."

"Liar! You've been having pains since right after dinner." Havah snapped her fingers.

"And *you* were in bed weren't you? I hope Arel's not upset."

"Who cares if he's upset? When a baby's ready to come, it's ready to come. There are some things *men* can't control."

"It's all Wolf's fault," said Sarah. "He'll never learn when to keep his mouth shut."

Shayndel sighed and rolled over onto her side. "Havah, do you remember when you helped Auntie Fruma deliver Bayla?"

At the end of the bed, Fruma Ya'el arranged the sheets and prepared a blanket for the newborn that would soon make its appearance. Then she laughed aloud. "Help? She curled up on the floor like a frightened puppy."

Havah's face warmed. "Mama, that was six years ago and my first time. I've helped you with lots of babies since then."

"And you delivered Katya's son Velvil all by yourself." Fruma Ya'el's face glowed with pride and then crumpled with sadness. "Such a waste."

There was no time for sorrow. Shayndel seized Havah's hand. "It's coming!"

At the same time, a sharp pain squeezed Havah's midsection. When it passed she saw Fruma Ya'el and Sarah's attention focused on her. Embarrassed, she shrugged. "Just a little indigestion."

"How many minutes apart is your 'indigestion'?" Fruma Ya'el raised an eyebrow.

"I can't do this again." Grabbing Havah's arm, Shayndel pulled herself up. She bent forward with a strained cry.

"You should've thought of that before you let Itzak share your bed. Knees up. Push." With a concerned glance at Havah, Fruma Ya'el helped Shayndel spread her legs.

Havah pressed her hands against Shayndel's shoulders and squeezed her eyes shut. Another band of pain radiated from Havah's lower back to her stomach. Finally it ebbed, and she opened her eyes in time to see the baby slide into Fruma Ya'el's waiting hands.

With one deft motion she clipped the umbilical cord and held up the wailing baby. "Mazel tov, Shayndel! You can plainly see it's a boy." Fruma Ya'el bathed the infant, swaddled him tightly in the blanket and then laid him in Shayndel's arms.

A sense of awe flooded Havah as she watched the infant suckle. She lightly touched his tiny hand and he curled his fingers around hers. "'*Adoshem* gave and *Adoshem* took. May the name of *Adoshem* be blessed.'"

After a short while the baby fell asleep. With an exhausted smile, Shayndel's eyes fluttered shut. "Would you like to hold him?"

Havah held out her arms, but as she did so, a vicious cramp gripped her. She bit her lip, doubled over and wailed. "Maamaa!"

"It's just as I feared. We greet two babies in one night." Fruma Ya'el placed her arm around Havah's shoulder. "Sarah, prepare the guest room for our second blessing."

"No, take me home," whispered Havah.

"It will be easier on all of us if you stay here where I can watch you both."

Hot liquid gushed from between Havah's legs and splattered the floor. All argument ceased.

Afternoon sun streamed through the window. Havah winced. "What time is it?"

"Four-thirty." Sarah pulled the shade.

Fruma Ya'el, who had dozed off in a chair beside the bed, raised her head and rubbed her eyes. "What do you care? You have maybe an important meeting to go to?"

How many hours had it been? Havah had lost track. Pain was a faithful husband, enfolding her in his raffish arms off and on throughout the night and into the day. Each embrace sapped more of her strength.

"How much longer, Mama?"

"Do I look like some kind of fortune teller to you?" Fruma Ya'el's smile looked artificial and her hands shook.

Havah's lover returned and devoured her. She bit her lip and moaned.

Sarah rubbed her shoulders. "You needn't be so brave, little sister. Scream if you have to."

"What if I disturb Shayndel?"

"She's had three children of her own. She'll understand."

"I should've gone home." In the next room the baby cried and then quieted. Havah closed her eyes and listened to his suckling noises.

"It's better this way." Sarah stood and stretched. "I should tend to supper. No doubt the men are hungry and I don't trust any of them in the kitchen."

A searing pain shot through Havah. She grasped the bed frame behind her and gritted her teeth. But when Fruma Ya'el reached inside of her, Havah's resolve not to scream crumbled.

When the pain subsided, the older woman pulled back and washed her hands in the basin on the bed stand. "It won't be much longer, my precious daughter. His head's in the right place, thank the Almighty."

Although Fruma Ya'el refused to discuss the details of Gittel's death in childbirth with Havah, Shayndel had. The baby boy had presented feet first, umbilical cord wrapped around his neck, and strangled to death before he could be born. Gittel hemorrhaged and poor Fruma Ya'el watched her daughter and grandson die, helpless to do anything about it.

Another pain slashed through Havah, racking her spine. Finally it released her and she fell back in the bed.

Outside the closed door she heard Arel and Sarah's voices, but could not make out what they said.

"Mama. My last words to Arel were angry ones. What if I should—"

Fruma Ya'el pressed Havah's blazing face between her cool hands. "Shah! Don't say it! Don't even think it!"

The door swung open. Fruma Ya'el jumped to her feet. "Out! This is no place for a man."

"She's my wife and he's my son." In two long strides Arel covered the distance to the bed.

"Stay . . . please." Comforted by his presence Havah nestled against him until agony riddled her again. Fruma Ya'el shoved her thighs apart.

"He's coming. Push, Havah. Push him out."

"I can't."

"You have to. Arel, make yourself useful."

Gently nudging her forward he slipped in behind her and wedged her between his legs.

Her face pale and haggard, Fruma Ya'el stood at the end of the bed, ready to catch the newborn. "Push hard!"

Havah warred against her body. A bluish face appeared between her legs. Fruma Ya'el seized the head. "Lay back."

Devoid of will or feeling, Havah collapsed against Arel's chest. She closed her eyes, squeezing back tears. It was too quiet. "He's dead isn't he?"

"No!" Fruma Ya'el hollered.

A loud slap and a high pitched squall preceded Arel's excited laughter. Havah held her breath until the warm bundle weighed down her arms. She opened her eyes and blinked. Flooded with awe and disbelief, she studied the infant from wet, dark hair to ten perfect toes.

"Arel? Our son's a girl."

Just outside the window a robin chirped as Havah marveled at her daughter nestled in the crook of her arm, studying her delicate features. Like a newborn kitten she squeaked, wagged her head from side to side, and with her rosebud mouth, tugged at Havah's tender nipple. Then, after a few energetic sucks, she sighed with satisfaction and fell asleep.

"She looks just like her mama," said Shayndel.

Faint light peeking through the curtain cast a tawny glow over Shayndel who stood at the foot of the bed with her infant son asleep on her shoulder.

"Did I wake you?"

"No, he did."

"You shouldn't be up."

"I only walked across the hall. Besides, I feel much stronger than I did after the twins."

"Just the same, you should be in bed."

"Move over." With an impish grin, Shayndel pulled back the covers and tucked in beside her. "There. I'm in bed."

Shayndel propped up her knees and laid her son against her thighs. Havah did the same with her daughter. Side-by-side the infants did not look as if they had been born only hours apart. While he was chubby, fair and bald, she was almost half his size with a full head of black hair.

"She's a tiny mite like you, Havah." Shayndel touched her fingertip to her niece's nose and sighed. "I'd hoped for a little girl this time."

"And I was so sure I'd have a son." Havah caressed her nephew's cheek. "Have you chosen a name yet?"

"Itzak wants to name him after his brother Evron of blessed memory, but wants to give him an American name as well. So his Hebrew name is Hevron and his American name will be Elliott. What about my niece?"

From the bedside table Havah lifted her prayer book and opened it. She took out and unfolded a child's drawing. Underneath the stick figures of a boy and a girl, written in Yiddish it said, "Tuli loves Auntie Havah."

"I wanted to name my son after him, but not my daughter. So I'll name her for Tuli's sisters, Ruth and Rukhel. Rukhel will be her Hebrew name and Rachel her American name. Her middle name is Esther for the Jewish queen of Persia who saved her people from annihilation."

"What does Arel think?"

With a bouquet of daffodils and lilacs in one hand, Arel burst into the room. After he set the flowers in a vase on the bureau, he hurried to the bed and swept his daughter into his arms.

"What do I think? She's my little American Jewish princess. Rachel Esther."

# CHAPTER TEN

*How could a delightful person like Catherine be remotely related to this disagreeable boy let alone come from the same parents?*

While they shared familial red hair and freckles, the similarities ended there. With a perpetual smirk on his narrow face, Quinnon slunk down in his chair and spoke in exaggerated cockney.

"Hey, Guv, what's the meaning of keeping me after class?"

To hide his revulsion, Ulrich turned his back to him and rifled through a stack of sheet music, took one from the middle of the stack and handed it to the youth.

"Here's the piece you'll play for your final recital. It's a folk tune I've transcribed that lends itself well to the violin."

Quinnon took the paper from Ulrich's hand and studied it. "Yid music?"

"I beg your pardon?"

"You expect a gifted solo artist to play this Jewish rubbish?"

To keep from losing his temper Ulrich counted to ten under his breath then swung around. His jaws ached with unsaid epithets.

"Mr. Flannery, your playing is at best—how shall I put this?—adequate."

"Then why should I bother with a recital at all if I have no talent?" Quinnon wadded the paper into a ball and viciously flung it to the floor.

"I never said that. You hit the right notes in all of the right places, but you lack passion. Passion, my good man, is what separates a great musician from an adequate one.

"For example, my friend Itzak Abromovich, without any formal training, plays with such enthusiasm Antonio Stradavari himself would stand and cheer!"

"All right. I guess I'll have a go at it, Guv." Quinnon bent down, picked up the paper and smoothed it.

"That's Professor Dietrich to you."

"Being's how you and me darling sister Cate is sweethearts, I'd say that makes us mates, eh, wot?"

Ulrich leaned into him until their noses met. Alcohol and stale tobacco odors sent a surge of aggravated nausea through him. "Sister or no sister, you come into my classroom drunk again and I'll see to your expulsion—*personally.*"

"You wouldn't dare!"

Ulrich smiled and lowered his voice. "Are you a betting man, Herr Flannery?"

# CHAPTER ELEVEN

Despite Fruma Ya'el's apprehension, Havah insisted she was well enough to celebrate Passover with the family. Having second thoughts, Havah leaned back on the hard chair and fought to keep her eyes open.

Wolf's flat voice droned on and on until Jeffrey broke the monotony. "'*Mah nish tahnah, ha layla ha-zeh mee kol halaylos?* Why is this night different from all other nights?' Did I say it right, Papa?"

With a pat to his son's head, Wolf continued to read from the Haggadah, the book of the Passover service. "'On all other nights we do not dip even once, but tonight we dip twice! And on all other nights we eat leavened or unleavened bread, but on this night we eat only matzo, unleavened bread.'"

Two-week-old Elliott Abromovich nuzzled against Itzak's chest and then wailed. Itzak chuckled. "Someone wants something other than matzo on this night."

Blushing, Shayndel picked up the baby and excused herself.

To see her, no one could guess she had given birth only two weeks before. Full of energy, in a matter of days she was out of bed, chasing after her twins with Elliott on her hip. Havah ached all over and she was still too weak to do more than feed Rachel every two hours.

Irritation apparent, Wolf cleared his throat. "'On all nights we eat any kind of vegetables, but on this night *maror*, bitter herbs.'"

"Papa, I have to go you know where." David's whisper was loud enough to be heard over a locomotive's whistle. He hopped up and down beside Mendel.

"Can't you wait?" Itzak whispered back, nearly as loud.

"Huh-uh."

"Sorry to interrupt again." Itzak stood, taking his sons' hands. "Mendel, why don't you join us?"

"I don't have to go, Papa."

"Keep me company. Please. Don't wait for us, Wolf."

Wolf frowned and took a deep breath. "'On all nights we eat sitting upright or reclining, but on this night we recline.'"

Before he could read on, Evalyne tugged his sleeve. "What's 're-cline?'"

"At this rate, we might be finished with this Seder in time for breakfast! 'Recline' means to lean back and relax, Evie."

"But we're not leaning back, we're sitting on chairs, and me and the boys are sitting on a lot of books, too."

"You have a bright daughter, Wolf," said Yussel.

"I'm smart like my auntie," said Evalyne.

One eyebrow raised, Wolf leveled his scorching glare at Havah. "Why don't you just ask your learned aunt?"

Exhausted and more uncomfortable by the minute, Havah bristled. "This is what my Papa told me when I was a little girl, Evie. In olden times, only royalty reclined at their fine tables while they dined. Servants sat on the floor to eat their meager portions. Now that we are free we have the right to eat like royalty."

"Is that true, Zaydeh?" asked Evie.

Yussel's proud smile warmed Havah and put her at ease. "I couldn't have said it better. Now I will tell you the story of Moshe Rabeynu, Moses our rabbi."

He continued to recite the story of the Hebrew slaves' deliverance from the Pharaoh from memory. Despite Havah's efforts to stay awake, the table blurred and disappeared. The next thing she knew, the floor hit her backside. Her cheeks blazed as Arel helped her to her feet and led her to the settee in the corner of the dining room.

"Someone needs to recline," he said.

Yussel stopped his story in midsentence and clanked his fork against his plate. "The end! Let's eat!"

With a solicitous eye on Havah, Fruma Ya'el gathered the dinner dishes. A plate balanced on her knees, Havah dozed on the settee in the dining room. Pale and too thin, she looked less than comfortable.

"Arel, take your wife home."

"I'm not through eating." Havah's eyes fluttered open. She sat up straight, took a bite of chicken and then grimaced.

"It's ice cold, isn't it?" Fruma Ya'el grabbed the plate.

On the floor beside the settee, the babies lay in their cradles. Elliott's lusty cry woke Rachel. In two swift motions, Shayndel rose from her place at the table, swept a baby up into each arm and plopped down beside Havah.

"It's too early for either of you to be up and about." Fruma Ya'el wagged her finger and clucked her tongue.

"Wife, enough with the speech making. Leave them be." Yussel interrupted her and then leaned forward as if searching for something. "We set a place for Elijah, but alas, I don't see him anywhere."

"Of course you don't, Zaydeh. You're blind," said Jeffrey.

Sarah's mouth dropped open. "Jeffrey!"

"Oy, after twenty years my secret's finally out!" Yussel cocked his head to one side. "Now who'll go look for Elijah?"

"Me!" Jeffrey ran from the room.

"No, me!" Evalyne chased after him, followed by Mendel and David.

Squeals and shrieks came from the living room. Minutes later, Mendel crept back into the room, his dark eyes wide with terror. His whispered voice quavered. "He's . . . he's here and he's a giant!"

Behind him, David peered around the corner. "It's not Elijah, you goofus."

A tall man with a red handlebar moustache followed the boys into the room. In one massive hand he clasped a black medical bag. He took off his derby, held it against his barrel chest and bowed.

"Do you remember me, Mrs. Gitterman?"

"Dr. Miklos! How could I forget you? You're the one who took care of Havah on the ship when she was so ill." Fruma Ya'el set down the dishes and wiped her hands on her apron. "Please forgive my grandsons' bad manners."

"I would hardly call it bad manners, Mrs. Gitterman. No, indeed not. How often am I mistaken for the great prophet Elijah?" His laughter echoed. "As for taking care of the little lady, all I did was give her some bicarbonate of soda and diagnose her condition. But I'll admit with the cholera epidemic, she worried this old doctor. She sure did."

"I thought you were going to live with your sister in Minnesota, Doctor."

"What can I say? She was a nuisance as a girl and she's only gotten older."

"How'd you find us?" Arel stood and embraced him.

"Remember your invitation, my young friend? You gave me your sister's address."

"It's a rare man who can read my brother's handwriting," said Itzak. "There's still plenty of food left. Please join us."

"Thank you, but no thank you. I'm on my way to dinner with a colleague. I just stopped by to let you know I'm in town and at your service."

Still holding a baby on each shoulder, Shayndel rose from the settee. "It's so good to see you again."

Dr. Miklos raised one eyebrow and cast a sidelong glance at Havah. "Not twins?"

A slight blush tinted Havah's wan cheeks. "They're cousins, but they were born a day apart."

"May I?" He took Elliott into his arms. "Two weeks old, I'd say. He's a strapping lad. A strapping lad, I must say."

After he kissed the baby's cheek he handed him back to Shayndel and lifted Rachel who looked even tinier engulfed in his arms.

"What beautiful eyes." For a brief moment a frown shadowed his face. "She's a lovely child; a beautiful girl like her mother."

Something about his smile seemed artificial to Fruma Ya'el as he bowed. "With your permission, I'll return in a few days to look in on my patients."

"Please." Fruma Ya'el's neck prickled. She followed him to the front door and seized his arm.

"What's wrong with my granddaughter?"

# CHAPTER TWELVE

With the grace of a prima ballerina, tall and lithe, Catherine, arms loaded with packages, twirled through the toy shop from one doll to the next. Her uncontained strawberry waves shone in the sun. Ulrich was helpless to do more than watch her childlike antics with delight.

"Oh, Ulrich, look! Aren't these dolls the most gorgeous things you've ever seen? What little girl wouldn't want one?"

"Catherine, Rachel's just an infant. All she wants is a dry bottom and a full tummy."

"She won't be one forever, you know. And whilst we're at it, why don't we buy an extra for little what's her name? You know, Havah's niece."

"Evalyne. According to Havah, she's quite a tomboy. She might not appreciate a doll."

"Poppycock!"

Catherine's childlike pout melted whatever resolve he might have had.

"A doll for Evalyne it is!" he said.

By afternoon's end, Ulrich was convinced Catherine had chosen a toy for every child in Kansas City.

"Frau Epstein, you are certainly having a lovely time spending my money."

In an instant the giddy child disappeared and she lowered her voice to a hissing whisper. "Don't you ever call me that!"

After her outburst Catherine sobered. No matter how much Ulrich tried to coax her out of her mood, his best efforts fell flat. Arms aching with the weight of packages, he led her to a park, found a bench and sat. He set his load on the ground and grasped her gloved hand.

When she pulled away her glove came off and exposed her calloused palm. He turned her hand over. Although rough and chapped, it was slender and graceful. She yanked it back and sat beside him, head bowed.

"Now you know."

"I know what?"

"I'm nothing but a scullery maid."

Fingertips pressed against her chin, he forced her to face him. She frowned and tried to turn from him, but he prevented her. With his thumb, he brushed a tear from her cheek.

"They're like fresh green leaves with little flecks of golden dew."

"What?"

"Your eyes, my dear, you have the most incredible eyes."

"You're not paying attention, Professor." She shoved his hand aside. "I'm no one you want to know."

He slid off the bench, sat cross legged in the grass and cupped his hands behind his ears. "I'm listening now."

Her lips quivered into a slight smile. She seized his hat and swatted him with it. "You're impossible."

Grasping her still ungloved hand, he kissed each callous.

"Don't do that. Hear me out first."

She wrenched back her hand and fingered her scarf fringes as she spoke. "Dad owned a distillery when I was a little girl. Fairly well off then, we were. On my seventh birthday, Mum and Dad presented me with Quinnon."

"My condolences."

"Influenza took Mum a year later. Dad drowned himself in drink and music. He often took us to recitals at your Royal College. That's where Dad hired Sherman Epstein, a young violinist, to teach us. Alas, I had no talent for it—all of that went to Quinnon. Sherman claimed he was a child prodigy and came to our house twice a week, every Tuesday and Thursday for lessons, until . . ." Her voice trailed off, she gulped and then continued ". . . until the day my father threatened to hang him if he didn't marry me because I was . . ." She brushed a tear from her cheek. ". . . in a family way. Then Dear Old Dad gave me a black eye and a sprained wrist as my dowry."

"Is that how you got that scar on your wrist?" He pointed to where her blouse cuff had come unbuttoned. "It must've been a nasty cut."

"It was just a scratch." She blushed as she fastened it. "It happened a long time ago."

Something in her voice, a mixture of anger and sadness, told him not to press.

"Forgive me. Go on."

"It's strange how swift Dad's judgment came. Quinnon found his strangled body stuffed in a whiskey barrel a fortnight later. Poor boy, he was barely ten. He still suffers nightmares."

After a moment of uncomfortable silence she whispered, "My . . . my son . . . died. Sherman made my life a bloody hell. I . . . I divorced . . . him."

"But didn't you tell me you're a widow?"

"Widow sounds more honorable than divorcée. But he is dead in any case. Not long ago they found his body in a house of ill repute in Whitechapel. Bullet through his brain and his 'lady friend' strangled to death.

"There you have it, Professor. I'm cursed. Run away now. Other men have."

Ulrich pulled her onto his lap and pressed his lips hard against hers. "Other men are fools."

# CHAPTER THIRTEEN

Nestled between Shayndel and Fruma Ya'el on the porch swing, Havah relished the evening breeze on her face. Lulled by crickets, locusts and the swing's rhythm, Rachel slept across Havah's knees. Her black hair curled under the ruffled bonnet from England. Black eyelashes fringed her pink cheeks. Could any child be more beautiful?

The door opened and Sarah stepped outside with a pitcher of lemonade. She set it down on a small table beside the swing. "I've never seen Evalyne so excited about a doll. She's calling her Miss Catherine. I must write and thank Professor Dietrich and his Catherine personally."

"Elliott will outgrow these beautiful clothes, if he ever has a chance to wear them." Baby on her shoulder, Shayndel brushed her fingers over his smocked linen gown.

"Can you believe they sent two baby carriages full?" Perched on the porch railing, Nettie grinned. "Havah, I bet if Zelda knew you had such a wealthy friend, she'd invite you to all her soirées."

"No, thanks." As Havah sipped her lemonade, she crunched a stray ice chip.

With a mixture of longing and joy in her eyes, Nettie reached over and caressed Rachel's cheek. "I hope my baby's as cute as these two."

"Nettie, you can't be with child!" Sarah bit her lip. "What if—?"

"I'm not going to lose this one."

"You said that last time and the three times before that."

Sarah, who sat on the railing, wrapped her arm around Nettie's shoulder, and then turned her attention to Havah. "Little sister, I've been thinking about it. Evalyne wants so badly to learn Hebrew. Would you teach her?"

"What does Wolf think?"

"I'll break it to him gently."

At the sound of the women's laughter the babies woke. Raising his head off Shayndel's shoulder, Elliott blinked. A moth flew by his head. He followed it with his eyes and cooed.

When it flew over Rachel's face, Havah's scalp tingled and her stomach tightened into a hard knot. She could no longer deny the truth.

# CHAPTER FOURTEEN

After a dinner of roasted mutton and colcannon, an Irish stew consisting of potatoes, cabbage and cream, Ulrich leaned back in his chair and watched Catherine stack the dishes. Candle flames flickered in her green eyes. Amber tendrils framed her flushed cheeks like a wild wreath; her coquettish lips beckoned him. In that moment, the desire to sweep her off to his bedchamber surged through him. Instead, he placed his hand over one of hers.

"I haven't had anything like that since I lived in Moldavia. Anzya was quite the cook. Leave the dishes, Catherine. I'll wash them."

"Really Ulrich, this house is too big for you not to have a wait staff. You should have a cook, upstairs and downstairs maids and a governess for Vasily."

"Let's discuss the matter over some after-dinner music, shall we?" He stood, led her to the library where he sat at the piano and tugged her hand until she sat beside him. Then he placed his fingers on the keys and played and sang. *"'Casey would waltz with a strawberry blonde and the band played on.'"*

"It's an important matter, Ulrich," said Catherine over the music.

"I had a delightful upstairs maid in Kishinev."

"You're talking about Havah, aren't you?"

"She was a brilliant slip of a girl."

You're still in love with her, aren't you?"

"Who says?"

"No one needs to." She pointed to the cluster of Havah's pictures on the end table. "I don't see any photographs of Anzya."

"She would never let anyone take her picture." He rose from the bench. With an exaggerated bow and a flourish, he extended his hand, palm up. "Mademoiselle, would you do me the honor of this dance?"

"You're daft." She stood and nestled in the circle of his embrace.

"So I've been told."

Tightening his arm around her slender waist, he waltzed her across the library. In the middle of a turn, her hairpins clinked to the hardwood floor. Her ungovernable waves of auburn hair cascaded over her shoulders.

He tilted his head and sang in her ear. *"'He'd glide 'cross the floor with the girl he adored and the band played on.'"*

"You've gone dotty, Professor Dietrich."

"Only when I'm with you, my little firebrand."

For a few blissful moments they whirled and danced, as her heart thumped against his chest.

"Ulrich, darling?" Her hot whisper against his neck made him quiver. "I've the most wonderful news."

"Do tell."

"Quinnon's procured a position with a small chamber orchestra."

"*Sehr gut.* Now he can repay you for all the sacrifices you've made for him. You probably got those nasty scars on your arms supporting his worthless carcass."

She stiffened, wrenched out of his embrace and turned her back to him. Then she moved to the door. He followed her and grabbed her hand. She spun around and tried to pull away, but he tightened his grip.

"Who did this to you?" he asked pointing to the marks on her exposed wrist.

"I told you before. I had an accident. Never speak of it again, do you hear?"

"Forgive me, Cate." Ulrich let her hand slip out of his.

"I thought you'd be pleased about Quinnon."

"Oh, I am. I am." He crammed his hands in his pocket.

"It's late. I should leave."

"Please. Don't go."

"I have to work in the morning."

"I know of a better job for you."

"Oh?"

"*Ja.* As you've said, I need a *hausfrau*."

"You want to hire me as your *hausfrau*—your housekeeper?" Her voice scaled up with each word. She whirled around to slap him. "I thought I meant more to you. You fiend! You cad! How dare you!"

He caught her hand in midair and then took a box from his pocket with his free hand.

"This is for you."

"You think you can buy me off with trinkets?"

"*Nein.*" He released her arm and opened the box.

Her mouth dropped open as he lifted a gold ring with a faceted green stone framed by diamonds from its velvet nest and slid it onto her finger.

"Perfect fit," he said.

Her lower lip quivered. "It's . . . it's . . ."

"It's an emerald to match your eyes."

"You're asking me to be your . . . your. . . ?"

"I'm asking you to be my *hausfrau*, my mistress, my *wife*."

# CHAPTER FIFTEEN

Mary Alice? Mary Alice?" Dodger's tearful voice rose with each thump on the door until she feared someone might call the police.

The man next to her pulled the covers over his head. "Tell whoever it is to go away."

With a groan she wrenched out of her "gentleman caller's" arms, tumbled out of bed and went to the door. She opened it a crack and peeked at the boy in the hallway. His blond hair hung in his eyes. A hand-me-down night shirt, two sizes too big, draped the floor.

"It's after midnight. Bad dream?"

The boy wedged his hand through the narrow opening and tugged at her bare thigh. "Come quick, Mary Alice. I've tried and tried to knock her up, but she won't open the door."

"Wait out there." She shut and latched the door. Although the kid knew what she and his mum did for a living, he did not need to witness it.

She took her orange silk dressing gown from the hook on the wall, put it on, then walked back to the bed and kicked her caller's ample rear end. "Time's up. Out with ya."

Instead of the hoped for compliance he rolled onto his back, reached up, grasped her wrist and wrestled her to the mattress. His moist breath in her ear sent shivers down her neck. He wrapped his leg around her knees and caressed her lips with his stumpy fingers. "I ain't had me shilling's worth yet."

She clamped her teeth down on his thumb. He yelled and let go of her. Springing off the bed, she tied her robe's belt tight. From a pile on the floor she picked up his clothes and hurled them in his face.

"Okay for you now, wench! You owe me and I'll be back for it!"

He sat up and pulled on his pants and socks. Then he tucked his shirt and shoes under his arm and stomped to the door. He yanked it open and snarled at the boy who tripped over the threshold.

"I'm sure she's all right, you little rotter." Mary Alice helped Dodger to his feet and led him down the hallway. "She's probably sleeping it off! You know how your mum is. Ivona likes to have a good time, that one!"

Upon entering the room she smelled the telltale stench. It was the same odor from a decaying mouse she found under her bureau. She turned to the boy who followed close behind, tugging at her robe, and gave him a gentle shove.

"Stay put, ya hear?"

"But—"

"Not a bloody word more."

Once assured he was going to mind, she approached the bed on tiptoe and covered her mouth with her hand. Ivona's vacant brown eyes bulged, her swollen black tongue protruded from her mouth, her wrists were bound with a thin cord and her palms were pressed together between her bare breasts as if in prayer.

With quaking hands Mary Alice dropped the blanket back over her friend's face and stepped in front of her to block the boy's view.

"Get out, Dodger!"

# CHAPTER SIXTEEN

A milieu of colors danced before Havah's eyes and the room spun with dizzying speed. Somewhere from the miasma she heard a woman's muffled scream . . . it was her own.

"My daughter's blind?" asked Arel in a hoarse whisper.

Startled by Havah's outburst, Rachel wailed from Dr. Miklos' shoulder. She quieted as he patted her back and swayed. "She's perfect in every other way. Indeed, she's a perfect child. Try to remember that, young Mr. Gitterman."

Fruma Ya'el grasped the doctor's forearm. "Isn't there something you can do? An operation maybe?"

"The medical books call it 'congenital blindness.' She was born this way. I suspected it the first time I saw her. I prayed I was wrong. I prayed so hard."

"Blind. My daughter's blind." Arel repeated it, his voice an agonized rasp. "She's alive, little brother." Behind the couch, Itzak leaned over and squeezed his shoulders. "Be thankful."

"Be thankful for *what*?"

"She's been spared the sight of your face."

"Everything's a joke to you, isn't it?"

Without another word Arel rose, stomped to the front door and yanked it open. His shoulders drooped like an old man. With his grim eyes on Rachel, he frowned, turned his head and stepped outside.

"Where are you going?" Havah sprang off the couch to follow him.

The door slammed behind him.

"Let him go." Itzak wrapped his arms around her.

"It's my fault." She dropped her head on his chest. "I'm a bad mother."

"Nonsense!" Yussel, who had been quiet in the rocking chair until that moment, pounded his cane on the floor. Then he leaned it against the chair and held out his arms. "Give her to me."

Once the doctor laid her on his lap, Yussel leaned forward and brushed his hands over her face. She, in turn, brushed her fingertips, like tiny feelers over his nose and lips, tugged his beard and cooed.

"The people who walk in darkness have seen a great light." With a satisfied smile he cuddled her against his shoulder. "*I* will teach her to see."

Downstairs the grandfather clock chimed midnight. Arel had not returned from his walk. Havah rocked Rachel and tried not to think about where he might have gone or what could have happened to him.

She let her mind travel to a spring day when she was a carefree child—to a time when both of her feet were whole and there were no scars—where there were only blue skies and lilacs . . .

"Havah, would you like to play hide and seek with us? We'll even let you be 'it' first." Nine-year-old Beryl Mayorovich winked at the other boys.

Eager to be included in their play, she shut her Hebrew primer and jumped to her feet, brushing leaves from her skirt. At last they wanted to be friends.

"Stand by that tree, cover your eyes and count to twenty. Count slowly so we have time to hide."

She turned her face to the tree, shutting her eyes tight. "One, two, three . . ."

"Some of the boys like to hide in the tool shed behind the synagogue." Beryl's peppermint breath tickled her ear.

". . . eighteen, nineteen, twenty. Here I come!"

Searching behind bushes and trees, she found no one. They must be hiding in the shed. Wasn't it nice of Beryl to share his secret with her? As she approached the shed she heard laughter. *Aha! He was right.*

"I have you now!" Havah stepped into the small, crude structure.

The door slammed and latched behind her. Darkness engulfed her.

# CHAPTER SEVENTEEN

Although Nikolai hated to write letters, his conscience compelled him to answer Havah's most recent correspondence. While he had feared something would go wrong due to her delicate health, he never dreamed her baby would be born blind. Even Ulrich, for all his wealth and affection, could not rescue them.

"These damnable kerosene lamps." Pen in hand, he squinted in the dim light at the blank paper.

Never skilled in bedside manner, the right words eluded him. He licked the nib and wrote. "*Dearest Havah, I'm so sorry . . . Nyet,* too familiar."

He crumpled the paper and tossed it in the waste basket beside the desk.

On a fresh page he wrote, *"Dear Friend . . . Nyet! Nyet,* too formal."

Again he crumpled the paper and tossed it. Once more he started over.

> *Dear Havah,*
>
> *It's with great sorrow I concur with Dr. Miklos. He is a most excellent physician. No doctor can do more for Rachel. We can't give her the optic nerves she was born without. Remember she's still a precious human being.*
>
> *Your friend,*
>
> *Nikolai Derevenko*

"This will have to suffice," he said as he folded the letter and put it in an envelope. "I'll post it in the morning."

With his task behind him he leaned back in his chair and listened to the quiet. He had the house to himself this evening as Ulrich had taken Catherine to the theatre. Although they had invited him to join them, Nikolai did not want to intrude; they deserved their privacy.

In an attempt to cheer himself, he picked up his flute from the table beside his chair, brought it to his lips and played an Allemande sonata. Usually music would lift his spirits, but tonight it only intensified his loneliness as he reflected on his life, beginning with the day he told his father he had chosen medicine over music.

Sergei Derevenko, a prominent violinist in the St. Petersburg philharmonic, eyed Nikolai with a mixture of anger and hurt.

"You'd rather slice people open and wallow in their blood and bile than delight thousands of patrons with your talent? I don't understand you, Kolyah."

"You never have. Why start now?"

"But how can you abandon your dreams."

"Don't you mean *your* dreams, Tatko?"

"Not one kopek will I pay for this nasty folly of yours, do you hear?"

The day Nikolai left St. Petersburg, Sergei locked himself in his room like an angry child.

During Nikolai's time in Heidelberg, Sergei attempted to lure his son back to music but every exchange between the two of them ended in hostility and chilled silence. All communication ceased for the next four years.

While he never regretted his decision, Nikolai did regret the rift that still existed between them. After commencement, more out of a sense of duty than guilt, Nikolai made one last journey to his father's home. Over *blini*, Russian pancakes and a samovar of spiced tea, they finally spoke of nothing that mattered. Following the meal they played a few duets as they had when Nikolai was a boy. By the end of his two week visit, neither of them proffered an apology and staunchly remained worlds apart.

Another sonata, soft and low, turned his thoughts to the creature who had taken advantage of and, ultimately, robbed him.

Sixteen years ago, a young man ready to take on and conquer the world, he studied under a tree until a shadow darkened the pages of his medical book.

She held a piece of paper in her hand. "Pardon me, sir. Could you give me directions to this address? My friend Valerica and I are hopelessly lost."

Her laughter echoed through the trees like birdsong. Sleek brown hair framed a lovely oval face. Her brown eyes with long black lashes imprisoned him at once.

"I'm sorry, Miss . . ." His throat closed as he fought to speak.

"Oh, please, call me Ivona! That's my name you know. How silly of me. Of course you don't know. My goodness, you're such a serious one." She grabbed his eyeglasses and propped them on her slender nose. "How do I look? Are you always this talkative, Mr.—"

"Derevenko . . . Nikolai . . . my friends call me Kolyah."

Two years later, Dr. Miklos slapped his back. "Congratulations, Dr. Derevenko, you have a son!"

"How is my wife?"

"She's as strong as a Romanian farmer's wife! She was born for having children. My services were never really needed. All she had to do was squat and push him out."

Despite the baby in the crook of her arm Ivona appeared to be anything but maternal—even her effusive chatter lacked sincerity.

"Oh, Kolyah! Look at him. He looks just like his father. I'm in love already!"

"He's perfect." Nikolai took the newborn in his arms with a sense of awe and kissed his soft cheek. "What do you think of the name Vasily?"

"Name him anything you like," said Ivona with the attitude of a child suddenly bored with her doll. "Can you imagine Dr. Miklos comparing me to a farmer's wife? The very idea!"

"You silly girl, it's a compliment. I hope it goes the same for me," said Valerica Dietrich who had assisted Dr. Miklos. Nine months with child herself, she maneuvered her awkward girth from her chair. "I'll leave you three alone. I've ignored Ulrich long enough." She leaned over and kissed Vasily. "Soon you'll have a playmate, little darling."

Three hours later, Valerica's panic stricken maid summoned Nikolai. After attending the arduous labor Nikolai filled out two death certificates. He spent the rest of the night trying to console a shattered Ulrich.

When he returned home, Ivona's shrill voice startled and stunned him. "You selfish pig! I've been here alone all night with your brat."

From then on her obsession with her looks and petulant self-absorption sickened him. His only consolation was their son to whom she paid little attention. So it baffled him to no end when she left him and took six-year-old Vasily with her.

"Enough of that, Doctor," Nikolai whispered and set his flute on the table. "Brooding won't change anything."

The doorbell rang.

"Who's coming to call at this late hour, I wonder." He glanced at the clock on the mantle, walked down the hallway to the front door and pulled it open.

A woman with a henna-dyed pompadour and a determined expression under a feathered hat stood on the step. Her cheap perfume's scent burned his eyes. How had she found him and why?

"Miss Tanner won't you come in?" He bowed at the waist.

"Lord love you, you remembers me!" She stepped inside and whistled through the gap between her front teeth. "Would you look at this place? Why a veritable palace is what this is! Oh, pardon me bad manners, Guv, that McKenzie bloke said you lives here." She coquettishly dipped her head which made the bright feathers on her hat dance. "I shoulda know'd the minute I laid eyes on ya in the artist shop. You looks alike you two."

"Who looks alike?"

"Why you and Dodger, of course."

"Your nephew?"

"Your son, Doctor."

The ground tilted beneath Nikolai's feet. After years of denied prayers and failed searches there stood Vasily on this very doorstep. His eyes seared through Nikolai like a hot poker.

"Eh, now, Dodger." Mary Alice ran her lace-gloved fingers through the boy's hair. "That ain't no way to greet your dad, now is it? At least say hello."

"*Zdravstvuiteh . . . Tatko.*"

The joyful reunion Nikolai yearned for never happened. The sunny six-year-old he remembered had turned into a sullen youth who refused to say more than *'da'* or *'nyet'* to anyone.

One afternoon, Nikolai entered the library to find him playing a simple melody on the piano. "You remember what Uncle Ulrich taught you."

Without responding or even looking up, the boy continued to play. Nikolai sighed, and then moved a chair so he could sit beside him.

"Solnyshko, please, it's been three days. I understand you miss your mother. It was a horrendous thing that happened to her."

Only then did Vasily stop. In the ensuing hush he stared at his hands, then brought one to his mouth and chewed his thumbnail. He spat out the bitten tip which landed on Nikolai's shoe.

"Ivona was nothing but a common whore and she got exactly what she deserved. I hated her and I hate you!" Vasily sprang off the bench and ran from the room.

Nikolai's heart banged against his ribs. At the top of the stairs the bedroom door slammed shut. His son's angry words echoing in his ears, Nikolai ascended the steps and opened the door. A porcelain pitcher sailed over his head and shattered against the wall. He raised his hands to shield his face.

"Go away!"

Vasily picked up the matching bowl and flung it. It clipped Nikolai's brow.

Stunned by the sudden blow he staggered backward. "Solnyshko, don't."

"Stop calling me that!" The boy shrieked and butted his head into Nikolai's stomach. "I'm not your 'little sun' anymore."

Dazed and winded, Nikolai grunted and dropped to the floor. "Every night I prayed you'd come for me, but you never came. She laughed at me." Vasily yanked open a bureau drawer and scattered its contents.

In a feeble attempt to stand, Nikolai rose to his knees. Overcome with dizziness he sank back down and leaned his throbbing head against the wall. Flashes of light danced around him and he fought to remain conscious.

Like the sudden end of a cloudburst, the boy calmed and knelt beside him. He dabbed Nikolai's cheek with a stray stocking and then stared at the red blotches seeping into the white wool.

"Why didn't you want me, Tatko? Why?"

Nikolai pulled the boy to him and whispered, "Damn her."

# CHAPTER EIGHTEEN

Although a seamstress she would never be, Havah enjoyed the Tuesday morning sewing circle for the company of other women. She grimaced at her uneven stitches on a pair of knickers. At least a boy would not care whether his seams were straight or not.

Meanwhile, Zelda Mayer droned on and on about the impending arrival of Sol's nephew Barry from the old country. "Sol's loaning him the money to attend the new medical school in Kansas City. Such a brilliant young man."

Havah could stand her boasting no longer. "Even if he was raised in a *shtetl*, right Zelda?"

Zelda's open mouth clamped shut and thinned into a taut line. Her icy violet eyes shot disdainful bullets at Havah. Then she settled back against the sofa cushions, jabbed her needle into her mending and whispered, "Peasant."

A muffled titter went round the circle. Hunched over her sewing, Nettie hummed a cheerful tune. After a few minutes of awkward silence, the ladies' conversations resumed.

On the pallet beside the sofa, Rachel slumbered next to Elliott. She looked like any five-month-old who cried when wet or hungry and cooed when content.

How could Rachel sleep so peacefully now when she had screamed almost all night? Havah ached with exhaustion and frustration. When she had begged for Arel's help, he pulled the covers over his head. He had to work in the morning, he'd said, and did not have time to be a nursemaid.

Around sunrise, the recalcitrant tooth poked through and Rachel drifted off. By then it was time to be about daily tasks. Havah cooked breakfast in silence. The only sounds until Mama and Papa joined them were the rustle of Arel's newspaper, the clink of his fork on his plate and the angry buzz in her head. When Mama urged her to go back to bed and leave the chores to her, Havah refused.

As the rain's litany against Sarah's window soothed Havah with its rhythmic patter, she wished she had not been so stubborn. It had almost lulled her to sleep when Nettie sprang from her chair and spun around in a clumsy pirouette. Her belly bulged under her loosened blouse. Round cheeks aglow, she held up an embroidered baby gown.

"It's finished and suitable for either a boy's bris or a girl's baby naming."

With a raised eyebrow, Fruma Ya'el glanced up from her mending. "Six months. You've felt life?"

"He's an acrobat, this one."

Something in Nettie's effusive tone gave Havah doubts, but before she could voice any of them a sudden burst of hail peppered the window panes followed by a thunderous crash. Rachel started awake and shrieked. Nettie dropped the gown, knelt and swept her into her arms.

The baby quieted and opened her eyes. One of them turned inward and never moved while the other oscillated aimlessly. Nettie cuddled her against her shoulder and whispered. "Poor little thing."

"Don't you ever call her that!" Havah threw the mended knickers to the floor, jumped off the sofa and took Rachel from her.

A shocked hush descended and the clatter of hail intensified. Stares from the other women pierced Havah. She squared her shoulders and pressed her daughter to her breast.

"I understand, Havah. Forgive me. Please, let me hold her."

Nettie lifted the baby back into her plump arms. As she did so, her eyes widened and she doubled over, still holding tight to Rachel.

"Oh God! Please! Not again!"

After nine hours of agonizing labor Nettie gave birth to a live baby boy. Not much larger than a newborn kitten, yet perfectly formed, he fit Dr. Miklos' palm. His tiny mouth opened in a silent cry.

Havah lifted her eyes from the baby to Dr. Miklos. His moustache drooped and he gave his head a slight shake. She bundled the soiled bed linens into a basket and hid her face behind it so Nettie would not see her tears.

"Give him to me." Nettie reached toward the doctor.

"Nettie, don't." The sheets fell from Havah's hands.

"Where else should a son die, but in his mother's arms?"

Dr. Miklos bound the baby in a clean handkerchief and laid him in the crook of her arm. Her voice quavered through a lullaby. Barely visible next to her left breast, his little head moved from side to side as if searching for her nipple. By the time she ended her song, he had wheezed softly and forever stilled.

*"Barukh dayan Ha Emes—Blessed is the True Judge."* George Weinberg chanted in a flat monotone, sat on the bed and laid his head on Nettie's stomach.

"Amen." Dr. Miklos sadly gathered his instruments into his bag.

"You should leave me, Georgie." Nettie stroked George's balding pate. "My womb is a graveyard."

"What do I need with children? I have you." He whispered as he lifted his dead child from her grasp. Kissing the top of his head, he held him against his chest. "I'll make the arrangements. You rest."

Side-by-side the two men left the room in silence. As the door shut behind them, Rachel, who lay in the cradle meant for Nettie's baby, woke with a lusty cry.

Havah's full breasts blazed. "Just a little while longer, Rukhel Shvester. We have to get home to Papa."

"Feed her *now*." Nettie grasped her arm. "Arel can wait."

Too tired to argue, Havah hoisted Rachel into her arms and sat in a chair beside the bed. She unbuttoned her saturated blouse.

Tension flowed from her and she felt her muscles go limp. Rachel's suckling sounds lulled her into a waking dream until Nettie broke into it.

"You're right, Havah."

"About what?"

"If you treat her like a normal child, she'll see herself as normal. But if she's treated as an object of pity, she'll sink into self-pity and live a life dependent on others."

"I wish Arel felt that way."

"He just needs time to adjust."

"It's been three months already."

"You tell him Rachel's his treasure. So be happy."

Nettie caressed the baby's head. "He was a bit older, my little Myron. Seven months."

"You and George had a son?"

"My *first* husband, my Avram, a watchmaker in our village in Poland, and I had a son. Ten pounds the midwife said. He nearly killed me, but I was just seventeen, and strong as young mare.

"Ah what happy times those were, Havah! I had everything, a home, a nice looking husband and an ox of a son. What more did I need?

"But was that enough for Avram? Ha! He dreamed of selling his fine watches to wealthy Americans. So together we managed to save every spare zloty—I with my sewing, him with his trade—until we collected enough for our passport and passage. Just enough.

"They crowded us into the cargo hold of the ship; crammed together like so much cattle. Oy. Can you imagine? Babies and their diapers. Old people. Young people. No place to wash. Sickness. Vomit.

"One day I held my son to my breast, but he refused it. Didn't have the strength to suck. Went to sleep that night. Never woke up. Avram joined him a few hours later. Cholera. Not even a proper burial. Me? Not so much as a belly ache. Why, Havah? Why didn't I die, too?"

Nettie's light brown braids appeared almost black against her pale gray cheeks. She shut her sunken eyes.

"The Weinbergs took me into their home in the Lower East Side, where they owned a butcher shop. Treated me like a daughter. They provided me with a dowry and a husband—their only son. Not so much to look at, my Georgie, but a good man just the same.

"A year later we moved from New York to Kansas City. 'Cow Town,' George called it. He heard it's a good place for a butcher and a better place to . . . to . . ." Nettie's voice trailed off, ". . . to raise . . . children."

George said the only time he saw Nettie smile over the next two months were the times Havah came to call. Nettie adored Rachel. Why could Arel not see his own daughter for the treasure she was? In her highchair, seven-month-old Rachel mushed a banana slice between her little fingers. She raised it to her nose and sniffed. With a single toothed grin she popped it into her mouth.

"Havah, close that window!" Arel slapped his palm down on his shifting newspaper.

She walked behind him and curved her arms around his neck. "A little fresh air will do us all good. Indian summer is what Mrs. Hutton calls it. Stay home, Arel. Let's take Rachel for a walk."

"I have to go to work." He took hold of her wrists and pried her arms off his neck.

After she shut the window, she buttered two slices of toast and plopped them onto a plate with scrambled eggs and placed it front of him.

"Your daughter pulled herself up yesterday!"

"Hmmm." Without look up from his paper, he shoved egg into his mouth. Then he gave the baby a sidelong glance. "Don't they make dark glasses her size?"

"Arel, did you hear me? Your daughter stood up yesterday. This is a milestone in her life and all you care about is hiding her eyes so you don't have to look at them."

"Okay. It's stupendous. Do you mind if I read my paper? It's going to be a long day. I have a new class starting tonight."

Havah's stomach churned. She grabbed Arel's paper and sent the pages flying. "Your daughter is growing up without you. The word 'papa' won't even be in her vocabulary because she never sees you."

Rachel's lower lip trembled and she raised her arms. "Poppeee."

"It's not like she'll ever *see* me." His brows knit in a fierce scowl. He dropped on all fours and hunted through the scattered pages. When he found the one he was looking for he smoothed it and held it out to her. "I've been reading. There are places for people like her."

"She has a name, remember? It's Rachel Esther. She's a person." Havah took the paper and, without looking at it, ripped it in half.

"Of course she is. I never said she wasn't. And in one of those schools she can be with other persons who are . . ." he lowered his voice, ". . . blind."

"Why don't we send Papa, too?"

Rachel's whimpers turned to screams. Havah lifted her out of the high chair. It toppled to the floor and Havah kicked it aside.

"Havah, have you lost your mind?" He stood and grasped her arm. Rachel's screams turned to shrieks. He took her from Havah's arms. "You're scaring her."

Choking on her anger, Havah hobbled up the stairs to their bedroom. There she opened drawers and pulled his clothes from the dresser. Then she hauled a suitcase from the closet. Laying it on the bed, she opened it and tossed in his wadded shirts. She shut it, lugged it to the top of the stairs and let it fall. It thumped, hitting each step and then popped open when it landed at the bottom. She hobbled behind it and grabbed Rachel from him.

"Get out! Get out of my house!"

Arel dropped to his knees, threw his clothes back into the suitcase and clasped it shut. Struggling to his feet, he took his hat from the hall tree and kicked open the door.

"Havah, listen to reason."

"I'll listen when I hear it."

"Calm down. We'll discuss it when I come home tonight."

"Don't come back until you decide to be a father!"

# CHAPTER NINETEEN

At first it stunned and hurt Havah when Arel did not return. She had expected more of a fight. For two days she did not know where he had gone and worried that he had met with an evil fate. By the third day, worry gave way to anger and resentment.

On the fourth day, the telephone rang. When she picked it up, his voice was slurred and she could hear Sarah's voice in the background. Once more he begged her to put Rachel in an institution. From then on, she ignored any and all telephone rings. Mama or Papa could answer.

Through the window over the kitchen sink, the moon was a blurred pearl behind a strip of grey clouds. Weary to her very bones from lonely insomnia, Havah regretted having invited Jeffrey and Evalyne to sleep over. In the week since Arel's last attempt to call, she had only dozed for short periods, usually, upright in the rocking chair beside Rachel's crib. She whirled away from the window when something smacked her between the shoulder blades.

Evalyne's high pitched squeals shrilled through her. Jeffrey stuck out his tongue and hurled a wad of mashed peas. The green mush landed on Evalyne's head.

"If you two can't behave, you'll have to go home."

"I don't like peas." Jeffrey wrinkled his nose and squished them with his fork.

"Auntie, how come Uncle Arel's at our house?" Evalyne made trails in her mashed potatoes with a spoon. "Why does he act like he's mad all the time? How long's he gonna stay?"

Havah lowered her voice to a deliberate whisper and slapped the table. "Enough! No more questions."

"But you said I could never ask you too many questions."

"I lied."

Jeffrey cocked his head to one side. "Are you gonna get a divorce?"

"She said, 'no more questions.' You're such a dope." Evalyne rolled her eyes and tapped her spoon on the side of her chair.

With a mounting desire to stuff rags into both their mouths and set them on fire, Havah grabbed Evalyne's spoon and waved it under her nose. "Is that any way to talk to your brother?"

"It is, when he's a dope."

Jeffrey's lips bunched into a tight knot. He picked up a saucer and held it over his head. Havah plucked it from his hand before he could throw it at his sister. In time to keep Havah from pummeling the twins with her bare fists, Yussel entered the room with Fruma Ya'el on his arm.

"Perfect night for a stroll, Havah," said Fruma Ya'el. "Go wake Rachel and we'll walk the twins home."

"Arel knows where we live." Havah sniffed.

"Don't wait too long, Daughter." Fruma Ya'el took a wash rag from the sink and wiped the twins' hands and faces. Then she tossed the cloth aside and grasped Yussel's arm. "Come along, children."

"Auntie said we could stay the night." Evalyne jutted out her lower lip as she followed her grandparents.

Still clutching the spoon and rescued saucer, Havah eased down onto a chair and listened for the front door's latch. An avalanche of emotions rushed over her and, with all of her strength, she flung the saucer at the ice box and watched it shatter.

One week followed another, but Havah hardly noticed autumn's progression toward winter. Her nightmares and sleepwalking that had dissipated after Rachel's birth returned with a vengeance. At night she would fall asleep in her bed only to wake in another room.

On a particularly frigid night in November she fell into a deep sleep in the rocking chair beside the crib. In her dream, she returned to Kishinev. Cossacks broke down the front door. One made a grab for Rachel. Havah clutched her daughter under one arm and with her opposite fist, punched him square in the nose.

It was not a Cossack who woke her from her nightmare but Fruma Ya'el, blood trickling from her nose. Sitting on her haunches, she lifted the terrified baby. Befuddled, knuckles smarting, Havah blinked at her fortress constructed of overturned furniture. With relief, she noted that there was no knife in sight.

Rachel calmed and nuzzled Fruma Ya'el's shoulder. Then Fruma Ya'el helped Havah from the corner and led her to the sofa and sat. Havah collapsed against Fruma Ya'el.

"I broke your poor nose, Mama."

"Shhh. A scratch." She pressed her palm against Havah's mouth. "No one, not even your husband, is going to take away your baby. I promise."

Later, in the few remaining hours of darkness, Havah settled into her empty bed. Determined to stay awake, she switched on the lamp beside the bed and unfolded Ulrich's most recent letter.

While it pleased her to read of Nikolai's reunion with his long lost son, at the mention of Ulrich's new bride Catherine, she bristled. He called this stranger his firebrand and described her as a delight to behold with music in her eyes.

Chiding herself for her jealousy, she crumpled the parchment and let it drop from her hand. He was her friend, *and* he deserved some happiness after long years of loneliness.

She stared at the vacant half of the bed, Arel's unslept half.

"Men! Who needs them?"

In spite of her desperate efforts her eyes fluttered shut. A boy with sky blue eyes and winsome smile came to mind.

She hugged her pillow and whispered, "Beryl, Beryl, why did you have to leave? Where did you go?"

At the end of the school day, nine-year-old Havah closed her textbook and gathered the rest of her books and papers. Ten-year-old Beryl Mayorovich stopped at her desk and yanked one of her long braids. With a leering grin, he crunched down his teeth on a peppermint stick.

"You're really smart, Fraylin Cohen. Too bad you'll never be anything more than somebody's wife."

Since the day he and the other boys locked her in the tool shed, she went out of her way to avoid them. In over a year, she had not spoken a word to Beryl. Arms clutched around her books she stood, pushed past him and walked out of the room.

Undaunted, he followed her to the yard. Ignoring his taunts, she quickened her pace to a run, but his legs were longer and he caught up to her. From behind he grabbed her shoulders. She tumbled backward.

Sprawled on the hard ground, her face heated and her wrenched ankle ached. The other boys formed a circle around them. Rocks poked her back and she blinked back angry tears.

Beryl's candy hung out the corner of his mouth like a red and white striped cigar. "Ha! You might even be *my* wife."

Despite the pain wending its way up her leg, she struggled to her feet and kicked his shin. He yelped and lunged at her. She ducked his oncoming fist. Thrown off balance, he tumbled, head first, to the ground.

Hands on her hips, she dug her toe into his side. "Beryl Mayorovich, I wouldn't marry you if you were Adam and I was Eve!"

After that day the boys stopped badgering her. It humbled them to admit she was not only the smartest student in the class, but the best fighter as well. Many of them, including Beryl, even asked her for help with their lessons.

By the tender age of twelve, Havah had developed the attributes of a young woman. Despite her disappointed protests, her father agreed with her teacher that her *Heder* education should come to an end. The boys would never learn Holy writ with such a comely distraction.

Her brother Mendel became her *lamed*, her teacher. While she missed her classmates' challenges, she enjoyed mornings with Mendel and flourished under his tutelage. A strict teacher, he never allowed her any leeway because of her gender or kinship.

Afternoons were hers to do as she pleased. More often than not she would read from the book of *Psalms*, a gift from Mendel. In the springtime, King David's words seemed sweeter when read under her favorite Hornbeam tree. It was on one of those gentle reading days that Beryl came to call.

The sight of him no longer repulsed her. Since the day he taunted her in the schoolyard, he had grown at least three inches. His round chin had squared in anticipation of manhood.

"Havah, I'd never have been able to read as well for my Bar Mitzvah without your help. But—" He sat in the grass beside her.

"Don't worry, Beryl, your secret's safe with me. I haven't even told Mendel or Papa."

"I don't care if they know." His gaze held her. He leaned forward, his breath warm on her face. "Havah? Would you betroth yourself to me?"

"You'll have to ask Papa."

"Does that mean yes?" His cheeks flushed.

"Yes." Her heart somersaulted and thumped against her ribs.

He stood, took her hand, and helped her to her feet. In silence they walked side-by-side. She kept her eyes on the ground, counting each grass blade, until they reached the house. Like a row of yellow dainty maidens with yellow bonnets, Mama's daffodils surrounding the tidy porch greeted them.

"Beryl, you'll stay for supper?" Without looking up from the lentils she shelled into a crockery bowl, Mama raised an eyebrow and her lips twisted into a slight grin.

"No, thank you, Froi Cohen. May I speak with the rebbe?"

"You've got a mouth?" She gestured to the open door.

In a corner of the front room Papa, prayer book in hand, swayed to and fro, his voice like murmuring wind as he chanted a prayer. The closer she tiptoed toward him, the louder he sang. It was his favorite game. Who would dare to disturb the rabbi in prayer?

Havah tapped his shoulder. "Papa, Beryl has a question."

"And this question can't wait until after my prayers?" With a mock growl, the rabbi shut his book.

Beryl's ruddy face blanched. "Rebbe . . . Rebbe . . ." His voice splintered and squeaked. "I would like to ask to . . . to marry your daughter."

In the doorway behind them, Havah's brothers cackled and made silly faces.

Tugging her braids, Mendel tittered. "Mazel tov! A match made in heaven."

"Imagine, our baby sister a bride. I hope Reb Beryl doesn't mind changing her diapers." David draped Mama's dishtowel over his head, clasped his hands and crooned in a high pitched falsetto.

Papa's scowl softened to a compassionate smile. He placed his hands on Beryl's shoulders.

"If your love is true, son, it will keep until your voice changes."

# CHAPTER TWENTY

Dinner settled like a lump of plaster in Arel's stomach. He could not remember a more desolate Sabbath dinner save one. It was the first Friday night after his mother died of brain fever almost twenty years ago. Papa slumped at the head of the table, tears in his unseeing eyes, Mama's chair, conspicuous and empty beside him.

Tonight, much like that long ago Friday, not a word was uttered during dinner aside from cursory prayers. Even the children ate in silence. Their guileless eyes assailed Arel with unasked questions. Everyone felt Havah's absence, but no one dared mention her name.

Almost a full month had passed since he moved in with Wolf and Sarah. In the room he shared with Jeffrey, lights off, Arel sighed and made trails on the sweaty window pane with his finger tip. All of a sudden the light switched on.

"Do you always sit in the dark, little brother?"

"Shut off the damned light." Arel turned to glare at Itzak.

"Tears are nothing to be ashamed of, little brother."

"Leave me alone! Go home to your beautiful wife and your three perfect children."

Shayndel entered the room and batted her eyelashes. "Do you really think I'm beautiful, little brother?"

"Enough! I'm going for a walk." Arel sprang to his feet.

"Not so fast. I have something to say," said Wolf as he entered with Sarah beside him. They blocked the doorway. "You don't look like you've slept much. Your razor hasn't seen much use lately either."

"If you want me to shave, I'll shave."

"Grow your lopsided beard to your ankles. It's your sloppy work that concerns me. I'd hate to fire my own brother-in-law."

"Go ahead, fire me." Arel tried to push Wolf out of the way. "I don't care anymore."

Wolf shut the door with his narrow backside and then folded his wiry arms across his chest. "When are you going to pick up the telephone and call that feisty little wife of yours?"

"I've tried. She won't speak to me."

"She needs you."

"She has my paycheck."

"Try again."

"Stay out of it, Wolf."

"You're under my roof."

"Throw me out. You won't be the first." He stepped backward and sat back down on the bed.

No matter how hard Arel fought it, he missed his wife. Every night visions of her eyes haunted him to wakefulness. During the day, her smile set his mind to dreaming. Why could she not listen to reason?

A book dropped into his lap. He looked up to see Sarah standing over him. "Before you write off your little girl, read this. It's by a lady who's blind and deaf."

"I see how it is. You're all on Havah's side!" Arel flung the book to the floor. He scowled from face to face. "I only want what's best for my daughter."

"What's *best*?" Shayndel's face flushed crimson and the blue of her eyes deepened with rage. "You call sending her to live with strangers *best*?"

She reared back her hand, but Itzak caught it in midair. He wrapped his arms around her, pinning her hands to her sides. With a smile he fixed his eyes, dark and piercing, on Arel.

"You owe me twice, for I could cheerfully slug you myself."

# PART II

## *Blind Men See*

# CHAPTER ONE

A world away from Kansas City in Odessa, Ukraine, Arel's nephew-in-law, Gavrel Wolinsky, wadded a piece of paper in his hand. Wind blew through a jagged hole in the dusty print shop's window. Glass shards and a large rock littered the floor. He waved his fist in the air.

"Orev! This garbage you write is going to get us all killed."

Hunched over his printing press, Gavrel's brother-in-law raised his ink smudged face. His mouth contorted into a determined grimace and his hazel eyes shot angry flames.

"Our family's blood cries out for revenge."

As a young man Gavrel lost his bride of one year to a fever. Not only was he devastated by the loss of his beloved but by the fact that she left him childless.

For some men not to have a child would mean only that there would be no heir to carry on the family name, but for Gavrel the lack heaped tragedy upon tragedy. He adored children and always kept candy for them in his shop in Svechka. They, in turn, flocked to him like hungry birds for the treats and to hear his stories. Not a day went by without a child's kiss on his lonely cheek.

His longing for family of his own was only a dream until four years ago when he married Leah Resnick. A year later, she blessed him with their daughter Pora. Within hours of the happy event apoplexy struck and took Leah's mother Tova.

From that moment he adopted Leah's younger brothers and sisters, Devorah, Lev, Reuven and Bayla. To finally be called Papa was one of the greatest joys in his life.

While seven-year-old Reuven did not remember his father, Gavrel remembered him well. Feivel Resnick was a hateful drunkard who beat his wife Tova often. Fruma Ya'el believed those beatings caused Tova's untimely death. Not one of his children shed a tear when villagers found his beaten and stabbed body in the woods.

Although he had closed his shop for the day, Gavrel could not break his promise to finish the Reuven's new shoes. He struck a match and lit the lamp on his work table.

From a stack of clean rags in a basket under the table, Gavrel took one off the top and buffed the high top shoes. They glowed in the lamplight. Then he hoisted Reuven onto a tall stool and pulled off his old shoes. Holding one up, he whistled.

"Not a minute too soon, little apple. Your toes were coming straight through the holes. You're growing so fast I'd better start on your next pair now."

"Papa, when I grow up I want to be a shoemaker just like you."

"I'll teach you everything I know, son."

A frown darkened Reuven's ruddy face and he tugged at a strand of his crimson hair. "Lev says someday you'll have a real son and won't want me anymore."

"Don't listen to him." Gavrel crushed the child against his chest. "If I have *ten* sons, not *one* of them will take your place!"

Steam rose from the dish pan. Sweat beaded Leah's forehead and soaked her kerchief. Gavrel's chest ached with yearning and remorse. She deserved better. He circled his arms around her waist.

"A perfect fit."

Turning in his embrace, she planted a moist kiss on his cheek. "Spoken like a shoemaker."

"How else should I speak? It's what I am. We may not be wealthy, but our children will never go barefoot in winter."

"Remember how angry Havah was at our betrothal. She even accused Mama of selling me into slavery."

"As I recall, you weren't too happy about it either. After all, I am old enough to be your father."

He surveyed their cramped apartment. With a front room that doubled as a kitchen and three cramped bedrooms, it was much too small for a family of six. Despite Leah's efforts to keep it tidy, it was always cluttered.

"Maybe Havah was right and your mother did sell you into slavery."

"Don't be ridiculous." After another kiss, Leah turned back to the dishes. "I'm happy with my life."

"Havah's letters are filled with stories of how much better things are for them in America. Your Uncle Itzak writes, too. I think we should heed them. What would you think about moving there?"

Leah swung back around, her eyes swimming with tears. "Just like that? What about my sister Devorah?"

"She and Orev should move, too."

"He won't."

With each letter from the city called Kansas, promise of a better life in America enthralled Gavrel. Since the night he spoke of it to Leah, he thought of little else. No matter what, he had to take his family away from Odessa, especially fourteen-year-old Lev.

Gavrel worried about him more than the other children. Almost every night the boy accompanied Orev to meetings and rallies. Afterward, he returned spouting hatred, threats and revolution.

Plans crowded Gavrel's mind as he slipped a few coins into a soft leather bag. He synched it tight with a cord. It was not much money, but it would add up. He stuffed it into a narrow space behind his tool drawer, and then shut it.

He climbed the uneven stairs to the apartment over the shop. Even through the closed door, he heard Leah and Lev's shouted voices. Gavrel pushed open the door and froze.

There stood his wife, pistol in hand, nose-to-nose with her brother. His indignant blush accentuated the silver scar that went from one cheek, across his mouth and down to his chin, a gift from his father's whip.

"Give it back! It's mine," cried Lev.

"I'll not have this in my house! What if one of the children should find it?"

"They won't. I'm careful."

"You call hiding it under a mattress you share with a seven-year-old careful?"

Gavrel's stomach roiled. He wedged himself between them and grabbed the gun. "Did Orev give you this?"

"I don't have to tell you anything."

"As long as you live under my roof you do!"

"You're not my father!" Lev shoved him and ran out the door, slamming it behind with a loud bang.

“Ugh. This goes in the garbage.” With her thumb and index finger Leah lifted the gun from Gavrel’s hand as if she held a dead mouse by its tail.

Turning his head, Gavrel noticed the three children huddled in a corner, their eyes wide with terror. His three-year-old daughter’s eyes filled with tears while five-year-old Bayla kept a protective arm around her.

“Don’t worry, Pora,” said Bayla. “I won’t let anyone hurt you.”

“Papa, are the Christians really coming to kill us?” Reuven watched the door. “Lev says they are.”

Gavrel retrieved the gun from Leah and put it in one of the sideboard cabinets. She shook her head, eyes wide with disbelief. “You can’t be serious about keeping it.”

“Maybe we shouldn’t be so hasty about getting rid of it.”

# CHAPTER TWO

To warm her chilled face Havah craned her neck over a pot of bubbling farina. The steam cleared her head for a moment and she breathed in the piquant aroma of cinnamon. She tossed in a handful of raisins.

After she spooned cereal into a bowl she set the pot back on the stove, and then eased down onto a chair. She closed her swollen eyes and took a bite. No taste. Her head throbbed. She swallowed and relished the warmth sliding down her raw throat.

Sleet clattered against the kitchen window. Rivulets trickled down the glass. The whole world was colorless and grey. Perhaps the sun would never shine again.

Dressed in a robe and ruffled night cap, Fruma Ya'el padded to the stove. She poured a cup of coffee, filled a bowl with porridge and then moved to the table. Her mouth gaped in a wide yawn. Then she reached over and pressed her hand against Havah's forehead.

"No fever, but you look awful."

"It's just a cold, Mama." She strained to speak but could not muster more than a painful whisper. "I was up half the night with Rachel."

"Is she cutting a tooth?"

Havah nodded. "She's asleep now."

"So go back to bed yourself. I'll look after the baby when she wakes."

Havah picked up a book from the table and rose from the chair. "I'm going to read when I finish my housework."

"Housework, 'shmousework.' Look at you. Let me make a bed for you in front of the fireplace. You can read and sleep to your heart's content. What's your book about?"

"Sarah gave it to me. It's written by a young woman who's not only blind but deaf as well." Havah sneezed, setting off sharp explosions in her ears.

Fruma Ya'el stood, grasped Havah's hand and led her to her rocking chair. "Sit. Enjoy the fire. It was nice of George to build it before he and Papa left for morning prayers, wasn't it? I'll be back in a minute with blankets and pillows. Rest is what you need and rest is what you shall have."

Too weak to argue, Havah melted into the chair beside the sofa. Fruma Ya'el walked down the hall to her room. The flames in the fireplace crackled and warmed Havah.

A few minutes later, dressed for the day and arms loaded with bed clothes, Fruma Ya'el emerged from her room. Then she tucked sheets and blankets around the sofa cushions. Once she completed her task, she fluffed two pillows at one end and sat down at the other.

"Your lounge awaits, Princess."

Havah rose off the chair and then eased herself onto the sofa. She snuggled against the goose down pillows. The soft linen caressed her chapped face. She lay on the makeshift bed and propped her feet on Fruma Ya'el's lap.

Fruma Ya'el slid the heavy woolen sock from Havah's disfigured right foot. Then with her thumbs she kneaded it from one end to the other. Havah's cramped muscles loosened from her tight shoulders to her misshapen toes.

"It's been hurting a lot lately, hasn't it, little sister?"

"It just aches a little more when it's cold."

"You shouldn't lie to your mama." Fruma Ya'el bent over and kissed Havah's instep.

"Ugh. How can you do that?"

"Love sees only beauty." Fruma Ya'el pulled the stocking around Havah's ankle and then covered her with a thick comforter.

Shifting her position, she laid the pillow across Fruma Ya'el's lap and then let her head sink into it. The fire's warmth lulled her. For a brief moment Arel appeared in a dream and caressed her cheek, his breath sweet against her lips. His lucent gray eyes consumed her until the doorbell rang and he dissolved like sea foam.

"Auntie Havah. Open up! It's cold out here." The frantic patter of small hands rattled the door.

"What's Evalyne doing here?" Loath to leave her cozy cocoon, Havah opened her gritty eyes.

"Let me answer that." Fruma Ya'el slipped out from under Havah's pillowed head, hurried to the door and pulled it open.

Flanked by Jeffrey and Evalyne, Wolf stood on the front porch. Evalyne hopped up and down on one foot.

"Hi, Bubbie!" she cried.

"Come in! Come in before you catch cold!"

"It's snowing!" Flakes stuck to Jeffrey's dripping mittens.

"So I see." Fruma Ya'el closed the door behind them, took their coats, scarves and hats and hung them on the hall tree.

"Wolf? Is something wrong?" Resentful of the intrusion, Havah tried to raise her voice and sound demanding. "Shouldn't you be at work?"

"Arel's minding the store."

The twins raced to the sofa to sit on either side of Havah. Jeffrey leaned against her. "You sound froggy, Auntie."

With a stern expression on his face Wolf walked to the couch and loomed over her. He shoved an open book into Evalyne's hands.

"Read what you read to me last night." With all the flair of a melodramatic heroine, the girl cleared her throat with an exaggerated "ahem." Then she turned so Havah could see the pages. Pointing to each word, she annunciated with rabbinic skill. "*B'rayshees barah Elokeem es ha shamayeem v'es ha aretz. In the beginning God created the heavens and the earth.*"

When she finished her recitation, Wolf seized the book, knelt and waved it under Havah's sore nose. "This is your doing!"

Even through her clogged nostrils his pungent cigar breath assailed her pounding head. Her queasy stomach threatened to empty. She coughed and whispered, "Can we please discuss this some other time?"

"Wolf, can't you see she's not well?" Fruma Ya'el put her hands on her hips and scowled.

Still down on one knee, Wolf passed the book back to Evalyne. A smile softened his angular face. "What I have to say should make you feel better. Last night Jeffrey had trouble with his Torah lesson. Instead of asking *me*, his papa, for help, he asked his *sister*. At first I wanted to send *you* back to Eastern Europe in a rowboat—without oars. But my sweet wife with her quiet, persuasive way urged me to listen to my children and not my pride."

Evalyne threw her arms around Havah's neck. "I'm going to be a scholar just like you!"

"Yay! Evie can go to Hebrew school in my place."

Wolf lifted him onto his knee. "Sorry son. It only means Evie will study with Auntie Havah while you go to Talmud Torah class at the synagogue."

"Drat." Jeffrey's lower lip jutted. "Why'd I have to come anyway if you just wanted to show Auntie how Evie can read gooder than me?"

"I want you to see."

"See what?"

"A true scholar admits when he's wrong."

# CHAPTER THREE

John Doe." The name blurred before Nikolai's eyes as he scribbled it on the death certificate. "Too young."

The day before, a disgruntled carriage driver had carried the limp child into the clinic at St. Thomas Hospital. He said he saw the boy, who he claimed was an orphan, run out into the street after a dog. The distraught driver had been unable to rein in his horses in time. There was nothing the doctors could do to save the boy whose broken ribs had punctured both lungs. He breathed his last before the driver could lower him onto the examination table.

"Write it down, Doctor. Death occurred at 3:23 P.M., Wednesday, 23 November, 1904." The other resident on duty, Dr. Musgrave flashed an uncaring smirk.

"What makes you so sure he's an orphan?" Nikolai looked around, but the driver had made a hasty exit.

"Come on, Derevenko, we see it all the time, just another unwashed urchin cluttering London's streets."

"Doesn't it disturb you that this child's life is over before it began?"

"It's not as if *I* killed the little blighter. 'All the king's horses and all the king's men couldn't have put him together again.'"

"How can you call yourself a doctor?"

"Listen, Nicky, if you bleed like this for every motherless bloke, you'll end up in a lunatic asylum banging your head against the bloody wall."

Dr. Musgrave's striking good looks and cavalier attitude seemed better suited to the theater than medicine. He snickered, took off his apron and tossed it into a hamper by the door. Then he took a comb from his pocket and raked it through his wavy hair. His stony green eyes flashed.

"I'm going to look for his parents," said Nikolai.

"You're bloody daft!"

"It could have been my Vasily on a table like this, and three months ago I would never have known."

"Do what you must, but don't say I didn't warn you," Dr. Musgrave's expression softened and he squeezed Nikolai's shoulder. "Once you've finished with the little rotter, what say you and I join me mate Quinn at the pub for a tankard of ale? A visit to the ladies of Whitechapel will do you good."

After hours of questioning people on the street, Nikolai drew his own sad conclusions. The other boys called the dead child George, after the prince, but no one knew his given name. Shop owners saw him as a thief and one more nuisance, a bug to be squashed and never given a second thought.

On the cold steel slab the boy looked angelic. His long dark eyelashes fringed his grey skin and his full lips were forever set in a sweet pout. Nikolai cupped his hand around the child's thin cheek.

"Good night, sweet prince."

# CHAPTER FOUR

After months of argument, Leah finally conceded to immigrate to America. Despite Orev's refusal to join them, she agreed the move was imperative for her brother Lev's sake.

It would take at least a year to save enough money for the journey. By then, perhaps Orev would reconsider. No matter what, Gavrel was determined to haul his family out of Eastern Europe.

Meanwhile, inspired by Havah's example and promiseful letters, Gavrel set his mind to learn to read and speak English so he and his family would not be cheated when they reached Ellis Island. Thus far, he had spoken to two potential teachers. One wanted too much money, while the other refused to teach a Jew at any price.

"Anything you want to say to Havah before I send this letter?" He glanced up at Leah who was intent on supper.

"Tell her how much we miss them and to have a happy Hanukkah."

"Take heart, my beloved, next year we'll all be together again."

"All of us?"

Although he wanted to reassure her, he could not. He folded the letter and stuffed it into the envelope. Then he stood and joined her at the stove. Potato pancakes, called *latkes*, sizzled in chicken fat in the iron skillet. Over her shoulder, he inhaled the pungent aroma.

"Mmm, you used onion."

"Next Hanukkah in the City of Kansas sounds wonderful." Leah's sorrel eyes shone. "I can't wait to see my Zaydeh again."

"I like Zaydeh Yussel," said Bayla, who stood on a chair to roll out sweet bun dough. Her dark ringlets were dusted with flour.

Reuven glanced up from his book and made a face at her. "You're too young to remember him."

"I do so remember him. He used to sing to us and tell us stories. And he can't see because his eyes are blind. And he has a special menorah his papa made a long, long time ago."

Gavrel pinched Reuven's freckled nose. "You lost that argument, little apple."

In the doorway to the bedroom he shared with Reuven, Lev leaned against the jamb, his scarred mouth twisted into a hateful smirk and said, "Orev says we're running off to America like a pack of scared rabbits. He says we should stand and fight Czarist tyranny. He says things will never get better for us Jews unless we fight for it."

"'Orev says this' and 'Orev says that,'" said Gavrel. "What does Lev think? Or is Lev just Orev's little puppet?"

"Must you two argue every night? Can't we have some peace with the holiday coming?" Leah's face flushed as she flipped the *latkes* onto a platter.

"Hanukkah is all about revolution. The Maccabees! They battled the Assyrians and won!" Lev grabbed one of the pancakes and popped it into his mouth.

"Leah! Gavrel! Open up!" Devorah cried from the other side of the door.

The spatula fell from Leah's hand. She fumbled the platter to the table, spilling *latkes* and grease onto her linen tablecloth, and ran to the door. When she swung it open she gasped. Devorah and her two year old daughter Tova stood in the doorway. The child sucked on her fingers and huddled against Devorah's skirts. Something in Devorah's red eyes gave Gavrel a sense of foreboding. With a lump forming in his throat, he knelt and gathered Tova into his arms, and then he stood and led Devorah to a chair.

"Has something happened to Orev?" Lev sprinted past them.

"Take the children to the girls' bedroom." Gavrel raced him to the door and then kicked it shut.

"I'm a man not a nursemaid."

"That's why we're entrusting our precious little ones into your care. Now go!"

Mumbling something under his breath about tyranny, revolution and leaving home, Lev took Tova in his arms and led the rest of the children from the room.

With one hand covering her face and the other pressed against her side, Devorah crumpled onto the chair. Once the bedroom door shut behind Lev she whispered, "We . . . we . . . had . . . a fight. It was . . . all my fault. I . . . ask . . . too many . . . questions."

Leah pulled Devorah's hand away from her face. A fresh bruise went from her ear to her chin, deepening from red to dark purple. "A curse on him!" said Leah. "Where else did he hit you?"

"He's so full of hate. The pogrom in Kishinev changed him."

"But he wasn't there."

"Havah was. Remember? They were betrothed."

"What difference does that make?"

"He swears I tricked him and took advantage of his grief at losing her."

Gavrel's scalp prickled. Until Havah's escape to Kishinev, Orev treated her more like prized property than a cherished bride-to-be. Gavrel remembered the way Orev stalked her. Less than a week after she fled Svechka and his clutches, he took advantage of fifteen-year-old Devorah's infatuation with him. When she was found to be with child a few months later, Reb Yussel married them in a clandestine ceremony.

"Devorah!" Orev's liquor-sodden shouts accompanied his heavy steps up the stairs. Then the door burst open. The odor of stale schnapps filled the air. Unkempt and unwashed, tobacco spittle clung to Orev's matted beard.

"Go home and sleep it off," said Gavrel.

Orev rammed his fist hard into Gavrel's stomach and hollered. "Devorah, you dumb *klafteh*! Get out here with my daughter! Now!"

Gasping for breath, Gavrel dropped to his knees. As the momentary pain subsided he straightened and grabbed Orev's collar. "They aren't going anywhere with a raving madman!"

Orev lunged and bashed his knuckles into Gavrel's mouth. The ceiling spun around him but he managed to keep his footing.

He pushed Orev against the wall. Wrenching him around in the direction of the door, Gavrel planted his foot against the younger man's backside and shoved. "Get out!"

"You'll be sorry!" Orev tripped and fell. His head thumped on the floor. He rolled over, snapped up his cap, stood and dusted off his trousers. Rubbing his head, he stumbled to the door.

The door banged behind him. Gavrel's mouth filled with blood. He made his way to the sink and leaning over it, he spat out a red glob. Behind him he heard jagged breathing. With the back of his hand, he wiped his mouth and whispered through swelling lips.

"Is that what you want to become, Lev?"

# CHAPTER FIVE

When Havah was a little girl she could not wait for Hanukkah. Each year her mother tried to make it a better celebration than the year before with sweets and special foods. She would start baking and frying at least a week before the first night. Every night for eight nights small gifts would appear for Havah and her brothers. A rag doll Havah had rescued from Natalya's ruins was one such gift. It enjoyed a place of honor on her bed and was one toy Rachel would never be allowed.

Miriam Cohen's final and most precious Hanukkah gift to her daughter was life when, a few weeks before the holiday, Cossacks attacked Natalya. Amid licking flames and crumbling walls she kissed Havah, whispered a blessing and then pushed her out into the frigid night.

"Run, Havah! Don't look back!"

But she did look back. She heard the gunshot and saw her mother collapse. Eerie light played across the black sky. Smoke filled her lungs.

In a clear, off-key voice, Evalyne sang the blessing over the fully lit menorah, bringing Havah back to the present. Behind the girl Wolf, his swarthy face aglow, winked at Havah.

"That's my girl! She's a credit to her teacher."

At Sarah's insistence, the family had gathered at Havah's for the final night when all the candles would be lit. While Havah cared little for celebration these days, Fruma Ya'el readily agreed. A party would do them all good. Havah bristled. Did they think she could not see through their scheme? Did they think she did not notice their exchanged winks?

Across the table Arel slouched between Yussel and Itzak. Gray shadows haunted Arel's eyes that were fixed on Rachel who slumbered in Havah's arms.

Although pressed and tidy, his clothes hung like draperies on his gaunt frame. He reminded her of beggars her mother used to invite in as a *mitzvah*, a good deed, for the holidays. She would clothe them with clean handouts that rarely fit but were better than their everyday rags.

*How long since he had shaved or cut his hair?* The left side of his face was covered with stubble and black spikes poked out between the scars on the right side. Steeped in her own exhaustion, Havah could not find it within herself to pity him. *Let him pay for his stubbornness.*

"Your daughter has grown, hasn't she?"

"Havah, please, not tonight."

"When, Arel? When she's seventeen?"

To evade his pleading gaze, she studied the menorah that sat like royalty on decorated oilcloth in the middle of her oak dining table.

Nine candle flames reflected in the silver stems of the candelabra that had survived three generations of Gittermans and a journey across the sea. It had been crafted to resemble a tree with nine branches swaying in the wind. A flowered vine twined around the trunk which was etched with the Hebrew words for "Behold your eyes are like doves." Just above the trunk, snuggled together like lovers, were two doves.

At their first meeting—Sabbath dinner with her adoptive family—Arel told her how his grandfather had crafted it in memory of his slain wife when Yussel was only five. While the story fascinated Havah, it was Yussel's son who fascinated her more. As he recounted the history, his luminescent gray eyes gleamed with enthusiasm and intelligence. Her grief fresh and wounds painful, she found solace in the rise, fall and lilt of his resonant voice.

"Havah? Where are you?"

Itzak's voice startled her into the realization that she was the only one standing. She blushed and sat.

"Try to eat something." Fruma Ya'el loaded her plate with *latkes* and applesauce. "Lately you don't eat enough to keep a gnat alive."

"Loneliness will do that to a person." Shayndel scowled at Arel. "You're both too skinny."

On Shayndel's lap, Elliott grabbed bits of food from her plate and crammed them into his mouth. Then he made a grab for Shayndel's water glass. It teetered, but Fruma Ya'el caught it.

"Look at those bright eyes!" Fruma Ya'el handed him a spoon. "Everything he sees he wants."

"At least he sees," Arel muttered.

While no one else seemed to hear him, his comment did not escape Havah. She crushed Rachel against her breast and glared at him.

Elliott reached over the table and poked his finger into a candle flame. At once he howled, and then popped his finger into his mouth. Shayndel whisked him up and hurried to the kitchen.

Startled by the noise, Rachel woke and screamed. One of her waving hands smacked the menorah. It toppled to the floor. Flames shot from the rug and licked their way up the lace tablecloth. Havah's heart pounded. She jumped off her chair, lost her balance and stumbled backward. Itzak grabbed a pitcher from the table and doused the blaze.

Arel rescued the baby. "You see! It begins already! She could've set the house on fire. We could've all been killed!"

"Where's your mind?" Itzak rapped his knuckles across Arel's forehead. "Elliott started it. They're babies. What does any baby know from candles and fire?"

"But my daughter isn't just any baby, she's afflicted."

Havah took the shrieking child from him. "So she should be sent away where we won't be bothered by her, is that it?"

"Dammit, Havah! Don't you see? We can't do this!"

"You mean *you* can't do this! Why do you hate her so much?"

Havah's words reverberated in Arel's throbbing ears as he stepped out onto the porch. How could she charge him with such preposterous things, of hating his own daughter?

Behind him the front door creaked and slammed shut. He flinched and turned his head. With Arel's coat over one arm and his other hand out to navigate, Yussel shuffled to the swing. He wore the same expression of consternation he did when Arel was a boy and he would deliver a fatherly lecture just before administering a spanking.

"You're leaving without this?" He thrust the coat toward Arel. Then he eased himself into it the swing.

"I don't need it."

"Put it on. Then sit!"

"Stay out of it, Papa."

"I've stayed out of it too long. Sit!"

With a snarl, Arel grabbed the coat from his father, wrapped it around his shoulders and sat on the porch swing. "I'm not a child, Papa."

"Then stop acting like one." Yussel settled back against the swing and pulled a toothpick from his pocket. "The night you were born everyone in Svechka heard me shouting for joy. After four daughters finally, a *son*."

The wooden pick snapped between his fingers. He let the pieces drop to the floor. "I suppose after your mama of blessed memory passed on, I depended on you too much. After all, you were only four-years-old."

"No, Papa, you didn't. I loved reading to you."

"My son, named for my father of blessed memory, I have always been so proud of you—until now."

"I see where you're going. You're against me, too." Arel bolted to his feet. "I don't have to listen to this."

"I'm not finished." Yussel pounded the swing's armrest.

"Papa, you don't understand." Feeling as if he were still ten yearss old, Arel pouted, sat back down on the swing and folded his arms across his chest.

"Let me tell you a story about a fool I knew back in Svechka. A proud man, full of grand ideas, he studied Talmud and spouted Torah. He had it all—lovely wife and two beautiful daughters.

"One horrendous night, calamity shattered his perfect world. His beloved who was with child fell down a flight of stairs. She and the baby nearly died.

"By the grace of *Adoshem* they lived. But the baby, oy, the baby, she was born too soon. Sickly. Scrawny. Not much to look at. To tell the truth, her looks didn't improve much as she grew.

"The man hated her. He ignored her, certain she'd die before she reached ten anyway. Her existence served as a reminder of his failure."

Although Arel could not remember the man, his anger burned against him. "Failure? It wasn't his fault his wife had an accident. He couldn't prevent his daughter's illness."

"Aha! Remind you of anyone you know?" Yussel laughed and smacked Arel's cheek with a stinging blow.

"You con artist. You made up the whole thing. There never was such a man."

"On the contrary, you're looking at him. The little girl? Your sister, Sarah. Are you so thick headed you don't see what you're doing to your daughter?"

"I only want what's best for her."

"What's best for *her*? Or what's easiest for *you*?" Yussel poked Arel's chest with his bony finger. Then Yussel reached over and pinched Arel's cheek hard. "My son is a fool. Rachel may be blind, but it's *you* who cannot see."

Golden clouds banded across the early morning sky as Arel dragged his feet along the deserted street, pulling his coat collar up around his neck to block the icy wind. After hours of aimless wandering, he stood at the front door, key in hand. His throat stung from his rehearsed speech. Was it too late?

Careful to be quiet and not wake anyone, he eased open the front door and stepped over the threshold. Instead of the empty living room he expected at six o'clock in the morning, Havah sat at the piano, her hair, an onyx avalanche skimming the floor. She held Rachel on her lap. The glow of sunrise gave them a celestial aura. Havah tapped a key and then Rachel tapped the same key with her pudgy finger and sang the note with faultless clarity. Each time it was the same. The child never missed a note.

Transfixed, he tiptoed to the piano and knelt beside them, focused on the baby. Despite her crossed eyes, she looked so much like her mother it startled him. Why had he not noticed before? With caution, he reached up and touched Havah's cheek. She leaned her head against his hand. The touch of her silken skin against his palm sent shivers of delight up his arm and down his back.

"Can you ever forgive this blind ignoramus?" he asked.

Just as she opened her mouth to answer, Rachel tumbled off her lap. He caught her in his arms and then, cradling her head in the hollow of his hand, he kissed her over and over again.

"I love you, my beautiful daughter. I love you so much my *perfect* daughter."

# CHAPTER SIX

Gray light streamed through smudged windows framed by dingy curtains. The striped wallpaper was once golden, but not during Mary Alice's lifetime. She smoothed the threadbare blanket on her bed. Then she sauntered to her pockmarked bureau, picked up a letter and read it for the fourth time that afternoon.

"Lord, love that boy. Imagine the likes 'o me hobnobbing with genteel folk for Christmas dinner. Whatever should I wear?"

From the bottom of a pile of clean clothes on the bed she pulled a 'proper' gingham blouse with a white collar and held it up for inspection.

"I should find me a respectable job. Sure. I could work in a kitchen, I could. Good afternoon, M'Lord. Does you like the crumpets? I made them meself. Old recipe from me sainted grandmamma. More tea, M'Lady?"

Her reflection in the cracked mirror grinned. The blue gingham blouse complemented her eyes. It was the one she wore once a month to visit her aging mother who believed her daughter worked as an upstairs maid in a country manor. Mary Alice sighed. Perhaps her conscience should bother her. But after years of watching Mum scrub chamber pots to earn a meager living, she wanted no part of it.

Her clientele paid her well enough and occasionally rewarded her efforts with baubles and trinkets. At any rate, the only chamber pot she cleaned was her own. Let the hoity-toity look askance at her. Her stomach stayed full and her debts were paid.

"Open up, wench!" The door shook under someone's pounding fist.

"Go away. I'm on holiday."

His voice, husky and liquid, commanded her. "There's no one else for me."

"It will cost you twice the usual rate, Guv'ner." She cracked opened the door and peeked out.

A sudden sharp pain doubled her over as he lunged through and the doorknob whacked her ribs. Before she could straighten, he rushed her, coiled his arm around her neck and forced her down on the bed.

He ripped her flimsy bodice, licked her lips and then thrust his alcohol sodden tongue into her mouth. Her heart raged and she writhed beneath him. His hot, rough hands scraped her bare breasts as with a savage smile he jammed his thumbs into her throat.

# CHAPTER SEVEN

Commingled cinnamon and clove aromas met Nikolai at the front door as he hung his coat and hat on the hall tree. He made his way down the hallway toward the study in anticipation of relaxing in his favorite armchair with the newspaper.

Earlier that day, a letter addressed to him had been delivered to the hospital. One emergency after another prevented him from opening it. The Russian postmark and handwriting, other than his father's, piqued his curiosity.

"Kolyah, come here. You must taste this." Ulrich beckoned him from the kitchen stove where he stood over a steaming kettle. "It's wassail, an English holiday tradition and Catherine's old family recipe."

Somewhat put off at being deterred from his mission, Nikolai forced a stiff smile and stepped into the kitchen.

"It smells wonderful, but I'd prefer something a bit stronger."

"You forget dear-old-dad owned a distillery. You should find this to your liking." Ulrich filled a cup.

"What's in it?" Nikolai set down his newspaper and medical bag to take the cup, sniffing the amber liquid.

"Cinnamon, cider, cloves, ale and more than a little brandy."

The hot drink burned Nikolai's throat and, at the same time, warmed him. He gulped it down and ladled out another. "I prescribe at least three more servings for this patient."

"Was it a rough day?"

"What's worse than rough?"

"You must be speaking of the infamous Dr. Musgrave."

"The man has the moral fiber of an alley cat and the bedside manner of Jack the Ripper. Not to mention, he's a bundle of strange and nervous habits. For instance, he drums his fingers on the table as he fills out reports, and he hums all the time—off key, I might add."

"Surely a surgeon of your caliber can find better employment. It seems to me your female patients alone would make for a lucrative private practice."

"No, thank you. There's not a true ailment in the lot, unless you count spinsterhood and hypochondriasis."

"What about Royal Hospital?"

"That might be a possibility. Where's Vasily?"

"He went Christmas shopping with Catherine."

After ladling out a third cup of wassail, Nikolai retrieved his bag and paper and headed toward the study. Once he reached his chair, he set the cup on the end table beside it, dropped the bag and sat down, easing back into the soft cushions. Awash in the warm glow of the drink, he unfurled the newspaper.

"Murder by Strangulation on the East End," read the bold headline. A photograph of the victim hit him with sobering force. His heart churned and the beat of it thudded against his temples.

Cup in hand, Ulrich entered the room and sat down at the piano. "The *Daily Mail*? Haven't you encountered enough suffering today, Doctor?"

"Have you read it?"

"The maniac strangled the poor girl and then bound her wrists in such a way as to make her appear to be at prayer." Ulrich tapped out the opening bars of Chopin's funeral march. "The sadistic bastard used catgut. Could be violinist or a cellist, you know."

"Or a doctor."

After one more glance at the photograph, Nikolai folded the newspaper. His own words sent his mind coursing back through the day. One memorable patient, a half dressed young woman, was brought in with a nasty gash on her shoulder. It was particularly deep and dangerously close to her neck. She claimed to have had an accident in the kitchen, although given her unmentioned bruises and scars, he guessed it to be the result of a domestic brawl.

Dr. Musgrave sutured the wound with his usual cavalier lack of compassion or respect. Red hot shame colored her cheeks. Once she left, Dr. Musgrave picked up a leftover piece of the thin catgut cord. He wound it around his index finger while making ribald jokes about her comely virtues.

With a disgusted growl, Nikolai downed his drink and stood to return to the kitchen for a fourth, then padded down the hallway. Catherine and Vasily met him, laughing and chattering about the holidays.

Although Christmas cheer was as far from Nikolai's mind as snow from the tropics, he could not help but smile at them. Vasily, his stocking cap askew, and hair sticking out every which way, reminded him of the boy who had been ripped from him. His arms were loaded with packages and, most notably, a large hatbox.

"Tatko, come see what we bought for Mary Alice. She's going to love it!"

Necessary words stuck in Nikolai's throat. Vasily pushed past him and raced Catherine to the study. Nikolai set his cup on the hall tree seat and followed them.

By the time he entered, she had removed the lid and taken a red velvet bonnet adorned with bright green feathers from the box. Then she set the garish bonnet on Ulrich's head and tied its yellow ribbon under his chin.

Under normal circumstances, Nikolai would have seen the humor. He could wait no longer. He picked up the newspaper from the end table.

"There's no graceful way to say it, and I hate to be the one to tell you, but Mary Alice is dead. She was murdered last night."

"You're lying! You just don't want Mary Alice to come for Christmas dinner and embarrass you." Vasily ripped the newspaper from Nikolai and flung it into the fireplace.

Half running, half stumbling, Vasily bolted from the room and out the front door. Without stopping for a coat Nikolai chased after him for a block until the boy tripped and fell. He sprawled on his stomach. Nikolai dropped to his knees in the wet grass beside him.

"Solnyshko, what kind of monster would lie about a thing like that?"

"Why wouldn't you? Ivona lied all the time." Vasily flipped over onto his back and sniffed. "Last year she told me you were mauled to death by a bear in Russia. She even showed me the letter from my grandfather Sergei Derevenko to prove it."

"That explains a lot." Nikolai took a deep breath and helped Vasily to his feet. "Listen to me, son. Please believe me when I say that I'll never lie to you and I'd have been honored to have Miss Tanner sit at my table any day of the week."

"You would?" Vasily wiped his nose on his sleeve and stared at him, mouth agape.

"You bet I would, Dodger." Nikolai took his handkerchief from his vest pocket and pressed it into Vasily's hand. "I'm forever in her debt. She was a lady in the truest sense."

The boy collapsed against Nikolai's chest. Vasily's heart wracking sobs both distressed and angered Nikolai. If Ivona were not already dead, he might have sought to kill her himself. Despite the boy's size, Nicolai hoisted him into his arms.

"Let's go home before I have to treat us both for pneumonia."

Later that night, after retiring to his bed, Nikolai tore open and read the letter from overseas. Of all people, it came from a boyhood friend and medical school classmate, Dr. Pavel Trubachov. Nikolai smiled as he remembered some of their youthful pranks.

"What have you to say for yourself after all these years?" whispered Nikolai. "Perhaps this is a wedding or birth announcement."

Pavel's handwriting had not improved since school days. If anything, it had deteriorated. Nikolai held the smudged paper close to the lamp on the bed table.

Pavel wrote of the tenuous political temperament in Odessa. With threats of war on the horizon and mutterings against the Czar, he feared the Jews would catch the brunt of it. The letter ended in a desperate plea for Nikolai to join him in the understaffed Jewish hospital.

No one needed to describe the devastation or urgency to Nikolai. Two years ago he had witnessed the senseless slaughter of innocents in Kishinev. The sight was still as fresh in his mind as ever.

If Pavel's invitation had arrived three months ago he would have accepted it without a second thought. Things were no longer simple. There was another person to consider. Would it be in Vasily's best interest to uproot him after so many upheavals in his young life?

"Tatko?" Vasily's whisper shook him from his unsettled thoughts. "May I sleep with you like I used to?"

In his loose fitting nightshirt that went below his knees, Vasily trembled beside the bed. His tousled hair fringed his swollen eyes. Wind chapped, his cheeks and lips were deep pink, giving him the appearance of a much younger boy.

"Of course." Nikolai folded the letter and laid it on the bed stand. Then he pulled back the covers. As the boy slipped in beside him, Nikolai snuffed out the candle and tucked the blanket around them.

"Tatko, what possesses a person to take another person's life? I don't understand."

"I hope you never do."

"Does being a physician make you feel powerful?"

"Sometimes. But there's a lot of suffering in the world, and one man can only do so much."

Conversation ceased. Sleep had almost overtaken Nikolai when Vasily murmured in his ear.

"I hate this place, Tatko. Can we go somewhere else?"

"Don't you like Uncle Ulrich and Aunt Catherine?"

"Of course I do, but I keep thinking about Ivona and Mary Alice and it makes me want to move away."

"Do you still speak Russian?"

"*Da*, yes, of course. Ivona's English wasn't very good. Why?"

# CHAPTER EIGHT

Hunched over his desk, Ulrich plodded through a stack of student music theory compositions. He detested the necessary evil of assigning grades. His fingers cramped around his pen and his stiff neck ached as he glanced at the mantle clock.

"How long can it take to pick up mail from the post office?"

In a direct answer to his question, Catherine entered the room. The swish of her crinoline petticoats was music to his formerly dormant heart. She set a parcel on top of his papers. "I'm home, dearest, and I come bearing gifts."

Ulrich's chair toppled behind him as he sprang to his feet, plucked her hat from her head and gathered her into his arms.

"I missed you terribly."

"Poppycock. I haven't been gone more than half an hour."

"It seemed like a fortnight." He pressed his ravenous lips against her temple.

"Aren't you the slightest bit curious to know what's in the package?"

"Not in the least."

"Set me down this instant, you naughty boy."

Struggling to regain some semblance of composure, he let her squirm from his disappointed grasp. After he righted the fallen chair, he picked up the package. It was addressed in Havah's incredible handwriting to "Mr. and Mrs. Ulrich Dietrich."

From its size and heft he guessed the present to be a book. When he ripped off the brown paper his eyes were met with golden Hebrew characters on a black background. This was not just any book. The earthy aroma of the leather binding filled his nostrils. He thumbed through the parchment pages with reverence. Leave it to the rabbi's daughter to send such a rare gift.

"Cate, do you know what this is? This is *Tenakh*, the Old Testament in Hebrew, the original tongue. Havah taught me to read it in return for English lessons. Of course, I have a long way to go.

"There's a note in the front. *'To Catherine and Ulrich in honor of your marriage. May you be blessed with happiness and healthy children. Havah and Arel Gitterman. 5 March 1905.'*"

Catherine's lips turned white. Hands pressed against her stomach she dropped down on the desk chair. Ulrich set the Bible on the desk and felt her forehead.

"Leave me be!" she said.

"What's the matter?"

"I just felt a bit faint. I'm better now." She took an envelope from her handbag. "This also came for you from the States."

"Havah wrote a letter, too?"

"It's not from her. It's from a Mr. J. W. Thomas. He says he caught one of your recitals in March." Catherine's color returned. "Why shouldn't he be impressed? You're undeniably brilliant."

"Do you read all my mail?"

Not waiting for her answer, Ulrich sat cross legged on the floor and pulled the folded stationary from the opened envelope. His heart pounded as he read the rambling script. "He refers to himself as an agent of considerable influence and is offering me an American tour of piano recitals starting at Carnegie Hall."

"You'll accept, of course."

"Of course, but only if you'll consent to accompany me, Frau Dietrich."

She slid off the chair into his lap, unfastened two of his shirt buttons and kissed his neck. "I'll go anywhere with you."

"What a touching sight," said Quinnon.

Ulrich turned to see the young man leaning against the door jamb. Both dismayed and aggravated, Ulrich struggled to his feet and helped Catherine to hers. "Ever hear of knocking before entering a room? It's all the rage these days."

"Door was open, guv-in-law." Quinnon set his violin case on the floor, sat in the desk chair, took a drag from his cigarette and exhaled a smoke ring.

Catherine curved her hand around Ulrich's fist. "Ulrich, I have the most wonderful idea. Let's take Quinnon to America with us."

# CHAPTER NINE

In over a month since Arel returned home, he never once mentioned putting Rachel in an institution. He sent off for books instructing him how best to educate her. Even though she was only a year old, he read to her every night when he read to Papa.

One morning, before leaving for work, he asked Havah to bring Rachel to the shop so she could see what her father did for a living. Since she had errands to run, Havah agreed.

Blended aromas of new fabric, camphor and machine oil greeted her like old friends as she opened the tailor shop door. They took her back to the Evron's shop in Kishinev. She blinked and reprimanded herself. *No sadness allowed today.* She maneuvered Rachel's pram to Arel's sewing machine.

He set aside a pair of unfinished trousers, lifted the baby and set her on his lap. Then he pulled a box from under his chair. His smooth shaven face flushed as he opened it. From it, he took a tiny velvet dress trimmed with shimmering lace and held it up to Rachel.

"It's purple for royalty. What do you think?"

"She'll be the most beautiful princess at the Purim ball." Havah admired his even stitches and artistry. "I'm glad one of us can sew."

When Rachel yowled her displeasure and batted at the dress, he gave it to Havah, then he guided the baby's curious hands to the machine's wheel while he pumped the treadle and made it spin. She hummed, imitating the whirring motor.

After she tired of that game, he stood and carried her around the shop, letting her explore the different fabric textures. He named each one for her—corduroy, seersucker, wool. With unusual dexterity for a toddler she brushed her delicate fingers over the materials and tried to shape their names in her mouth.

"My daughter's a genius."

The scar from his Kishinev beating prevented the right side of Arel's mouth from extending into a full smile. Once more Havah's mind went back to Evron's shop where cruel beasts with their crowbars and sticks thrashed Arel to the floor. Despite her heavy coat, she shivered.

"Havaleh? You're there again, aren't you?" Arel's whisper tickled her ear and brought her back to the present. "We're safe. It's over."

"Never." She took Rachel from him and tucked her into her pram. "It will never be over."

Arel's stormy eyes misted and he pressed his scarred lips against hers, then he pulled back and looked around for any unannounced customers who might have witnessed his public indiscretion.

He straightened his tie and cleared his throat. "Have you met Sol's nephew yet?"

"You mean Barry, the future doctor? I haven't. Have you? He's all Zelda talks about. Do you know she's already found him a date for the Purim party?"

"He came in this morning to be fitted for a suit. He's not what you'd expect from Zelda's royal family. It might interest you to know that he grew up in a village in Moldavia, not far from Kishinev. He's working at Mayfair sweeping floors and stocking shelves."

"That's where we're headed next for tooth powder. I'll look for him."

The long narrow shop smelled of leather, licorice, and chocolate, but for the most part, it reeked of Sol's cigars. Havah moved between rows of shelves filled with dolls, toy trains and stacks of canned food until she found the tooth powder.

Behind the counter Sol Mayer smiled at her, his cigar clenched between his teeth. Smoke tendrils framed his bulldog jowls. He took a peppermint stick from a glass jar and held it out to Rachel who wriggled in her pram.

"Looks like the little *maideleh* needs one of these."

"What she really needs is a n-a-p. But c-a-n-d-y might keep her quiet for a while." Havah opened her coin purse.

"Put your money away, Mrs. Gitterman. My treat." Sol walked around the counter and knelt. He handed the candy to Rachel who popped the tip of it into her mouth.

"What do you say to the nice man, Rukhel Shvester?" Havah snapped her purse clasp shut.

"Senk oo."

"Amazing!" Sol patted the child's head. "Wendy didn't start talking until she was almost three. Of course she hasn't stopped to take a breath since. Just like her mother." He brushed his hand over his balding head and winked at her. "I had a full head of hair when I married Zelda."

His deep blue eyes twinkled. Havah felt as if she had seen them in another place and time.

"Is that your nephew?" She motioned toward a young man sweeping the floor with wide strokes in one of the aisles. Unlike Sol, the boy's curling hair, like an unpruned bush under his *yarmulke*, obscured his face.

"Barry, come meet Mrs. Gitterman."

"Yes, Uncle Shlomo, just as soon as I—" When Barry raised his head and approached them the broom fell from his grasp. "Havah!"

Her stomach and heart flipped in unison. "Beryl Mayorovich!"

# CHAPTER TEN

After weeks of contemplation, discussion and another entreaty from Dr. Trubachov, Nikolai tendered his resignation to St. Thomas Hospital. As he came from the administrator's office he felt a burden had lifted. At the same time, he dreaded a burden of a different nature.

"Good morning, Doctor."

A musical voice took Nikolai from his musings. An attractive nurse whose dimensions stretched her starched uniform to its limits cocked her head and flashed a dimpled smile. He followed her with his eyes to the other end of the long corridor until she turned and entered a patient's room.

When he returned to his original path he looked up in time to avoid a collision with a uniformed police officer.

"Don't blame you a bit. A man would have to be in his grave two years not to notice that one," said the officer with a wink.

"Is that Russian?" He pointed to Pavel's letter on Nikolai's clipboard. "I can't read a lick of it. You wouldn't be Dr. Derevenko, would you?"

"Are you here to arrest me?"

"No, no, Doctor, nothing like that. Allow me to introduce myself. I'm Sgt. McKenzie of Scotland Yard at your service."

"In that case, I am Dr. Nikolai Derevenko, at *your* service, sir." He extended his hand.

"I thought so! If I may say so, your son is the spitting image of you. My condolences on the loss of his mum. Tell me, how is the little tyke?"

"Very well, thank you. I owe you, Sergeant. Are you here to visit a sick friend or maybe one of our pretty nurses?"

"No, my visit's strictly business. I'm looking for Dr. Corbin Musgrave. Would you happen to know him?"

"As well as I know dysentery."

"Where might I find him?"

"Follow me. I'm headed that direction. It's time to wake him."

"Beg your pardon. Did you say, 'wake him'?"

"He often sleeps here after a late night."

"Then he worked a late shift?"

"I suppose you could call it that, but not here at the hospital."

Nikolai led Sgt. McKenzie down the corridor to a room. As he opened the door the faint odor of vomit and stale alcohol assaulted him. He switched on the light.

"Have you no respect for the dead?" said Corbin in a slurred voice. "Turn off the bloody light."

Sprawled on the bed in a rumpled suit, Corbin took a pillow from under his head and covered his face. He turned over on his side and groaned.

"Does this happen often?" asked Sgt. McKenzie.

"Only a couple of times a week," said Nikolai as he poked Corbin's shoulder with his fountain pen. "Musgrave, wake up. You have a visitor."

Corbin rolled over onto his back, let the pillow fall to the floor and opened his enflamed eyes. Then he sat up, grabbed a pan from the bed table and threw up.

"Is this some sort of joke?" asked Corbin.

"I never joke," said Sgt. McKenzie.

"Have I done something wrong, Officer?"

"You tell me, Doctor."

Corbin pushed his disheveled hair off his forehead and glared at the sergeant, then at Nikolai. "What's this about?"

"Were you at Whitechapel last night?" asked the sergeant.

"Bloody hell. What if I was?"

"Just answer the question, please."

"Yes, I was there." Corbin grinned. "Damned good time of it, too."

"Another of them was murdered last night. Maureen O'Brien. She was strangled and her hands were bound like the others. Only this one was disemboweled."

"Well that's a bit different, isn't it? There's more where she . . . wait a bloody moment. My God. Surely you don't think that I had something to do with it."

"Your fingerprints were found at the crime scene."

"Mine and a hundred others I warrant."

"The murder weapon was a scalpel. A Mr. Quinnon Flannery discovered the body."

"Did you question him? He can tell you I'd never do such a thing."

"We've already tried to speak with him. He was quite hysterical and had to be given a sedative."

"Then speak with him again when he's calmed down. When I left Miss O'Brien, she was very much alive. Tell him, Derevenko. I may be a randy scoundrel, but I'm not a bloody murderer!"

# CHAPTER ELEVEN

Despite Devorah's protests, Gavrel refused to allow her to return home with Orev after he beat her. Although he had apologized and swore it would never happen again, Gavrel did not trust the volatile man.

The only person who believed Orev was Lev. Gavrel and Lev had argued most of the afternoon, until Lev stormed out. Gavrel regretted his angry words as he looked out the window at the empty street below. His instinct to protect Lev only drove the boy further away.

After a tense supper he helped Reuven with his lessons while Leah and Devorah washed the dishes and planned what sweets they might bake for Purim. Bayla, Pora and Tova played in a corner with homemade dolls.

"I'm going to be Queen Esther," said Bayla.

"What's so great about that? All the girls dress up like Queen Esther." With an angry sigh, Reuven shut his book and stuck out his lower lip. "Why do I need to be a scholar if I'm only going to be a shoemaker?"

"You have to be become Bar Mitzvah," said Gavrel, "a son of the commandment."

"But Papa," the boy counted on his fingers, "that won't be for another five years."

"You're good at arithmetic, my son. And in those five years, you'll make this Papa proud. And furthermore—"

Downstairs the doorbell sounded as the shop door opened and banged shut. The stairs creaked under heavy footsteps. Gavrel leaped from the chair and swung open the door. Disappointment filled him when the young man who stumbled over the threshold was not Lev.

"Hyram!" Devorah dropped her dishtowel and ran to him. "What's happened? Where's Orev?"

Gavrel grasped Hyram's arm and led him to a chair where he slumped over. Gavrel's heart cratered to his stomach when he noticed fresh bloodstains on Hyram's shirt.

The children gathered around them. With a sense of foreboding, Gavrel squeezed Reuven's shoulder. "Take the girls to the other room."

"Aw, I always have to go to the other—" Reuven wrinkled his nose until Gavrel tightened his grip. "Yes, Papa."

As soon as the door closed behind them, Hyram's words tumbled from his lips. "We had a rally tonight at the University. Christian hecklers came. They cursed at us, but made no threats of violence. I begged Orev to ignore them. He had a gun. I tried to take it. It fired."

Her face ashen, Devorah crumpled at Hyram's feet.

"Lev? Where's Lev?" asked Leah.

"He's at the hospital with Orev."

"Is he . . . hurt?"

"No. He's okay."

"What about Orev?"

"There was so much blood. I don't see how he could still live."

"My poor sister. Maybe Orev is still alive." Leah knelt beside Devorah.

With eerie calm Devorah pushed away Leah's hand, stood, smoothed her kerchief and returned to the sink. "My husband died a long time ago."

"The bullet nicked the carotid artery. I couldn't stop the bleeding." The doctor removed his stethoscope from his ears.

Lev dropped down beside the stretcher and starred into Orev's vacant eyes. His gray complexion reminded Lev of one of those pictures painted on the outer wall of the Orthodox church in Svechka of the man they called Christ, the one the goyim claimed the Jews killed.

Laying a gentle hand on his shoulder, the doctor whispered, "Son, no physician on earth could have saved your brother."

Overcome with anger and grief, the boy pulled his knees into his chest. Helpless sobs wracked him. He wanted to kill all of the Christians. He flinched, pulled away from the doctor's hand and bared his teeth.

"I watched you. You didn't try to save him. You stood there and let him die."

In place of the hatred he expected, the physician's eyes brimmed as he pulled a sheet over Orev's head. "He was a dead man as soon as the bullet penetrated his neck."

"Don't you mean a dead *Jew*?"

# CHAPTER TWELVE

Not one corner of the synagogue hall was left undecorated. The linoleum floor, polished to a high gloss, and the freshly painted walls reflected the glow of the brass light fixtures. Paper chains crisscrossed from one corner to the other. Childish paintings adorned each wall, commemorating the victory of the Jews over wicked Haman in Shushan in ancient Persia.

"Auntie Havah, you're beautiful! I've never seen that dress before." Evalyne skipped around her.

"I agree." Sarah brushed her hand over the lace. "You're the most beautiful Queen Esther here. Lavender is such a pretty color. I'll bet Professor Dietrich had it made for you, didn't he?"

"No. It belonged to his first wife." The taffeta skirt rustled and flared as Havah did a clumsy pirouette. "When she died he couldn't bear to part with her things. After the pogrom in Kishinev, I had nothing, not even clothes, and hers fit me. He said, 'Perhaps God had me save it for such a time as this.' Even my wedding dress was hers. Perhaps one day Rachel will wear it."

Arel, followed by Jeffrey, rushed into the hall carrying Rachel who squealed and tried to pull off her sequined headband. He laid the wriggly child in Havah's arms.

"Diaper changed, Mama. Are you children ready to present your Purim play?"

"I'm ready!" Jeffrey paraded back and forth in his striped robe.

"Yes, I think you are. You will be a strong Mordekhai!"

Jeffrey wrinkled his nose. "I'd rather not be Wendy Mayer's uncle."

"It's only play acting. You aren't really going to be her uncle."

The stage had been set at one end of the hall. With Wolf's help,

Itzak had built a small, yet convincing, palace. Two little faces with red noses peeked through the painted cardboard windows.

"Mendel and David, that castle is for the play." Itzak's laughter bounced off the high tiled ceiling.

"But we want to be in the play, too." David pouted.

"Maybe next year, my little *tzaddik*. This year, you make good clowns." Itzak lifted a boy into each arm.

"Tell you what." Arel winked at Itzak. "You boys can be my chief noise makers. Whenever it's time to boo Haman, I want you to jump up on the stage and make your groggers rumble. Can you do that?"

David clapped his hands. "Yes, Uncle Arel. We'll be the best chief noisemakers that ever was!"

"I hope you know what you're doing, little brother," said Itzak.

In the past month, Arel and the children had been working on a reenactment of the Book of Esther for Purim. Zelda insisted that her Wendy play the lead role. After all, the Mayers gave the most money to support the synagogue. With some resistance, Arel accepted the rabbi's edict and cast Wendy as Esther, the Jewish girl responsible for freeing her people from Persian tyranny centuries before.

"You're a beautiful Queen Vashti, Evie." Havah righted Evalyne's skewed crown. Although her niece had more talent than the other girl, she kept her opinion to herself. Admittedly, Wendy had the looks for the part.

"Aw, I'd rather be Haman." Evalyne frowned. "I wish I was a boy."

"You'd rather be a villain? Silly girl."

"Make way for Queen Esther!" Clad in an extravagant evening gown, with a glittering rhinestone tiara in her hair, Zelda entered the room waving her arms like a reigning monarch in a parade.

Havah rolled her eyes. "Leave it to Zelda Mayer to make a children's Purim play into a high society social event."

Behind her, in a costume that must have cost a small fortune, Wendy scuffed the toes of her patent leather shoes along the floor and whined with every step.

"I don't feel good, I don't want to be Queen Esther and I don't want to be in no dumb old Purim *shpiel*."

"Ouch! Ouch!" Rachel covered her ears and buried her head on Havah's shoulder.

"Let's go, kids. It's almost time for curtain." Arel's jaw rippled and his lips puckered as if he had just eaten something sour as he took Evalyne and Wendy by the hand.

"The chairs are filling fast. Wolf and I will save one for you." With a nod to Zelda, Sarah excused herself.

"You should buy this poor child some dark glasses." Zelda clicked her tongue and patted Rachel's head.

Havah bristled. "Why? It's not as if the light hurts her eyes. Don't look at her if it bothers you so much."

"Some people would rather be embarrassed, wouldn't they?" Zelda smiled in such an ingratiating manner Havah entertained the idea of snatching her bald, one painful handful at a time.

"There's nothing to be embarrassed about," said Havah.

"Have you seen my nephew?" Zelda's nattering continued. "He should be here with his lady fair any minute. She's such a delight. Her father owns a large grocery store on Tenth Street, you know."

"Kansas City's a big place. I'm sure a handsome man like Barry can find a wife without your help."

"I'll thank you mind your own affairs, Mrs. Gitterman."

"Perhaps you should follow your own advice, Mrs. Mayer. Oh, look, isn't that your nephew and his 'lady fair' now?"

At the entrance, with a young woman clinging to his arm as if he alone stood between life and death, Beryl's expression reflected all the delight of a man with a toothache. The girl's round face, framed by straight hair parted in the middle and plastered to her head, matched her equally round figure. She gazed up at him and grinned, revealing a pronounced overbite with a wide gap between the middle two teeth.

When he caught sight of Havah, his face brightened and he hurried to join her, almost to the point of dragging his date. The suit Arel had tailored for him accentuated his broad chest and shoulders. His dimples deepened.

"What a beautiful dress, Mrs. Gitterman."

Zelda curved her pincer grip around his free arm. "It is beautiful. That is if you like clothes fifteen years out of fashion. Honestly, Havah, bustles are so passé."

Frederic Chopin's Nocturne in C Sharp Minor soothed Havah's jangled nerves. The ivory keys were smooth and comforting under her fingertips. Although she would never be a pianist of Ulrich's caliber she played well enough to entertain an audience of one. Closing her eyes, she relished a soft breeze carrying the scents of daffodil and hyacinth through the open window.

She raised her fingers from the keyboard and pressed her palms against her stomach. Spring flowers and hot tea could not ease her guilty ache. *Of all the places on the Almighty's creation, why did Beryl end up here?*

Slippered footfalls padded down the stairway and across the living room until she felt Arel's breath on her neck. "Can't you sleep?"

Not wanting to discuss the reasons for her insomnia, she opened her eyes, tilted back her head and said, "The kids did a wonderful job tonight."

"I don't know about 'Queen Vashti,' though." Arel placed his hands on his hips, scrunched his nose and spoke in a falsetto voice. "'Tell him I'm not coming and that's that. Dopey old King Akhashverosh can just have his silly old party without me.' Somewhat different from the original script I'd say." He sat down on the bench beside her.

"At least Evie was creative and didn't cry when she forgot her lines, like the king."

"True. But he's only six, and he did have a rough night. First he forgot half of his lines and then Queen Esther threw up in his lap."

"Wendy said she didn't feel good. Zelda should learn to open her mouth less and her ears more."

"And what about my two noisemakers?"

"They played their parts better than anyone. Poor Rachel woke up screaming and I'll wager no one heard her above Mendel and David."

"I saw you leave."

"I had to. She was hysterical."

"Barry left, too."

"So?"

"I can't say that I blame him. If I'd been stuck with such a cow, I'd want to escape with a beautiful woman like you, too. He's a handsome man," said Arel. "Why didn't you mention him before?"

"I never thought I'd see him again."

"But you were almost betrothed."

"It was a childish promise. It didn't mean a thing."

"He's still in love with you, Havaleh."

Her tongue stuck to her mouth like paste. She twined her bathrobe hem around her fingers. Then she let go of it, reached up and pressed her hand against his scarred cheek.

"You're the one who fills my thoughts, Arel Gitterman."

"Am I?"

# CHAPTER THIRTEEN

"'*The blossoms are seen on the earth, the season of singing has arrived.'* Well said, King Solomon. Ah, spring, glorious spring." Ulrich stopped to sniff the lilacs blooming on a row of bushes along the sidewalk before stepping up to his front door. Distracted by the sweet smell of flowers and thoughts of his upcoming travels, he stumbled over a trunk in the foyer.

"Dammit!" A burst of pain sent him to his knees. "Catherine! Cate!"

Not his wife but Nikolai came to his aid, a slight smirk on his face. "Sounds serious. Need a doctor?"

Ulrich rolled up his pant leg to inspect a red lump forming just below his knee. "I'll live."

"I have a saw in my medical bag. I can amputate if necessary."

"Always the quintessential surgeon." Ulrich struggled to his feet and hung his hat on the hall tree by the door. "Where is my little firebrand?"

"She took Vasily out for some last minute shopping."

"Shopping? From the looks of her luggage I'd say she's exhausted every shop in London. Fine lad, Vasily. Perhaps I'll have one someday soon."

"Something you haven't told me, Ulrich?"

"Not that I'm aware of. But who knows? We'll be on a luxury ocean liner on the high seas. Moonlight suppers on the deck. The perfect prescription for romance, I'd say."

"With Quinnon as the antidote. Why on earth are you taking him?"

"Trapped like a mouse under the *hausfrau's* broom. Catherine won't go unless baby brother comes along."

"If you push him overboard, make it look like an accident."

"Promise."

Nikolai's smile faded. "I'll miss you, my friend. We've been through a lot together."

"You've made up your mind then?"

"I have to get Vasily away from here."

"Why not America? Florin Miklos has sent more than one offer. With political turmoil and Russia's war with Japan things could get ugly."

"I am Russian."

"So you are."

"At least there I might be able to help effect positive change for people."

The determination in Nikolai's eyes and set of his jaw told Ulrich to keep his fears to himself and leave his friend's safety in greater hands. Still a nameless heaviness weighed on him. He forced his lips into an unwilling smile.

"Then let's drink to it."

They walked, side by side in silence, to the library and sat in Havah's favorite red brocade chairs. Ulrich took the sherry decanter from the table between them, poured two glasses and handed one to Nikolai.

"To you and to our former classmate Pasha Trubachov. May the two of you turn Mother Russia right side up."

*"Na Zdrovia."* Nikolai emptied his glass.

*"L'Khayim."* Pausing, Ulrich lowered his eyes and watched the light glint off the bronze liquid. "Where will you live?"

"With Pasha and Oxana until we find a place of our own."

"Who's Oxana? Is she his wife?"

"No, she's his sister."

"Are you sure he isn't just playing matchmaker?"

Again a hush fell between them. Ulrich set his glass on the desk as they stood and faced each other. Ulrich seized Nikolai's shoulders and pulled him into an embrace. "Kolyah, *mein bruder*, take care of yourself."

"Stop it." Nikolai shoved him.

"Right you are. We've had enough of this sentimentality!" Ulrich pivoted on his heel and picked up a folder from his desk. "Mr. Thomas sent a piece of music I want you to hear. It's called *Maple Leaf Rag*, as American as *Stars and Stripes* and guaranteed to lift the lowest of spirits!"

With a flourish, Ulrich set his sheet music on the piano stand and sat on the bench. It had taken a few days of practice, but once he mastered it, he fell in love with the new form. His fingers leapt and danced across the keys. When he finished, he grinned. "Like it?"

"Bravo!" Nikolai applauded. "Who's the composer?"

"He's an American Negro by the name of Scott Joplin."

Cigarette pinched between his teeth, Quinnon entered the room and sat down on the sofa. Draping one leg over the sofa's arm and the other over the back he lay against the cushions and blew smoke rings that drifted upward and dissipated in midair.

"No doubt Frederic Chopin is whirling like a bloody dervish in his grave."

Ulrich rose, walked to him, took the cigarette and snuffed it out in an ash tray. "Are you close to being ready to leave? We depart in two days."

"Packed, practiced and passionate, Guv. All the excitement has given me a nasty headache." Quinnon pressed the back of his hand against his forehead. Then he sat up and took a rolled up copy of *The Daily Mail* from his pocket. "By the way, Dr. Derevenko, it seems your friend and fiend Dr. Musgrave won't be getting his comeuppance from the courts after all. According to the article in here he was murdered before he could be hanged, poor chap."

"You sadist. You're loving this." Ulrich ground his teeth.

"Well, it's not as if I killed him. A cellmate at the Clapham station, a client, if you will, of the late Mary Alice Tanner, took it upon himself to beat the doctor to a bloody pulp. Either way, justice is served."

# CHAPTER FOURTEEN

Gavrel's ledger lay open on his work table. He tallied the numbers and sighed. If he was ever going to take his family out of this place he needed customers. More often than not his profits were used to buy leather to make more shoes, leaving a meager sum for household needs.

The night before, Leah pointed out the fact that Devorah had not been to the *mikveh* in three months to be cleansed from her monthly impurity. This morning, Leah banished the children to his care so she could tend her ill sister. He did not need a doctor to tell him the nature of her ailment. How much further could he stretch his income and still have some left over to pay their fare?

The girls played quietly at his feet. He marveled at his little rainbow. Pora had his sandy blonde hair while Tova's curls were the same color as ripe cherries and Bayla's silken braids were blacker than slate.

On a high stool, Reuven read from his prayer book until he stumbled over a word. Then Lev, who hovered over him like a vulture stalking his prey, smacked the back of his head.

"Wrong, wrong, wrong! You *schlemiel.* Can't you tell a *tav* from a *khet*?"

"The letters are too small. Papa! Make him stop yelling at me."

"Lev, no one learns by violence and ridicule." Gavrel struggled to keep his voice low and gentle.

Lev's freckles stood out like dark pencil dots on his reddening cheeks. "You always take his side."

"Son—"

"I'm not your son."

"So you've told me."

Gavrel's stomach roiled. He had to talk to the boy sooner or later. Shutting the ledger, he rose from his stool. Then he gripped the boy's narrow shoulders. Lev's muscles tensed under Gavrel's hands. His eyes darkened and narrowed. His scarred lips parted and he bared his teeth like a rabid wolf.

"Go ahead, hit me. You know you want to."

"No, I don't, but I do have an important matter to discuss."

"Yeah?"

"You haven't been to school in a year."

"So what? School's a waste of time."

"I've found a job for you . . . in America."

Clapping her hands, Bayla jumped up from the floor. "Yippee! We're going to Kansas!"

Gavrel flattened his palm against the air. "Not us, chatterbox, just your big brother."

The color drained from Lev's face as Gavrel continued. "I've saved enough for passage for one. Uncle Itzak is ready to teach you his trade and you'll have a bedroom to yourself."

"No, no, no!" Bayla's screams riddled Gavrel's heart. "Please, Papa. Don't send Lev away."

"You just want to get rid of me." Lev stomped toward the front door. "I hate you!"

At the same time, bells clanged as the door swung open. A lanky stranger stepped over the threshold. "I've heard this is where to find the best shoes in Odessa. Did my friend Lev tell me the truth?"

While clean shaven and smelling of soap, the man looked like a beggar in want of food. His suit coat hung from his angular shoulders like rumpled curtains and his baggy trousers were threadbare and patched. Gavrel doubted he could afford shoelaces, let alone shoes.

As often was the case, Bayla spoke first. "Who are you?"

With a kind smile, the man folded his tall, thin frame to its knees. "I'm Dr. Trubachov. Where did you come by such beautiful gray eyes?"

"My mama. She doesn't live here. She's in heaven."

"You must miss her very much."

"I don't remember her."

Dr. Trubachov eased back to his feet and took Gavrel's hand. "My condolences on the loss of your wife, sir."

Curving his other hand around Bayla's cheek, Gavrel said, "My bride's very much alive and I . . . I'll explain later. As for shoes, business hasn't been so good so I can't afford to extend credit."

"That's not a problem." To Gavrel's amazement, the doctor pulled a ragged wallet from his coat pocket and from it a wad of currency. "Just tell me what you need."

In stunned silence, Lev watched from a bench by the table. He had not uttered a word since the man's entrance. His eyes darted from Gavrel to Dr. Trubachov and then to the money.

"I'm not much of a clotheshorse, I'm afraid." The doctor sat beside Lev and removed what remained of his worn out shoes—one knobby toe peeked through a hole in his sock.

From his work table drawer Gavrel took a ruler, a piece of parchment and a pencil. Then he knelt and traced around Dr. Trubachov's long narrow feet to make patterns.

"Can I sit on your lap?" Bayla tapped his shoulder.

Lev smacked her behind. "Bayla, don't be rude."

Pavel held out his hands to her. "I never could resist the raven-haired maidens."

"Do you have a little girl like me?"

"I wish that I did, but I'm not married."

"How come you're so skinny? Where's your beard?"

Gavrel shook his head. "If you're not careful, my friend, she'll still be asking questions when the sun rises in the morning."

With her finger in her mouth Pora tiptoed to him and then climbed up beside Bayla.

"Me, too. Me, too." Tova's cherry ringlets bobbed and jumped about her round face.

Gavrel expected irritation, but the doctor seemed to relish the childish attention lavished on him. He answered each of Bayla's questions with humor and patience.

"Finished." Gavrel rolled up his patterns and set them on the table. "Dark or light brown leather, Dr. Trubachov?"

"Whichever will last the longest. As you can see I don't have shoes made often." Then the doctor sobered. "I must confess. I have an ulterior motive. You see, I have a business proposition for young Mr. Resnick here. It's a decent job if he's willing."

"Doing what?" Lev raised his eyebrow.

"I need an orderly—someone to sweep the corridors and treatment rooms at the hospital."

Arms folded across her chest, Leah rustled into the room. "Why should I let my brother work for you?"

Astonished by her abrupt lack of hospitality, Gavrel scowled. “You’d rather have Lev brawling in the streets? Do you want him to end up like Orev?”

“We agreed to send him to Itzak and we hardly know this man.”

“He’s a doctor.”

“And a *goy*. Don’t forget that.”

“He’s a *goy* who cares for Jewish people in a Jewish hospital. If we reject this man because he’s not a Jew, we’re no better than the Christians who hate us because we are.”

# CHAPTER FIFTEEN

In deference to Catherine's violent seasickness, Ulrich had spent the first three nights of their journey sleeping on the sofa in their stateroom. At last her stomach settled. Whistling *The Band Played On*, Ulrich walked across the saloon with a bottle of champagne in one hand and two crystal glasses in the other.

Eyeing Quinnon at a nearby table, Ulrich stepped up his pace. With his usual disregard for protocol, Quinnon sat with his feet on the table, cigarette in hand. A young woman, dressed in a low cut silk evening gown, sat beside him.

"Where are you going in such a hurry, Guv?" asked Quinnon. "As if I didn't know." He winked twice, blew a smoke ring and then put his cigarette out in a large already overflowing ashtray.

Ulrich stopped. "I should think your time would be better served practicing. Our first concert is in a few days."

"You know what they say about all work and no play, Guv. They serve the most excellent cognac on this bloody boat." Quinnon took a swig and wrapped his arm around his companion. He lightly stroked her neck with his index finger. "Have you ever studied a woman's neck? Hers is particularly exquisite, isn't it? There are seven beautiful vertebrae." He curved his hand around her throat. "The hyoid bone ties it all together, tongue, larynx and so on."

"*Por favor, señor*, no do this," whispered the woman. Her imploring eyes glistened as she tried to push his hand away.

"As you can see, she's not much of a conversationalist, Guv." Quinnon kissed her cheek. "No habla mucho English. But who needs talk, eh, wot?"

Ulrich set the bottle and glasses on the table, grasped Quinnon's wrist and pulled it away from her neck. She ducked under Ulrich's arm and said, "*Gracias, Señor.*"

Quinnon took his feet off the table, sat up straight and grabbed the bottle before Ulrich could. "'Laurent-Perrier,' you have good taste, Professor. I'm sure my psychotic sister won't care one way or the other."

"How dare you speak of her like that? After all she's done for you, you miserable ingrate." Ulrich took the bottle out of his hands. "You should fall down on your knees and thank her."

"You really don't know much about your precious bride, do you?"

"I know enough."

"Do you think she's really been seasick, dear brother in law? It could be morning sickness, you know."

In spite of himself, Ulrich smiled at the possibility. "I hadn't thought of that."

"You're pleased at the idea, aren't you? Well, Daddy, did she happen to tell you she murdered her own son?"

An hour later, Ulrich stood on the deck beside Catherine. Quinnon's accusations played like a canon in his head. Why would he tell such a heinous lie about his own sister? Perhaps there was some truth in what he said. Ulrich thought about the scars Catherine refused to discuss. Could there be a darker secret? He had to know.

The full moon's reflections flickered on the waves like radiant sea creatures. A salt laden breeze ruffled Ulrich's hair and chilled him through his thin shirt. He relished the cool ocean spray on his face.

"It's such a lovely evening, isn't it dearest? Let's open that champagne now." Catherine leaned her head on his shoulder.

He shook his head.

"What's the matter, Ulrich? You've hardly spoken since you came back."

"Are you with child, Cate?"

"No, of course not."

"How can you be sure? Have you seen a doctor?"

"I'm sure."

"Did you kill your son?"

"Yes."

Ulrich's heart raced. A hundred questions surged through his mind. What kind of woman had he married? Perhaps she was more like her brother than Ulrich wanted to believe. Bile rose in his throat.

"What of our children? Will you murder them, too?"

"How dare you!" Catherine stepped back and slapped him.

She leaned over the rail and covered her face with her hands. Remorse filled him and he pulled her to him. "I should know better than to listen to that slimy little weasel. Tell me what really happened, Cate. Please."

She lifted her head, her face wet with tears. "I suppose you have a right to know." She pulled her shawl around her trembling shoulders. "You are my unfortunate husband after all."

"You're freezing. Let's go inside and open that champagne."

A slight smile spread her lips. In silence they walked back into stateroom where Ulrich led her to the sofa. He sat, popped the cork on the champagne, poured two glasses and took a sip.

"On our wedding night Sherman beat me with that damned whip of his." Catherine sat beside him. She took her glass, held it for a moment and then set it back on the table beside the sofa. "He whipped me until I couldn't tell you my name. Do you know what it's like to watch your own blood splatter and hurt so badly you pray for death?

"If that wasn't enough he cursed me, called me a whore and our child a bastard. Then he took me to a 'doctor' to get rid of it. By the time that butcher finished what he called surgery there was nothing left inside me. Do you understand, Ulrich? I'm not with child and I never will be again. I *can't* give you an heir."

Shame paralyzed him. He searched for words to comfort her but she pressed her fingers against his lips. "Don't say anything. It's time you know about the scars on my wrists.

"After the surgery, Sherman took me home and left me to die with only Quinnon to try to nurse me back to health. Once the fever broke and I regained a bit of strength, I tried to end it all, but the razor didn't cut deep enough."

"A poor workman never blames his tools," whispered Ulrich.

"What's that supposed to mean?"

"Nothing, nothing at all, I'm sorry, please, go on."

Catherine took a sip of champagne, stopped for a moment and then gulped down the rest. She coughed and then took a deep breath. A tear trickled down her cheek and she wiped it off with the back of her hand.

"The police put Quinnon in an orphanage and locked me up in a lunatic asylum. You can't imagine what a horrid place it was. At first they gave me so called medicines that kept me in a state of illness and delirium. They shaved my head and sucked me dry with leeches.

"After a year the doctors deemed me sane enough to throw me back on the street. By that time Quinnon had flown the orphanage. It took me five months to find him and make a home for us, but I did it. No one helped me."

Ulrich stared at the scars on her bare wrists. At once a mixture of anger and sorrow filled him. He wanted to take her in his arms, comfort her and tell her that her past made no difference to him. Instead he poured himself another glass of champagne.

"Ulrich, please say something."

# CHAPTER SIXTEEN

Nikolai stood on the deck of the ship as it eased up to its berth in Odessa Harbor. Crewmen fore and aft threw lines to men on the dock who hauled across heavy hawsers and secured them to bollards; a long stairway led from the harbor to the city.

"Tatko, look at all those steps."

"Those, my son, are the Richelieu Stairs, two hundred of them, I'm told," said Nikolai. "They're impressive aren't they?"

"Do we get to climb them?"

"As far as I know, there's no going around them."

Nikolai hefted a small trunk, which contained all of their possessions, onto his shoulder. He curved his free hand around Vasily's arm and together they pressed through the crowd descending the gangplank.

"Kolyah! Kolyah!" cried a familiar voice.

Over a sea of hats, Nikolai caught sight of Pavel who looked almost as if he were constructed of pipe cleaners. On the landing of the tenth flight of stairs he waved his cap like a banner. Then, two steps at a time, with the speed of a gazelle, he bounded toward them until he reached the end of the stairs. Seizing Nikolai's shoulders, Pavel kissed him on both cheeks.

"How long has it been? Fifteen years? You've hardly changed." Nikolai dropped his trunk and embraced Pavel.

"I might be little older, but I'm not too sure I'm any wiser," said Pavel.

When they reached the fifth landing Nikolai set down his trunk to catch his breath. "I would hate to be a dock worker and have to climb these stairs every day."

"After supper, I'll take you on a tour of our beautiful city."

"Feel free to leave out the stairs. We've seen quite enough of them already. Pasha, are you sure this isn't an imposition? From what you've written you don't have much room. Vasily and I can find another place to stay."

"Oxana wouldn't hear of it. She's spoken of little else since I told her of your coming."

"How can I refuse?" Nikolai said, his chest burning as exhaustion from the long journey overtook him. He relished the promise of a hot meal and a warm bed.

Almost to the eighth flight Pavel motioned for him to stop and wrapped a protective arm around Vasily. Despite the frigid air, Nikolai's back was drenched with sweat. A few yards away a group of young men crowded the landing shouting threats and obscenities. Their hateful words made him cringe at vivid memories of Kishinev.

"Odessa stinks with you filthy *Zjids*!"

"Christian bastards."

"You Christ killers should be purged from the earth!"

"Never again!"

Someone waved a club and the inevitable brawl began. It was hard to tell the Jews from the Christians. Pavel pushed his way into the midst of the frenzied mob. "Stop! Hasn't there been enough bloodshed?"

A right hook to his jaw sent Pavel head over heels down several steps. He landed prone, eyes shut. Nikolai yanked off his spectacles and tossed them to Vasily. Before he could reach Pavel, a vicious blow to his ribs knocked him to his knees. Fists struck his head and he raised his arms to protect himself. Then someone grabbed him from behind in a stranglehold until a youthful voice cried out.

"Hyram, let him go. It's Dr. Nikolai."

The arm that was choking him fell away and Nikolai slumped to the ground. One of his eyes had already begun to swell. A sharp pain in his side challenged his efforts to breathe.

"Tatko?"

Nikolai forced open his uninjured eye and coaxed his split lip to smile. "Still here, Solnyshko."

With Vasily's help he managed to sit. Who in this place knew him? He spotted a redhaired boy bent over Pavel who was still unconscious and sprawled across the stone steps. Nikolai crawled to them and felt the other doctor's neck for a pulse.

"The patient's still alive." Pavel groaned. "Painfully so."

Relieved he had not arrived in time for his friend's funeral, Nikolai turned to the boy. "You're Lev Resnick from Svechka." He gently pressed his thumb against a bruise forming under Lev's eye.

"You remember me?"

"You sang at Arel and Havah's wedding with a voice like a screech owl."

"It was changing."

"All men go through it, my friend. It's a rite of passage, like your Bar Mitzvah."

"There's nothing bleeding or broken." Pavel sat up and grimaced. "Kolyah, you look terrible."

Lev helped Pavel to his feet. "Dr. Trubachov. Why did you put yourself in danger? It wasn't your fight."

"It's what my Lord would have done."

"Then your Lord's a fool."

Nikolai and his son followed Pavel under an arched entryway and down an alley between two dilapidated stone buildings to his apartment door. Pavel leaned against the wall by the door, then fumbled through his pocket. His face took on a sudden grey tinge. "I can't seem to find my key."

"Pasha, are you all right?" asked Nikolai.

"I'm just a little lightheaded. You worry too much, just like a doctor."

"Must be all the time I spent in medical school."

"Worry no longer. My sweet sister will tenderly dress our wounds and . . ."

Pavel's smile vanished and his eyes rolled back in his head. His body went limp and crumpled to the stone sidewalk.

Nikolai pounded on the door. "Miss Trubachov! Open up"

The door swung open. A woman with braided blonde hair tightly wound around her head glowered at him through thick-lensed spectacles. Tall and slender like her brother, her full lips seemed out of place on her narrow face.

"Dr. Trubachov isn't here. Come back later," she said.

The pain in Nikolai's side intensified his irritation. He pointed to the ground. She screamed and dropped to her knees. "Pasha!"

Pavel rolled over onto his back and his eyes opened halfway. "Kolyah, why you hit me?"

"You struck my brother?" the woman asked, astonished.

"Chitchat later." Nikolai crouched beside her. "Let's take him inside."

"*You* struck my brother?"

"Woman, are you deaf? I said help me take him inside."

"Tatko didn't hit him, you old witch," cried Vasily.

Nikolai flicked Vasily's head with his thumb and forefinger. "Solnyshko, bring in our luggage while the lady and I put Uncle Pasha to bed. Hold your hand under his arm, Miss Trubachov."

"Stop ordering me about like a servant." She scowled over her eyeglasses.

Pavel rallied enough to stand and wobble between them, his arms draped over their shoulders. Behind them, Vasily grunted as he dragged the trunk.

Upon entering, smoke burned Nikolai's already stinging eyes. A pile of blackened pierogis sat in the middle of the table. His disappointed stomach growled.

It did not take long to survey the cramped apartment. The front room doubled as living room and kitchen. There was only one window that looked out onto the cracked and broken cobblestone street. Doorways on opposite sides of the room led to two bedrooms.

"That one's Pasha's." Oxana indicated.

Dingy flowered wallpaper added to the bedroom's dismal atmosphere. Two narrow beds, one along each wall with a wooden stand between them took up most of the space. In one corner of the room sat a small wooden desk with an oil lamp and a straight-backed chair.

Once they had maneuvered Pavel to one of the beds, he folded his gangly frame down onto it and gingerly eased himself onto his back.

"There's no need for all this fuss," said Pavel in a slurred whisper. "A night's sleep and I'll be good as new."

Nikolai pointed to the lamp. "Turn up the flame and bring it to me, Miss Trubachov."

"Why should I?"

"Just bring me the infernal lamp!"

She hissed at him, but did as he asked. He held the lamp aloft over Pavel's face so it shined in his eyes. She observed Nikolai with icy disdain. "Well, Dr. Derevenko, what's your diagnosis?"

"Concussion, as I suspected. A few days in bed and your brother should be back to his impetuous self. I'll sit with him tonight to make sure there are no complications."

"I suppose you expect me to thank you?"

With a shrug of his shoulders, Nikolai scooted the desk chair to the bedside and sat. His side ached mercilessly. She switched her thin hand over the other bed where Vasily had already fallen asleep.

"This is our only spare bed," she said. "You'll have to share with your boy. Good thing you're both small. I'm sure it's considerably less than you're used to."

"Are you always this hospitable?"

"Rest assured, Dr. Derevenko, this arrangement is my brother's idea, not mine."

Nikolai rubbed his forehead. Then he took a pillow from the bed and tucked it behind his aching neck. "My son and I have been in Odessa less than twenty-four hours. Since our arrival I've been pummeled, kicked and nearly strangled to death. I'm hungry, bruised and in sore need of a bath. If my being here upsets you, Miss Trubachov, rest assured I'm too damned tired to care."

# CHAPTER SEVENTEEN

The next afternoon, while walking with a friend, Lev reenacted the brawl on the Richelieu stairs. "You should have seen Hyram. He's a warrior—even when he's outnumbered four-to-one. *Wham!* He punched one in the nose. *Boom!* He socked another in the stomach."

The other boy dodged Lev's fist. "Watch it!" He leaped off the sidewalk. "You're dangerous. What did your father say? Was he angry?"

"Gavrel's not my father."

As they neared the shoe shop, Lev heard someone crying. He peeked around the corner of the building. Devorah and Hyram sat side by side on the ground in the alley. To Lev's dismay the cries came from Hyram.

Devorah lightly touched Hyram's bandaged nose. "Lev's telling everyone what a hero you are."

"I'm no hero. I'm a coward. I reacted in anger to words . . . mere words. I could've . . . I *should've* walked away."

With mounting indignation Lev tiptoed closer. How could he say such things? Orev would never have walked away. Who knows? Maybe Hyram meant to kill him so he could have his wife. Just look at them. Huddled together like two birds in their nest and Orev only a month in his grave.

"But Lev said the goyim struck the first blow." Devorah pulled her woolen shawl around her and leaned her head on Hyram's shoulder.

"I . . . I couldn't tell." Wiping his eyes on his sleeve, Hyram hung his head. "He looked awful."

"Who?"

"Dr. Derevenko. I didn't even look at him."

"How could you have known who he was? You'd never met him."

"It wouldn't have made any difference. I became someone else, some*thing* else, an animal with no soul. I could've killed Dr. Derevenko, if Lev hadn't yelled when he did."

"But he *did* yell and you *did* stop."

He buried his head on her shoulder. "What if there comes a time when I don't?"

"You won't."

"How can you be so sure?"

"I just know, that's all." She took his hand and held it against her belly. "We know."

With his other hand Hyram pulled off her kerchief and exposed her shorn hair. He curled a lock around his finger. "It's as red as Reuven's." He leaned over and kissed her lips. "I don't have the right, with Orev so soon gone, but . . . would you consider becoming my wife?"

"Yes."

# CHAPTER EIGHTEEN

If Arel harbored any ill feelings or jealousy toward Beryl, he certainly did not show it. In fact it baffled Havah that, since Purim, the two had become good friends. Had she not done everything in her power to avoid him? She watched from a second story window as Beryl, four books under his arm, walked down the porch steps. He looked up, smiled and tipped his hat. She frowned turned away and nearly ran into Arel who stood behind her holding a stack of books.

"Beryl's some kind of a reader," he said. "He borrowed these just a week ago."

"He always was."

"He says you out-read him three books to one in *Heder*."

"He's generous."

"Why won't you talk to him?"

"I'm going to bed." She turned and limped across the landing to their room. Pain shot from her foot to her hip.

"It's only seven-thirty." He followed her and then pressed his palm against her forehead. "You feel kind of warm."

"I'm just tired."

She sat on the bed, took off her shoe, rubbed her swollen ankle and groaned. Arel sat down beside her, pulled her foot onto his lap and massaged it. Then, as Fruma Ya'el had taught him, he took bands of cloth from the top drawer of the bed stand and wrapped them tightly around her foot and ankle.

"Why don't you let Dr. Miklos take a look at it? You might've broken it this time."

"What can he do? Turn it back into a normal foot? Make me less clumsy? If it were broken it would be much more swollen and black.

And if we called him every time I twisted it, we'd have to give him his own room."

While she did not want to admit it, the bandage did bring her some relief. She took her foot off his lap and slipped it under the bedcovers. Their softness enveloped her and she had almost drifted off by the time he stood to leave.

"Good night." The floorboards creaked as he walked to the door. Then he stopped. "Incidentally, Beryl's joining us for *Shabbes* dinner tomorrow night."

Suddenly wide awake, she glared at him. "What?"

Again he asked, "Why won't you talk to him?"

"Why do you want me to?"

"You talked to him at the synagogue at Purim. What did he say to offend you? Do I need to talk to him about it?"

The telephone rang. Grateful for the interruption, she buried her face in the pillow and pulled the blanket over her head. "If it's Shayndel, tell her I've gone to bed. I don't want to talk to anyone."

Downstairs the ringing stopped. A moment later, in a voice loud enough for the whole house to hear, Arel said, "I'll get her."

When he entered the room, she sat up and waved her finger. "Don't you listen? I told you I don't want to talk to anyone."

Without a word, he pulled back the blanket, lifted her into his arms and carried her to the dining room. Then he lowered her onto the chair and handed her the receiver.

Yanking it from him, she leaned toward the mouthpiece and shouted, *"Hello!"*

"Ouch! Is this any way to greet an old friend?"

"Old friend?" she asked. The voice sounded familiar. Where had she heard it before?

"Does your nephew still have the silver dollar I gave him or did he spend it on candy?"

Her breath caught in her throat. Imagine, the president of the United States calling a peasant girl from Moldavia. She choked and stammered. "Mr. President?"

"Theodore Roosevelt at your beck and call, madam."

"How did you find me? I mean why did you call? Do you want us to pay you back for our train fare?"

"Of course not, dear lady. It's always a pleasure to help an American citizen find her way home. As for this call, it's at the behest of a mutual friend."

"I don't understand."

She had lived in the United States less than two years and nowhere near the capitol. Who could she possibly know who would be a friend of President Roosevelt?

His voice resonated even through the static on the line. "Last night, we at the White House had the great pleasure of being entertained by a marvelous pianist who tells me you are a woman of valor and great courage, Mrs. Gitterman. I have no doubt he speaks the truth. Even now he's chomping at the bit to rip this telephone from my hand. I've no choice but to surrender."

"I am honored, Mr. President."

"Nay, my dear, it's I who am honored. Godspeed to you and yours."

"*Shalom Alayikh*, Peace upon you, Havaleh," said another familiar voice.

Her heart pounded. She closed her eyes and whispered, "*Shalom alaykhah*, Ulrich."

"Havah, I have a great favor to ask of you."

"Anything."

"Catherine, her brother Quinnon and I will be in Kansas City in less than three months for a series of recitals. Would you possibly have room for us?"

"As if I'd let you stay anywhere else?"

"My last recital will be at the home of Sol and Zelda Mayer. They're Jewish. Do you know them?"

After she finished chanting the blessing over the Sabbath candles, Havah slipped her lace scarf off her head and sat down. "Good *Shabbes*."

"You always did have the voice of a morning dove." Beryl's even teeth shone in the flickering light. "Is it true, Mrs. Gitterman? Did the President of the United States really call you?"

"Yes, it's true, now can we talk about something else?"

Although speaking to Mr. Roosevelt and Ulrich was a crowning moment, she preferred to treasure it in the privacy of her heart. She certainly did not want to discuss it with Beryl. His presence made her itch. She dug her fingernails into her arm.

As the bread was passed around the table, Dr. Miklos took a large piece and held it to his nose. "There's nothing like the aroma of fresh baked bread. I appreciate the invitation, Mrs. Gitterman. It's not often I dine on such grand fare or with such fine friends and with such a great lady the President himself took the time to call her.

"What about my young protégé here?" The doctor squeezed Beryl's shoulder. "I have great expectations for this fine young man. Already he's making great strides in his medical education and only after one month of study."

"I, too, thank you for inviting me, Reb Gitterman. My aunt and uncle no longer light the candles or keep the Sabbath." Beryl's eyes stayed focused on Havah. She flushed and looked down at her lap.

Yussel shook his head. "It's a pity how some of our people are more interested in being Americans than Jews. Our traditions and ways of the faith mean nothing to them anymore."

Havah scratched the back of her neck. She stared at the food on her plate, her appetite gone.

"Is something wrong, Havaleh? I put extra raisins in the *tzimmes* just for you." Fruma Ya'el scooped enough for a small mouthful onto a spoon.

To appease her, Havah took the bite, gagged and, when Fruma Ya'el was not looking, spit it into her napkin.

"I'll eat whatever she doesn't want, Mama. So, Dr. Miklos, tell me, have you had a chance to go to a baseball game since you've been here?" Itzak piled a heaping spoonful of the carrot mixture onto his plate.

"I went once. It was great fun, great fun, indeed."

"Come with us to the Blues game tomorrow," said Yussel as he stuffed a large chunk of bread into his mouth.

With a slight shake of her head, Fruma Ya'el rolled her eyes. "Why should you want to go a baseball game, old man? You can't even see it."

"Jeffrey describes everything to me. I enjoy the crowd sounds and most importantly, I love those Cracker Jacks. We should all go and make it a family outing."

"Count me out." Havah rubbed her heel on her itchy leg. "A bunch of grown men hitting a little ball with a big stick and running in circles is just plain silliness."

"Mama, I don't feel good." David whined and pushed his plate away.

Beside him, Mendel curled up on his chair. "Me, either."

"I'm itchy all over." Evalyne tugged at Sarah's sleeve.

On Shayndel's lap Elliot whimpered. She cupped her hand around his flushed cheek. "He has a fever and a rash."

"This one, too," said Sarah as she pressed her hand against Jeffrey's forehead.

"And this one," said Fruma Ya'el of Rachel who fallen asleep on her lap. Red bumps dotted the child's face.

Dr. Miklos leaned back in his chair. "As you will learn to recognize, my future Dr. Mayer, what we have here is a common childhood malady known as chickenpox."

Mendel sat up and fixed his dark eyes on the doctor. "Did we catch it from chickens?"

"No, it's only called chickenpox. It's a silly name isn't it? But it's easier to remember than varicella. You probably contracted it from Wendy Mayer or a dozen other children I've seen this past week." The doctor's laughter filled the room. He dabbed his moustache with his napkin and then stood. "Take these children home and put them to bed. I'll drop by to see each of them."

"Make the itchies go away." David scratched a blister on his arm.

Dr. Miklos picked him up and held onto his hands. "If you're good, mind your mama and try extra hard not to scratch, I'll take you for a ride in my new motor car."

"Can you make it go really fast?"

"Well, the Oldsmobile will go up to forty miles per hour, but we don't want people to think this old doctor is a speed racer, do we?"

One by one, the adults filed from the room, each with a sick child in tow. Over the doctor's shoulder, David pointed.

"Looky, Dr. Miklos, Auntie Havah gots chicken spots, too."

Four hours later, after he had gone from house to house to tuck in each of his small patients, Dr. Miklos returned, Beryl in tow, to Havah's bedside. While he claimed it was merely a routine house call, Dr. Miklos' feigned smile did not fool her. Doctors did not make such visits after midnight for no reason.

She clenched her teeth around the glass thermometer and glared at Beryl. He pulled the thermometer from her mouth. "It's little over one hundred and three, as hot as my mother's oven the day before Shabbos."

"Why make such a fuss over a silly children's disease?" Havah clawed at a bump behind her ear.

"There's nothing silly about it." Dr. Miklos sat on the bed and took her hands in both of his. "They tell me you nearly died from German measles, another so called children's disease."

"How can I lie here in bed when my baby's sick?"

"Her grandmother has things under control. She is a capable woman." He took his stethoscope from his bag and handed it to Beryl. "Listen to her chest and tell me what you hear."

Havah pulled the blanket up around her neck. "You'll do no such thing!"

"Cooperate." Arel, who had not left her side for more than a few moments at a time, pushed the covers aside and then grasped her bare shoulders to prevent escape.

When Beryl pressed the stethoscope's cold bell against her chest she shuddered.

"So? What do you hear, 'Doctor' Mayorovich? Beethoven?"

With a foreboding frown he returned the stethoscope to Dr. Miklos who listened as well. His eyebrows made a tight hedge across the bridge of his nose. "I suspected as much. Mr. Gitterman . . . Arel . . . may I speak with you . . . outside?" He stood and moved toward the door.

"What can you say to him that you can't say to me?" Havah rose up on her elbows and then, seized by a fit of coughing, fell back against her pillow. "Why do I get so sick when no one else does?"

"The truth is you'll always have to take precautions, my dear. You most definitely will, no thanks to the Czar and his filthy henchmen."

Despite her heavy quilt, Havah could not get warm, yet her face blazed as she watched them leave. Brawny Dr. Miklos ducked to keep from hitting his head on the top of the door. Slender Arel, at his side, barely reached the doctor's shoulders. She strained to hear their whispers when the door shut behind them, but to no avail.

Beryl cleared his throat. "Does Arel know about Purim?"

"Do you think he'd be as friendly to you if he did?" Her chest ached and she itched everywhere possible.

"I shouldn't have kissed you."

"I love him."

"You should. He's a good man. Forgive me."

"I forgive you. Now go away."

"Not until I tell you."

"What's left to tell?"

"We heard about the pogrom in Natalya from Reb Nukhum. He said he alone escaped."

"Reb Nukhum the butcher? He's alive?"

"No, he hung himself." A tear rolled down Beryl's cheek. "It took a long time for me to accept the fact that you were dead. I begged the Almighty to strike me dead to punish me for abandoning you."

"You didn't abandon me. We were children. You had no choice. Your parents moved."

"Isn't that the real reason you're angry with me?"

"No."

"What else have I done?"

"Nothing." She scratched her neck and drew a painful breath. "Everything. Don't you understand? In *you* I see *them*.

"That last night Mama lit the Shabbes candles. Papa sang the prayers. David complained to Mama there was too much salt in the soup. Mendel discussed the next day's lesson with Papa and, like always, they argued.

"The sun went down and the world went up in flames."

# CHAPTER NINETEEN

After his brutal introduction to Odessa, Nikolai spent a week in bed with bruised ribs followed by a grueling two weeks of work under less than sanitary conditions. Moldavanka, with its dilapidated buildings and threadbare laundry hanging over uneven balconies was the Jewish section of the city. Even less welcoming than the neighborhood, Oxana's unpalatable cooking, served with a side of hostility, left Nikolai longing for London and worried about Vasily who looked like he had dropped at least a kilo from his slight frame.

When the opportunity presented itself, Nikolai took the boy on an outing. The sun shone on the majestic buildings with their curved walls and colonnades as they explored the city. Afterward, they had lunch in an expensive restaurant where Vasily wolfed down his food like a man who had not eaten for months.

On the way home Vasily chattered excitedly. "Today's been fun. I've never seen so many statues. The opera house is my favorite. I've never seen a round building before. Which one was your favorite, Tatko?"

Before Nikolai could answer, Vasily tripped on the uneven sidewalk. Without thinking, Nikolai reached out to catch him. Vasily crammed his hands into his pockets and frowned. "I'm not a baby."

"You'll always be my baby."

At that, Nikolai wrestled him into an embrace, tickled him under his arms, kissed both of his cheeks and then knocked off his cap. It bounced along the stones. Vasily skipped after it, caught it, made a face as he put it back on and pulled it down so it almost covered his eyes.

"Let's get home. You know how upset Oxana gets when we're late for supper."

"Yuck," Vasily pinched his nose between his fingers. "Is Uncle Pasha poor, Tatko?"

"I suspect he lives in this neighborhood to be close to work. As I recall, his family had considerable wealth. If he's poor, it's because he gave everything away."

"It's what his Lord would have done, right Tatko?"

"It's not such a bad motive if you ask me, Solnyshko. The world would be a better place if more people acted like him."

"If you say so."

In the ensuing silence, their footsteps beat a steady rhythm until Vasily tripped again and tumbled to the ground.

Nikolai knelt beside him and inspected his scraped knee. "Nothing serious, but I have noticed you're limping."

"My shoes are too tight."

"No wonder, as much as you've grown. Good thing for you there's a shoe shop close by."

"It's Sunday."

"In this neighborhood people worship on Saturday and work on Sunday." He helped Vasily to his feet and pointed. "It's two blocks that way."

Along the way, they passed a ragged old man sitting on a folded blanket, a prayer shawl draped around his thin shoulders. His black hat almost hid his eyes and his scraggly white beard reached to his spare waist. He leaned against a wall and in a relentless, almost prayerful chant, cried out, "A kopek. Please kind sir, could you spare a kopek for a poor old man?"

Nikolai took a step backward, fished a few coins from his pocket and placed them in the old man's gnarled hand. "Here, good father. May it serve you well."

The old man clamped his bony fingers around the coins and, without showing even a hint of gratitude, he spat on the ground. "Murdering goyim."

"He doesn't deserve your charity," said Vasily once they were out of the beggar's earshot.

"Perhaps not, but he *needs* it." Nikolai peered over his shoulder at the old man who resumed his imploring cantillation. "I've heard it said 'we don't always get what we deserve nor do we always deserve what we get.'"

When they rounded the next corner, Nikolai stopped in front of a ramshackle stone building. He pointed to the sign above the entrance.

"Wolinsky and Sons Distinguished Shoes, it looks like we've come to the right place, Solnyshko."

He opened the door and stepped inside, breathing in the scent of leather. Shoes in all shapes and sizes sat in pairs on a bench. Some had tags attached with names of the intended recipients. Others had tags stating the expected price.

"Dr. Nikolai. Welcome. Welcome." A man with sandy hair and a bushy beard to match looked up from his work table.

"I'm sorry, have we met?"

"Yes, but it's been a couple of years and only once at that. It was at Arel and Havah's wedding. Our family in America owes you a debt of gratitude."

"You confuse me with Ulrich Dietrich."

"Not at all, Doctor, you saved our Havah's life."

"Remember me, Dr. Nikolai?" A little girl popped up from under Gavrel's work table. "I'm Bayla. I remember you." She pointed at Vasily. "Is he your little boy?"

Vasily stiffened. "I'm not a little boy."

"You're not as big as your papa."

"I'm bigger than you."

"Why is your hair white?"

"Why is yours black?"

"I don't know. All my sisters and brothers have red hair, but I have black hair like my Mama. She's an angel now. Your papa has white hair, too."

"Hush, Miss Chatterbox." Gavrel swatted her behind with a shoe sole.

Sudden tears made her gray eyes glisten and her lower lip quivered. Gavrel chuckled and tapped it with his index finger.

"If you're not careful, little sister, someone's liable to step on that lip. Then it will be this long," he said stretching his arms wide.

Her pout turned to giggles. "Silly Papa."

"What brings you to my humble shop, Dr. Nikolai?"

"Vasily's outgrown his shoes."

"Boys have a way of growing before we have a chance to blink."

"Girls grow, too." Bayla tugged at his sleeve.

Scooping her up in his burly arms, Gavrel growled and pretended to bite her ear. "Girls, too, even girls who twitter and chirp all day like birds and chipmunks."

The afternoon sun streamed through the window and warmed Nikolai. He loosened his tie and unbuttoned his collar. "If you need to close for the day, I can bring Vasily back tomorrow."

"You're here. The boy needs shoes. Who knows? I might even have a pair already made to fit him." He stood Bayla back on her feet and pointed to a chair. "Sit, Reb Vasily."

Vasily sat on a low stool, took off his shoes and uncurled his cramped toes.

After Gavrel measured the boy's feet he took a pair of thick soled shoes from under the table. "I *do* have some that should fit. Fine grade black leather, they're like new. Lev wore them less than a month before he outgrew them. No charge if you don't mind shoes that have been worn by Jewish feet."

"Is there a difference between Jewish feet and Christian feet?" Cocking his head to one side and twisting his lips to the other, Vasily put on the new shoes.

"Some people seem to believe so. How do they feel?" Gavrel motioned toward the shoes. "Walk in them."

For the first time that day Vasily walked without a limp. "They're wonderful. May I really have them?"

"Of course! A promise is a promise and I always keep my promises. You and the boy will stay for dinner. My Leah is the best cook in Odessa."

Nikolai's stomach betrayed his polite protests. Opening his wallet, he pulled out a ruble and pressed it into Gavrel's hand. "The workman is worthy of his hire."

"Thank you, Doctor." Gavrel smoothed the crumpled bill, kissed it and stuffed it into an envelope. "I'd refuse, but this puts us one ruble closer to America."

Wishing for a window to open in the stuffy bedroom, Nikolai pushed his wet hair from his forehead. He took off his spectacles and wiped them on his shirt. Then he rolled up a pair of socks and threw them into the trunk in the doorway.

"You don't have to do this, Nikolai," Pavel sat on the bed. "You're more than welcome to stay."

"Would your sister agree?"

"About Oxana, you have to understand. I'm not the easiest person to live with and I did put her in a ticklish situation."

"There's nothing to explain, Pasha. Suffice it to say we appreciate your generosity, but this apartment isn't big enough for four."

"Give her chance to warm up to you. It's only been a three weeks."

"It seems more like three *years*," said Vasily as he folded a shirt and stuffed it into his suitcase.

"We're not going far. You'll be able to wave at us across the courtyard, and Mr. Sharp Tongue won't have to share a bed with his old tatko." Nikolai hurled a pair of trousers at Vasily, hitting him square in the face.

With tender care, Nikolai put his flute in its case and tucked it into the trunk between shirts and socks. Pavel picked it up and opened the case. "One tune and I'll leave you to your packing. I promise."

Nikolai rarely passed up opportunities for musical respite. He took the instrument from the case, held it to his lips and shut his eyes. The lilting melody of a Yiddish lullaby carried him back to an evening in Kishinev. Evron Abromovich, at his side, accompanied him on the clarinet. Ulrich's fingers floated across the ivory piano keys, golden under flickering candlelight. Itzak's onyx eyes shone as he caressed his violin with his chin. With the children gathered around her, the youngest on her lap, Havah sang in a winsome soprano voice. "*'Shlufje, yiddileh, shluf'—Sleep, little baby, sleep. Ay-lee lu lee-lu.*"

"Raisins and Almonds," Pavel whispered. "Beautiful, Kolyah."

"Yes, they were." Nikolai blinked open his eyes, put the flute back in the case and laid it in the trunk.

"Forgive me, Kolyah, I didn't mean to stir up the past." Pavel stood. "This damned anti-Semitism will destroy Mother Russia." He embraced Nikolai and then headed for the door.

"Watch your step." Pavel sidestepped the trunk. "Someone's liable to break their neck if they're not careful."

After he left, Nikolai smoothed the blankets on Pavel's bed and slipped two ruble notes under his pillow. "Let's hurry and leave before Oxana comes home from the market."

Vasily snapped his suitcase shut. "If we're lucky, we'll miss dinner."

"Sort of makes you miss Aunt Catherine. Speaking of whom, I received a postcard from her today from America. She's had a case of the sniffles and says that Uncle Ulrich is treating her like an invalid."

"He'd better be careful. She might poison his strudel."

"Women are a joke to you, aren't they?" Startled, Nikolai turned to see Oxana, holding a stack of neatly folded shirts. Her disapproving scowl made her look more severe than ever. "I washed your dirty clothes for you. So you see women are good for something."

Swallowing the words he really wanted to say, Nikolai cleared his throat. "Miss Trubachov, the woman we were laughing *about* is the wife of a dear friend."

"Oh, so it's all right to make sport of her."

His cheeks scarlet, Vasily frowned at her. "We love Aunt Catherine, which is more than I can say for—"

Curling his arm around his son's shoulder, Nikolai held his hand over Vasily's mouth.

"Is that so?" She flung the shirts at them and spun on her heel.

Nikolai followed after her. "Oxana! Watch out you're going to—"

In her haste, she somersaulted over the trunk in the doorway. Nikolai winced at the popping sound of breaking bone. She landed flat on her back, her foot twisted at an odd angle beneath her bottom. He dropped to his knees beside her.

Her face turned ashen. She glared at him. "Go ahead and laugh."

Being as gentle as possible, he straightened her leg and removed her shoe. Her ankle had already begun to swell. "Can you wiggle your toes?"

Snarling at him she slapped his hand before he could pull off her stocking. "Find my brother, you animal."

"Pavel's at the hospital, which is where you're going."

He bent down to pick her up, but she scooted away from him. "You're not carrying me anywhere."

"Have it your way."

With Vasily taking one arm and Nikolai the other they helped her to her feet, but as soon as she tried to stand her ankle buckled. They let her crumple to the floor in a moaning heap. Nikolai knelt and, ignoring her protests, tore her stocking.

"Does this hurt?"

"Of course it hurts you stupid oaf."

"I understand that you're angry, but tell me, can you move it?"

Her cheeks flushed with futility. She bit her lower lip and shook her head.

"Vasily, bring me the broom in the corner." Nikolai pointed.

"Don't you touch that," she yelled.

Despite Oxana's barrage of epithets Nikolai broke the broom handle in half. Then he took one of the clean shirts she had thrown at him and tore it into strips.

Once he had splinted her ankle, he gently picked her up and headed for the door. As he stepped out into the alley, he heard shouting and breaking glass. It sounded like it came from the next street. Black smoke spirals wreathed the amber sky.

Oxana's arms tightened around his neck and she huddled against him. He hurried along the sidewalk, his bruised ribs aching. Thank God it was only a couple of blocks to the hospital.

When they arrived, Nikolai heard painful cries from the clinic. Opening the double doors he held his breath. Bloodied women, injured children and battered men lined up for treatment. Pavel hunched over the table bandaging a little girl's head.

Without a glance at his sister, he seized Nikolai's shoulder with his free hand. "Nikolai, thank God you're here early. Police broke into their homes and smashed everything in sight. The whole damned city's on fire!"

Nikolai later learned that the pogrom and been precipitated by a mutiny of Russian sailors aboard the battleship Potemkin. Its presence in Odessa's harbor fomented a riot among dock and factory workers that had been on strike for over a month. Bundists, Bolsheviks and Mensheviks all seized their opportunities. Once violence erupted amid the crowd, mob rule took over. Mindless bloodshed begat bloodshed and ultimately shifted to Moldavanka and the Jews.

Until the flood of victims abated, Nikolai and Pavel worked without stopping to eat or rest. There had been no time that night to find out if the Wolinskys escaped the violence, although thoughts of them weighed heavily on Nikolai's mind. When Lev showed up to work the morning after the pogrom, angry but unscathed, Nikolai breathed a sigh of relief.

"Have you read this?" Lev tossed a crumpled leaflet on the treatment table.

Upon smoothing and reading the page, Nikolai recognized the idiotic ravings from a similar publication two years before in Kishinev. The same author, Krushevan, urged the beating of "Jews, students and wicked people for hurting the Fatherland."

"I'd rather be an orphan," said Nikolai.

Later that evening, he sat at Gavrel's dinner table. Fatigue and frustration destroyed what little appetite he had. He set down his fork, fished his wallet from his pocket. "Gavrel you must leave this place. Let me help you."

"Help yourself." The shoemaker clamped his massive hand over Nikolai's.

"Eat," said Leah as she filled his plate with potatoes. "You'll stay here tonight."

"But you barely have enough for yourselves. I can't impose."

"Look at you. You can't keep your eyes open. We've found room for your son and we'll make room for you, Doctor Nikolai."

In a corner, Vasily, sitting cross legged on the floor, played English word games with the children. Pora huddled close and watched him sketch faces on the letters on her slate. Reuven and Bayla competed to call out the letters' names and sounds. Vasily's face glowed with evident pride in their accomplishment.

"You see? Your boy earns his keep." Gavrel gathered up little Tova who had fallen asleep on the floor with a piece of chalk in her hand. He sat down in the chair next to Nikolai. "Very soon my babies will be ready to take on the United States of America."

Tova's auburn eyelashes grazed her cheeks. The divinity of her peaceful expression stabbed Nikolai as, unconcerned by imminent peril, she slumbered against Gavrel's vast chest.

A sense of urgency nearly choked Nikolai. "Don't wait, Reb Wolinsky."

"'Don't wait,' he says. Do I look like I can pack up and traipse off across the sea with this gaggle of geese? Business is slow." With a sidelong glance at the children, Gavrel lowered his voice. "The pogrom didn't help matters."

"That's all the more reason to leave."

"What about Devorah?" Leah lifted Tova and hugged her against her shoulder.

"She's only in her sixth month. She and the baby won't be in danger if you leave in the next couple of weeks."

"With all due respect, Doctor," said Leah as she headed toward her sister's bedroom, "you're *meshuggenah*." The door slammed behind her.

Oxana's bedroom, with its high ceiling and faded wallpaper, boasted one of two windows in the otherwise dark apartment. Vasily sniffed the musty air. Staring out the window, she lay on the bed, her mouth a taut line. With her arms folded across her chest, she had not moved a muscle in ten minutes.

He fluffed the pillows under her splinted foot. "Does it feel any better?"

She answered with icy silence.

"You should open the window, Miss Trubachov. Tatko says a person should breathe fresh air at least an hour every day."

Finally, she turned her head and glared at him. Without a word, she rolled over and resumed her former position.

Inspecting the bowl of lentil soup on the bed table, he heaved a sigh. "I guess you didn't care much for it. Does it have too much salt? Not enough?"

How much longer did he have to endure before either Uncle Pavel or Tatko would come to rescue him? He looked over her shoulder and out the window. There was no one in sight, save an old woman hanging laundry on a makeshift clothesline strung between two balconies. He turned to the bed stand and picked up a framed photograph of a lanky boy with spindly legs and a girl with ribbons in her long braids.

"Is this you? *Nyet*. It couldn't be. This girl's smiling."

Oxana said nothing. Vasily's resentment intensified. She did not need a nursemaid. He set the photograph back on the table and continued his chatter to ward off the hostile silence.

"I love children. I'm going to have a house crammed full of them when I grow up."

She took off her spectacles and laid them on the bed table. Then as if he did not exist, she nestled her head against the pillow and closed her eyes.

"Fine. Don't talk." With a kick at the rag rug beside the bed, he shrugged his shoulders, picked up the soup and turned to leave.

"The soup is . . . good," she whispered.

The bowl fell from his hands, splattering the floor. Lentils dotted the wall. He braced himself for a tongue lashing.

"Come back here and talk to me." Her eyes opened and she pointed to a ladder back chair beside the bed.

"What about the mess?"

"It can wait. It gives this shabby room extra color anyway."

Reluctantly he moved to the chair, sat and chewed his thumbnail. She gently slapped his hand. "Don't. It's a nasty habit."

To avoid her prying gaze, he stared at his feet and tucked his hands under his thighs. A cockroach scurried across the knot holed floorboards and disappeared between the cracks. He traced its path with his toe and wished he could follow it.

"Do I scare you?"

"No."

"You just don't like me and would rather be anywhere else in the world than with this sour old spinster, right?"

Heat blistered his cheeks. At a loss for words he slipped out one hand and gnawed at his pinkie nail. Then he spied a hairbrush on the bureau. He rose from the chair and lifted the brush by its ornate bronze handle. In itself it was a piece of artwork with roses painted on a porcelain background. He stroked the tuft of soft bristles.

"I'll brush your hair for you if you'd like."

"You'll what?"

"I used to brush Ivona's hair. One hundred strokes every night."

"Who's Ivona? Is she your mother?"

"No, that is, I mean, yes, but not exactly. She's dead."

For a moment Oxana's blue eyes riddled him with questions. Then she leaned forward and unbraided her hair. It cascaded down her narrow back. He wedged in behind her.

"You must miss her," she said.

"I don't."

"But she was your mother."

"She pushed me out and tossed me aside like garbage." He yanked the brush through Oxana's hair.

She grabbed it away from him. "And what about your father?"

At that moment, Nikolai entered the room carrying a pair of crutches. He tossed them down on the bed. "There's no need to interrogate my son."

"I'm sorry. I didn't mean to meddle." Oxana's sallow cheeks flushed and for a brief moment she looked like the little girl in the photograph.

"Did I just hear an apology?" Nikolai's rigid expression softened. "Let's get some fresh air into this musty room." He opened the window and took a deep breath. "For a moment you seemed almost—pleasant. Something's different." He tilted his head. "Your hair, it's—very nice."

# CHAPTER TWENTY

Havah's delirium from chickenpox complicated by pneumonia lasted an entire day. When her fever broke it left her depleted and too weak to even sit up by herself. Thus she languished in bed while Fruma Ya'el pumped her full of tea, tonics and rich foods.

To help ease Arel's worries, Nettie offered to take Rachel. Once Fruma Ya'el and Dr. Miklos deemed Havah well enough, Nettie brought Rachel home for short visits.

One morning Nettie burst through the door with the toddler in the curve of one arm and a carpet bag hanging from the other. Motherhood fit Nettie like a well-made dress. Her satisfied glow eased Havah's guilty conscience. Sitting on the bed, Nettie let go of Rachel who, in turn, nestled against Havah and popped her thumb into her mouth.

Still exhausted by the slightest exertion even after two weeks, Havah hugged Rachel and then fell back against the pillows.

"Here's something to fatten you up." Nettie pulled a tinfoil wrapped parcel from the bag. "My bubbeh's famous cinnamon buns to celebrate!"

At once Rachel sat up and clapped her hands. "Bun! Bun!"

"Nothing gets by this." Nettie tapped Rachel's nose. "Like a bloodhound, she is."

Havah took one of the rolls and bit into it. "Mm. Raisins. What's the occasion?"

"Why, your good health, of course." Nettie pinched off a piece of her roll and gave it to Rachel. "And my new baby."

"Your new baby? Oh, that's right. George told Arel about your puppy."

"That flea-bitten mutt? *Feh*. No, Havaleh, I'm going to have a baby."

"When are you due?" Trying to hide her dismay, Havah munched on the roll.

"Any day now."

Since her miscarriage, Nettie had lost a considerable amount of weight. Havah eyed her slender form and flat stomach. "You shouldn't tease a woman who's just escaped the clutches of death by chicken-pox."

"I'm not in a family way. My baby's true mother is barely fourteen."

"Who is she?"

"How should I know? She's one of the poor emigrants Dr. Miklos takes care of in McClure Flats. It's a shame the way they live. Sometimes there are as many as six of them crammed into a shack the size of my bedroom."

"You went to that pest hole?"

Populated by impoverished emigrants from Italy, Sweden and Russia, McClure Flats was a filthy place, rampant with rats and typhoid. Havah ached for those who had probably spent their life savings just to journey to this land of promise only to find cruel poverty. Had it not been for Ulrich's generosity, she and Arel might have ended up in one of those crude shanties.

"No, I didn't go there. Dr. Miklos made all the arrangements," said Nettie. "All I know is that before her family left the old country, some Russian boys attacked her. They pushed her into an alley, beat her, did their business, and left her to die."

"They should all be smitten with a rash that never heals."

"Dr. Miklos took her to City Hospital last week."

"It doesn't bother you this baby's father is a *goyisheh* pig?"

"Why should it? The father, he should drop dead a hundred times, may be a gentile, but the mother's a *yiddisheh maydeleh*, a good Jewish girl. Did she ask for this cruel fate? Doesn't the baby deserve a chance at a good life?"

Downstairs the telephone rang. A few moments later, Fruma Ya'el entered the room, a wide smile on her face.

"It's a boy! He weighs eight pounds."

"And he's healthy?" Nettie jumped off the bed.

"Go to the hospital, Mama. See for yourself."

Dark braids pulled to either side of her head made the girl in the hospital bed appear to be much younger than fifteen. Her huge eyes swam with tears and pierced Nettie's heart. Why must her joy come at this child's expense?

"You will take good care of him?" the girl whispered.

Nettie nodded as she cradled the swaddled infant in her arms. "Would you like to hold him?"

"No! Never. Take him. Take him and go." The girl buried her head in the pillow.

The next day, the girl and her family disappeared without a trace. Rumor had it that they bought tickets to St. Louis with the money Nettie and George paid them for the baby.

Eight days later, Nettie dressed the baby for his bris in the gown she had made a year before. "He's almost too big for it."

"How many bottles did he down last night? Two? Three? I'll bet this little horse has gained a pound already." George gathered him up into his arms and whispered. "My son."

"Do you think she'll be all right?"

"Who?"

"His mother."

"You'll be just fine."

The summer breeze warmed Havah's face and she breathed in the aroma of fresh cut grass. Leaning on her cane for support, she walked down the sidewalk beside Arel who carried Rachel on his shoulders. Mendel and David skipped ahead of them.

Fifteen-month-old Elliott toddled behind his brothers. His sandy hair shone in the sunlight. Havah pointed. "Look at how well he walks. Rachel won't take so much as a step."

"You heard what Dr. Miklos said." Arel reached up and tweaked Rachel's nose. "She's more cautious than a sighted child. When she's ready, she'll walk." Then he lowered his voice. "Besides, she talks better than Elliott."

Just as Havah opened her mouth to reply, Elliott tumbled to the ground and wailed. She dropped her cane and hurried to him. Squatting next to him, she examined his tiny hands and kissed his upraised scraped palms. His grey eyes spilled over. "Up."

"Don't you even think about lifting him, Havaleh," said Shayndel. "You haven't been out of bed a whole week." She scooped him up in her arms and twirled him around. He squealed with delight when her straw hat flew off her head. With the baby straddled on one hip she chased after it, her golden braid falling to her knees.

As Havah picked up her cane and stood, she felt like a shriveled old woman by comparison. Only a few years ago she could have beaten Shayndel in a footrace and still have had enough energy to dance. She stared at her feet. Those days would never again be hers.

Itzak scooped up Elliott and then hoisted him up onto his shoulders. "We're going to be late. The Weinberg's invitation said two-thirty and it's a quarter after now. Mama and Papa are way ahead of us." He pointed to Yussel and Fruma Ya'el who walked hand in hand. Mendel and David skipped alongside, chirping like two robins with their wings aflutter.

"Don't worry, big brother. There'll be plenty of goodies. The ladies have been baking all week." Arel offered his arm to Havah.

She hooked her hand around it. "I can't wait to see the baby. Sarah says he's adorable and even looks a little like George."

"Yeah. He's bald," said Itzak as he sped by them.

Arel squeezed Havah's hand and slowed his pace. "You're so pale. I should take you home and put you back to bed."

"No you don't. I'm sick of seeing the world sideways." Havah's legs ached just as Dr. Miklos had warned they would after so many days on her back. "I didn't sleep well last night, that's all.

Finally they stopped in front of a single story house where George sat on the porch swing. A cocker spaniel with doleful eyes lay beside him. It raised its head and barked, then leaped off the swing, trotted to Arel and stood on hind legs, front paws scratching his knees.

George followed and swatted it. "Down, girl. Down Kreplakh."

"Keppy!" Rachel squealed and clapped her hands.

Kreplakh whined and ran in circles around Arel wagging her tail.

George wiped the sweat from the top of his head with his sleeve. "I haven't seen her get this excited in over a week. All she's done is mope since Rachel went home."

The door swung open and Nettie stepped out with a bundled baby in her arms. "Havah, it's good to see you up and around, but we need to put some color back in those cheeks." She led Havah to the sofa. "Sit. Arel, the food's in the kitchen. Fix your wife a plate."

"I wish I could've been at shul this morning for the *bris*." Winded from the short walk, Havah was grateful to lean back against the sofa cushions. She followed Arel with her eyes until he disappeared into the crowd gathered in the dining room.

"There was nothing to see," said Nettie with a shrug. "A little snip and it was all over. Benjamin slept through the whole thing. It'll mean more to him when you come to the synagogue for his bar mitzvah."

"I like the name Benjamin."

"George's grandfather of blessed memory was also Benjamin. Would you like to feed him?"

Without waiting for an answer, Nettie laid little Benjamin in Havah's arms and handed her a warm bottle. Benjamin nuzzled Havah and then latched onto the rubber nipple. His warmth and mewling sounds lulled Havah. She had almost drifted off when she heard Itzak say, "Would you look at that!"

With one hand grasping the scruff of Kreplakh's neck, Rachel toddled toward her on two feet. "Keppy go Mama."

When she reached her destination, Kreplakh licked Rachel and then laid down and let the girl use her as a step stool to climb onto the sofa.

"Havah, I don't suppose you want a dog?" Nettie whisked the baby off Havah's lap to make room for Rachel.

"Do I have a choice?"

Although the gentle animal did not seem to mind Rachel's hold on her fur, Arel decided it was not the best arrangement. He fashioned a harness and leash out of leather strips and rope.

"It's more comfortable for Kreplakh and better grip for Rachel," he said with a proud smile.

At first Fruma Ya'el railed against having a dog underfoot. She insisted an animal in the house would lead to disease and pestilence. However, by the end of the second day, Havah caught her sneaking leftover meat scraps to the dog.

When she was not guiding her little charge, Kreplakh would shadow Havah. If she saw an obstruction in her path she would nose it out of her way. Whenever Havah had one of her frequent nightmares, the dog would jump up on the bed and lick her face until she woke.

One such night Havah, afraid to go back to sleep, limped down to the living room. As she sat down on the sofa, Kreplakh curled up beside her. Her warmth comforted Havah.

That morning the postman delivered two letters. One was a postcard from Ulrich and Catherine, the other a missive from Gavrel, partly in Yiddish and partly in rudimentary English.

*"Young Vasily it is teacher to me good. By after holiday of high we speaking then. Then we to America come with have money enough."*

She read the clumsy lines aloud. His determination to be ready for America made her smile.

In Yiddish he told of a skirmish in Odessa's harbor and how the Almighty had spared them. Although he made light of the "little pogrom, hardly enough to mention," it made her shudder. She sensed there was more that he did not want to tell them.

Yussel, in robe and slippers, shuffled into the room. He lowered himself onto the sofa and stroked the dog's head. His disheveled hair hung over his forehead and tears wet his beard. He pounded the couch's arm.

"They shouldn't wait. They cannot wait! They must come now!"

Havah placed her trembling hand over his on Kreplakh's head. "Bad dream, Papa?"

"Bad dream? It was horrible, dreadful, unimaginable. The Angel of Death cast his shadow. Children screamed. Then silence. Louder than death."

"Hush you foolish old man." Fruma Ya'el padded into the room. "Listen to you. 'Louder than death.' Our daughter doesn't have enough trouble with her own nightmares? You have to disturb her with yours?"

Nameless terror gnawed at Havah. "Papa's not disturbing me, Mama. I had the *same* dream."

# PART III

## *Night of Madness*

# CHAPTER ONE

Ulrich and Catherine's confrontation aboard ship created such a strain on their relationship he worried the marriage might end before it had a chance to begin. A series of 'sick headaches' kept her bedridden. She refused to attend most of his concerts in New York, save one at Carnegie Hall. He slept alone for fear she would shatter like porcelain if he laid a hand on her.

Once they reached the White House, things improved; a fact he attributed the president's wife, Edith. Shortly after their arrival, she invited Catherine to her chambers for a visit. Following the chat, Catherine's smile returned.

Ulrich wanted desperately to know what Mrs. Roosevelt said. But it did not matter, for that night Catherine welcomed him with open arms. At last in the privacy of a presidential guest suite he melted into her under silken sheets.

Afterward, her hair on the pillow surrounded her flushed cheeks like flames and he ached with love for her. "What's been vexing you so, Catherine?"

"I was so afraid you didn't want me anymore because I can't have children."

"How could I not want you?" With his hands on either side of her face, he used his thumbs to brush away her tears. "I'll drink you like fine wine for the rest of my life."

At Catherine's insistence Ulrich submitted to a day trip from Boston to Wrentham. The night before, after his concert, she and a Mrs. Macy had arranged it. Although he had no recollection of the exchange, Catherine maintained that he cheerfully consented.

"Wasn't it nice of Mrs. Macy to send their carriage for us?"

"Very nice, indeed."

The romantic notion of touring the States had already lost its allure amid trains, carriages, misplaced belongings, sleepless nights, hurried concerts and pretentious soirees. Lulled by the summer breeze and the clop-clop of horses' hooves on the dirt road, Ulrich's eyelids drooped. Just as he nodded off into exhausted sleep, her voice snapped him back.

"Ulrich, you're a dreadfully dull companion."

"Am I?"

"Wake up, you. We're nearly there."

"I'm not asleep." Reluctantly he pried opened his eyes. "See?"

"You were so."

Her lower lip jutted like a petulant child's and her strawberry spirals, along with certain other attributes beneath her light cotton blouse, bounced in tandem with the carriage, arousing his most ignoble urges. He tucked his finger under her chin and leaned forward for a kiss.

"My lunatic sister has found love at last," said Quinnon.

Draped across the opposite seat Quinnon pushed his hat off his face and sneered. Then he struck a match against the sole of his shoe and lit a cigarette fished from his waistcoat pocket. He took a long drag then blew a succession of smoke rings.

Catherine flinched. "Why *did* you insist on coming along?"

"Family togetherness, sister dear. And who'd pass up the opportunity to meet a true sideshow freak?"

"One impertinent word from you during this visit and I'll dissect you with a fork and use your intestines to restring your violin." Leaning forward, Ulrich grabbed him by his lapel with one hand and balled his other into a fist.

Cigarette clenched between his teeth, Quinnon grinned. "What difference does it make what I say? She's deaf as a fence post."

Ulrich tightened his grip. "And she won't see it when I pulverize your—"

"Ulrich, please." Catherine gasped. Then with a forced smile she continued to talk. "I can't wait to finally meet Miss Keller. She's an amazing woman. You simply must read her book, Ulrich. I saw her at your recital in Boston last night, but couldn't reach her for all the people gathered around her. Mrs. Macy's her teacher you know."

"Perhaps they can suggest some resources to pass on to the Gittermans for their little Rachel." Ulrich released Quinnon's lapel and eased back against the seat cushions.

"Always looking out for your former mistress and her blind brat, eh Guv?" Quinnon sneered. "Maybe you're the little tyke's daddy after all."

"Quinnon," said Catherine. "Ulrich would never—"

"Oh, wouldn't he? Have you ever noticed the way he fair lights up whenever he speaks of her?"

The carriage stopped in front of a three story house with a balcony and screened-in porches on two sides. Grateful for the diversion, Ulrich stepped down, then he reached for Catherine who pushed his hands aside and jumped from the carriage unassisted.

A stout woman with dark eyes bustled toward them, her hand extended. "Professor and Mrs. Dietrich, how lovely of you to come. Helen and I are delighted."

"It's wonderful to see you and your amazing prodigy again, Mrs. Macy." Ulrich bowed and kissed her hand.

"*Guten Morgen*, Professor." A young woman with chestnut hair and pleasant smile followed Mrs. Macy. Although she was obviously blind and deaf and her high pitched monotone was hard to understand, he marveled at her poised self-assurance.

At her side, a Great Dane let out a low growl. Then, with a ferocious bark he lunged at Quinnon, knocked him down and pinned him under its paws.

"That's odd. I've never seen him exhibit such aggressive behavior." Mrs. Macy grabbed the dog by the collar. "I apologize. He seems to have taken a dislike to you, sir."

"Smart dog," whispered Ulrich.

# CHAPTER TWO

"Where will you go, Barry? What will you do? What about medical school?"

"Dr. Miklos is helping me with the entrance requirements for Johns Hopkins. I'll finish medical school in Baltimore."

"Just like that?" Aunt Zelda snapped her fingers. "You leave without so much as a thank you?"

"Thank you."

"After all your uncle and I have done for you!"

Her never ending palaver reverberated in Beryl's ears like a tin can tumbling over rocks on a windy day. To avoid her prying glare, he averted his eyes to the rosebud pattern on the china serving bowl beside his wine goblet and traced it with his finger.

Finally Aunt Zelda stomped her foot under the table. "Sol, say something to *your* nephew!"

Despite his amiable smile, Beryl could not help but notice the twitching veins in his uncle's neck. With a pronounced shrug of his shoulders he raised his glass and winked at Beryl. "*L'khaim.*"

Wendy raised her water glass. "*L'khaim* means 'to life.' Right, Daddy?"

"You are absolutely correct, princess."

"But Barry, dear, Maryland is so far." Like a melodramatic heroine, Aunt Zelda pressed the back of one hand against her forehead and fluttered her other one in front of her face.

"Zeldie Malka." Uncle Sol emptied his wineglass and then refilled it. "Let the boy eat in peace."

"Zeldie Malkie. Zeldeeeeeeee Malkeeeeeee. Zeldie Malkie. Zeldie Mommy!"

Wendy's singsong prattle both amused and irritated Beryl. He sawed off a piece of steak and popped it into his mouth. Then he washed it down with wine and caught a glimpse of his aunt's pinch-lipped pout. She reminded him of the drawings of ladies in the *Kansas City Star* touting the latest fashions—elegant and flat as the paper itself.

"Don't worry, Aunt Zeldie Malka, I'll write. You'll still be able to boast to your friends about your nephew the doctor."

"Well!" Her mouth dropped open, then she pursed it shut, dabbed her lips with her napkin and cleared her throat with a dismissive cough. "Sol, dear, have you received an answer from Professor Dietrich yet? I'm sure he'll accept our invitation."

"On the contrary, I received a telephone call from him just today. He says 'thank you, but no thank you.' They will be staying with friends. I wonder who he knows in Kansas City."

"Did you think to ask him?"

"A man's entitled to his privacy. If he wanted me to know specifics he'd tell me."

"No wonder you never know what's going on around you, Sol. You lack curiosity. You don't suppose he turned us down because we're Jewish do you?"

Beryl chased a green bean with his fork and muttered, "Maybe he's just a good judge of character."

"Don't mumble, Barry. Only old people mumble." She shoved a bowl of kugel across the table. "You've hardly touched your dinner."

"I'm not hungry."

"Nonsense." She spooned a heaping pile of noodles onto his plate. "A doctor must take care of his own health."

"Dammit. Stop trying to run my life."

"Barry Mayer, what's come over you?"

"Mayorovich. *Beryl Mayorovich*. Just because *you're* ashamed of whom you are and where you came from doesn't mean I am."

"This is what comes of spending time with common *shtetl* peasants like those Gittermans."

"Zeldie, they're honest, hardworking people and good customers, too." Sol emptied his third glass in one gulp.

Wendy rose up on her knees. "Mrs. Gitterman's a pretty lady. She met President Roosevelt when she went to Elves Island in a big boat. She showed me the hanky he gave her and it has gold letters on it. A 't' and a 'r.'"

Sol chuckled and tweaked one of her ringlets. "I think you mean Ellis Island, Wendy."

"Yeah, Ellie's Island."

"Ha! I for one don't believe it," said Aunt Zelda with a sniff. "She just told you a fairy story. Anyone can embroider 'T.R.' on a handkerchief."

"Not Havah." Beryl pulled a yellowed piece of cloth embroidered with clumsy Hebrew characters from his breast pocket. "Unless she's improved a lot, she couldn't sew two even stitches in a row if her life depended on it."

Zelda took the cloth from his hand. "Where did you get this?"

"We were—school friends."

"I can't believe it." She shook the cloth under Sol's nose. "Did you know about this?"

"When I left Natalya, Rabbi Cohen only had two sons and his wife was in a family way. My brother often wrote about the rebbe's pretty daughter who went to Heder like a boy. But until this minute I had no idea Mrs. Gitterman was the same Havah."

Beryl took the crude handkerchief back and stuffed it into his pocket. "What do you have against her? What's she ever done to you?"

"I just don't like her," said Aunt Zelda.

"Well, I *love* her!"

# CHAPTER THREE

Spread like a cloth across the table, the print on the four-page broadside shimmered before Nikolai as though through steam from a kettle. He shut his eyes, snapped them open and reread. "'Search their apartments. Confiscate their weapons.'"

Almost three months had passed since the pogrom. While life in Moldavanka appeared to have returned to some semblance of peace, the atmosphere crackled with underlying tension.

At the hospital Nikolai treated a disturbing number of gunshot wounds. Although he applauded the Jews' efforts to defend themselves, he feared they would prove to be futile.

The night before at Gavrel's home, Nikolai read the unspoken angst in the shoemaker's eyes. Still the man refused monetary assistance.

"I give charity," said Gavrel, his jaws set like iron. "I don't take it. Besides, I should pay you for the lessons your son gives. Listen to my children. They speak English like they were born to it."

"Your damnable pride will be your death sentence."

"So be it!"

Gavrel hit the table with his fist. The noise echoed in Nikolai's ears as his mind returned to the one-room apartment he shared with Vasily. Aside from a stove, sink and small icebox, it was sparsely furnished. A cluttered desk sat in one corner next to a bed that dipped in the middle. The only other furniture was a pockmarked set of table and chairs.

Savoring his spiced tea, he gazed out the open window. Threatening clouds rumbled overhead. They reflected the heaviness which beset him and weighed on his chest like jagged boulders. Oblivious to the approaching storm, a group of boys played tag in the courtyard. Their laughter warmed him; it was music in its purest form.

Across the table, Pavel leaned back in his chair until the front legs left the floor, his fingers linked behind his head. "Do you have any idea how long it's been since I've heard my sister laugh?"

"What's so funny?" A clap of thunder and a sudden burst of rain sent the children scurrying into an alley. Nikolai propped his elbow on the table and rested his head on his hand.

"You are, my friend."

"Me?"

"You've enchanted her somehow. You're all she talks about. 'Have you spoken to Kolyah?' or 'Is Kolyah well?'"

"She called me 'Kolyah'?"

A damp wind fluttered the bright, colored curtains that Oxana had made to add life to his dreary quarters. The thought of her using his nickname brought him unexpected pleasure.

With a wink Pavel set the front legs of his chair back on the floor and leaned forward. "Lest I forget, you're invited for supper tonight. After two months of living as bachelors you and Vasily could use a home cooked meal."

"No offense, Pasha, but your sister's cooking leaves a lot to be desired no matter where it's been prepared."

Nikolai turned back to the window. Rain spattered the pavement. The children had vanished except for two small boys who chased each other through the puddles, splashing and cackling. He swallowed the last of his tea. "We're moving back in with you."

"Why?"

"For Oxana's sake."

"You just said you hate her cooking."

"My stomach aside, she shouldn't be alone. First, it's garbage like this," Nikolai rolled up the paper and waved it like a baton. "Gullible people eat it up because they need a scapegoat. Then, like a volcano, hatred erupts into violence."

"But we're not Jewish."

"No, but we live in the heart of the ghetto."

"Where else should I live? Our Lord was a Jew."

"When the bloodthirsty mob claiming to be Christian breaks down your door do you think they'll notice the cross around your sister's neck or stop to consider what their Lord would've done?"

# CHAPTER FOUR

The yeast-laden aroma of fresh baked hollah coupled with the lemony scent of sponge cake wafted over Havah as she settled into the rocking chair. Cuddled against her shoulder, Rachel popped her thumb into her mouth and closed her eyes. Kreplakh curled on the floor, her eyes following the chair's motion.

In her mind Havah listed the tasks she needed to complete before sundown. Dinner had been prepared the night before. Sarah would bring potatoes, Nettie and George the wine and Mama had made *tzimmes*. Havah needed only to put the chicken in the oven at four.

"We're ready to greet the Sabbath Queen."

"With four hours to spare." Shayndel stretched out on the sofa with her head against one of its arms and her feet on the other. She flashed a self-satisfied grin.

"I'd still be scrubbing the floors if it weren't for your help," said Havah as she propped her aching foot on the hassock.

"At next Friday's dinner, you can repay me at my house."

Rachel's rhythmic breathing lulled Havah until a loud knock at the front door startled her. Kreplakh bounded to it, barking and furiously wagging her tail.

Rachel sat up and clapped her hands. "Arf! Arf!"

Havah eased off the chair and sat the baby on the rug. She pointed to Elliott, asleep on the sofa beside Shayndel. Amid the dog's barking and the insistent knocking at the door he had not even flinched. "How can he sleep?"

"He slept right through that awful storm the other night. Good thing, since we already had Mendel and David in bed with us." Shayndel swung her legs over the side of the sofa and leaped up. "I'll get it."

She ran to the door, pulled it open and greeted a man holding a large package.

"Is this the residence of Mrs. Gitterman?" His cap's wide bill obscured his eyes. He tilted his head.

"Yes." Shayndel took the parcel from him with childish enthusiasm. "It's heavy!"

"I'm Mrs. Gitterman." Pain shot through Havah's swollen ankle as she limped to the door. "Please come inside."

"Thank you." He took off his cap and tucked his chin in a sort of bow. Freckles speckled the rounded bald spot on top of his head. He straightened and eyed her foot. "You should have that looked at. Pardon my saying so, ma'am, but you don't look much older than my little thirteen-year-old daughter."

"Thank you for your kind concern, sir. I'll certainly look into it," said Havah.

"I'm sorry, I didn't mean to . . . I mean it's none of my business." The man's acne-scarred cheeks reddened.

"Who's the package from?"

"Lessee here, it's postmarked 'Boston, Massachusetts.'" He took a clipboard from under his arm and held it out to her. "Please sign on the line."

She signed the paper and handed back the clipboard. He pulled his cap back over his eyes, tapped it with his fingertips, mumbled "good day" and then turned on his heel like a uniformed soldier.

Shayndel shut the door and hurried back to the sofa, pushing the box along the floor. She helped Havah tear off the brown paper and pry open the seal.

Atop layers of tissue sat an envelope addressed to her in Ulrich's sweeping scrawl. After fishing a soggy wad of wrapping paper from Rachel's mouth, she ripped open the envelope and unfolded the parchment stationary. "*'Dearest Havah, Catherine and I will be there before you know it. Please accept this gift my lovely wife has chosen. It's the latest in Paris fashion.*'"

"Look now." Shayndel seized the letter. "Read later."

A bit annoyed because she longed to hear Ulrich's voice as she read the words, Havah reached under the tissue. With a gasp she lifted layers of pink and violet organdy overlaid with golden lace.

Shayndel brushed her hand over the gown. "I'll bet even Zelda doesn't have anything like this in her fancy wardrobe."

Holding it up to her shoulders, Havah climbed up onto the hassock and admired her reflection in the mirror over the mantel. Waves of pleasure flooded her when she noted how the gown's colors complimented her hair and complexion. Then she stepped down and draped the dress over the back of the sofa.

"What else is in here?" Shayndel tossed the tissue paper to the floor and reached into the box. "It's too heavy for just one frock."

Her smile faded and she shook her head as she pulled out a large book with thick pages. "This is just what you don't need. You're running out of room for the ones you have now." She opened it. "This is a strange book. There's no print or pictures, just bumps."

"Do you know what this is? It's Braille." Havah took the book from her and brushed her fingertips over the raised dots. There was also a typewritten note tucked between the thick pages. "They're from Helen Keller *herself*! Rachel, look! Books for—where is she?"

Only a pile of torn paper remained on the floor where Rachel had been playing. Havah's anxiety mounted as she searched from one side of the living room to the other. She had been so intent on Ulrich and Catherine's gift she had ignored her daughter. There was no sign of either the child or her dog.

From outside she heard barking. When she was not paying attention Rachel and Kreplakh must have wandered to the backyard. At least Mendel and David could watch her.

Havah dropped the book back into the box and hurried through the dining room, the kitchen and out the backdoor. Her chest tightened when she saw only the twins and the dog.

The frenzied cocker spaniel stood on her hind legs, scratching at the elm tree and yelping at a tabby cat who sat on lowest branch, calmly licking her paw. Havah ran to the tree, swatted the dog, grabbed the cat and tossed it, yowling, over her neighbor's fence. "Where's Rachel?"

"I dunno." Mendel shrugged.

She knelt, grasped his shoulders and shook him. "What do you mean you don't know? Kreplakh's out here so Rachel has to be out here, too."

Huge tears rolled down his cheeks. David patted Mendel's back and said, "Auntie, we haven't seen her for a long time today."

"I'm sorry, Mendel, it's my fault." Hugging him, she looked over his head at Shayndel who had followed her and then out at the empty yard. "I should've made sure the doors were all closed."

"We'll find her, she can't have gone far," said Shayndel.

"What if she fell into a ditch or was hit by an automobile or trampled by a horse."

*"Shah!"* Shayndel pressed her hand over Havah's mouth. "Don't even think it. You search the house. The boys and I will search the street."

Havah watched them walk down the sidewalk calling for Rachel. Choking on the panic rising in her throat, she swatted Kreplakh's nose.

"Bad dog."

Back inside the house she searched the living room. Elliott still napped on the sofa, softly snoring like an old man. Kreplakh cocked her head and then scampered around Havah's feet, sniffing at the floor. Barking, she ran up the stairs. Moments later she ran back downstairs and nipped at Havah's ankles.

"Stay away from me!" She shoved the dog aside with her good foot, hurried to the dining room and looked under the table. The child was not there. "Rachel, where are you? Answer me, right now, this minute!"

Silence answered her and the walls whispered crushing accusations.

"I know. She's in Mama and Papa's room." Why had she not thought of that sooner? They were at the park with Evalyne and Jeffrey, but they often hid treats for their grandchildren. Rachel always knew where to find them and the door was open. Havah crawled under the bed.

"I know you're under there, Rukhel Shvester."

The only thing she found under Mama and Papa's bed was an empty box that usually held the hidden candy. There was no time to whine. She rose, squared her shoulders, stepped out into the hallway and slammed the bedroom door behind her.

"Rachel! Rachel!"

Havah's hope diminished with each unanswered call. If Rachel was still in the house she would answer. She had better hearing than most.

Havah hobbled up the stairs with Kreplakh at her heels. "Go away! Rachel, please, *please* answer me." Peeking around the nursery door, she gazed at the empty crib.

The dog chomped down on her skirt hem and growled. Havah kicked her and headed for her own room. Kreplakh jumped up on the bed, barked and then jumped off, ran to the closet. Sniffing and whining she scratched at the door.

"You want in the closet, you stupid mutt?"

With a force that almost pulled her shoulder from its socket, she opened the door. There in the laundry basket amid petticoats and bed linens, with her thumb in her mouth, was Rachel, sound asleep.

* * *

The next day, Havah's swollen ankle throbbed with vengeance. She chided herself for using her lame foot as a weapon on the innocent dog. When Arel commented that her limp seemed worse than usual she denied it.

Rather than lessen as she hoped, the pain increased as the week wore on. Even Yussel heard and mentioned her labored gait. By Thursday she could no longer fasten her shoe.

On her way to put Rachel in her crib that night, Havah's leg buckled. The baby's head just missed the iron crib bars as she slipped from Havah's grasp to the floor. Pain paralyzed her leg and she collapsed.

The ceiling light snapped on and hurt her eyes. She turned her head away from the glare and shut them. Footsteps jostled the floorboards beneath her. Fruma Ya'el's palms cooled Havah's fiery cheeks.

"You're going to be fine, daughter. I promise."

Something in her calm whisper said otherwise. Rising up on her elbows, Havah opened her eyes and looked from the older woman's panicked expression to her enflamed leg. Swollen to twice its normal size, it looked more like salami than a human limb.

Six hours and two injections later, Havah's pain subsided to a dull ache. Dr. Miklos looked at her with concerned blue eyes through her morphine haze.

"The worst of it has passed. This should help you sleep, because sleep is exactly what you need."

"But . . . it's . . . Friday." Havah struggled to push words through her numb lips. "I promised Shayndel I'd help her clean her house."

"Warm compresses every two to four hours, take your medicine and you should be up and about in a couple of days, not before."

"What is it?"

"We doctors call it Causalgia. To put it in layman's terms it's a nerve injury from the frostbite you suffered."

"No matter what you call it, I'm a cripple."

"You're young and new discoveries are being made every day."

"There's no cure, is there?"

The doctor's smile under his sweeping moustache faded. His shoulders sagged. He shook his head with resignation.

"No."

# CHAPTER FIVE

As Nikolai walked home from the hospital, the damp summer night air clung to him. There was no wind and not a sound, not even a baby's cry or dog's howl could be heard. He massaged his stiff fingers and, when he reached door, searched his waistcoat pocket for his key. The door opened.

"You're late," said Oxana. "Vasily and Pasha have both gone to bed."

"You were worried about me?"

"Of course not."

"Did I wake you?"

"No. I couldn't sleep."

She hopped to a chair in the corner of the front room, sat and picked up a large piece of cloth stretched over a wooden hoop. Then she turned on one foot and sat.

"You're not using your crutches."

"I detest them."

"No matter, the cast comes off tomorrow."

Her waist length hair shone like an amber sunset and her thin cheeks flushed as she hunched over her embroidery. Mesmerized, he watched the needle between her slender fingers. Had he ever seen anything more beautiful?

"What's it going to be?" he asked.

"I haven't decided. Perhaps it will be a blouse or maybe a dress."

"It will be lovely on you either way."

"You needn't flatter me, Doctor. 'She's plain as a slice of bread' my father used to say."

"And you believed him?"

"I have a mirror."

"You should clean it every so often." He shrugged, rubbed the back of his neck and bowed. "Good night, Miss Trubachov."

"Come here. Sit." Setting her sewing on the table, she pointed to the floor in front of her.

"How can I resist such a tender invitation?"

"I mean . . . I . . . you look tense. Let me massage your shoulders for you. I do the same for Pasha after he's spent long hours in surgery. He says it helps him sleep. See?" She held up her hands. "No weapon."

"What makes you so sure I've been in surgery?" He stripped off his waistcoat and sat on the floor.

"Why else would you be home this late?" She pushed with the flat of her hand against his forehead until he leaned his head back on her knees. "Was it successful?"

"How do you know I wasn't with a lady friend?"

"You hate women as much as I abhor men." She plucked off his eyeglasses and set them on the table.

"Whatever gave you the idea that I hate women?"

"For you it's Ivona. For me it's Grigory. He married another woman on what was supposed to have been our wedding day."

An aroma Nikolai had not noticed before drifted over him. It was lilac. He drank in the scent as his taut muscles relaxed under her kneading fingers.

"The operation was a success," he said.

After that night, Oxana often waited up for him with spiced tea, a neck massage and stimulating conversation. Her medical knowledge surprised and challenged him. Under different circumstances, he had no doubt she could have surpassed her brother as a physician.

Little by little other things about her took over his waking thoughts. When he least expected it he found himself contemplating the violet flecks in her pale blue eyes. At other times, he remembered her infrequent laughter.

He realized that her sour disposition masked not only deep wounds, but intense shyness as well. So it surprised him when she agreed to accompany him and Pavel to the Wolinsky's home for a Sabbath dinner.

As they walked along the uneven sidewalk, Oxana tripped and grasped Nikolai's hand to keep from falling.

"I'm so clumsy. I should've stayed home."

Despite the fact that she towered over him, his hand dwarfed hers. Her slender fingers felt delicate against his palm.

"No . . . I . . . that is . . . we would miss you."

"Nonsense, no one would notice whether I was there or not." She pulled back her hand and smoothed back a lock of hair from her forehead.

Ahead of them Vasily regaled Pavel with his plans for the future as a world renowned painter. Nikolai stopped and reached for her arm.

"Oxana, there's something important I have to tell you."

"What?"

"You're not wearing your eyeglasses."

"I dropped them this afternoon. One of the lenses is broken."

How different she looked without glasses. In a moment, all traces of her former austerity vanished. Her parted lips beckoned him like a rose in bloom. His tongue and throat turned to dust.

"What do you have to tell me, Kolyah?"

He looked up to see Pavel and Vasily walking toward them. "Nothing . . . nothing, it can wait."

After the Sabbath meal, the Wolinsky's shabby apartment took on the cast of a Chardin painting, all muted light, color and shadow. As Oxana helped Leah and Devorah clear the table, Nikolai settled back his chair and let the Hebrew prayers possess him. Although he did not understand the words, he sensed their meaning through Gavrel's passionate tone. Flanked by Reuven, Hyram and Lev, Gavrel transformed from humble shoemaker to celestial singer. Vasily sat on the floor with his sketchbook propped up on his knees. Bayla snuggled beside him. Hands folded across his chest, Pavel dozed in a rocking chair.

"May I sit on your lap, Dr. Nikolai?"

Not waiting for an answer, Pora climbed up and nestled in the crook of his arm.

"Me too! Me too!" Three-year-old Tova hopped up and down beside them, her scarlet curls bouncing.

"Omayn!" Gavrel shut his prayer book. "Girls, girls. Let the good doctor rest."

"Let them be, Reb Gavrel. It's been years since I've enjoyed such sweet company. Solnyshko won't sit on my lap anymore."

Intent on his sketching, Vasily merely grinned. Bayla tittered.

Between the wine, the heavy meal and the glow of Oxana's unframed eyes Nikolai felt quite giddy. Opportunity for private conversation with her kept eluding him and his heart pounded with impatience.

"Papa, you didn't finish prayers." Reuven's eyes widened, suggesting that something terrible might follow Gavrel's infraction.

Lifting the boy with one arm, Gavrel tweaked his nose and spun him around. "Not to worry, little apple, the Almighty's heard these prayers a thousand times over and will hear them a thousand and one more."

"I'm leaving," said Lev and headed for the door.

"It's *Shabbes*." Gavrel's smile faded.

"So?"

"Where're you going?"

"Out."

"You belong with your family."

Lev opened the door, stepped out and slammed it behind him. The stairs leading to the shop creaked under his boots. Gavrel's lips formed a thin white line as Lev's footsteps pounded the shop floor followed by the loud bang of the front door.

"Papa? Do you think Lev will get hurt like Orev?" Reuven whispered loud enough for everyone in the room to hear. "Promise you'll never leave me, Papa."

"None of that, little apple." Gavrel cupped his huge hand around the boy's head and pressed it against his shoulder. "Someday you'll be a grown man and you'll leave me."

"Promise me, Papa." Reuven's eyes filled with tears.

"I promise." Gavrel planted a loud kiss on the boy's round cheek and then set him on his feet. Gavrel picked up two documents from an end table and waved them in the air. "Good news! Hyram sold the printing press and I've found a buyer for my shop. He'll take possession in two months. Then we pack and move to America."

"Me, too." Tova jumped off Nikolai's lap and toddled to where Devorah sat and patted Devorah's rounded belly. "Baby, too."

"All of us are going, Miss Echo," Gavrel laughed. "Our Uncle Itzak and his friend Sol have already found a place for us to open our shoe shop in Kansas City."

"But we can't call it 'Wolinsky and Sons' anymore," said Reuven.

"That's true, little apple. Hyram shows great promise as a shoemaker. So what shall we call our new shop?"

Reuven scratched his head. "What about 'Wolinsky and Family?'"

"A genius, this boy!"

Bayla pouted and wrapped her arms around Vasily's neck. "I'll miss you. I wish you could go, too."

"You've taken such good care of us, Dr. Pavel and Dr. Nikolai," said Devorah. "What will we do without you in America?"

"You'll still have me," said Nikolai. "Dr. Miklos asked me to consider hiring on as his partner. He says he has more patients than he can handle and has never been adept at surgery."

Oxana, who had been chatting with Leah at the table, let out an audible gasp. "Is that what you wanted to tell me, Kolyah?"

"No . . . I . . . yes . . ."

Nikolai's heart thumped in his ears and he wished for his tongue to shrivel and drop from his mouth. He had not meant to blurt out his news in such a crass manner. "Please, Oxana. Let me explain."

"That's Miss Trubachov to you, Dr. Derevenko."

Her cheerful blush faded and her eyes became distant clouds. She took her shawl from the chair back, stood and crossed the room to the doorway in three long strides. "Pavel." She tapped her brother's brow. "Take me home. I'll be downstairs."

Groggy from his after dinner nap, Pavel rubbed his eyes and flashed Nikolai a lethal glare. "You cad."

"Pasha, don't you see? This place . . . I've Vasily to think about. But your sister—"

"Leave my sister out of this, Derevenko." Fists clenched, Pavel rose and followed Oxana from the room.

Nikolai started toward the door when Gavrel seized his arm. "Wait, Dr. Nikolai, there's something I have to show you."

"Show me later."

With a wink, Gavrel nodded toward the door. "That can wait. You'll win her over. This can't."

His fingers dug deep into Nikolai's arm as he led him to the kitchen cabinet and swung open the door. "Behold our ticket to freedom."

The first thing Nikolai saw was a pistol on a stack of dishtowels. Icy sweat beaded down his spine and trickled to his waist. Had his friend joined forces with the rebellion?

"That's your ticket to freedom?"

"No, no. Not the gun." Gavrel slipped one hand under the towels and pulled out a leather folder. "This is our passport, bought and paid for."

"Why are you showing this to me?"

"Promise me if anything, God forbid, should happen—to me—you'll take my family with you." Gavrel's desperate gaze, almost a premonition, pierced through Nikolai. "Doctor, I won't rest until you promise me."

Another precious family, the Abromoviches, Evron, simple tailor and his wife Katya haunted the Nikolai. He would never be able to shake their blood soaked images.

"I promise."

Nikolai hurried along the deserted sidewalk with a single thought. He had to talk to Oxana. He had to make her understand.

Just ahead he saw Pavel and Oxana, arm in arm. Nikolai stopped and held his breath. He had been the brunt of her snide remarks which he took in stride, but her heartbroken sobs seared him.

"Oxana, please, listen to me," he said as he caught up to her and tapped her shoulder.

She flinched. "Go away!"

"Haven't you done enough damage with your talk, Derevenko?" Pavel wrapped a protective hand around her shoulders.

For a moment the two men glared at each other. Then Pavel dropped his hands. He smirked and whispered, "Get on with it, man. Then pack your bags."

Head down, Oxana turned her back to Nikolai and followed after Pavel.

"Oxana, look at me," said Nikolai.

"Why? Have you changed?"

He grabbed her arm. "Oxana, please."

"Are you deaf?"

With her fingernails clawing chunks of his flesh, she pried off his hand. Once free, she redoubled her pace. He raced her to the apartment door. She grasped the handle, but he pressed his palm against the door.

"Damn you. You are the most insufferable, impossible, disagreeable woman I've ever met."

She spun around to face him. "You left out dull, dowdy and ugly."

He shoved her and pinned her shoulders to the wall.

"Let go of me!"

"I will, but not until you give me an answer."

"To what?"

"To this." He pressed his mouth hard against hers.

She pulled back and slapped him. He tightened his grip and forced his lips over hers again until her shoulders went limp. When he let go she dropped her head on his chest. He ran his fingers through her disheveled hair.

"Oxanochka, come with me to America."

"Are you asking me . . . to . . . to marry you?"

"I'm not asking, I'm begging."

# CHAPTER SIX

Even with all the windows open, the breeze fluttering the curtains did little to cool Havah. She held a sweaty glass of lemonade against her forehead with one hand and gathered her skirt and petticoat up over her knees with the other.

The rest of the family had gone to the park. She begged off, claiming truthfully that her leg hurt, Rachel had the sniffles and she had bread dough rising in the kitchen. Sprawled on the sofa, she relished a respite from Fruma Ya'el's solicitous hovering.

Lying on the sofa with her head in Havah's lap, Rachel whispered, "No, no no," in protest to oncoming sleep. Her wet hair clung to her flushed cheeks.

To Havah's other side, the dog's warmth was an unwelcome addition. She gave the animal a gentle nudge and then fished a piece of ice from her glass. With a pitiful whimper the dog licked it from her hand.

"Poor Kreplakh. You can't ever take off your fur coat."

She pushed the dog off the sofa, struggled to her feet and then bent to gather the baby in her arms. "Off to bed with you, Rukhel Shvester, then Mama's going to take a nice cool bath."

A loud knock at the front door startled Rachel awake. She wailed. At the same time, the dog dashed to the door where she barked and scratched.

"Oh dear, it's probably the milkman coming to collect this month's payment." Havah turned on her heel, twisting her already aching leg.

The pounding, crying and barking grew louder. Her anger mounted with each knock.

"I'm coming already. A *bissel* patience." She pulled open the door and Kreplakh scampered under her, causing her skirt to wind around her legs.

"You stupid mutt!"

In a frenzy of twisted petticoats she attempted to free herself without dropping the baby, but tripped over the dog and lurched forward. A man's arm caught her and then encircled her, pressing her face against his chest. She fought against the intruder.

"Haveleh? Have you so soon forgotten me?"

His unmistakable voice and the familiar aroma of bay rum stopped her struggle. "I . . . I didn't expect you until next week. The house is a wreck."

*"Shh. Zei ruhig.* Hush." Ulrich scooped her up, baby and all, into his arms and carried them to the sofa. Once he lowered them to the cushions, he took his handkerchief from his pocket and handed it to her. "I hope those are tears of joy to see us."

"Us?"

With a graceful flourish, Ulrich waved toward the door where a woman and man stood in the doorway. "I present to you my beautiful wife, Catherine Dietrich."

Catherine looked miserable. Her hair stuck to her sweaty cheeks. Even the silk flowers on her stylish hat seemed to wilt in the heat. Something in her half smile filled Havah with nameless guilt.

"There, there, Cate," said the young man beside Catherine. "It's only natural for your husband to forget us. After all, he hasn't seen the little mum in at least two years."

Ulrich's back noticeably stiffened. While he had written volumes about his bride, he had included little of her brother aside from the fact that he was traveling with them.

"Havah Gitterman, allow me to introduce my dear brother-in-law, Quinnon Flannery."

Havah tightened her arms around her daughter. Quinnon's lips, dark against a pasty complexion, stretched into a crooked smile as he shifted his stare from the baby to Havah.

"You never told us what an exquisite creature your little paramour is, Guv."

Upon returning from the park, the children flocked like noisy ducklings around the Dietrichs who had brought expensive presents for each of them.

Fruma Ya'el refused Ulrich's offer to treat everyone to fancy restaurant dinner. "It's *Shabbes.* The roast is in the oven. Havah's made her Hollah."

At the mention of the Sabbath loaves that had been Havah's specialty in Kishinev, Ulrich conceded. "Cate, my dear, you're in for a treat."

Beside him on the sofa, cuddling Elliott, Catherine glared at Havah and nodded.

Later Havah sang the prayer over the candles to usher in the Sabbath.

"Voice of an angel," said Ulrich with a rapt smile.

Once more, Catherine's green eyes, like piked icicles, pierced Havah.

Throughout the evening, Ulrich doted on Rachel. He held her on his lap as he gave an impromptu concert at the upright piano. Between each piece he kissed the top of her head and uttered praises.

"Look how she hangs on every note. There's music in your daughter, Havah. I'll hire the finest teachers for her."

With a sidelong glance at Rachel and an unmasked scowl at Ulrich, Catherine excused herself, claiming exhaustion from their travels.

Hours later, sweat soaked Havah's pillow. The thought of having somehow offended her friend's wife tortured her. She had hoped they would be friends, but everything she did or said seemed to displease Catherine. Between Arel's louder than usual snoring and her own racing mind, Havah gave up on sleep. A walk outside might cool her and clear her head.

After she made her way downstairs and out onto the porch, sultry night air closed in on her. She started to unbutton her dressing gown until she saw Catherine sitting on the swing.

Lifting her thick hair with one hand, Catherine fluttered a Chinese fan behind her neck. "Beastly hot night, isn't it, Mrs. Gitterman?"

"The newspapers say it might rain tomorrow, but I have my doubts." Havah lowered herself onto the swing.

For the next few minutes the only sounds came from Catherine's fan and the swing's creaking chains. While Havah tried to think of something to say she plaited her hair into a long braid and glanced over at the other woman who looked straight ahead.

"My sister, Gittel, had beautiful red hair like yours."

"Had?"

"She died three years ago in childbirth. The baby died, too."

"How tragic. Did your brother-in-law remarry?"

"Yes. He married me."

"Arel?" Catherine finally turned her head, mouth slightly agape. "It's a long story."

"I'd love to hear it. Your daughter . . . Rachel, she's . . ."

"Blind?"

"I was going to say beautiful. She looks just like you."

"You think so? Everyone says so, but she has Arel's chin with its little dimple." She reached for Catherine's hand. "Ulrich is *not* Rachel's father."

# CHAPTER SEVEN

Although her vision was somewhat blurry without her eyeglasses, for the first time since childhood Oxana liked what she saw in the mirror. Her blue eyes shone and her flaxen hair cascaded over her shoulders. The white lace at her throat accentuated her ivory complexion.

Even the dingy apartment glowed, crowded to its limits with the Wolinsky family. The table was heaped with food and the aroma of savory pot roast mingled with sugary sweet scents. Leah and Devorah had been cleaning and cooking all week long, refusing to let her help.

Perhaps her new friends could teach her how to cook. It would not do for her to poison her husband. She grinned at her reflection once more and pinned the lace veil to her hair.

"Father Alexi should be here by now. Nikolai's late, too."

"Calm yourself." Pavel kissed her forehead. "Soon you'll be a wealthy American doctor's wife."

"Who said anything about wealthy? We barely have enough money between us to make the journey. Won't you please come with us, Pasha?"

"You know the answer to that. There's still so much to do here."

"I know. It's what your Lord would've done."

"You won't have time to miss me. Mark my words, you'll be wealthy. Nikolai's a skilled surgeon. With his pretty wife at his side to encourage him, I predict he'll make a fortune. Have I told you what a beautiful bride you are?"

"You've had too much wine, big brother. It's obviously impaired your vision."

Despite her feigned irritation she basked in his lavish compliments.

"My mother of blessed memory worked on this dress for a month." Leah adjusted Oxana's veil.

Devorah fingered the lace. "I remember. She said it would be her legacy."

"I'm honored to wear it." Oxana held out the skirt and twirled. "It's elegant, but I'm afraid I don't fill it out very well."

"You look like a fairy princess." Pora waved her arms as if she could fly. "Mama says when I grow up and be a bride, I'm going to wear it, too."

Someone pounded on the door. "Kolyah, it's about time!" Oxana swung it open.

Not Nikolai, but Father Alexi, arrayed in black cassock and skewed skufia, ambled over the threshold with priestly pomp. He brushed his sleeves as if to divest them of dung.

"I would've been here much sooner had it not been for a riot in the street. The Jews, they are animals!"

Bayla, one arm around Leah's waist, pointed to the golden crucifix around his neck. "What's that and why is that man all stretched out like that without any clothes? Why are you wearing a dress and that funny hat?"

Father Alexi's cheeks, half obscured by his beard, reddened. Ignoring the girl, he slowly swiveled his head until his gaze rested on Gavrel in his traditional ceremonial clothing. With a low hiss, he shook his head and whispered, "*Zjids*. Jews."

"Let's get on with it then. Are you the groom?" He sneered at Pavel.

"No, Your Honor." Pavel frowned, wrapped his arm around Gavrel's shoulder. "My friends and I expect him any minute."

"I've other appointments to keep. I'll not wait long."

"You *will* wait. When Dr. Derevenko arrives, he and my sister will take their vows." Desperate to see Nikolai, Oxana peered out the window and scanned the street. She trembled with indignation. If he had listened to her, they would already be married. Sign the papers and say the words. He insisted on following a silly Russian tradition which required the groom to come from afar to claim his bride. It was his decision to dress at the hospital and then, flanked by his loyal knaves, Lev and Vasily, come for his fair maiden.

She wound a lock of hair around her finger until it cut off her circulation, and clamped her teeth down on her quivering lower lip. "It's two-thirty. He promised he'd be here at two."

With raised eyebrow and obvious disdain, Father Alexi pressed his palms together. "It's closer to three. Perhaps he's had second thoughts and decided to stay at home."

"This is his home."

"You're living in sin and expect the holy church to sanctify your marriage?"

Pacing in a small circle, Oxana wrung her hands. "It's happening again. Nikolai's taken Vasily and—"

"His flute's still here. He'd never abandon her." Pavel's playfulness did not hide his own misgivings or his sidelong glance out the window. "He is a doctor. Maybe there's been an emergency."

"He'd have sent Vasily to tell us."

"I'm hungry." Pora stood beside the table and eyed the macaroons.

"Me, too." Tova hopped on one foot.

"Hyram and I will go out and search for him if you'd like," said Gavrel.

"I hear singing." Reuven cocked his head. "It sounds like Dr. Nikolai."

Again Oxana looked out the window. Relief at Nikolai's arrival turned to anger and disappointment. He stumbled between the boys, one arm draped over Lev's shoulder, his other hand tucked inside his coat. Pavel swung open the door in time to catch Nikolai who stopped his off-key singing and pitched forward.

Ready with a tongue lashing, she rushed to Pavel's side. "You're drunk!"

"I wish." Nikolai pulled his hand from under his coat, wet with blood.

The floor swayed beneath her. She screamed as all strength drained from her knees.

"Leah, take the children home." Gavrel swept Nikolai like a child into his arms.

"Stay here." Nikolai tried to wrestle out of his hold. "It's not safe."

"Lev, clear the table. Oxana, change your clothes." Pavel prevented her from collapsing, his hand like a vise around her upper arm. "You can cry later."

Another arm encircled her shoulders and Leah's calm voice whispered in her ear. "It's going to be all right."

Like an obedient child, Oxana followed her to the bedroom where Leah helped her take off the wedding gown. The sounds of clanking dishes and scooting furniture came from the other room as Pavel continued to bark out orders.

"I'm twenty-nine. There'll never be anyone else." Oxana put on and buttoned her blouse with numb fingers.

"Don't dig his grave just yet." Leah slapped Oxana's cheeks with a wet washrag. "What if—?"

"What if the Messiah should come today? We'll all dance. Be strong, my sister."

The cool water and Leah's words cleared Oxana's mind. Once dressed, she took her new glasses from the bed stand, squared her shoulders, braced herself for the worst and then returned with Leah to the front room.

The food had been hastily piled on the stove and chairs. Eyes shut, face paler than his hair, Nikolai lay on the table where Pavel had cut off his blood soaked shirt. Oxana brushed her hand across his clammy forehead.

"Superficial." He opened one eye. "Nothing to worry about."

"Wrong diagnosis, Doctor." Pavel blotted the wound. "A bit further to the right and you'd be trading your flute for a harp."

Oxana startled when the priest stamped his foot and shook his skeletal finger under her nose. "What did I tell you? Moldavanka is a dangerous place for good Christians."

"Good Christians, as you call them, did this." Nikolai winced and made a feeble gesture to the two boys. "Tell His Honor the Reverend Father, Solnyshko. Tell him."

Lev's cap, cocked sideways on his head, half covered a bruised eye. Blood from a cut above his eyebrow made trails down his dirt caked cheeks. "It should've been me."

"They came after us, calling us terrible names, especially Lev." Vasily wiped his nose on his arm, leaving a red streak on his sleeve. "I—I never saw the gun. Tatko pushed us down and then I heard it."

"I see my services won't be necessary." The cleric turned to leave.

Nikolai struggled to sit up. "You came here to perform a marriage. Get on with it!"

Pain shot through Nikolai's chest and shoulder as he woke from ether induced sleep. He blinked and looked around the room. Oxana hunched over her sewing in the chair in front of the window. Moonlight diffused through the ruffled curtain behind her cast a halo of light over her face and illuminated the folds of her clothing, reminding him of a Vermeer painting.

"What are you making?"

"It's a shirt for Vasily. He's growing so fast he needs new clothes almost every week." She dropped the shirt. "You're awake."

"How long have I been out?"

"A day and a half." She stood and stretched.

"And *you* haven't shut your eyes in all that time."

"What makes you think I'd lose sleep over the likes you, Dr. Derevenko?"

"Forgive me."

"For what?"

"I spoiled your wedding day."

"Nonsense. You made it more—memorable."

"Where's Vasily?"

Vasily, who had been sleeping on the floor at the foot of the bed, stretched and stood. His tousled hair hung in his eyes and a bandage covered his swollen nose. He rubbed his bruised eyes. "You're alive, Tatko. I was so scared."

"We'll soon be out of this hellhole, Solnyshko. How's your friend?"

"Lev's just fine, save a few contusions and a black eye. It's only fair to warn you he's proclaiming Dr. Nikolai to be the greatest hero since Moses." Pavel entered the room and moved to the bed, hypodermic syringe in hand, and peered under Nikolai's bandages.

"A work of art if I do say so myself, almost as creative as my sister's embroidery. I thought you'd enjoy a little nightcap about now." Pavel poised the syringe.

Wincing at the needle's sting, Nikolai held his breath and then slowly exhaled. "The last thing Lev needs is another hero."

Vasily's bruised eyes brimmed with tears. "Does it hurt badly, Tatko?"

"Not bad at all."

"Your father's a shameless liar, Vasya." Pavel reached into his waistcoat pocket, drew out a bullet and held it up between his fingers. "This missed his lung and arteries by a centimeter and splintered his left scapula. I'm quite sure it hurts like hell."

# CHAPTER EIGHT

After weeks of traveling from one unfamiliar place to another, Kansas City was the last stop on Ulrich's tour. He had planned it that way to leave time to spend an extended visit with his dearest friends. What could be sweeter than studying with the blind rabbi who saw more with his heart than most saw with their eyes? No ovation thrilled him more than making music with Itzak or watching the children dance and clap their hands.

Despite their ticklish introduction, Catherine and Havah became fast friends almost overnight. Peevish and snide, Quinnon seemed to have grown more so since their arrival. The way his rapacious green eyes followed Havah disturbed Ulrich. For Catherine's sake he kept his observations to himself. To voice them did no good in any case. In spite of her own irritations with her brother, anything she considered an affront against him met with the ferocity of a lioness.

The night of Ulrich's concert at the Mayer mansion, Quinnon fell ill with aches and fever. Ulrich suspected he was faking, but relished the idea of a concert without him.

"Poor dear." Catherine laid a cool cloth across Quinnon's forehead. "You shan't be able to play tonight."

"But . . . but . . . Ulrich's counting on me." Quinnon writhed beneath the blankets.

Ulrich leaned against the doorjamb. "No need to worry your poor fevered brow. I've the perfect substitute."

"The passionate Itzak Abromovich, your Yid friend? You'll have to let me know if Mr. Stradavari shows up to stand and cheer."

The Mayer's mansion door opened wide. Sol, his bald head and dark eyes gleaming, pulled his cigar from his mouth and snuffed it out in the pedestal ashtray in the entryway. "You look particularly lovely tonight, Mrs. Gitterman. Is it my imagination or is that a new frock? Isn't it lovely, Zeldie dear?"

More than Sol's compliment, Havah relished the shocked expression on Zelda's face.

"Why, why, yes, it's beautiful," said Zelda. Her gaze traveled from Havah's diamond necklace, a twenty-first birthday present from Ulrich to her satin pumps. "However could you afford such a stylish gown?"

"It was a gift from a dear friend." Havah curtsied, enjoying the triumph of the moment.

"And of course, you already know Mrs. Gitterman's friend, Professor Dietrich," said Sol.

"Friend?" As Zelda's eyes darted from Havah to Ulrich, her lips quivered.

Dapper in his tuxedo, he held Rachel on one arm and took Zelda's hand. He bowed and kissed it.

"It's a pleasure, Frau Mayer. My dear friend Havah has told me so much about you."

"Friend?" she whispered.

"Are you all right, my dear?" asked Sol. "You look like you're going to faint."

"Uncle Ulrich and Aunt Cate sent Auntie's gown all the way from Paris, France." Evalyne, who held Catherine's hand, skipped from foot to foot with six-year-old impatience and pointed. "See, my cousin Rachel's dress matches."

"Frau Mayer, my wife called and made thirteen reservations, did she not?" With a curt bow, Ulrich clicked his heels and released her hand. He winked at Havah.

"Yes—yes—she did—I mean—I—I—" Zelda's face turned deep red. "The—Gitterman's seats are in the front row."

"*Sehr gut.* Then there should be no problem with seating for these—how did you so eloquently put it—'shtetl peasants?'"

The Mayer's huge ballroom boasted a massive crystal chandelier, polished walnut wainscoting and flocked wallpaper. Paintings of bowls of fruit and flowers in ornate frames hung on the walls. A grand piano took up a small corner of the room. At least a hundred folding chairs had been set up in anticipation of an audience which had begun to gather.

As people moved past, Havah caught snippets of conversation and whiffs of strong perfume.

"Zelda's outdone herself."

"He's actually Austrian, you know."

"Do you think Russia will win the war against Japan?"

As Havah turned to find her seat one of the many pictures, a yellowed photograph, captured her attention. From an ornate brass frame a bearded man seemed to smile at her. He wore a yarmulke on his head and an embroidered prayer shawl around his broad shoulders. His eyes looked vaguely familiar. Where had she seen him?

"Havaleh?" Arel whispered. "It's time. Is something wrong?"

"No, I was just admiring Zelda's house."

"Does my little Daniel fear she might be devoured by the wealthy lioness?" Yussel took a piece of chewing gum from his pocket, unwrapped it and popped it into his mouth.

"Don't be silly, Papa. When have I ever been afraid of her?"

"You've never been inside her den before."

Arel squeezed Havah's hand in the crook of his arm. "Come along, Mrs. Gitterman. I'll protect you."

Crowd conversation hushed. Zelda, who had yet to regain her composure, looked ready to swoon over the piano. Her stare seared Havah as she took a chair between Arel and Catherine.

With a loud cough, Zelda cleared her throat. "Without further ado, it's my privilege to introduce Professor Ulrich Dietrich from Germany by way of London, England."

The audience applauded. Ulrich bowed. "It's my great pleasure to be accompanied tonight by Herr Itzak Abromovich, cabinetmaker extraordinaire and one of the best friends a man could wish for."

Havah was almost sure that Zelda would faint when Itzak stepped up to the piano, violin in hand. He and Ulrich started off the concert with a few Jewish folk pieces. The audience thundered its appreciation. Rachel, who had fallen asleep on Catherine's lap, woke with a shriek.

Rising from the bench, Ulrich took the child in his arms and carried her back to the piano, cuddling her on his lap. Her crying ceased and she snuggled against him. "Uncle Uree."

"This bright young lady is a future virtuoso." Taking her tiny hands in his he positioned them on the piano keys. "Would Rukhel Shvester like to play piano?"

"Yes! Yes! Pee-ano!"

Pride surged through Havah as her daughter, not yet two-years-old, played "Twinkle, Twinkle, Little Star" without missing a single note.

"Bravo! Bravo!" Arel jumped to his feet. "That's my little girl!"

The entire audience rose, applauding Rachel who buried her head in Ulrich's coat. Once she calmed, Ulrich sat her back on Catherine's lap, grinned at Havah and then addressed the audience. "I'd like for Rachel's mother to sit beside me as she did when I played for her in the old country."

Zelda pursed her lips until she appeared to have no mouth at all. Havah smiled at her as Ulrich swept her into his arms and then lowered her onto the bench. He poised his hands over the keys. "I'll begin with Nocturne in C Sharp Minor. Mrs. Gitterman's favorite."

For the remainder of the concert Havah sat beside him. With the first few notes, Zelda and her social pretentions disappeared. Chopin, Mozart and Bach transported Havah's soul to another place—a place where a lonely orphan learned great things from a gentle pianist.

Ulrich's voice brought her back to the ballroom as he spoke again to the crowd. "If you'll indulge me further, I'd like to end this concert with a little surprise. Frau Mayer?"

"But of course, Herr Dietrich." Zelda blushed, batted her eyelashes and fluttered her lace fan.

Beryl entered the room carrying a large parcel. He set it on the floor beside Ulrich and opened it. Together they pulled out an armload of cloth bears.

"These are for each of the youngsters in Havah's family and for our host's daughter, Gwendolyn Mayer." Ulrich held up one of the bears.

"With these little fellows comes a letter I'd like to read, if I may." Not waiting for an answer, Ulrich winked at Havah and, with a dramatic flourish, unfurled the parchment White House stationary.

*"'My Dear Mrs. Gitterman, I will forever remember our chance meeting at Ellis Island.*

*"'It is a rare individual who leads a difficult life and leads it well. I see in you, dear lady, someone who has the courage to do both. Keep your eyes on the stars and your feet on the ground. Godspeed to you, little Havah.'"*

Ulrich placed the letter, along with an autographed portrait of the President in Havah's hands. To her ultimate delight, Zelda's mouth dropped open when Ulrich read the signature on the photograph. *"'To Havah, an American woman of valor. Best wishes from your friend, Theodore Roosevelt.'"*

* * *

"Havah, dear, I don't know what to say." Zelda twisted her pearls around her fingers. Perspiration beaded on her rouged cheeks.

Sol wrapped his arm around her shoulder. "You could start with 'I'm sorry.'"

Beryl curved his arm around her other shoulder. "How about 'I was wrong.'"

"Yes. Yes. All those things. Can we please be friends, Havah?"

Havah's head pounded with both the thrill of vindication and crippling pain coursing from her ankle to her knee. A hundred hateful words came to her lips, but she thought better of them and said, "For two years you've insulted me and my family. Now, because you learn I have a wealthy friend with influence, you want to make nice? No, thank you."

She turned away from Zelda, leading with her cane and hobbled across the room to join Arel at the piano. A crowd swarmed around Ulrich who held Rachel on his knee.

"Ladies and gentleman," he said, "this little lady is what we musicians call a prodigy. Observe."

He played a few notes of *Mary Had a Little Lamb* and she copied without a mistake. "She has what musicians refer to as absolute pitch. Mark my words, she'll surpass me as a concert pianist by the time she's ten—another Mozart."

"Mozart needs her diaper changed." Itzak pointed to the spreading wet spot on Ulrich's lap.

"Come to Auntie Cate, sweetheart," said Catherine as she lifted Rachel from Ulrich's damp knee.

"I'll change her." Havah dug a diaper from her bag.

"Poppycock. You'll do no such thing." Catherine took both diaper and child and left the room.

Arel took his watch from his vest pocket. "We should collect the family and leave."

"Everyone's having such a good time." Havah yawned and tried to keep her drooping eyes open.

"You're not."

"Let me take her home," said Beryl. "Uncle Sol won't mind if I borrow the Rambler. You can stretch out in the back seat, Havah."

Arel shrugged. "It's your decision, Havah. But if you ask me, it's a good idea."

Her leg burned and the thought of sinking into a soft bed appealed to her. She curved her fingers around Beryl's arm and limped beside him toward the door. Taking the cane from her, he gathered her up into his arms.

"Put me down!"

"If I do, we won't make it out to the curb until sunrise."

"Everyone's staring at us."

"Let them. This is one argument you're not winning."

Zelda raised her hand and waved. "Toodle-oo, Havah dear. See you soon. Call me when you can meet me for lunch."

"I liked her better when she hated me," said Havah.

Beryl picked up his pace. "Is it wrong to confess I won't miss her?"

He helped Havah into the back seat of the automobile and then tucked a blanket around her legs. "Comfortable?"

She winced. "Yes."

"Someday modern medicine will find a cure for it, Havaleh."

"I won't be alive to see it. When do you leave for Baltimore?"

"In the morning."

"You'll be a wonderful doctor, Beryl."

"Havah, I wish things were different." He slid into the seat and shut the door. "I should never have left Natalya."

"Take me home."

Neither of them spoke as he drove. Havah listened to the car's engine and relished the warm wind on her face. When the car stopped Beryl got out and opened the back door for her. He leaned in, pressed his hands against her cheeks and kissed her. Then he pulled back, his hands still warm on her face. "I'm sorry, Havah."

"I'm not."

Havah admired her reflection one last time before undressing. She hated to take off her stylish dress and spoil the magic. She slipped it over her head, smoothed the lace and hung it in the wardrobe. Then she lifted her nightgown from its hook and pulled it over her head. As she did so, she caught a glimpse of Quinnon's yellow eyes in the mirror behind her reflection.

"It's an evening frock fit for a princess. Ulrich's little princess."

Hastily she grabbed her robe and put it on over her night clothes. She spun around and pointed at the door trying not to let him see her fingers shake.

"How dare you? Get out!"

"That's what they all say. They don't mean it." He leaned against the doorjamb, took a long drag from his cigarette and blew a smoke ring. "*You* don't mean it."

"Please," she whispered and stepped toward the doorway.

Before she could run for it, he slammed the door with his heel. Then he flicked his cigarette butt to the floor and ground it underfoot. After that, he fished a match from his trouser pocket and struck it on his shoe. He lit another cigarette and tossed the burning match to the wardrobe. The silk dress's hem ignited.

"Pity if anything should happen to your dress. Ulrich paid dear for it. But nothing's too good for his mistress."

She screamed, dropped to her knees and beat out the flames with her hands.

"How careless of me. Let me make it up to you, dearest." He knelt beside her, exhaled smoke in her face and then put out his cigarette against the cabinet door.

His breath reeked of schnapps and tobacco as he glided his tongue over her cheeks and nose and then forced it between her lips. She shrank back and huddled in the corner.

"Please, Mr. Flannery. Think about what you're doing."

"I've thought of little else since I met you, you tasty morsel."

On hands and knees, he crawled to her, closing her in. One by one he pulled out her hairpins and then stroked her neck with his fingertips. She shuddered.

"Stop! Arel! Ulrich! Help!"

"Tut-tut. What good will that do? You and I both know we're the only ones here."

He grasped her shoulders and forced her down on her back where he pinned her to the floor. Again he forced his tongue into her mouth. This time she bit down hard. He shrieked, blood oozing from the corners of his mouth, and he released her. She rolled out from under him. He sat up on his haunches and laughed.

"You bloody whore!"

She hurried toward the door, but he covered the distance, grabbed her hair and yanked her back to the floor. Her head thumped against the boards.

Once more he shoved her to her back. Heart pounding, she smashed her head into his nose. He clapped his hands over it and squealed with maniacal glee.

"The princess is a fighter. I like that."

She crawled to the bed, pulled herself up on the post and hobbled toward the doorway. He leaped from the floor and wedged himself between her and the door with a lopsided grin on his face. Blood from his nose outlined his teeth.

"Surely you don't want to leave the party, my dear?"

He smacked his fist across her mouth. Blood filled it. She spat it in his face.

Undaunted, he settled his hands on her throat and closed his fingers around it. "Flawless. Like fine china."

"Don't. Please." Icy prickles stung her throbbing scalp. She choked and dug her fingernails into his cheek. His grip tightened.

"'Please,'" he sang in falsetto.

"'Don't.' You're mine, princess—for eternity." Downstairs the front door opened. She heard Catherine's laughter and Rachel's sleepy whimpers. "Let's put you to bed, you little angel."

Arel called out, "Havah, you missed the best part of the evening."

"Let her sleep, Arel," said Ulrich. "You can regale her in the morning."

Havah tried to cry out but Quinnon's cruel thumbs crushed her windpipe. Her lungs constricted and her heart thudded against her ribs. Little by little the will to fight left her. Her hands fell limp and heavy at her sides. A curtain of darkness fell and the voices downstairs faded. From somewhere behind the curtain, Shimon beckoned her.

Numb with exhaustion and sick with worry, Ulrich paced the long hospital corridor, playing the last eight hours in his head. Shortly after he and the Gittermans had returned from the concert they found Havah, lifeless as a broken doll on the bedroom floor. The room was in a state of chaos and Quinnon was nowhere to be found. Ulrich guessed he had bolted through the open window.

By the time the police apprehended Quinnon in a bordello, he was unconscious and bleeding. The officer at the scene said that Quinnon's last victim, a quick thinking prostitute, used her derringer to stop him in the act.

"It's all my fault," said Catherine who paced beside Ulrich.

"Of course not, liebling. You had no way of knowing."

"Poppycock. I insisted on bringing him, didn't I?"

"Then I'm equally guilty."

"Cathy!" Quinnon's screams came through the treatment room doors.

"You don't have to go," said Ulrich.

"He's still my brother." She dabbed her eyes.

Ulrich followed her into the treatment room where Quinnon lay on a metal table. Blood soaked through the white sheet over him.

"Your wish has been granted, Guv," he said with spectral smile.

"My wish?"

"Admit it. You're enjoying this. You want me dead. I murdered your little princess."

"How could you do such a horrid thing?" Catherine gasped.

"For you."

"You killed Havah—for me?"

"I killed all of them for . . . for . . . you, Cathy." He closed his eyes.

"He took two bullets, one in the liver and one where he lives." The doctor held the bell of his stethoscope to Quinnon's chest. "His heartbeat is fading. I give him quarter of an hour at the most, two or three minutes at the least."

Catherine leaned over her brother. "What do you mean, you killed 'all of them'?"

He flashed a proud smile like an orator preparing a recitation of his life's accomplishments. "Dad first . . . then . . . Sherman . . . bastard . . . deserved to . . . to die."

Her lips turned white. Ulrich wrapped his arm around her, fearing she would faint. "Let me take you home."

She straightened and pushed him away. "The others—what about the others?"

"Whores . . . every . . . one," whispered Quinnon with a rasp. "I rendered a . . . a . . . service."

Loath to hit a dying man, Ulrich crammed his fists into his pockets. "Why did you bind their hands with your violin strings after you killed them?"

"Fun."

"You filthy animal!"

"Save your sanctimony." Quinnon spat through a sudden gush of blood. “The police might’ve . . . caught me . . . but for you . . . and your Russky friend. ‘Catgut’ . . . ‘could’ve been a . . . musician,’ you say . . . ‘or a doctor,’ he says. Poor Musgrave. Innocent patsy. Wrong place . . . right time.”

Catherine put her hands over her ears and turned away from him. “Enough!”

His giggling stopped abruptly. He arched his back and gasped. In a pitiful child’s voice he cried, “Cathy. I’m afraid.”

His eyes fixed into a surprised glassy stare and his breath escaped as a soft whistle through his open mouth. Catherine’s face paled. She pressed her handkerchief over her mouth and dropped down into a chair.

“I’m sorry, Mrs. Dietrich.” The doctor pulled the sheet over Quinnon’s face. “There was nothing anyone could’ve done for him.”

Ulrich squeezed Catherine’s shoulder. “I’ll make the funeral arrangements as soon as possible.”

She batted his hand away, squared her shoulders, stuffed her handkerchief into her purse and said, “Toss his worthless carcass in the bloody dust bin.”

# CHAPTER NINE

More than one patient under Nikolai's care had developed morphine dependence and he was determined it would not happen to him. After three weeks, despite Pavel's objections, Nikolai demanded that his dosage be gradually lessened. Bored with bed rest and weary of his bride's hovering care, he picked up his shirt and tried to put it on. Pain shot through his shoulder and an involuntary groan escaped him.

Oxana rushed into the room and took it from him.

"Kolyah, are you mad?"

"I'm a doctor."

"And a terrible patient. Pasha says at least six weeks, maybe longer."

"The hospital's understaffed. While I'm lounging he's working day and night." With more willingness than he cared to admit, Nikolai settled back against the pillow.

"Quit trying to make me your widow." She sat on the bed.

"It hasn't been much of a honeymoon, has it?" Curving his hand around the back of her head he pulled her down until her lips pressed against his.

"You are my honeymoon." She curled up next to him.

"My poor unconsummated bride, let me make it up to you."

After Ivona had left him, Nikolai forced himself to forget a woman's warmth. Intoxicated by Oxana's slender body against his, he trembled and unbuttoned her blouse. Excitement filled him with each unfastened button.

"Nikolai, it's midafternoon," she whispered but made no attempt to stop him.

"Who cares? Vasily's with Lev. Pasha's at work. We are alone."

"What if I hurt you?"

"I'll take my chances."

His excitement turned to abject frustration when someone pounded on the door. Oxana sprang off the bed, refastened her blouse and hurried to answer. Nikolai heaved a dejected sigh.

"Shalom! Shalom!" Gavrel's voice boomed from the front room.

"It's a wedding party!" Bayla skipped into the bedroom, her black braids bobbing.

"Whose wedding?" Nikolai asked.

"Yours and Miss Oxana's, silly."

"We already had a party."

"True, Dr. Nikolai. But as you must recall, it was cut short." Gavrel appeared in the doorway.

Nikolai rubbed his shoulder. "I remember—painfully well."

Bayla hopped up and down. "Papa asked Dr. Pavel if you were well enough and if we could bring the party to you and he said yes so here we are. Leah roasted two whole chickens and made her best noodle kugel and sponge cake and we have presents and everything—"

Clapping his hand over her mouth, Gavrel swept her up in his arms. "You're going to make Dr. Nikolai's ears fall off, chatterbox." He set her back on her feet and swatted her bottom. "Go help the ladies with their surprise."

"Surprise?" Nikolai noticed Oxana had not returned after answering the door. "What surprise? Really Gavrel, this is too much."

"It's a big, big surprise," sang Bayla as she skipped from the room.

Cheeks flushed and cap askew, Hyram swaggered through the doorway, a bottle in each hand. "What celebration would be complete without a good kosher wine? My grandfather's special recipe. Handed down for generations. Sweet. Potent. Sometimes deadly. Like a good woman."

Grabbing one of the bottles, Gavrel took a long swig and wiped his mouth on his sleeve. "And how much of this good kosher wine has my young brother-in-law sampled already?"

Two more bottles in tow, Pavel entered the room. "I heard there was going to be a party and didn't want to miss it. And to immortalize the day, we've brought our friend, the photographer extraordinaire."

Behind Pavel a rat-faced man with scraggly beard and bulbous eyes entered carrying a camera. Pushing past the others he set it on a tripod at the end of the bed. Nikolai hunched down and pulled the blankets around his neck.

Arms raised, Lev entered the room and bowed. Then he sang out in Hebrew and Russian. "Blessed is she who is arriving!"

Flanked on either side by Leah and Devorah, Oxana entered. Once more she wore Leah's wedding gown. Her hair, plated into six braids that hung past her waist, was adorned with ribbons and flowers.

"In Svechka, we had a wonderful custom. The night before a wedding all of the women and girls of the village would take turns brushing and decorating the bride's long hair one last time. Of course Oxana won't have to cut off all of her hair like I did." Leah ruefully smoothed her stray wig hair back into place.

"Stand beside your husband and look directly into the lens." With a knobby finger, the photographer beckoned Oxana. "The groom must sit up straight and tall."

"Dressed like this?" asked Nikolai.

"A story to tell your grandchildren," said Pavel.

"Yes, I can hear it now. 'Your grandmother wore lace and your grandfather wore bandages.'"

As soon as he had taken the picture, the photographer hoisted the camera onto his thin shoulder. "Your photograph will be ready in a few days." He touched his hat and left.

The Wolinsky family gathered around the bed. Gavrel raised his glass of wine. "To Dr. and Mrs. Nikolai, may you live to see many years of happiness."

"Omayn," cried Lev.

"What's different, Lev?" asked Nikolai. "Have you grown taller?"

"I'm wearing long pants."

"I thought you looked more like a man, and a fine one at that."

"If it weren't for you Dr. Nikolai I—what you did—"

"Stop it. I'm no hero, flesh and blood, that's all."

Reuven crept up to the bed and squeezed Nikolai's hand, a mixture of childish curiosity and sadness in his eyes. "Dr. Nikolai, why aren't other Christians like you and Dr. Pavel? Why do they hate us Jews so much?"

"It's ignorance, son—witless, gullible ignorance."

# CHAPTER TEN

Catherine recalled little of Quinnon's funeral other than her collapse on the way to the carriage from the graveyard. After a week shrouded in a laudanum haze of low whispers and nightmares, she refused the drug.

One morning a few days later, she woke to an empty bed. She looked at the clock on the bed stand. Ten o'clock. She vaguely remembered Ulrich saying something the night before about a meeting, but had paid no mind to details. Everywhere they went he held meetings with adoring patrons.

Downstairs Yussel and Fruma Ya'el's voices rose and fell. While Catherine could not understand Yiddish, she could tell by the tones of the voices that it was not a friendly discussion about the weather. The sooner she left the Gittermans, the better off they would all be.

"There's no time like the present to start packing." She stretched and yawned.

Within an hour she had scrubbed and dressed.

Quinnon's trunk sat at the foot of the bed. With disregard to Ulrich urgings to donate it to charity, contents unseen, she undid the latch and lifted the lid. The scent of cedar and tobacco greeted her as she opened the lid and rummaged through her brother's shirts and trousers. Under a sweater she found a thick folder. She recognized it as the one he used to carry under his arm when he went to school. It never occurred to her that it might be anything other than compositions and sheet music. When she took it out, grisly newspaper photos scattered to the floor. She knelt to gather them, grimacing at images of her brother's unfortunate victims. A leather-bound diary caught her eye. As she thumbed through it, her breath caught in her throat.

*"I laughed and laughed. Sherman looked so surprised whilst his blood dripped into his foul mouth. Cathy will be pleased."*

Suppressing a scream with one hand, she flung the journal to the floor with the other. Havah limped into the room with Rachel in her arms. Setting the child on her feet, she bent down and picked up the journal. She thumbed through the pages and then shut it.

"It's not your fault, Catherine."

"How can you say that, Havah? My brother nearly murdered you."

"And you think you're responsible?"

The bruises on Havah's neck were still dark and visible through her high necked blouse. Although Dr. Miklos did not think the damage was permanent, after three weeks she still had a slight rasp in her voice.

"I just thought if Quinnon and Ulrich could spend some time together, they would become friends. If only I hadn't been so stupid. If only I'd listened to Ulrich and left Quinnon in London."

"If, if—forget about 'if.' He was your brother and you loved him."

"Auntie Cate." Rachel wrapped her pudgy arms around Catherine's waist. "No cry."

Catherine sat back on the carpet and gathered the girl onto her lap. Reaching up, Rachel brushed her fingertips over Catherine's lips, and then nestled her head between Catherine's breasts. "Sweet."

"My daughter knows a good person when she sees one."

At that moment, Ulrich entered the room, grabbed the journal from Havah and tossed it into the wastebasket near the bed table. "Let the dead bury their dead."

"Uncle Uri," cried Rachel, squirming out of Catherine's arms. "Music."

"Not now, Rukhel Shvester." He helped Catherine to her feet. "Aunt Cate and I have packing to attend to."

A tear trickled down Havah's cheek. "I wish you didn't have to go."

"With the invention of the telephone, the modern world's a smaller place. We'll call at least once a month."

"It won't be the same."

"I should think you've had your fill of the Dietrichs."

"Never."

"In any case, my wife misses her home."

"Poppycock," cried Catherine. "I don't care if I ever lay eyes on it again."

"You can't be serious," said Ulrich. "It's your homeland. Are you sure?"

"Of course I am. What's there to go back to?" Her eyes and chest burned. "You're laughing at me. Did I say something funny?"

"Funny? No. Providential? Yes."

Taking Rachel's hand, Havah turned toward the door. "I'll leave you two alone."

"No, this concerns you, too." Ulrich held Catherine in his gaze. "If my bride says yes we may be imposing on your hospitality a while longer."

"Stop speaking in riddles," said Catherine.

"All right, I'll come to the point. At my last recital a man named John Cowan approached me with a proposition. He asked me to teach piano next year when he opens his Conservatory here in Kansas City. What should I tell him?"

Havah's warmth beside him in the bed comforted, yet troubled Arel. His mind swarmed with unanswerable questions. Why had he not seen the signs and protected her? Because he trusted Ulrich, he had blindly accepted Quinnon as a guest. While he saw that his wife was uncomfortable with the odd young man, Arel never uttered a word. Although, he valued Ulrich as a friend and would forever be in his debt the prospect of the man living in the same city bothered him. At one time he considered the handsome German a rival for Havah's affections. Yes, he was married to Catherine now, but would close proximity to Havah rekindle the flame?

Finally, Arel drifted off to sleep until Havah's cries startled him awake less than an hour later. Befuddled and groggy, he groped the empty space beside him. He rubbed his eyes, sat up, and switched on the lamp. Frantically he searched for her.

"Not again!" Her cry came from Rachel's room.

Had something happened to the baby? At once wide awake, he swung his legs over the side of the bed and hurried across the hall. Havah hunched over the crib, grasping the iron bars.

"Did you hear it, Arel?" Her voice quavered.

"Yes, I heard you cry."

"Not me. *Her.*"

Thumb in her mouth, eyes closed, Rachel barely stirred.

"She's sound asleep. You just had another one of your nightmares."

"This was different. It was another baby in another place. She was in the kind of pain no child should ever suffer. It rips out your heart because there's *nothing* you can do to stop it."

# CHAPTER ELEVEN

The growing turmoil and anti-Semitism in Odessa troubled Nikolai. Once he deemed himself strong enough, despite Pavel's protests, he concentrated on helping the Wolinsky family pack in hopes of expediting their departure. In return, Leah and Devorah insisted on providing meals.

"You needn't feed us," said Nikolai. "When would you eat, Doctor?" Gavrel wrapped a bed sheet around a lamp. You and Froi Oxana are here every day. You look exhausted.

"When you and yours are out of this place I'll sleep."

Devorah gave him a gentle nudge. "Dr. Nikolai, you're a doctor, not a housewife. And you're still not well."

"And a woman in your condition shouldn't be standing."

She blushed and pulled her shawl around her swollen stomach. Plunging his hands into the soapy water, he mumbled a hasty apology. A sharp pain shot through his shoulder and he uttered an involuntary groan.

"Above all else, my husband is a doctor. Despite his indelicacy, he's right. Go sit and put your feet up." Oxana seized the dish towel from Devorah. "I may not be able to cook, but I can make short work of these dishes. Kolyah, sit before you faint and embarrass me."

Closer to passing out than he cared to admit, he eased into a chair next to Devorah's. She sat with eyes closed and feet propped up on a crate. Her unborn kicked and made her apron jump. He hoped the child would wait until after the long journey to America, but from all signs he could tell Devorah would not last another two weeks.

"In America I'm going to be a ballerina." Pora twirled past one of the boxes. She tripped and stumbled into Nikolai's knees.

Following her with clumsy pirouettes, Tova cried, "Me, too!"

Outside, voices rose in victory songs. Nikola peered out the window. Arms linked, young men danced and students waved flags. Something about the merrymaking gave him a sense of dread.

Lev burst through the front door. "Gavrel! Leah! Have you heard?"

"It's official!" Close behind him, Vasily waved his hands in the air. Hyram stumbled over the threshold, cheeks flushed.

"The Czar signed a paper granting the people—all the people—freedom." He knelt beside Devorah and laid his head on her stomach. "Do you hear, my son? We're no longer slaves in Egypt."

Gavrel's already menacing scowl at Lev deepened. "Where have you been? You missed breakfast. Your sisters have been worried sick."

Dodging cooking pots and toys, Lev scooped up Pora and swung her around. "Listen to the cheering. At last we're free."

"Free. We're free, Mama." Pora giggled and clapped her hands.

"We'll soon be in America where everyone's free already," said Leah.

"Don't you see, Big Sister? We don't need to leave. Now we have freedom to speak, the freedom to assemble. The police can't arrest us for having our meetings." He kissed her cheek and playfully tweaked her nose.

"Just like that?" Gavrel snapped his fingers. "The Czar signs a piece of paper and, like magic, the Christians will suddenly love and embrace us as brothers. If you believe this, you're more naive than Pora."

News of the Czar's signature on the edict spread throughout Odessa and brought anything but peace. The hospital courtyard teemed with Jewish families who had taken refuge behind the formidable stone walls when the celebrations disintegrated into violence.

Nikolai clenched his teeth as he sutured a child's wound—a gash the length of his forehead that would leave a scar he would carry for the rest of his life. He was six, maybe seven. Reuven's age.

As he bandaged the boy's head his vision blurred and he pitched forward slightly. Pavel took the bandage roll from him.

"Nikolai, you're gray. Go lie down for a while."

"There aren't enough doctors to go around as it is."

"You won't be much good to me dead. At least take a fifteen minute break. Doctor's orders."

"Fifteen minutes." Nikolai found a spare gurney. "That's all."

Despite his resolve, fatigue overtook him and he nodded off. His dreams took him to his boyhood spent ice skating in St. Petersburg by day and playing his flute with the Philharmonic by night. He was his father's prodigy. He remembered his first solo, a Bach Sonata in A minor. For an exhilarating moment he held the audience in his twelve-year-old grasp until he missed a note. He writhed under Father's disapproving glare.

"Kolyah!" Father grasped his shoulders and shook him. "What were you thinking? Daydreamer! You . . ."

Father faded in a mist and another voice took his place.

"Dr. Nikolai? Are you all right?"

"Hyram? Thank God." Nikolai coaxed his eyes open. "Your family's in the courtyard, I trust."

"No. Lev and Gavrel—after you left yesterday morning—they had a terrible fight. Gavrel slapped Lev and he ran off. Leah refuses to leave the apartment until she knows he's safe. He thinks so much of you and Dr. Pavel. I thought maybe he came here."

"I haven't seen him, have you, Pasha?" Nikolai sat up and searched the clinic, then snapped open his pocket watch.

Slouched in a nearby chair, Pavel shook his head. Stretching his long legs he straightened and stood. "We'll help you find him."

Oxana dropped the instruments she had been scrubbing. "Kolyah? Pasha? You can't go. It's too dangerous."

Nikolai rose from the gurney and pulled her into a tight embrace. The scent of her hair and the warmth of her trembling body filled him. He grasped her shoulders and gave her a gentle shove.

"No matter what happens to me, promise me you'll look after Vasily. Don't let him go outside these walls."

Before he loaded a bullet into one of the revolver chambers Gavrel studied it. He marveled at its size. How could something so small do so much damage? Could he take a human life? One by one he loaded the rest of the bullets into the gun and then set it on the table.

Outside, the screams and shouts grew louder. How long would it be before pogromists would come for him—for all he held dear? Apprehension plagued him and he gnawed the inside of his lip until it bled.

*Where had Lev gone? Damn that boy. Did he, at this very moment, lie dead in the street?*

"Papa?" A small finger poked his lower back. "Reuven. What did I tell you about staying in the bedroom?" Gavrel spun around and dropped to his knees.

"I—I have to go." Reuven's lower lip trembled.

"Can you hold it?"

Crushing him into his arms, Gavrel curved his hand around the back of Reuven's head. The softness of the child's hair tickled his palm. Like a man dying of thirst, Gavrel drank in Reuven's youthful scent. In the crook of his arm, the boy's head bobbed up and down. Releasing him, Gavrel rose and picked up the gun. The sight of it in his hand chilled him. He set it back down and grasped Reuven's hand. Ushering him to the bedroom, Gavrel forced a smile. Certain he fooled no one, he knelt beside Leah who held their daughter against her breasts.

"Papa, I'm scared." Pora wriggled out of Leah's embrace and held out her arms. "Are we going to die?"

"What kind of silly talk is that for a little ballerina? The storm will pass," Gavrel whispered.

Devorah, beside Leah on the bed, looked uncomfortable. She stretched her legs out in front of her. Tova laid her head on her mother's rounded belly and walked her fingers in a circle.

"Baby brother," she sang.

Pora, innocently satisfied with Gavrel's wooden comfort, snuggled against Leah. "Mama, tell us a story. Tell us about America."

"In America, Pora's going to be a dancer," said Leah, her voice low and strained. "We're going to see Aunt Havah and Uncle Arel again, and we're going to meet our special cousin Rachel who can't see and plays the piano."

"Me, too," said Tova.

From downstairs came crashing sounds of shattering glass. Leah continued. "In America, everyone is safe and—"

"Silence!" Gavrel jumped to his feet and ran to the kitchen.

He held his breath as he listened to the sound of heavy boots on the stairs. Taking one last look at his precious family huddled on the bed, he lifted the revolver, cocked it and aimed at the front door.

All too familiar with Lev's impassioned temper, Nikolai prayed they would find him alive as he and Pavel followed Hyram and fought their way through the crowd of rioters.

"I pity them," said Pavel.

"You pity whom?" asked Nikolai.

"The Russians, the Czar, the police."

"What pity does that pack of rabid mongrels deserve?"

"One day they'll have to answer for the way they've treated the apple of God's eye."

Nikolai's heart thumped when, a few yards away, he saw a group of angry Russian men surrounding Lev. One man shoved him, a second man kicked him. Lev doubled over. Two more blows to the head and he fell hard to his knees.

"Let them answer with blood!" Hyram went for the pistol in his belt.

"Don't." Pavel seized his arm. "You might hit Lev."

Wrenching from his grasp, Hyram started toward the fray. Nikolai wrestled him to his knees. Pavel shoved his way into the press. Nikolai yelled at him to stop. Sunlight glinted off a dagger, held high in the air by a scraggy hand. Then, amid a milieu of legs, fists and epithets the hand and knife made a swift descent. The men scattered, leaving Lev, Pavel and one other man.

Nikolai scrambled to his feet and rushed to where Pavel stood, face to face with the stranger, who held tight to the dagger's handle. Pavel curved his hand around the man's twisted fingers and smiled. Blood trickled from the corner of Pavel's mouth as he whispered, "May God have mercy on your eternal soul."

Eyes wide and mouth open in a silent scream, the man jerked the dagger from Pavel's chest and half-stumbled, half-ran after his cronies. Pavel's knees buckled. Nikolai caught him and eased him to the ground, then sat on the pavement, cradling Pavel's head in his lap.

Hyram went to his knees. "Do something, Dr. Nikolai."

"I . . . I can't." Blood, hot on Nikolai's lap, saturated Pavel's shirt. "It pierced his heart."

"Why, Dr. Pavel? Why?" Lev wailed.

Between gurgling breaths, Pavel rasped. "It's what—"

"Nooooo! Don't say it!"

". . . my . . . Lord would have . . . done."

In the hours following Pavel's death Nikolai merely functioned. There was no time to allow himself the luxury of grief or to console Oxana. The body had to be delivered to the morgue and papers filled out. Once business had been taken care of, Nikolai, Lev and Hyram headed for the shoe shop. Nikolai prayed under his breath with every step. His heart raced as they arrived. The new sign that had proudly advertised, "Wolinsky and Family, Distinguished Shoes" lay in splintered pieces on the sidewalk. Shattered glass crunched under his feet. All that remained of Gavrel's handiwork were scraps of leather and broken tools. Nikolai strained to hear voices or movement from the apartment overhead. He heard only ear-piercing silence. Maybe Leah changed her mind and decided not to wait until Lev came home. Perhaps Gavrel put his foot down and insisted on taking his family to safety. The decrepit stairs creaked beneath them. Nikolai's ragged breath resounded in his ears as he looked to the apartment's entrance. Light streamed through the half opened door.

Hyram's voice cut though the quiet. "Devorah? Leah? I found Lev, he's—he's safe."

"Oh God!" Lev covered his eyes as Nikolai pushed open the door.

Two strange men lay dead close to the entryway. The odor of sulfur permeated the air. Reuven's muffled cry came from the other side of the room. Nikolai ran to the stove where Gavrel lay on his side behind it, blood seeping into the floorboards beneath him. Reuven huddled against him, his dark eyes wide and pleading.

"Please, Dr. Nikolai, make Papa well."

"I'll do my best, son." Nikolai fell to his knees beside them and pressed his fingers against Gavrel's neck, a faint pulse at best. With difficulty, Nikolai pushed him over onto his back.

"Don't lie to the boy," whispered Gavrel and grasped Nikolai's wrist with surprising strength.

Lev collapsed on the floor and laid his head on Gavrel's chest. "If I hadn't run away—"

"Hush. I . . . said things . . . I had no right. I'm sorry I hit you. Take care of your . . . brother."

"I will . . . Papa."

"Papa. A title . . . worth dying for. Doctor . . . remember . . . you gave me your . . . word." Gavrel's suddenly limp hand fell from Nikolai's wrist.

"Farewell my friend." Nikolai took off his coat.

"Papa, wake up!" Reuven screamed and clung to Gavrel's neck.

"He's dead, little brother." Lev pried off Reuven's arms.

"He promised he wouldn't leave me. He promised he wouldn't die." Lying on his stomach, Reuven drummed his feet and beat his fists on the floor. "He lied."

With one hand over Reuven's mouth and the other arm around his waist, Lev lifted him and carried him to the other side of the room.

Nikolai covered Gavrel's face with his coat, turned his head and gasped at the sight of Leah's body propped against the wall like a discarded toy; bare legs sprawled in front of her at odd angles. Gulping outrage on top of nausea, he smoothed her torn skirts over them. He could only imagine what those sadistic beasts did to her before allowing her to die. From behind her came a piercing cry. Gently he pulled Leah away from the wall and then laid her on the floor. Like a small animal caught in trap, Bayla crouched in the corner, her gray eyes wide with terror. Red stains spattered her threadbare dress. He ran his hands through her blood matted hair. There was not a scratch on her.

"Thank God," he whispered as he lifted her into his arms.

At first her little body went rigid, then she popped her thumb in her mouth and fell limp against his shoulder. From the bedroom came a tortured wail. Holding his hand over Bayla's face, he rushed toward the sound. Sprawled across Devorah's body, Hyram looked up at Nikolai.

"The children . . ." the words turned to dust in Nikolai's throat when he caught sight of Tova and Pora's bodies beside Devorah's.

"Please," whispered Hyram. "Leave me alone with her for a while."

"Don't be too long." Nikolai's voice sounded thready and distant to his own ears. He turned on his heel in the doorway and collided with Lev who tried to push past him.

Nikolai blocked his way. "Don't, Lev. Remember them the way they were. Take your sister to the other room and wait for me."

Bayla clung to Nikolai's neck and whimpered.

"You know me, little sister." Lev lowered his voice to a gentle whisper. At last she loosened her stranglehold on Nikolai and nestled into Lev's outstretched arms without a sound.

Lightheaded, Nikolai staggered to the kitchen, dropped to his knees and vomited until there was nothing left. Once the dizziness subsided, he stumbled to the cabinet where Gavrel kept the passport and his lifesavings. It surprised Nikolai to find them untouched. An envelope with familiar handwriting caught his eye. A wad of American currency fell out as he opened the enclosed letter.

*"28 September 1905*

*"Dear Herr Wolinsky,*

*I don't know if you remember me."*

"Could anyone could forget, you, my friend?"

*"Itzak informs me that you and your family are soon to sail to America. As you know, I assisted the rest of your family in their journey nearly two years ago. I hope it won't insult you if I presume to do the same for you. Please accept this small sum."*

"Ulrich, you don't know the meaning of small sum."

*"Treat yourself and your family to first class tickets. I look forward to seeing you again in a few short weeks"*

Folding the letter, money and passports, Nikolai crammed them into his waistcoat pocket. As he did so a child's arms circled his waist and he heard Reuven's hoarse whisper.

"Dr. Nikolai, are you taking us to Bubbe and Zaydeh's?"

"I promised your Papa, didn't I?"

Nikolai hefted him into his arms, carried him to the front room and lowered him into a chair beside Lev and Bayla. Then he returned to the bedroom where Hyram stood beside the bed, expressionless and strangely calm.

"The baby," said Hyram. "He was Orev's son, not mine."

"Let's get out of here."

"I can't leave them." Hyram pulled his pistol from his belt and aimed it at Nikolai.

Almost welcoming the prospect of a bullet boring through his forehead, Nikolai whispered, "Hasn't there been enough killing?"

"Goodbye, Dr. Nikolai." Hyram turned the gun away from Nikolai, pressed it against his own temple and shut his eyes.

"Hyram, think. Your death won't bring them back." Nikolai lunged toward him, but was not fast enough.

Blood, bone fragments and brain tissue peppered Nikolai's face.

# PART IV

## *Shalom Alaynu, Peace On Us*

# CHAPTER ONE

Oxana's stomach coiled into a hard knot. Stopping in the doorway of what had, up until two weeks ago, been her bedroom, she stared at the feathers and shredded bed linens strewn across the floor. She flexed her tense shoulder muscles as she wandered from room to room surveying the shabby, dingy apartment she had shared with her brother, husband and stepson. Neither paint nor colorful curtains ever did anything to brighten it, no matter how hard she tried. It was too cramped for one person to live in, let alone four.

Looters had left little more than debris. What they did not steal, they destroyed. Someone had even carted off the cast iron stove. She hoped they crippled themselves in the process.

Traces of her brother remained. A spare medical bag he kept for home emergencies lay opened in the corner—its contents scattered. Kneeling, she turned it right side up and foraged for anything salvageable for Nikolai.

A stethoscope and a pair of forceps were all she found. She dropped them into the bag. *No doubt murdering scavengers took the scalpels.*

Amid the broken medicine vials she spied a book, or what was left of one. She recognized the frayed leather cover and remembered how Pavel used to pore over it. He delighted in reading whole chapters aloud to her despite her cranky protests.

"I've better things to do with my time than listen to your religious blather," she would say with disgust.

Her empty ears ached to hear his voice. She would not care if he read it from cover to cover. Doubling over, she pounded the floor.

"Damn you and your precious Lord, Pasha!"

With her index finger she traced the engraved cross, an extravagant gift from Pasha that hung around her neck on a golden chain. It would keep the love of the Lord close to her heart he told her when he fastened it. Her disheveled mind flashed back to the day she and Nikolai wed. The priest who officiated wore an elaborate crucifix, the so called symbol of charity, yet he made no attempt to hide his disdain for her Jewish friends. Pinching the pendant between her thumb and fingers, she yanked—the chain snapped and fell to the floor.

The front door opened and slammed shut. She froze and braced herself for what might happen next. A peculiar tickle rose in her throat and her tongue tingled.

Nikolai, in a voice hoarse and heavy with exhaustion, called her name. His footsteps reverberated against the emptiness. Entering the room, he crossed the distance and knelt beside her. She leaned her head against his chest and listened to his heartbeat; its steady thump soothed her.

He rested his chin on top of her head. "You shouldn't be out alone. It's almost dark."

"How long were you in surgery?"

"Too long." His chin trembled as he lowered his voice to a husky whisper. "I can't do it anymore."

He let go of her and picked up Pavel's tattered Bible. He held it up to the retreating light by the broken window, squinted, and read aloud. "*'Rescue my soul from the sword; from the power of the dog.'* Why didn't the Lord rescue him from the sword?"

With a snarl he hurled the book. Loose pages falling, it bounced across the floor.

Stunned, she stared at him. Three day's growth stippled his cheeks and chin and his hair had not been combed. His red-rimmed eyes reflected more than fatigue. He was her Nikolai, yet he was not.

"Isn't he your Lord, too, Kolyah?"

"No."

# CHAPTER TWO

Afternoon sunlight refracted through the stained glass dining room window like watercolor and cast brilliant colored patterns on the oak paneled walls. The brightness contrasted the pall that had settled over the people seated around the table. Dishes piled with food remained for the most part untouched. Havah gripped Nikolai's telegram, having read it multiple times, wishing the words, like magic, would change. If only she could wake up from this nightmare.

The messenger, a youth with a cheerful smile, had delivered the telegram that morning. Seeing it was from Odessa, she signed for it in haste and ripped open the envelope with joyful expectancy. The next thing she remembered was coming-to on the sofa surrounded by her weeping family.

She watched those gathered at her table. Fruma Ya'el, Elliott asleep on her shoulder, buried her face in his hair. "Those poor babies."

Yussel pounded his cane on the floor and shook his fist. "*A klog tsu meine sonim!* A curse on my enemies!"

Rachel huddled against him. She patted his lined cheek and her sightless eyes brimmed as if she somehow understood the magnitude of the tragedy.

"All of them, I brought them all into the world," said Fruma Ya'el. "I saw their faces even before their own mamas."

"Is there anything we can do to help?" asked Ulrich.

"Bring the dead back to life," said Arel.

"Arel," cried Shayndel. "Shame on you. After all the Professor's done for us."

"We have three weeks to make some decisions," said Itzak as he took the telegram from Havah. "Ulrich, I apologize for my little brother."

"No offense taken," said Ulrich. "In any case, Catherine and I will be in the new house by next week. We'll have plenty of room for Nikolai and his family."

"Mama, may I be excused?" Evalyne tugged at Sarah's sleeve.

Sarah nodded. "Go upstairs and play. Take your brother and cousins with you." Havah waited for the usual protests from the other children—none came. The boys slid off their chairs and filed out behind Evalyne like old men in a funeral procession.

From a serving bowl filled with tzimmes, Havah dug out a raisin and rolled it between her thumb and forefinger. She popped it into her mouth and crushed it between her teeth. It had no taste.

"Nu? Who will take the children? We shouldn't wait until they step off the train to decide." Yussel pushed his plate aside.

"Nettie and George have offered to take Bayla and Reuven," said Sarah.

"They're wonderful parents," said Wolf.

"And what of Lev? Does he not also need a home?" Yussel scowled.

Sarah flushed. "Yes, Papa, I didn't mean—"

"I know what you meant. The Weinbergs would give them a good Jewish home, but we are talking about my grandchildren. I'll not see them separated."

With her hand on her stomach, Shayndel rose from her chair, her usually pink cheeks tinged with grey. She took a deep breath, let it out gradually and said, "It's true, Lev can be a pill, but he's my nephew and he's welcome in my home."

Leaning forward with his hands flat on the table, Arel spoke in a ragged whisper. "Havah and I had a long talk last night. We want them. *All* of them."

"They're my sister's children."

"Are you forgetting she was my sister, too? Besides, you don't really want Lev."

"I never said that!"

"*Yes, you did.* You just said it. 'Lev can be a pill.' You never liked him. Admit it."

"*Shah!*" Itzak pounded the table. "Listen to you, bickering like a couple of children Yourselves."

"May I speak?" Trembling, Havah rose and gripped the chair back for balance. "I'm not born into this family so I don't know how much is my right to say."

"Since when did that stop you?" Wolf raised his wine glass and winked. "Speak, Mrs. Scholar, before your husband and his sister come to blows."

"Bayla was the first baby I ever saw born. To me, she is a special child."

"So what?" cried Shayndel. "She's still *my* niece and what about *your* health?"

"My health has nothing to do with this."

"Are you kidding? Sometimes you can hardly walk. What happens when you have one of your episodes?"

"It's true. I'm not as strong as you, but Arel and I—" Havah swallowed and groped for his hand. "We know what it is to have lived through such a slaughter."

"It's behind us now." Arel pulled her onto his lap.

"Behind us? I relive it every day."

Around the table, no one spoke. Shayndel hung her head. "Forgive me, Havaleh."

"I have but one child. Dr. Miklos says I can't have any more. Shayndel already has her hands full with three and one on the way."

Itzak's mouth dropped. "Is this true?"

Shayndel nodded.

"Why didn't you tell me?"

"I've been waiting for the right time."

"I don't know whether to shed tears of joy or of sorrow."

"Sometimes the best we can hope for is *shalom*," whispered Yussel.

## CHAPTER THREE

Someone's baritone voice boomed out the first lines of *The Star Spangled Banner* in broken English. Lev listened. Other voices, some off key, joined the song amid weeping and joyful shouts.

"It's America, Mama," cried a child in excited Yiddish.

All over the decks children shouted in their native languages.

Lev shielded his eyes from the sun with his hand and gazed out at the approaching harbor. He stretched his arms over his head, then dropped them and held onto the ship's railing. Sunlight shimmered on the water like sapphires. Looming over the horizon of buildings, a giant statue of a regal woman with flowing robes raised her torch in her right hand. Her serene face and the cheering crowd mocked him. He longed to apologize to Leah. If he had not argued and stomped out like a selfish fool, she would have sought the safety of the hospital courtyard instead of waiting for his return. The death of those babies would forever be on his head. What would be better about this new land?

Beside him, Reuven hopped on one foot, waving and pointing at the statue. "We're free!"

"Free from what?"

# CHAPTER FOUR

Arel turned his collar against the frigid November wind. The ground rumbled as a train pulled out of the station. Crowds thronged the street. Horses pulling carriages pranced alongside a smattering of shiny automobiles.

"I could have sworn Kolyah told me they'd be arriving at four o'clock." Ulrich clasped his watch and slipped it into his waistcoat pocket. "It's past four-thirty."

Startled when his horse balked, a milk truck driver yelled at two little boys who had run out in front of it.

"Watch where you're going, ya little brats."

With a scowl directed at the milkman, a woman in a broad brimmed hat with bobbing flowers pulled them to safety. First she gave them tearful hugs, then took a paddle from her bag and swatted their behinds.

"You watch where you're going, sir, or I'll most assuredly report you to the police." She cast another scowl at the milkman, grabbed the boys' hands, squared her shoulders and hurried toward the streetcar.

"Ulrich, I'm afraid," Arel whispered.

"Of what?"

"What kind of father will I be to them? They deserve better."

"Don't underestimate yourself, my friend. As far as I can tell, you're a wonderful father."

"You think so? If it hadn't been for Havah I would've made the worst mistake a father could make."

"She is a prize at that." Ulrich slapped Arel's back.

The last time Arel saw his sister Tova's children had been two years ago. He barely remembered what they looked like. He remembered the night after she suddenly passed away. Lev was only eleven. Arel found the boy weeping and reciting the mourner's Kaddish in the cemetery. He corrected the boy by telling him he should not pray without a minyan. What a ridiculous thing to tell a heartbroken child.

"A child's tears rend the heavens," Arel's mother used to say when either he or his sisters would scrape a knee or cut a finger.

The heavens must be ripped to shreds by now. No ocean could separate him from the pain.

Lost in his thoughts, he did not notice the thin man with dirty blond hair approaching them until the stench of alcohol and body odor brought him back to the present. The stranger's lips spread in a grin full of decaying teeth as he thrust a grubby finger in Arel's face.

"Hey, didn't I see one of them little round Jew bonnets under your hat?"

"There's a bath house not far from here. My treat." Ulrich took a handful of coins from his pocket. Then he grasped the man's wrist, flipped his hand open and dropped them onto his grimy palm.

The man shoved the money into his threadbare trouser pocket, his rheumy eyes riveted on Arel. "Jew Boy! I'm talking to you!"

"You say nothing worthy of my hearing." Arel pushed past him, his heart thumping faster with each step.

"You come back here, I ain't finished."

"Hey, you, Kike. You best be listening when your betters is talking."

Another man blocked his path. Greasy hair of an indiscriminate color framed the pockmarked face of a stringy man in a tattered coat who did not smell any better than his cohort.

Despite the cold, Arel's cheeks blazed and sweat streamed between his shoulder blades. His tongue was as heavy as a slab of cement. Clenching and unclenching his fists at his sides, he pondered the craters in the face of his tormentor.

"Arel, it's time." Ulrich tugged his arm. "If you gentlemen will excuse us, we have a train to meet."

"Not so fast Mister Wiener Schnitzel. We's got to learn this here Jew boy a lesson." The man snatched Arel's hat and tossed it to his friend.

"Nice sombrero. Mine now." The other man slunk from behind Ulrich, wearing Arel's hat. "Cat got your tongue? Say something, you dumb Jew!"

Arel ground his teeth and fingered the honeycomb of scars on his face. "Is this not America, the land of the free and the home of the brave?"

"Herr Gitterman, the train's coming with the children. Forget these filthy *khazers*, these pigs," cried Ulrich in Yiddish. "I'll buy you a new hat."

A strong gust blew the hat into the street. The man chased after it with a drunken swagger. He tripped and fell flat on his face. Horse's hooves sealed the hat's fate.

The other man grasped Arel's lapels and leaned into him. His breath reeked of stale whiskey. "I don't like your kind in my country. Why don't you just pack yourself on that there train and take your sorry Jew carcass back to where you come from."

"Never again," whispered Arel.

"What'd you say, Jew boy?"

Union Depot disappeared. Arel stood, once more, before murderers in Evron's house in Kishinev. He trembled, not with fear or cold, but with rage and repeated the words as loud as he could.

"Never again!"

Arel closed the distance and smashed his head into the bridge of the stranger's nose.

The man grunted in pain as his nose gushed blood. Arel sent blow after rapid blow into the pitted face. The bum fell sideways and sprawled on the sidewalk. He spewed more curses and sat up, clutching his broken nose. Arel knocked him backward with a left hook to his cheek. With vengeful euphoria, Arel straddled his would-be assailant and pummeled his face.

Spectators gathered around but Arel hardly noticed. With each blow, he added a name.

"For Havah. For Tuli."

The man's cries for mercy fueled Arel's frenzy. "Mercy? You bastard. You child murderer. For Tova. For Pora."

With the last blow, the man's eyes rolled back in his head. Blood gurgled from his parted lips. A gloved hand grasped Arel's poised fist.

"Enough!" Ulrich hollered.

Arel's knuckles smarted as he stood and gazed at the unconscious derelict. The strength of anger drained from him until the second *khaser* grabbed him from behind. Arel choked and struggled to pry the gnarled fingers off his neck.

The man shrieked and released him as suddenly as he had attacked. Arel spun around to see that Ulrich had trapped the man in a stranglehold. With murderous intent, Ulrich squeezed and lifted until the spindly man's kicking feet dangled an inch above the pavement.

"You're mine, Yankee Doodle." Ramming him against a lamppost several times, Ulrich smacked one of the man's cheeks, and then backhanded the other.

"Excuse me," said a deep voice Arel thought he had heard somewhere before.

He turned to see a uniformed police officer standing behind Ulrich, holding a club that he tapped rhythmically against his palm. Ulrich released the tramp, wiped his hand on his coat and extended it with the aplomb of a duke at a high society soirée. The tramp fell to the ground.

"Good evening, officer. Ulrich Dietrich, professor of music at your service. This is my good friend, Herr Gitterman."

"Pleased to meet you, Professor Dietrich, I'm Lafayette Tillman, a music lover myself. I studied it in college. As for your friend, we've met." A smile spread across Officer Tillman's dark bronze face as he turned back to Arel. "Apparently Mrs. Hutton was right, Mr. Gitterman. You are a brawler after all."

The bum's mouth dropped open as he looked from Ulrich to Arel to Officer Tillman. "Who woulda ever thought a kike and a nigger would be all chummy like?"

"Why don't *you* tell me what happened—*boy*?" Officer Tillman seized the man's ragged collar and leaned into his face until they were nose to nose.

"Okay. Yeah. I'll tell you, officer. This here crazy Jew boy and his foreigner buddy attacked me and my pal." The man's peeling lips curled into an ingratiating smile. "We was just being neighborly."

"I see what you mean. They *are* foreigners," said Officer Tillman with a wry smile. He let go of the man's collar and pulled a pair of handcuffs from his coat pocket. He snapped them around the man's wrists and ratcheted them tight.

"Maybe they misunderstood. When you said, 'Welcome to America' in your 'neighborly' way they heard, 'I'm a bigoted ignoramus whose parents never married. Slug me.'"

The locomotive juddered to a halt in front of Union Depot. White billows poured from the iron smokestack and its shrill whistle announced the train's late arrival. According to the telegraph operator it had been detained in Chicago by an early winter blizzard and it took all night to clear the tracks. As weary travelers stepped off of each car's stairs they were greeted by friends or relatives. Ulrich searched the sea of faces for Nikolai.

"Lev," Arel yelled, tightened his woolen scarf around his head and fought his way to his nephews. "Reuven."

Ulrich remembered the sullen youth with the scar across his lips who moved to meet Arel halfway. At his side, a round faced boy skipped, waving his cap and shouting in Yiddish. "Fehter Arel! Uncle Arel!"

"Little apple." Arel swept up the smaller boy on one arm and encircled Lev's shoulder with the other. "Where's Bayla?"

"She's with Missus Doctor Nikolai." Reuven pointed to a slim woman with wireframe spectacles.

Bayla clung to Oxana's neck and wrapped her legs around her slender waist. When Arel approached with his arm outstretched, Bayla shrank back, buried her face on Oxana's shoulder and whimpered.

Ulrich walked to Oxana, bowed and extended his hand. "Welcome to Kansas City, Frau Derevenko."

"Professor Dietrich." Oxana offered a mitten clad hand and spoke English with apparent difficulty. "My husband, he telling me of you all of time."

Ulrich understood why Nikolai, in his early letters, described her as an intolerable shrew. There was fire and strength in her eyes. Her stature and straight posture communicated stubborn determination.

"Fabrications, my dear Frau Derevenko," Ulrich answered in Russian which seemed to put her at ease.

"Tatko tells the truth." An adolescent stepped from behind her, kissed her cheek and grasped Ulrich's hand. "It's good to see you again, Uncle."

Ulrich stared at the boy's familiar gray-blue eyes and blond hair. "Vasily, you've grown a good ten inches."

"Only four, sir, but I'm as tall as Tatko."

"Taller, I'd say. Where is he?"

"He's gone for the baggage, although they don't have much to speak of." Vasily adjusted Bayla's hood and nodded his head toward Lev and Reuven.

Shielding his eyes from the coppery morning sun's glare, Ulrich spied a slight man who at first glance appeared to be a vagrant, lugging a steamer trunk with one hand and carrying a carpetbag in the other, teeth gritted at the obvious pain of exertion. Pale stubble covered his chin and hollowed cheeks and dark circles framed his gaunt eyes.

"Kolyah?" Trying not to appear alarmed, Ulrich rushed to help him.

The trunk dropped from Nikolai's shoulder. Ulrich drew him into an embrace and shuddered. Nikolai's heavy coat did not disguise his skeletal frame.

"You've lost weight," Ulrich whispered.

"My wife's a terrible cook."

"Tell him, maybe he listens to you," said Oxana with deep scowl. "He is no eating. He is no sleeping."

"I should never have taught her to speak English." Nikolai grimaced and rubbed his shoulder. "Now she nags in two languages."

"I heard about that wound. It's a brave thing you did." Ulrich patted Nikolai's back. "How is it?"

"It's better."

"He's lying, Uncle Ulrich," said Vasily. "Tell him, Tatko, it aches all the time. Uncle Pavel says, I mean *said*, he didn't give it enough time to heal."

"We have better things to do than stand here in the cold discussing my health," said Nikolai.

Reuven tugged at Arel's coat sleeve and pointed to a lengthening wet streak saturating Oxana's skirt. "Bayla *pished* again."

Tears streamed down Bayla's chapped red cheeks and she stuck two fingers in her mouth, making her seem much younger than her six years.

Forcing a smile, Ulrich picked up the trunk. "I've a splendid idea. There's a water closet and a restaurant inside the station. Frau Derevenko and Bayla can change into some dry clothes in the ladies' room. I'll telephone Havah and Catherine to tell them the children arrived safely and that we'll be even later than we thought. Then it's hot apple pie and coffee for everyone."

"Apple pie?" Reuven slipped his hand into Ulrich's. "Papa loves apples."

# CHAPTER FIVE

Every night for the past month, the same dream haunted Lev. From the midst of flames and black clouds of smoke, Leah held out her hands and screamed his name. When he reached for her the blaze engulfed him and his own cries woke him.

The aroma of coffee and eggs frying wafted over him. He studied the room's high ceilings, long glass windows and blue-striped wallpaper. What right did he have to live in such luxury? Unable to deny his grumbling stomach, he sat up, swung his legs over the side of the bed and put on his new robe. He relished and resented the soft terrycloth against his skin. With a yawn he padded down the hallway and then descended the stairs. At the foot, Kreplakh bared her teeth and growled. He delivered a vicious kick that sent her yelping between a strange man's legs and under the sofa.

In Yiddish, the man said, "Careful, son, the pup's done nothing to deserve that, indeed she hasn't."

"I should let her bite me?" Lev scowled.

"Come say hello to Dr. Miklos," said Reuven from the stranger's lap. "He's nice."

"Good to finally meet you, Reb Resnick. Your Uncle Arel's told me all about you." Dr. Miklos extended his meaty hand. "I'm an old friend of Dr. Trubachov."

"He's dead." Lev crammed his hands into his pockets.

"It is a tragedy—a waste."

"What do you care?"

"Lev, don't speak to the doctor like that. He's a friend," said Havah as she entered the room with Bayla clinging to her skirts. Lev blinked back tears. His little sister's vacant stare made her look as blind as Rachel.

"He's not my friend." Lev knelt and held out his arms to Bayla. "Come to big brother."

For the briefest moment he expected her to smile and skip to him the way she used to. On the contrary, her eyes remained distant and cloudy as she moved to him like an old woman and then buried her face in his chest. As he stood, she whimpered and tightened her arms about his neck.

"What have you done to her?" He frowned at Havah.

Havah returned his frown. "How could you ask such a question?"

The last time Lev had seen his uncle's wife was at their wedding in Kishinev three years ago. She was shorter than he remembered, and looked like every other rich American woman he had seen on the train.

With a ragged sigh she turned to Dr. Miklos, who seemed to be speaking words of comfort. While Lev did not understand all that the doctor said, he recognized his name and the name Sigmund Freud from Dr. Pavel and Dr. Nikolai's conversations.

"Talk about me in your English now like I'm a baby, but soon I'll speak it better than either of you."

"Of course you will, son." Dr. Miklos smoothed his moustache with his thumbs. "You're a bright lad."

Warm liquid streamed down Lev's pajama pants. Bayla shivered against him.

"Not again." Havah grasped the girl around the waist. "Let me change her. You'd best change, too, Lev. Leave her with me."

Tightening his arm around his sister, Lev pushed Havah's hand away. He swayed back and forth, resting his cheek on Bayla's forehead. "I'll never leave you again, little sister."

After another night of fitful sleep, Lev woke from his nightmare. He tried to cover himself, but the blanket was tangled around Reuven. With a loud grunt he yanked it out from under the boy, who rolled over and kicked him.

"Hey! I was having a good dream. I dreamed that Papa was here with us."

"Shut up and get your feet off of me."

The thick comforter's warmth relaxed Lev and he closed his eyes. He had almost drifted to sleep when Reuven's whisper tickled his ear.

"Why don't you like Auntie Havah?"

"Who says I don't?"
"I like her. She's nice."
"You like everybody."
"No, I don't."

Yussel shuffled down the hallway to the kitchen, scraping his cane and sliding his right big toe along the floorboards to navigate his way to the icebox. He opened it, reached in and found the cold, smooth milk bottle. He set it on the table. Next he took a drinking glass from the cabinet, then found a chair and sat. He poured just enough milk, praising himself for not spilling a drop.

The aroma of Fruma Ya'el's lemon sponge cake teased his nostrils. He walked his fingers across the table until he felt the plate. One piece left. Surely, if he ate it, there would be no squabbling over who took the last one.

Telltale sounds told him it was somewhere around midnight. A mournful train whistle blew in the distance and the neighbor's dog howled softly. Havah wept in her sleep. Kreplakh, ever vigilant beneath Rachel's crib, snuffled and let out a subdued yip.

Hot tears welled in Yussel's eyes. He clenched his hand around the chilled bottle. "How many, *Gott in Himmel*? Will you take them all? Or maybe you'll just take their eyes or their minds." He tilted his head, resting it on the chair back and raised the milk bottle in the air. "Kill *me*. I'm old, dried up and blind."

Silence answered him. He set the milk on the table and crammed a chunk of cake into his mouth. Someone tiptoed through the door behind him. He heard the light switch click followed by a startled gasp.

"Can't sleep either, eh, Arel?"

"What are you doing sitting here in the dark, Papa?"

"Nu? Need I explain?"

The cabinet door creaked open and banged shut. Arel's footsteps padded to the table. The chair squeaked when Arel sat down. Liquid sloshed. The bottle clinked against the glass.

"Any more of that cake, Papa?"

"This is it." Yussel pushed the plate. "Here, take it."

"No, you keep it."

"I need it like I need a hole in the head. Take it."

"Okay." The plate rasped across the table.

Leaning back in his chair, Yussel sipped the cold milk and listened to his son chew. "What's troubling you tonight, Arel? Aside from the fact that you've three new children who've lost everything."

Arel slurped and gulped. The glass clunked against the table and the fork clanked lightly against the china plate. "I'm worried about Reuven."

"Why? He seems perfectly happy."

"Exactly."

# CHAPTER SIX

After news of the Odessa pogrom swept through Kansas City's Jewish community, the area rabbis decided to bring all the congregations together for an evening. Arel, along with Itzak, Wolf and Yussel, went leaving the women at home despite Havah's protests.

Following the meeting, Arel watched the people pour out of the building. Some gathered in small groups along the sidewalk and talked. Others wept or walked away in silence.

He pulled his hat down around his ears. "I'm ready to go home. A nice cup of hot chocolate by the fire sounds good."

"You look bushed, little brother," said Itzak. "It's quite a job taking on an extra family, eh?"

"It's not just that. Havah had a horrible nightmare last night. One of those where you practically have to beat her to wake her up. I'm glad she stayed home tonight."

"I don't know about that." Wolf put his hands on his hips to mimic Havah. "I dare say she'd have gone head to head with all of those rabbis, lawyers and chairmen, *and* had the final say." His smile faded. "All kidding aside, you're right. She's better off baking cookies with the kids than listening to a bunch of bigwig *makhers* make fools of themselves."

"I don't remember the last time I saw so many Jews in one place," said Arel. "At least as many as lived in Svechka and then some."

"That explains all the arguing," said Itzak.

Yussel tapped his cane on top of Itzak's shoe. "The suffering of our people in the old country is nothing to laugh about."

"True enough. But how did the quarreling honor their memories? What did it accomplish? Surely you see the humor in that, Papa."

"I don't see humor in any of it." Yussel spit on the pavement. "My grandchildren are dead and all we hear is talk. And now even my son-in-law makes light of it."

Itzak's dark eyes flashed. "My brother, his beloved and their babies perished two years ago in Kishinev. Now more of our family has been murdered in Odessa. Do you think I'd make light of it?"

Arel took hold of Yussel's arm. "Let's go home and argue before we turn to ice."

"Make light of it?" Itzak continued as they walked. "I'd like to slug them all. Talk, talk, talk. What do they hope to accomplish with all their talk? That reform rabbi, Mayer, is an idealist. 'The Jews should unite' he says. 'Patient suffering and forbearance,' he says. We couldn't even unite for one memorial service."

"What of Mr. Ringolsky's idea?" asked Wolf. "'The Jew's only hope is to escape from Russia?' Just how does he propose to make this happen?"

"He's such a self-important lawyer maybe he has enough money to buy every Jew in the Pale of Settlement a ticket," said Arel. "And what of Mr. Block's idea? He wants to arm the Russian Jews so they can defend themselves. *Feh.* Like a bandage helps a corpse. Gavrel, may his memory be blessed, died with a gun in his hand."

# CHAPTER SEVEN

While spacious enough to accommodate a baby grand piano and some furniture, the living room in the Dietrichs' newly constructed Kansas City home was modest in comparison to those in Kishinev or Streatham. Under protest, Ulrich had allowed Catherine to have incandescent lights installed. He still detested the wires that ran from switch to fixture, and pronounced them cold and unfeeling.

With a mixture of gentle reverence and sadness he played *Silent Night* as he watched Catherine, Oxana and Vasily hang decorations on the tree. Fresh evergreen scented the air and candlelight made the walls glow. The scene had the ambience of a Vermeer painting yet, like roasted pig at a Jewish wedding feast, everything seemed out of place.

Oxana lifted a painted, egg-shaped ornament from a lacquered box that looked like an angel. "Pasha . . . he make this for me when I was little girl—he love Christmas."

"Your English is improving every day, Mother," said Vasily as he selected another ornament and hung it on a bough.

"It's high time for some Christmas cheer." Catherine jiggled a silver bell that tinkled as she hooked it to a lower branch. Rising, she brushed pine needles from her skirts. Her petticoat rustled as she headed toward the kitchen.

"Yes," said Ulrich. "Methinks Kolyah could use a large dose of Dad's wassail recipe."

"Come Solnyshko." Oxana grabbed Vasily's shoulder. "We help."

"But, Mother, Aunt Cate doesn't need help. She's just going to get drinks."

Even though the boy stood nearly as tall as his stepmother, it only took one sidelong glance from her to silence him.

As they disappeared through the double French doors, Ulrich tilted his head. "You found a good one this time, Kolyah."

Slouched on one of the red brocade chairs in front of the fireplace, Nikolai raised his head and stared at Ulrich. "Forgive me. I'm not good company tonight."

"Just tonight? You haven't been much company any other night since your return. When was the last time you shaved?"

"When was the last time you defecated?"

Ulrich raised his fingers off the piano keys, rose and moved to the fireplace. He sat on the other red chair, leaned across the table between them and whispered, "What happened over there?"

"It was in all the newspapers."

"To *you*, Kolyah, what happened to you? What was different this time?"

"It was just exactly like Kishinev. My friends were massacred and there was nothing I could do about it. Isn't that what you wanted hear?"

Something in Nikolai's haunted eyes betrayed him. Ulrich wanted to press for more but Oxana, Vasily and Catherine entered the room. Ulrich stood and turned on his heel to greet them. As he did so he grasped Nikolai's shoulder.

"We'll talk later."

Nikolai recoiled under Ulrich's hand. Because it might cause a scene to push his friend any farther, Ulrich let go of Nikolai's shoulder and walked back to the piano. He forced a festive smile and took a cup of steaming wassail from Vasily. Setting the cup on the table beside the piano, Ulrich wrapped an arm around him.

"Vasya, has your father ever told you the story of your grandfather's Christmas visit to Heidelberg?"

"No, sir."

"Kolyah, I'm surprised at you. You'd deprive your own son of one of the greatest stories of the nineteenth century?" Ulrich glanced over at Nikolai who did not turn or give the slightest response.

Oxana whispered in Russian, "I apologize for my husband's rudeness."

At that Nikolai raised his head and turned to glower at her. He opened his mouth, then quickly shut it and turned back to the fireplace.

"Not at all." Ulrich gestured toward the sofa. "Ladies and gents, gather round and Uncle Ulrich shall regale you with young Kolyah Derevenko's antics."

Once Catherine and Oxana were seated, Ulrich sat down to the piano and played a soft rendition of *God Rest Ye Merry Gentlemen.* "It was Christmas of 1888."

"'89," said Nikolai.

"You want to tell this story, Kolyah?"

Nikolai answered with stony silence. Ulrich shrugged and continued.

"Sergei Derevenko, violinist extraordinaire, had nothing but disdain for Kolyah's choice to pursue medicine, not music, and came to Heidelberg with his chamber orchestra to entertain the university students. But really it was to dissuade his errant son."

"But Uncle Pasha said Tatko's a brilliant doctor," said Vasily.

"True enough, Vasya, but your grandfather had other plans for your father. He invited him to participate with his orchestra, no doubt to help him see the error of his ways. And to be fair, your father never missed a rehearsal and practiced his part for an hour each day. Your grandfather was pleased.

"Everyone in the orchestra was to dress as Dedushka Moroz, the Russian version of Kris Kringle. Sergei had been kind enough to provide the costumes replete with white beards.

"Then came the big night. For some reason your Tatko missed every cue and even refused to lift his flute to his lips. Sergei went to confront the rebel with a swift baton tap to his shoulder. Can you imagine the old man's surprise when a skeleton, borrowed from the anatomy laboratory, fell to the floor in all of its bony glory?"

"Guess you showed him, Tatko," said Vasily.

# CHAPTER EIGHT

"This would be pretty on you, Bayla. I wish I could sew. It's a good thing your Aunt Sarah is a seamstress. I'll bet she'd make dresses out of this for you and Evalyne and Rachel, too. What do you think about that?"

Havah unrolled a bolt of calico, knelt, and held it up to the child's face. Bayla's empty gray eyes showed no glimmer of recognition nor did she seem to be the slightest bit interested in the pink fabric. Havah set the bolt back on the table.

"Good morning, Mrs. Gitterman." Sol Mayer looked up from a stack of papers on the counter and smiled. He took a pencil from behind his ear. "It's a beautiful day."

"It's cold and cloudy." Havah pulled her shawl around her shoulders.

"It's always a beautiful day when a pretty face like yours graces my store. How may I help you today?"

Her cheeks heated. "The children . . . they need clothes. How much do you want for this calico?"

Reuven picked up a toy automobile from the shelf. He sat on the floor and rolled it along the rough boards. Arel took another car from the shelf, squatted beside him and made rumbling noises.

"Little boys never grow up," said Havah.

"I just want our boy to feel at home." Arel stood, brushed the dust from his trousers and patted Reuven's head. "Shall we take that car with us, son?"

"Are you rich, Uncle Arel?" asked Reuven.

"I suppose by old country standards I am."

Clearing his throat with an exaggerated cough, Sol dragged a cardboard box from behind the counter. "Before you spend your hard earned cash, take a peek in here."

Almost as tall as Bayla, the box brimmed with toys and clothes. Reuven followed and, with a cry of delight, found a tin automobile close to the top.

"My Zelda, of all people, took up a collection at the synagogue," said Sol as he directed Havah's attention to a rack of clothes behind the counter. "These are brand new. Zelda insisted. She said the children should have good clothes for services. Sarah gave her the sizes. There's a suit for your Lev, another for Reuven and one for the doctor's son, even though he's not Jewish." Sol winked. "Then feast your eyes on these beautiful dresses for Bayla and Rachel. Zelda handpicked these. I don't know what's come over her but I can't remember the last time I saw her so excited."

Arel fingered the seams of one of the suits. "Fine tailoring."

Havah blinked at the dresses. Some of them were silk with hand-tatted lace. "I'll be sure to thank Zelda when I see her."

Sol held up his hands as if to stop an oncoming train. "No, no. Don't do that. It'll bring about my demise if you do. She insisted on keeping it a secret."

Bayla took a doll with glossy black ringlets from the box. For a moment, Havah saw a flicker of a smile. Sitting on the floor, Bayla hugged the doll, pressing its porcelain cheek against hers.

"She still hasn't spoken?" asked Sol, shaking his head.

"No, not a word." Havah fished some coins from her purse.

"Gitterman money is no good in my store today. How many yards do you need?" He whisked the calico bolt off the table, shoved his papers aside and set it on the counter.

"We can't accept. You've given us so much already."

"Ten yards should do it. Let's make it fifteen for good measure. Get it? Good measure?" Sol chuckled. He took a large pair of shears from a drawer and cut the cloth. "Is there something wrong with the boy?"

Havah turned and watched her nephew limp between the rows of shelves. "Reuven, come here."

"Am I in trouble, Auntie?" He hobbled to her, wincing with each step.

"Of course not but you're walking like me. Did you hurt your foot?"

"No."

She knelt and pushed against the tips of his shoes with her thumb. "You're growing. Your shoes are too small." She unbuttoned them and pulled them off his feet. "It's time for a new pair. We'll save these for Elliott."

Sol pointed to a row of leather shoes on a top shelf. "Pick whatever you want, son. Happy Hanukkah."

"They're mine." Reuven snatched his too small shoes from Havah's hands and huddled in a corner, shaking and sobbing. "Papa made them. Papa! Papa! I don't want new shoes! Never! Never! *Never!*"

# CHAPTER NINE

Flames crackled between the logs in Florin Miklos' potbellied stove. His new clinic, wainscoted with walnut and half covered with beige flocked wallpaper, reflected the fire's warmth. Nikolai settled back against a leather upholstered chair and sipped champagne.

Florin's new gramophone held a place of honor on his treatment table. Florin leaned back in his swivel chair and propped up his stockinged feet beside the gramophone, his toes keeping time to the music.

"It's a shame the ladies couldn't join us tonight," he said. "Poor Catherine, what a shame to be ill on New Year's Eve. Such a shame."

"She can barely breathe." Ulrich paced the perimeter of the room. "Nikolai, are you sure she's going to be all right?"

"You've got to stop worrying over every sneeze, Ulrich," said Nikolai.

"She looked so pale."

"It's simply fatigue."

"There's influenza going around."

"She has no fever. It's a common cold. In a couple of weeks, with rest and proper nutrition, she'll make a full recovery. Don't take my word for it, let Florin examine her."

"I'm sure your diagnosis is accurate, doctor. It was kind of Oxana to stay home and look after her," said Dr. Miklos.

"She's an excellent nurse," said Nikolai. "Pavel taught her well."

Florin's broad brow crinkled. "I dare say the doctor could stand a dose of his own prescription. You don't look at all well, Kolyah. No, not at all well."

The grandfather clock in the corner chimed twelve times. Firecrackers popped in rapid fire succession, gunshots rang out and tin whistles shrilled. Nikolai listened to people singing and laughing outside. All these things gnawed at him and intensified his emptiness.

"To the Miklos Medical Office and Surgery and to 1906, may it be a year of peace and healing for us all." Florin raised his glass and inclined his head toward two medical certificates on the wall behind the desk. "To Dr. Nikolai Derevenko, my esteemed partner and surgeon par excellence."

Nikolai took a deep breath. "Florin, I hate to disappoint you, but I'm no longer fit for—"

Frenzied banging at the front door interrupted him. Setting his glass on the desk, Florin rose and hurried from the room. In a few minutes he burst back in with a little girl cradled in his massive arms. Blood from a wound on her leg made ever widening stains on his shirt.

Ulrich dropped his glass and moved the gramophone from the treatment table to the desk. Nikolai stood and went to the sink where he scrubbed his trembling hands and then prepared his surgical instruments.

Meanwhile, at Florin's side, a skinny boy in denim overalls hunched his shoulders and wiped his nose on his sleeve. His eyes, wide with terror, were trained on the girl.

In a dialect Nikolai strained to understand, the boy's words tumbled over each other. "I . . . I didn't mean no harm. Just celebrating New Year's Eve and all. We—me and my cousin—was just a-shootin' at the lamppost when—I missed and the bullet got Penny."

A revolver fell from his hand. He plopped down beside it. "Our folks is gone 'til tomorrow. Pa's gonna wup me. My sister ain't gonna die, is she? Please, God, don't let Penny die."

"We won't let Penny die, son, I promise." Florin laid the quivering girl on the treatment table. "Most certainly, Dr. Derevenko will see to that."

"My leg hurts." She clung to him. "Don't let him cut off my leg."

Noisy celebrations continued in the street just beyond the clinic walls. Nikolai moved to the treatment table, removed the girl's shoe and cut off her stocking, and was relieved to see that the wound did not look as bad as he had anticipated. The bullet had lodged in her calf and its removal would be a simple matter. Blood loss and shock were his biggest concerns.

"No one's going to cut off your leg, *lapochka*," he whispered and patted her pallid cheek.

"You promise?" She stopped crying and held onto his hand, her hazel eyes round with fear.

Not realizing it, he kissed her palm and whispered, "You will dance again, little Pora."

"Hey, Mister," said the boy as he scrambled to his feet. "We ain't rich or nothing but we ain't poor neither. I ain't asking for no handout, ya hear?"

"You misunderstand, son. Pora is Russian for, how you say, OK." Florin patted his shoulder and cast Nikolai a questioning glance.

"Come on son, let's go out to the waiting room." Ulrich knelt and picked up the gun, then tried to hand it to the boy.

"Unh uh." The boy crammed his hands into his overall pockets. "It ain't mine and I don' never wanna see it agin. I'm gonna stay right here with Penny."

"Your germs might make her sick," said Florin. "You wouldn't want that, would you?"

"Oh no, sir."

"Be a good lad and go with Mr. Dietrich to the waiting room."

"Yes, sir."

Ulrich stuck the gun in his trouser pocket, stood, grasped the boy's arm and ushered him out of the room.

As soon as the door shut behind them Florin, his piercing gaze still on Nikolai, whispered in Russian, "What's wrong with you, Kolyah?"

Huge tears welled in Penny's eyes and spilled down her cheeks. "You're going to cut off my leg, ain't you? That's why you're talking all funny like."

Nikolai squeezed her hand and gritted his teeth as unexpected rage drilled him. "I will kill anyone who dares to try. All of your arms and legs will be here when you wake up. I promise. Do you understand?"

"Doctor Derevenko, have you lost your mind?" Florin reached across the table and seized Nikolai's arm. "I'm putting the patient under before you scare her to death."

Florin's voice sounded tinny and far away. Nikolai's chest burned as he watched him place an anesthesia mask over Penny's nose and mouth. With each drop of ether he felt as if he would suffocate. He stared at her plump leg and choked. Even for a first year intern it was basic surgery, yet sweat loosened his grip on the scalpel as he held his breath and poised it over the wound.

# CHAPTER TEN

*Thorns snagged Havah's skirts and slashed her legs as she trudged through the forest. Smoke billowed above the trees and engulfed the red moon. An arm grabbed her from behind. With every ounce of strength she tried to wrestle free of the monster. The louder she screamed the tighter it gripped. She kicked it with her heel. It cried out and slapped her.*

"Havah, wake up!"

"Arel?" She fought to open her eyes and then raised her hand to her stinging cheek. "Did you have to hit so hard?"

"You kick like a mule." He sat up, turned on the lamp and rubbed his shin. "I'm glad you don't have hooves like one."

"Did I wake anyone else?"

"Mrs. Hutton hasn't called the police yet, so we're okay."

"I can't sleep now." Havah sat up and picked up a book from the bed stand.

"What are you reading?"

"*The Bishop's Carriage*. It's a wonderful romance. I can't wait to see what happens next."

"This." He kissed the back of her neck and slipped his hand down the front of her nightgown. She shuddered with delight, pressed her back against him and closed the book.

"I'm the big bad wolf." With a low growl, he nibbled her earlobe.

"Don't hurt her," whispered a child's voice. "Please."

Startled, Havah looked up to see Bayla, almost dreamlike in the pale lamplight, clutching her doll. Arel let out a sigh and Havah patted the blanket.

"It's okay, Bayla. Uncle Arel wouldn't hurt me."

"No. No. No." Bayla hugged her doll, stepped backwards and shook her head.

Havah slowly rolled out of the bed, cautious not to frighten the child. Once she reached Bayla, Havah sat on the floor and pulled the child on to her lap.

"It's my fault," whispered Bayla, her eyes wide.

"What's your fault?"

"Mama died."

"Did you make her sick?"

"No, but then Orev died."

"Did you shoot him?"

"No. But . . ."

"But what?"

"Then . . . then . . ." Bayla buried her face in Havah's nightgown. "Papa . . . and . . . Leah . . . and . . . and . . . I promised Pora I wouldn't let anyone hurt her."

Arel knelt beside them and bundled Bayla in his arms.

"Do you have power to stop floods?"

"No."

"Can you make lightning flash or winds blow?"

"No."

"Could you have stopped those bad men from hurting Pora?"

"No."

"Then what makes you think it's your fault that they died?"

"Because it happens every time I love someone," whispered Bayla.

"Listen to me," said Arel. "You're just a little girl. None of it was your fault. You're safe now."

For the first time since her arrival, Bayla smiled. She laid her head on Arel's chest and closed her eyes.

# CHAPTER ELEVEN

Two sweaters and a coat could not warm Nikolai. Searing pain hindered his every breath and his head throbbed. He leaned against the high backed chair and watched rain fall outside the bedroom window as he played his flute. Music did little to soothe his savage breast. Nothing could.

"*Raisins and Almonds*, I always loved that melody."

"Who's there?" Nikolai's heart pounded. The voice sounded like Pavel's. He set down his flute and looked around the empty room.

Only the rustling wind answered.

"Dr. Nikolai, can I sit on your lap?"

The flute rolled off his knees and as he bent to retrieve it he looked up at a little girl with sandy braids.

"Pora?"

"I'm a ballerina." She grinned, her hazel eyes sparkling, and spun around on her toes.

"Me, too."

"Tova?" He dropped the flute again, rubbed his eyes and stared at the tiny child with scarlet curls at his other side.

"Goodbye, Dr. Nikolai."

The girls melted into the wall.

"The old man might've been right, Kolyah. You should've just joined his orchestra and avoided all that nasty blood. Ugh. There's nothing nastier than the blood of children."

"Pavel?"

"It's all on your hands you know—my blood—their blood."

"I'm dreaming." Nikolai stared at his clean palms.

"That's what I admire about you. You never let your emotions control you."

"Stop, it, Pasha!" Pain tightened Nikolai's stomach. Acid vomit burned his throat.

"Dr. Nikolai Derevenko," said Pavel. "You were always the fortress of self-restraint, the epitome of reserve."

Pavel's apparition disappeared, then reappeared by the window and grinned.

"Tag, you're 'it,' Doctor!"

Nikolai sprang from the chair, then lifted it and hefted it over his head. Pain shot through his shoulder. "Stop it now or I'll—"

"You'll what? Break my nose, crack my skull? How do you propose to do that? I'm dead."

The chair fell from Nikolai's hands. His knees buckled and he dropped to the floor. Moaning, he slammed the back of his head against the wall to block out Pavel's accusations.

"Kolyah?" Oxana's cold hands on his blazing cheeks startled him. Her slender face replaced her brother's. "Have you lost your mind?"

"It was . . . he was . . . Pasha—here." He fought to catch his breath.

"You're going to bed, my husband."

With her arm to support him, he struggled to his feet. It was all he could do to take five steps and collapse on the bed. He grasped her hand.

"You should divorce me."

"Why bother? I'll be a widow soon enough."

By midnight alcohol rubs and cold compresses failed to lower Nikolai's fever. On the contrary, it seemed to rise with each passing hour. The room smelled of camphor mingled with bile and vomit. Ulrich's head and tense shoulders ached from sitting up most of the night. He bathed Nikolai's forehead and hollow cheeks with a wet cloth. How could a person be so thin and still live?

His voice a painful rasp, Nikolai whispered, "Please . . . I . . . beg . . . you . . . Florin . . . let me die."

"Request denied Kolyah," said Dr. Miklos. "I expect you back at the clinic first thing Monday morning."

"I can't."

"Of course you can't. No doubt, you can't. But when you've recovered and regained your strength, the tools of our trade will be there."

"I'm not coming back. I quit." Nikolai's eyes rolled back.

Florin dabbed spittle from the corner of Nikolai's mouth with a towel. Then he took the thermometer from a glass of alcohol on the bed stand and held it under Nikolai's tongue. After three moments of anxious silence, he withdrew it and winced.

"One hundred five degrees." He returned the thermometer to the glass. "It can't go much higher."

"You've got to fight, Kolyah!" cried Ulrich. "Don't let the bastards win."

Nikolai opened his eyes. "Take good care of them for me. Send . . . Vasily . . . to art school . . . tell him . . . I'm proud of him. Always was." He closed his eyes. ". . . tell Oxana . . ."

"*Gott verdammt*, Kolyah."

Tell her yourself." "Tell me what, Kolyah? Please," whispered Oxana, who had labored with tireless desperation all night, slumped in the chair beside the bed, her narrow cheeks grey with exhaustion. Despite her obvious determination and iron will, she looked nearly as fragile as her husband.

Ulrich laid a gentle hand on her shoulder and whispered in Russian, "Go to your room and rest, Frau Derevenko. Catherine's prepared your bed."

"My place is here with him." Oxana kept her eyes fixed on Nikolai.

"If you don't get some rest, your place will be a pine box," said Florin. "He needs your strength, dear lady. He has none of his own."

She took Ulrich's offered forearm and rose with some effort. "You'll call me if there's any change, Dr. Miklos," she said with a weak, yet demanding voice.

"Get some sleep. He'll be here when you wake. He'll be here, I promise."

"*Spasibo*. Thank you."

Ulrich watched her stoop-shouldered reluctance as she left the room, then he shut the door behind her. When he was certain she could not hear, he whispered, "Are you sure you can keep that promise, Doctor?"

"No."

Leaning back until he propped the high-backed chair on the other side of the bed on two legs, Florin yawned. His tangled red hair, bushy mustache and beard stubble gave him the appearance of a lion. He set the chair down on all fours. It groaned under his weight. He leaned forward and pressed the back of his hand against Nikolai's flushed cheek.

"Stop, Pasha, don't . . ." Nikolai clawed Florin's hand and opened his eyes. Hacking coughs shook Nikolai's spare shoulders and jarred Ulrich with each desperate gasp.

Nikolai rose up on his elbows. “Gavrel, forgive me!”

Several times in his delirium, Nikolai called on the dead to absolve him. Then, like a bird shot in midflight, he dropped back against the pillows.

“It’s so cold,” he whispered. A coughing fit, so violent it shook the bed, seized him. When it subsided, he seemed to stop breathing altogether.

Florin mopped his dripping forehead with his shirt sleeve. Then he tucked in his stethoscope’s earpieces and pressed the bell against Nikolai’s rawboned chest. For several minutes he listened, shifting it from one side to the other, his eyes moist and wide. As he removed the earpieces, he let the stethoscope drop from his titan fist to the bed.

“Get Mrs. Derevenko and the boy before it’s too late.”

Dizzied by rage and disbelief, Ulrich searched the doctor’s face.

“You mean he’s. . . ?”

“It’s out of my hands.”

# CHAPTER TWELVE

Havah's leg blazed. Flipping onto her back, she held her breath and let it out in short exhalations. She closed her eyes and listened to the rain drumming on the pavement outside, hoping it would lull her back to sleep. But no, the sound reverberated in her head and grew louder. She turned onto her side, pulled her knee up to her chest and massaged her calf. Nothing she did stopped the pain. She sat up and reached for her cane by the side of the bed.

Arel rolled over. "Nightmare?"

"Just the one that never ends."

"Did you take your medicine?"

"It doesn't help."

"You've been awake since the telephone call?"

"I can't stop thinking about him. It will never end, will it Arel?"

"Someday good people like Ulrich and Dr. Nikolai will change things."

"Do you believe that?"

"Don't you, Havah? He saved your life."

"But he couldn't save himself. I don't know what I believe anymore." She ran her fingertips over Arel's scarred cheek. "Go back to sleep. It's only four o'clock."

"Where are you going?"

"To the kitchen for some hot chocolate. Would you like some?"

Only his snoring answered her invitation. How could anyone fall asleep that fast? She envied him.

She donned her dressing gown and went across the hall to peek in on the girls to make sure the storm had not disturbed them. Both of them, cuddled in Rachel's crib, slept peacefully.

While Bayla's bedwetting and easy tears continued, at least she had found her voice—a sign of trust and acceptance the doctors had said. Havah kissed the slumbering child's forehead and tucked the blanket around the girls. Why were children forced to experience such torture? Even the Baal Shem Tov would be hard pressed to answer such a question. Havah tiptoed from the room.

Rain dashed against the windows and pelted the roof. Leaning most of her weight on her cane, she held tight to the banister with her free hand and hobbled down the stairs.

Pain stabbed her with every step. Dr. Miklos had told her if she had Causalgia it could spread to her other leg, the good one. She had not said anything to Arel but it had already begun to happen. What purpose would it serve? In time, he would know. With extra mouths to feed, he had enough to worry about.

Upon entering the kitchen she glanced out the window over the sink. The young elm pitched and weaved with the wind and rain. She marveled at how fast the weather could change in this place. Only a week ago the lawn had been covered with snow. Days later the temperatures rose and the snow melted.

In a sudden flash, a white figure darted behind the tree.

"Mrs. Hutton's cat. Poor thing's liable to drown in this. I can only hope."

The thunder seemed to voice its agreement in Yiddish. She grinned at the thought. What language did the Almighty speak? Was Hebrew truly the sacred tongue as the sages taught? Perhaps He spoke German since Ulrich seemed to hear Him so well.

She sat on one chair and propped her leg onto another. To take her mind off her pain, she shut her eyes and played the awareness game she had devised to imagine what Rachel and Yussel's world must be like. First, she concentrated on feeling and touch. A chill breathed through the window and stung her cheeks. Strands of hair tickled her nose. Next she focused on scent. Supper's chicken soup aroma still saturated the air like a fragrant cloud. Then sound; Kreplakh yipped in her sleep. The walls creaked and whined, sounding incredibly human. A floor beneath the bedroom, Arel's snores were loud enough to be heard over the storm and mixed with the noise of rain into a gentle rhythmic rumble that calmed her. Her head slumped forward and a delicious wave of sleep washed over her.

She had almost succumbed when the voice she had thought was the wind cried again. Opening her eyes she cocked her head. The voice was clear and familiar.

"I hate you, God," cried Lev.

She jumped off the chair and switched on the lights. Then she hobbled to the back door and swung it open.

"Lev Resnick, have you lost your mind?"

"Leave me alone."

Her feet sank into mud as she sloshed through the yard.

"What kind of mother would I be if I did?"

Raindrops splashed off his eyelashes. His purple lips quivered. He squinted at light from the window.

"My mother's dead. I don't need you. I'm a man."

"Then act like one."

With his nightgown whipping around his spindly legs and his smooth skin, Lev was merely a taller version of Reuven. Had he been a small boy, she would have gathered him into her arms and carried him inside. Not knowing what to do, she crossed her arms and looked up at him. "Let's go inside. You'll catch your death."

"Good. Let me catch pneumonia and die like Dr. Nikolai."

"He's not dead."

"Don't lie to me. I heard the telephone."

"Lev, do you really think I'd lie about that?"

"What about the call? You were crying."

"I was crying for joy. The doctor said it was a miracle. Dr. Nikolai rallied and his fever broke."

Lev slumped over Havah's shoulders and crushed her in a shivering embrace as he emptied himself in torrents of pent up emotion. From their first meeting Lev, then nine, had regarded her with open hostility and suspicion. Joy mingled with sorrow surged through her, for he did not pull away when she embraced him. She offered no comforting words. To say anything would be like interrupting the sacred *Kol Nidre* prayer on the Day of Atonement.

Finally he quieted, raised his head, wiped his swollen eyes with the back of his hand and whispered, "I'm cold."

"So am I. Let's make some hot chocolate."

"I'd like that."

Arm in arm they walked toward the house until a stringy vine tangled around her ankle. Muddy lawn slapped her face. Spitting out wet grass and dirt, she pushed against the ground and forced herself upright.

He bent and offered his hand. She grasped it and pulled herself to her feet. A sharp pain pierced through her knee and her legs buckled. He hefted her into his arms.

"You're almost as light as Bayla."

Once back inside, he lowered her onto a chair. Looking down, his smile suddenly turned to horror. Her face burned. Desperate attempts to cover her gnarled foot with the wet hem of her robe failed. She turned her head from his prying eyes and twisted a lock of wet hair around her fingers.

"Who did this to you, Aunt Havah, the bastards in Kishinev?"

"They didn't," said Fruma Ya'el who stood at the doorway with a stack of towels and dry clothes. "I did."

Although Lev did not mean to stare, his young aunt's cruel disfigurement fascinated, sickened and angered him. How could his gentle grandmother do such damage and why?

Questions coursed through his mind as he exchanged his wet clothes for dry since she refused to answer them until he did. Leaving his pajamas in a soggy heap on the bathroom floor he hurried back to the living room where Bubbe had lit a fire in the fireplace.

On the sofa, Havah, a blanket tucked around her like a cocoon, curled up with her head in Bubbe's lap. Her face was paper-white next to her black hair. In her sleep she looked as fragile as his mother's porcelain dishes that were destroyed in Odessa. She mumbled something that he did not understand.

Bubbe held her finger to her lips, then patted the sofa to her other side. In a sudden rush of exhaustion, he couched beside her. She drew him close with one arm and kissed his forehead. For a while the crackling of the fire was the only sound in the room.

"Life hasn't been kind to you, has it, Lev?"

He shook his head and, without realizing it, balled his hands into tight fists. She curled her hands around his, massaging them with her thumbs.

"You blame the Christians for everything, don't you?"

"They're beasts. Look what they've done to us."

"What about Dr. Nikolai or Professor Dietrich, do you blame them, too?"

"Of course not, they're different."

"And who did this to you—a priest maybe?" Bubbe traced his scar across his mouth with her fingertip. "How many times did I hide you under my bed just so that father of yours, he should . . . *shah* . . . it's bad luck to speak ill of the dead."

"I'm glad someone killed him. I wish someone had done it sooner."

"Hush!" She pressed her palm against his mouth, and then spit between two fingers of her other hand. "Don't tempt the Evil Eye."

Lev's hands relaxed and he grinned. For all his grandmother's wisdom and practicality she still clung to peasant superstitions. Nonetheless, she had been his greatest ally when it came to his vicious father. Many times she had rescued him from certain death until Papa sobered up. Lev saw only kindness in her brown eyes and the crinkled lines around them.

"Why did you chop up Aunt Havah's foot?"

"Do you know what frostbite is?"

"Sure."

"I've never seen it that bad. Her toes were blacker than tar. It's a wonder she has any feet at all. Her fever was so high. What else could I do?"

"You had no choice, Bubbe."

"Remember that, Lev."

# CHAPTER THIRTEEN

Vasily scrutinized the sketch propped on his drawn up knees. Satisfied he had captured Mrs. Gitterman's likeness, her smile at once joyful and melancholy, he finished the last few pencil strokes and then smudged in the shading with his fingertips. Even though he had never seen her ebony hair unbraided or unbound, he rendered it as he imagined it, cascading over her shoulders in a riot of curls.

Leaning against the sofa in front of the fireplace, he stretched out his legs and warmed his stockinged feet. He set the leather-bound sketchbook Mary Alice had given him for his thirteenth birthday on the floor, the same birthday he received a set of oil paints from a mysterious Russian doctor she met in the art store.

In the short time he had been in Kansas City, the Gitterman home had become Vasily's sanctuary. Here he could count on noisy children to occupy his mind. Bayla's squeals from the back yard assured him she would be all right. He basked in the sound of her voice above all others, chattering in both Yiddish and English. Upstairs, Mrs. Gitterman sang a lullaby to Rachel who protested being put down for her afternoon nap.

Brushing eraser crumbs from his trousers, he cupped his other hand to catch them as he rose, padded to the kitchen and tossed them into the wastebasket. He looked out the window and watched the children play the American game called baseball.

Jeffrey tossed a ball to Reuven who swung a long wooden stick called a bat. Reuven chortled with glee when he tapped the ball out into the yard where it rolled between Mendel's legs and on past him to the fence. Reuven dropped the bat and raced over three folded towels, the bases, strategically placed in a diamond pattern around the yard. David scurried after the ball, picked it up and threw it to Jeffrey. It sailed over Jeffrey's head, missing Evalyne's outstretched hand. Reuven slid on his backside into an old sofa cushion called home plate.

Lev hoisted Reuven up onto his shoulders, danced around and yelled, "Hurray! It's a home run!"

Vasily breathed in the new-grass scent on the air sweeping through the open window and held it in his lungs. Winter's stubborn chill would soon surrender to spring. He exhaled.

Behind him uneven footsteps roused him from his thoughts. His heart suddenly thumped as if he had been running the bases with the children. He turned away from the window.

"The floor isn't a good place for something so elegant." Mrs. Gitterman's onyx eyes twinkled. She cradled his sketchbook in the crook of one arm.

From Tatko's stories of her willful strength, Vasily had expected her to be taller and stouter, yet she stood half a head shorter than he and looked delicate enough to shatter at the slightest touch.

He tried to think of something clever to say, but his tongue stuck to the roof of his mouth. "Thank you," was all that he could muster as he took the proffered tablet from her.

She took a bottle of milk from the icebox and set it on the kitchen table. Then she cut two slices of yellow sponge cake. "Would you like some?"

"Yes, please."

On tiptoe, she reached for glasses from the cabinet. He plopped his book on the table and nearly upset the milk as he rushed to help her. The music of her laughter tickled his ears.

Once the glasses and plates were safely set on the table, she sat. "It was kind of you to come and visit the children, Vasya."

"They're my friends." He sat on the chair across from her.

"You should be out playing with them."

"I'm not very good at athletics."

"Neither am I, now, anyway." She poured milk into the glasses. "I used to run faster than some of the boys."

Without meaning to, he stared at her feet. He recognized her soft brown leather shoes. "Reb Wolinsky made those for you. He said they were special for a special person."

"They're tailor made for a cripple."

"I'm sorry I—"

"No, I'm sorry. That was mean of me. He was such a dear man."

Her tears flooded Vasily with remorse. The last thing in the world he wanted was to make her cry. He took a bite of cake, washed it down with cold milk and tried to think of something to say.

"This cake is wonderful, Mrs. Gitterman. May I have the recipe?"

"You certainly may, but only if you call me Havah. Mrs. Gitterman sounds old and dried up, doesn't it? Do you cook? You never cease to amaze me, Vasya. Remind me to write it down for you before you leave."

"I have to cook or starve. Oxana—Mother—is dangerous in the kitchen, Mrs.—" He could feel the heat on his face. To speak her name made the back of his head prickle. Could any name given under heaven be more beautiful? "Havah."

"May I see your drawings?"

"Yes, of course. I mean, please."

By the time he answered she had already opened the book to her portrait. Her smile thrilled him.

"It's like looking in a mirror."

"You really like it?"

"Yes, really."

"Then it's yours." He carefully tore out the page and handed it to her.

"I must have Itzak make a proper frame. May I ask you a favor?"

"Anything."

"Could you draw one of Arel, too?"

Reality crashed in on Vasily and he tried to hide his disappointment. He would rather she had asked him to clean her toilet than draw her husband.

"I have lots of school work." He downed the final bit of his cake.

"School work comes first. It can wait until you have time." She picked up the book and opened it to what had been the next sketch after her portrait. "Oh, Vasya, this is amazing."

In the drawing, Gavrel sat at his work table, hammer poised over an upside down shoe, his head cocked to one side, mouth wide open with laughter. Leah stood behind him, arms wrapped around his neck, her cheek pressed against his, shining with adoration.

"And I thought their betrothal was a mistake." Shaking her head, Havah turned the page and pointed to a colorful portrait of Mary Alice in all of her feathered glory. "Is this your mother?"

"No, she was kind of like my Aunt. Ivona would be a waste of paper." He gnawed at his thumbnail.

Havah curled her hand around his wrist and pulled his thumb away from his mouth. "You're left handed, aren't you?"

"So are you."

"I didn't used to be." She held out her right hand so he could see the scar that made a pale pink trail from one side of her palm to the other. "I can't write with this one anymore."

She turned back to the book and flipped the page to a drawing of four-year-old Pora in her nightgown on her bare tiptoes, arms arched over her head. Next was a sketch of little Tova on the floor with a bowl in her lap and a spoon in her mouth.

"You're so much like your father. He adores children. The little ones in Kishinev, Tuli and the others, he treated them as if they were his own. He should live to see your children's children."

"He won't."

"He lived through pneumonia. You'll see. He's strong."

"He's dead inside."

"You don't really believe that, do you?"

In that moment, she turned to the caricature he had never intended for anyone to see and covered her mouth. The book dropped from her lap to the floor creasing the page. He slid off the chair, picked up the book, smoothed the paper with the heel of his hand and gazed at his artwork.

A tangled mess of white hair hung unevenly about Tatko's sunken cheeks. Half in shadow, his expressionless eyes, deep within skeletal hollows, shone like glazed marbles. A serpent wound about his neck like a muffler.

"It's a terrible drawing," whispered Vasily.

Havah knelt beside him. "You're very talented."

# CHAPTER FOURTEEN

Nikolai studied his reflection in the oval mirror above the large china basin. He ran his fingers through his hair that had changed overnight from pale blond to silver white. Gray hollows framed his fatigue-dulled eyes. Shaving soap made a frothy beard and obscured his gaunt cheeks.

From a doctor's perspective his own recovery bewildered him. He had been at death's door, ready and willing to pass through and beyond. Sunlight glinted off his razor. With surgical precision he shaved off a month's growth. Then he bent over the basin and splashed off the soap. He straightened and, sickened by his cadaverous visage he turned from it, examined the prominent veins in his wrist and poised the blade. Perhaps Hyram had chosen the best escape after all. A simple longitudinal incision would end his woe.

"All hail the great physician who set out to save the world," said Ulrich.

Startled, Nikolai glanced up to see Ulrich's reflection behind his. He stood in the doorway and raised his coffee cup.

"Get out!" shouted Nikolai.

"I pay the rent." Ulrich stepped into the room and kicked the door shut. "I see why Ivona left you."

"You see why that cheap tramp left *me*?" Nikolai threw down the razor and spun around.

"It's a pity she's dead. Vasily would be better off with a prostitute than a dispassionate doctor whose heart pumps antiseptic."

Ulrich closed the distance between them in one stride and slapped Nikolai. Nikolai's cheek stung and chest tightened. He balled his trembling hand and punched Ulrich's stomach.

With a loud grunt, Ulrich doubled over. The cup fell from his hand, splattering coffee across Catherine's pale blue carpet. Momentary remorse filled Nikolai until Ulrich coughed and then straightened, a smirk on his lips.

"You let them down, you pathetic failure."

Ulrich's words struck like a hail of bullets. How could he say such things after seeing for himself the horrors in Kishinev? Anger surged through him as Ulrich's verbal barrage continued.

"Stop!" Nikolai slammed his fist into Ulrich's face.

Ulrich stumbled backward over a chair and landed on his back. He rolled over, rose to his knees and grabbed the chair. He flung it, hitting the back of Nikolai's legs. Nikolai's knees exploded with pain as they hit the floor. Then Ulrich surprised him with a left hook to his jaw. The room went dark.

Nikolai came to soaking wet and squinted up at Ulrich who stood over him holding an empty wash basin. Nikolai raised his hands, palms up. Ulrich set the basin aside, reached down, grasped Nikolai's forearm and helped him to his feet. Then he pulled a revolver from his trouser pocket and put into Nikolai's hand.

"Here, take this. It's faster than a razor."

Dazed, Nikolai rolled it over in his hand. Ulrich curved his fingers around Nikolai's so they both clasped the butt and pressed barrel hard against Nikolai's temple. Nikolai tried to pull the gun away but Ulrich held fast.

"Don't fight it," said Ulrich.

Nikolai shut his eyes.

"Get it over with." Ulrich intoned.

Taking a deep breath, Nikolai pressed his finger against the trigger.

"Give Vasily a day to remember," whispered Ulrich.

At the mention of his son's name Nikolai wrestled his sweaty hand from Ulrich's grip. The gun clattered to the floor.

"Damn you." Nikolai shoved Ulrich against the wall and drew back his fist.

"Go ahead, if it makes you feel better." Ulrich's eye and lower lip had already begun to swell.

Nikolai's rage-fueled strength suddenly dissipated. He unclenched his fist and sank to the floor. "I . . . I don't know what's come over me."

Ulrich sat beside him, took his handkerchief from his shirt pocket and dabbed at a cut above his eye. "It's not your fault, Kolyah."

Ulrich's face blurred and images flooded Nikolai's mind. He could no longer blot out the shocked expression on Devorah's face. Once more Hyram smiled as he pulled the trigger. The shot still reverberated in Nikolai's ears.

"It wasn't enough to rape and kill—they sliced her open and ripped her unborn son from her. And those innocent girls—they hacked them to pieces—their limbs—dear God—how can I ever cut into human flesh again?"

When his tears subsided and he could speak, he whispered, "Ulrich, I almost pulled the trigger. I . . . could've . . . you . . . you tried to kill me."

"Nah. The gun's not loaded."

# CHAPTER FIFTEEN

In the month since their daughter's birth Shayndel and Itzak referred to her only as little sister and refused to tell anyone what her name would be.

"Why the secrecy?" Havah asked. "You'll just have to wait," Shayndel would say and wink at Itzak who merely shrugged his shoulders and smiled.

"You see, Havaleh," he said. "My hands are tied."

Havah had even resorted to bribery with Mendel and David. Despite her offer of candy, both of the boys swore they did not know their sister's name. Since she had never known either of the twins to be able to keep a secret, she knew Shayndel had not told them.

Finally the day of the naming ceremony came. Every living person Havah held dear from the family who had adopted her and claimed her as its own, to the friends who had shown her true faith without religion, gathered around Itzak and Shayndel. Havah's heart swelled with so much gratitude she feared her chest would burst.

"Life is such a gift," said Catherine, her emerald-green eyes fixed on the newborn bundled in a prayer shawl in the crook of Yussel's arm.

*"Eloheinu v'elohei, imoteinu k'yemi ha'yalda ha'zoht l'aviha—"* Yussel chanted the prayer. "—our God and God of our ancestors, sustain this child for her father and mother. Let her be called in Israel Tikvah daughter of Itzak and Shayndel."

After the final amen Fruma Ya'el shook her head. "Who in our families was ever named Tikvah?"

"No one that I know of," Itzak replied.

"Nu? How does this name honor the dead?"

"We've had enough of the dead, Mama." Shayndel's plump cheeks flushed. "We want to honor the living."

Fruma Ya'el's frown softened. Then she lifted little Tikvah from Yussel's arms and cuddled her against her shoulder. "She should live to enjoy prosperity and happiness."

"Tikva's a beautiful name. It means hope," said Havah.

"Hope," whispered Nikolai under his breath.

His face had lost its deathly pallor, yet his warm smile could not mask the somber chill behind it, nor did his spectacles hide his haunted eyes.

"They never leave you, do they, Dr. Nikolai?" asked Havah. "Those ghosts are like uninvited guests that appear when you least expect it."

"I tried to save them." He hung his head. "I failed."

"Never say it again, do you hear? You're a hero."

"She speaks for all of us," said Arel.

"As a friend of mine so aptly put it, Kolyah, you're only one man, not God. Now break out that magic flute of yours and accompany me." Ulrich sat down at the carved upright piano he had given the Abromoviches in honor of their new princess.

Just as Ulrich played the first few notes of *Raisins and Almonds* Reuven tugged at Yussel's sleeve and asked in a stage whisper, "Zaydeh, why do people kill other people?"

Yussel leaned forward on his cane. "I don't know, little apple. All I know is the Almighty is merciful."

"How can you say that, Zaydeh? When we light candles for our dead, it'll start a bonfire. You call *that* mercy?" cried Lev, his voice brittle and heavy with disgust.

An uncomfortable hush fell over the room. Havah shifted her gaze from Lev to Yussel who tilted his head and smiled, undaunted by Lev's outburst.

"Lev, come here." He beckoned with his index finger.

"Why?"

"Obey your grandfather." Arel pointed.

Lev glowered at him, shrugged his shoulders and moved to where Yussel waited. "Okay. Here I am, Zaydeh. Now what?"

Yussel set his cane aside and covered Lev's eyes with his hands. The boy flinched and tried to pry them off.

"What do you feel?" asked Yussel.

"Your bony hands."

"You have a sharp wit. Take care not to stab yourself with it. What else do you feel?"

"This is stupid."

"Perhaps." Yussel held his hands firm. "Humor an old man."

"I don't understand. What do you mean what do I feel?" Lev crammed his hands into his pockets.

"What do you feel on the skin of your arms or your face or your hands? Are the pennies in your pocket smooth or rough?"

"Fine. I'll play your game. I feel sweat between my *tokhes* cheeks."

"Um! Lev said *tokhes*," whispered Evalyne and covered her mouth.

"It is warm in here, Evie. There's a little moisture between mine as well." Yussel nodded. "Perhaps we should move on to sound. Tell me what you hear, Lev."

"I hear Bayla and Evie's giggles."

"Anything else."

For a moment Lev stood still, bit his lip and cocked his head. "Kreplakh's snoring under the sofa. Tikvah's bawling."

"Good, Lev. Now, what do you smell?"

"What do I smell?" Lev's voice scaled up an octave with each word.

"You have a nose?"

"Sure."

"And it works?"

"All right. All right. I smell . . . mm . . . sponge cake and apple pie. Coffee. Aunt Cate's lavender perfume and Uncle Wolf's nasty cigar."

"You see, Lev, not all smells are pleasant. Not all sounds are sweet. But . . . *we are* alive. *That*, my son, *is* God's mercy."

# EPILOGUE

Havah stood on the front porch and watched Lev, Reuven and Bayla, dressed in their new clothes for the first day of school. It took all of her strength to resist the inclination to sweep Bayla up and carry her back into the house, but Arel's words from the night before prevented her.

"Don't you see, Havah? Being with other children will help her heal."

"Rachel and Elliott are other children."

"They're babies."

"But she's still having nightmares."

"Havah. Havaleh, you of all people know that keeping her at home won't make the bad dreams stop. It will hurt her more if we hold her back. She'll be too far behind the other kids in school."

"I can teach her at home. Besides, the school year's almost over."

None of her arguments would change his mind. When Dr. Miklos who had stopped in for a visit agreed with him, Havah conceded.

Havah came back to the present when Bayla sat down on the sidewalk, one arm tight around her doll and popped her thumb in her mouth, all because Reuven made fun of her for taking her doll to school. If only Arel could see this, he would know she was right.

"Aw come on, Bayla," said Reuven. "Take your dumb old doll. You're gonna make us all tardy."

Bayla's sniffs turned to sobs.

"It's okay, chatterbox. Reuven just doesn't understand." Lev crouched beside her. He held his ear against the doll's lips. "What's that, Miss Tova? Dolls need to learn to read and write, too?"

"Aw, dolls don't learn nothing." Reuven rolled his eyes. "They're just made out of sawdust and stuff."

"Oh, yes, I'll tell him." Lev grinned and winked at Havah as he continued to listen to Miss Tova.

"Tell *him* what?" Reuven scowled.

"She says to tell you that dolls don't learn *anything*." He knocked off Reuven's cap. "Ha! Miss Tova speaks better English than you." He hoisted Bayla up onto his shoulders. "Now we really need to hurry."

"Wait for me!" Reuven grabbed for his cap and stumbled after them.

Bayla turned and waved. "Goodbye, Auntie Havah. See you after school."

"I guess Poppy's right." Havah eased down on the porch swing.

"Poppy at work," said Rachel who sat on the porch floor willowing her fingers through Kreplakh's fur.

"That's right, smarty girl, Poppy's at work."

The fragrance of daffodils wafted over Havah and sent her mind back to Natalya where her mother filled vases with them. Every autumn Havah helped her transplant the bulbs. Their little house would be surrounded by a glade of yellow the following spring. Since then Havah had vowed, no matter where she lived, her home would be surrounded by her mother's favorite flower.

"Putt-putt car coming, Mama." Rachel stood and pointed. "I don't hear anything." Havah looked down the empty street. "I swear, Rukhel Shvester, you could hear a flea buzz in St. Louis."

"Me and Zaydie gots special ears."

She grinned and crawled backwards down the porch steps. Ever vigilant, Kreplakh ran ahead of her, then sat and waited for her mistress to take hold of her harness. Then she guided Rachel to the sidewalk.

Although Havah trusted the dog to protect her daughter, she feared the child might let go and run out into the street. She rose from the swing and walked behind them.

A familiar automobile turned the corner at the end of the block. The sun glinted off the Rambler's glossy hood and chrome wheel spokes. Its engine backfired as it came to a stop in front of the house.

A woman wearing a wide-brimmed hat tilted fashionably to one side adorned with a large bow emerged from under the car's canopy. Her dress boasted yards of expensive lace.

Instead of the usual formal and haughty greeting Havah expected, the woman knelt, pinched Rachel's cheek and said, "Good morning, Rukhel Shvester. Say hello to your Auntie Zelda."

With a mixture of joy and astonishment, Havah marveled at seeing Mrs. High Society with her perfectly coifed hair and fine jewelry here in her living room, cuddling Rachel in the rocking chair, and singing a familiar lullaby from the old country in a tender, melodious voice.

*"'In dem bais ha migdash*
*In a vinkle kheyder*
*zitz de almoneh bas Tzion aleyn.'*
*In the temple*
*In a small corner*
*Sits the widow alone, daughter of Zion.'"*

When Zelda finished the song a thousand questions raced through Havah's mind, but it seemed irreverent to ask any of them. Nestled against the lacy bodice, Rachel had drifted off to sleep. Zelda's violet eyes were distant clouds and her cheeks glowed in the sunlight.

"It's been a long time since my Wendy was this small," she whispered. Then, almost in the same breath she said, "Barry's at the head of his class in medical school and he's engaged to be married."

Havah started as if a door had just slammed behind her. So this was the reason for the visit. It would be just like Zelda Mayer to make a special trip to gloat over her triumph and boast about her nephew the doctor.

"Of course," said Havah. "He's brilliant."

Not gloating at all, Zelda cocked her head and winked. "It never occurred to you he'd stop mooning over you and find someone else, did it? We women are funny little creatures, aren't we? We're jealous of others who have what we claim we don't want. Ah, how I've envied you, Havah."

"Me?"

"Why should I envy you? I have it all, don't I?"

Havah nodded.

"I'd give it all up for just one ounce of what you have."

"But I'm—"

"Crippled? No, dear. I'm the one who's crippled." Lowering her voice, Zelda stroked Rachel's cheek and continued in Yiddish. "When Papa chanted Torah, I heard the voice of God."

"The man in the photograph?"

"It seems out of place in my grand mansion, doesn't it?"

"I didn't mean—"

"Of course you did, Havaleh. Let me speak while I have the courage."

The language of Zelda's youth flowed from her like fresh spring water. Her face had lost its harshness and her liquid gaze held Havah captive.

"Mama was his *beshert*, his other half. Not a day went by that I didn't hear them sing their deep love for each other and for me. It was a perfect life, Havah. Perfect and simple.

"We heard about pogroms in other places. Papa assured me the Almighty would protect us. Why should I doubt him? He was a cantor. He'd devoted his life to serving Adoshem. Why should he not be rewarded for his faithfulness?"

Zelda's smile faded into a painful grimace. She reached over and grasped Havah's forearm.

"On my sixteenth birthday, Mama made a special dinner to celebrate. But before I could take a bite, those hyenas broke in, shouting curses.

"'Hide, Zeldie!' Mama yelled. It was the last thing she ever said to me. They ravaged her over and over. Papa tried to stop them but they beat him senseless. When he came to, it was too late.

"Papa refused to eat or sleep. He died by his own hand. The next day I buried Zeldie Malka, the shtetl peasant, with him. I found a job as a seamstress for a well-to-do shop owner's wife and set my cap for her son."

"Sol?"

"Then he went by Shlomo Mayorovich. He fell in love with me. I fell in love with his money. He was my passport and ticket to America. What would Papa think about his only daughter now, Havah?"

"He'd say his daughter is a woman of valor."

"Do you think so, Havah? I wonder. And what of my mama? She worked so hard to teach me to be a good Jewish wife. Our last Sabbath together she even let me wear her lace scarf and say the prayers over the candles. I felt so grown up. I still have that scarf. It was the only thing beside Papa's picture I managed to save."

"Do you still remember those prayers?"

"Why, yes, I do."

"Would you, Sol and Wendy join us for Shabbes dinner Friday?"

"We'd love to."

"And would you say the blessing over the candles, too—Zeldie Malka?"

"After the hateful way I've treated you, Havaleh, you'd bestow such an honor on me?"

"My papa used to say that everyone deserved a second chance."

"So did mine."

"Tell me, Zeldie, what did I ever do to make you dislike me so?"

A warm gust of wind rustled the curtains and blew a lock of hair across Zelda's nose. She made no attempt to pin it back in place.

"Don't you see Havah? You're the mirror I turned my back on. How, after all you've been through, have you kept the faith?"

Havah's mind returned once more to the cruel night in November that changed everything. Up until then, the greatest tragedy in her life had been having to say goodbye to Beryl. Her ears still ached with the sounds of the gunshots that robbed her of her innocence and of those she cherished most, her parents, Shimon and Miriam and her brothers, Mendel and David. She could still feel the icy ground and sharp thorns that ripped her bare feet as she ran all night through the woods with nothing to protect her from the frigid wind but a nightgown. With each painful step she heard Shimon's voice in her head. His words comforted and encouraged her then, even as they did now.

"The answer is simple but not easy." Havah knelt, took Zelda's smooth hands in hers and gently stroked them with her thumbs. "As one must, one can."

# ACKNOWLEDGEMENTS

After I wrote *Please Say Kaddish for Me*, Havah and her friends continued to tell me their stories. It became apparent that a sequel was in the offing. I want to take the time to thank those who encouraged me along the way.

To Kent Bonham who listened tirelessly to my updates and offered suggestions, some of which I actually used. Thank you for your stellar book trailers and dependable friendship.

The bell clangs for thee, Douglas M. MacIlroy, my dear friend. Your technical knowledge, unyielding focus and honesty made this book more than I dreamed.

Without your guidance, Annie Withers, I would never have found the path to publication.

To Louella Turner who was the first to put my work in print.

Regina O'Hare, dreams do come true. Thank you for being a part of mine.

Thank you, Marie Gail Stratford lending your most excellent bio writing skills.

Victorial Bernal Forbes, because of your photographic gifts I'll always be smiling back at you.

*Todah rabbah* to Teri Gitterman Kallevig who loaned her name and Moldovan origins to Arel and Havah.

Holly McClure, we shared a divine appointment one Saturday morning at an Ozarks Writers League conference. It's one of those milestones I cherish.

*Todah rabbah* to my rebbe and friend Shmuel Wolkenfeld for my continuing Jewish education.

To Jean L. Hays for her keen eye for proofreading—thank you, Taffy.

Lois Hounshell, you listened to me read my manuscripts from their roughest beginnings to the present. Your unselfish friendship is one of my greatest treasures.

Many thanks go to Jeanie Loiacono, my unwavering agent, who never stopped believing in my writing, my artwork or me.

Thanks go again to William Connor for putting Havah, her family and friends in print.

Last but never least, a special thank you to my husband Jan Fields who has encouraged me to write even when it meant spending more time alone that he would've liked.

# ABOUT THE AUTHOR

Rochelle Wisoff-Fields is an author and illustrator. A woman of Jewish descent and the granddaughter of Eastern European immigrants, she has a personal connection to Jewish history, a recurring theme throughout much of her writing. Heavily influenced by the Sholem Aleichem stories, as well as *Fiddler on the Roof*, her novels *Please Say Kaddish for Me*, *From Silt and Ashes*, and *As One Must One Can* were born of her desire to share the darker side of these beloved tales.

A Kansas City native, Wisoff-Fields attended the Kansas City Art Institute, where she studied painting and lithography. She maintains her blog, *Addicted to Purple*, and is the author of *This, That and Sometimes the Other*, an anthology of her short stories, which she also illustrated. Her stories have also been featured in several other anthologies, including two editions of *Voices*. Wisoff-Fields and her husband, Jan, have three sons and now live in Belton, Missouri.

# ROCHELLE WISOFF-FIELDS

FROM OPEN ROAD MEDIA

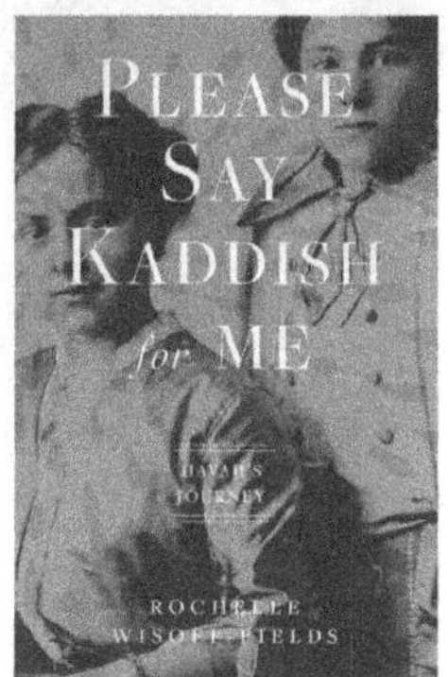

OPEN ROAD
INTEGRATED MEDIA

Printed in the USA
CPSIA information can be obtained
at www.ICGtesting.com
LVHW040848141023
760983LV00002B/7